**Also available from Delores Fossen
and HQN Books**

A Wrangler's Creek Novel

The McCord Brothers

To see the complete list of titles available from
Delores Fossen, please visit www.deloresfossen.com.

DELORES FOSSEN

THE LAST RODEO

HQN™

HQN™

ISBN-13: 978-1-335-63200-5

The Last Rodeo

Copyright © 2018 by Delores Fossen

The publisher acknowledges the copyright holder of the
individual work as follows:

Cowboy Blues
Copyright © 2018 by Delores Fossen

Recycling programs
for this product may
not exist in your area.

This edition published by arrangement with Harlequin Books S.A.

For questions and comments about the quality of this book,
please contact us at CustomerService@Harlequin.com.

® and TM are trademarks of Harlequin Enterprises Limited or its
corporate affiliates. Trademarks indicated with ® are registered in the
United States Patent and Trademark Office, the Canadian Intellectual
Property Office and in other countries.

www.HQNBooks.com

Printed in U.S.A.

CONTENTS

THE LAST RODEO

CHAPTER ONE

BE A COWBOY, they said. It'll be fun, they said.

Lucian Granger was doubting that fun part right about now.

One second his butt was firmly anchored in the saddle, and his hand was gripped on the thick braided rein. The next second, no part of him was touching anything but air.

The bronc gelding orchestrated the hardest buck in the history of hard bucks and sent Lucian flying. Even though Lucian had been thrown before, it'd never been this hard or this high and with this kind of force behind it. His life did indeed flash before his eyes, and Lucian was pissed off that he could possibly die from a horse with no balls.

Hell's Texas Bells. What kind of cowboy did that make him?

Lucian instantly got the answer to that question. It made him a *hurt* cowboy, that's what.

First his tailbone collided with the rock-hard ground in the corral, sending up a cloud of dust. Then his shoulder hit, the jolt of it slamming all the way to his eye sockets and rattling his teeth. Every part of his body went to full-throttle pain, and his breath was still somewhere on the back of the ball-less Appaloosa named

Outlaw. The horse was now smirking at Lucian with a "guess we know who won that round, don't we?"

If the horse had actually had balls, Lucian would have removed them there on the spot.

"Boss man, that was only four seconds," Skeeter Muldoon called out to Lucian. The ranch hand was holding a stopwatch while perched atop the corral fence. "You gotta stay in the saddle a mite longer if you're gonna win a bronc-riding buckle in the rodeo."

Skeeter was the oldest hand they had on the Granger Ranch and was as reliable as they came, but Lucian considered neutering him, too, for pointing out the obvious.

"You all right?" he heard his brother Dylan ask.

It was a simple enough question, but Lucian figured Dylan was laughing his butt off. Lucian would have been doing the same had their positions been reversed. It was their form of brotherly affection.

"I'll live," Lucian assured him, but when he tried to sit up, he wasn't 100 percent certain that was true. The pain shot through him again, and that's when he realized he'd dislocated his shoulder.

Shit.

He didn't have time for this. He had a meeting with a cattle buyer in an hour and appointments stacked up after that.

While Lucian was still sitting on the ground and fighting to drag in a decent breath, Dylan climbed over the corral fence and moseyed toward him. Emphasis on the *moseying*. Again, it was a sign of affection that Dylan wasn't showing a whole bunch of concern.

Well, either it was affection or else Dylan was enjoying that Lucian had just had his butt busted—again.

When you were the big brother/boss, family and folks

in their hometown of Wrangler's Creek, Texas, liked taking you down a notch. That was especially true when
those folks—or rather, some of them, anyway—called
him Lucifer. Not behind his back, either. To his face.

Since he didn't want to continue this dignity-reducing
moment any longer, Lucian accepted Dylan's hand when
he extended it to help him get to his feet. But the dignity
reduction only continued when the pain did a lightning
strike through his shoulder.

Dylan sighed. "You dislocated it again."

Lucian didn't like the addition of the laid-back "again,"
but then, there wasn't anything he did like about this, so
there was no use getting into specifics.

"Want me to get Miz Jordan for you?" Skeeter called
out.

Jordan was not only Dylan's wife, she was also a
nurse, which meant that Lucian must have looked pretty
damn bad for Skeeter to even suggest it. Mainly because
Skeeter's long-distance eyesight was so off that it was
hard for him to see a barn door, much less Lucian's gri-
mace. Perhaps, though, Skeeter had heard the string of
raw profanity grumbling from Lucian's teeth-rattled
mouth.

"Jordan's not here," Dylan informed him. "Want me
to drive you to the hospital?"

Lucian would rather have his butt busted once more.
"Get Karlee."

But he soon realized that getting his assistant wasn't
necessary. Lucian spotted his assistant, Karlee O'Malley,
walking toward the corral. No moseying speed for her.
She was hurrying, and she had her hand cupped over
her eyes to block out the glare from the morning sun.

She was no doubt seeing him just fine and piecing together what'd happened.

"Did you dislocate your shoulder again?" she asked. Along with the accelerated speed, she also had some concern in her voice.

Even though Karlee was wearing dressy office clothes—heels, a slim gray skirt and top—she threw open the corral gate and traipsed through the dust and muck to make her way to him. She was frowning when she reached him and immediately started removing his protective vest, and then unbuttoning his shirt. Normally, that wouldn't have been part of the job description of an assistant, but since Karlee had worked for him for nearly ten years, her list of duties were, well, pretty wide-ranging.

Thankfully, her skill set handled the wide range just fine.

Too bad she thought her talents would be put to better use because two weeks ago she'd given him her thirty days' notice with the excuse that she wanted to start her own cattle brokerage business. That meant he had two more weeks to try to convince her to stay.

Once she had the buttons undone, Karlee eased off his shirt as quick and efficient as any hot-to-trot lover. She wasn't his lover though. Never had been, never would be. Because that quick and efficient label didn't only apply to shirt removal. It was the way Karlee handled everything else. No way would he risk losing her over a soured relationship. And that's exactly what would happen.

All of his relationships soured.

Especially the one that had mattered most.

She examined his shoulder, and then looked up at

him with those Irish-green eyes that could be either warm or cool depending on the situation. Right now, they were on the chillier end of the spectrum because she likely didn't approve of the shoulder injury or how he was about to ask her to handle it.

"No hospital?" She didn't wait for an answer because she knew it would be no. She huffed at his unspoken no. "This is risky, you know? Just because I did this for you once before and for my brothers too many times to count, it doesn't mean it's a smart thing. You need to see a doctor."

"Just pop it back in," Lucian growled.

Her eyes went from plain ordinary chill to an Arctic frost. Karlee frosted and frowned at him a few more seconds while she debated what to do.

"Hold him," she said to Dylan, and Dylan hooked his arms around Lucian's chest and waist. "What's your safe word?" she asked, turning back to Lucian. "The one you use when you're playing rough with your sweet things?"

What the hell did that have to do with this? But Lucian only managed to get out the "what" part of that before Karlee gave his arm a hard push, moving the shoulder back in place.

And causing him to curse every single word of profanity in his entire vocabulary. He added some new ones, too, though they came out so garbled that it was like cuss stew.

Once he got past the eye-watering, excruciating pain, Lucian realized the reason Karlee had asked about the safe word was to distract him. It had worked, and his shoulder was already starting to feel a little better. The sharp stabbing was now more like a sharp toothache.

"All fixed up now?" Dylan asked him. "I think you just wanted to feel a woman's touch." He didn't wait around for Lucian to glare at him for that bad joke. Dylan gave them a wave and headed for the barn where he'd likely been going when he saw Lucian take the throw from the gelding.

Lucian tried to put his shirt back on, but after a couple of grunts from pain, Karlee helped with that, too, and then they started back toward the house. She also took hold of his wrist.

"No, I'm not giving you more of a *woman's touch*. I'm checking your pulse in case what I just did ruptured a blood vessel," she let him know. "If that happened, your pulse rate will change."

Lucian figured she knew how to do that because she'd practically raised her three younger brothers. Being a big sister seemed to give her a special set of expertise like doctoring duties, ESP and a built-in lie detector. Those things were far superior to his big-brother talents.

As a big brother, he knew how to come up with bail money when needed. That was about it. Of course, being the oldest had also gotten him the title of head honcho/boss for Granger Enterprises after his parents had divorced and moved away from Wrangler's Creek. That boss label included not only the ranch but the businesses, as well.

So yeah, there was that.

Too bad it came with so much pressure that sometimes Lucian felt as if it was eating him up on the inside. No way, though, would he ever admit that to anyone. Because it would be a sign of weakness. His father was weak. He wasn't.

"When are you going to give up this wacky notion of winning a bronc-riding competition in the Wrangler's Creek Charity Rodeo?" she asked.

"I'll give up when I win."

Though he was sure Karlee was skeptical that would ever happen. She had a reason for that skepticism, too. He'd been competing in the bronc-riding event since he was eighteen, which meant this next one would be his nineteenth try. Those same folks who called him Lucifer also called him a dumbass, hardheaded idiot when it came to the charity rodeo competition.

"Since I know you're not going to want me to reschedule any of your meetings for today, I've already sent your agenda to your phone," Karlee said, jumping right into business.

Lucian didn't mind the shift in conversation. They'd already wasted enough time on his fall and the rodeo training.

"You have a meeting in forty-five minutes here at the ranch, but then you have to leave for Austin," she went on. "Today and tomorrow, there's a dinner, a lunch and five other meetings. Six if you want to deal personally with the issues with the new feed supplier."

Lucian shook his head, but then winced when the motion tugged and pulled at his sore shoulder. "No dealing with a feed supplier. If it's ranch business, continue to give it to Dylan."

His brother had been running the majority of the ranch operations for a while now, and Lucian wanted to keep it that way. Well, unless the feed issue got worse, and then he'd step in—something that would likely piss off both Dylan and the suppliers. But Lucian didn't put hurt feelings and stepped-on toes ahead of the bottom line.

And the bottom line was success.

Because failure was a sign of weakness.

"The painters start on the interior of your house in San Antonio tomorrow," Karlee continued as they went in through the back of the house. "So, when you finish up in Austin, you probably shouldn't go there because of the fumes. I'll hang around if you want to come back here so we can get some work done. Oh, and I put a suit on your bed for you to pack—which I know you won't do, but the dinner tomorrow night is business formal."

Lucian didn't know what the hell that meant, but he was certain of one thing. He wouldn't be packing, or wearing, that suit.

He wasn't sure he'd ever even bought a suit, which meant his mother, Regina, likely had. She was always trying to turn him into something he wasn't. As the family CEO, she always thought he should dress like a guy who sat behind a desk. He did an ample amount of desk sitting, but he was still a cowboy. Besides, ties and suits were uncomfortable.

"I'll make sure my boots don't have cow shit on them," Lucian grumbled. "That'll be business formal enough."

Karlee sighed and made a sound of resigned disagreement.

Lucian huffed and made a sound of "you're wasting your sigh."

"When you get back from this trip," she went on, "I've arranged for some more interviews for my replacement. This time, I want you to actually interview them and not dismiss them because you don't like something superficial about them."

It wasn't superficial if he got a bad vibe about them. And he'd gotten bad vibes about all six that Karlee had lined up to do the impossible—take her place.

When they went into his office, Lucian immediately saw the blinking lights on his landline, indicating there were multiple calls that had come through in the half hour he'd been out in the corral. He also checked his cell that he'd left on his desk for his ill-fated ride, and he saw the string of missed calls there, too.

"What's all of this about?" Lucian asked, tipping his head to the lights. He got a reminder that head tipping hurt as much as head shaking. Shrugs were probably out, too. "This isn't still about that city council stuff, is it?"

Karlee looked at the message screen of the landline. "Yes. It's still about that *stuff*. Two of them, though, are from your mother."

His mom had also left a voice mail on his cell. That didn't necessarily mean there'd been an emergency. Regina had once left him six messages to ask if he remembered how much salt went into Aunt Kitty's potato bread recipe. His mom had assumed he would know the answer because once when he'd been about ten or so, Aunt Kitty had baked some while visiting the ranch.

"I'm sure some of the calls on your cell will be from the city council, as well." Karlee took out some ibuprofen from his desk and went to the bar to get him a bottle of water. "Along with the mayor, the historical society and the garden guild, you've managed to rile every single person in any position of authority in Wrangler's Creek with that *demand* you sent them."

"That was yesterday." Except for the garden guild. He hadn't known about that. "And I *requested* that they approve the new road I want. It wasn't a demand."

Karlee gave him the flattest look in the history of flat looks. "You told the city council if they didn't rule in your favor by the end of the week that you'd pull the funding you'd pledged for a new park. A *park*," she emphasized. "What's next? Taking candy from little kids?"

Lucian scowled at her. "I didn't pledge that funding. Dylan did." Though it had been a good idea. "And the city council's been farting around for over a month on my *request*. I want that road so it'll be easier for me to get cattle in and out of those back pastures. Hell, I even said I'd pay for it. All they have to do is sign the papers to approve it."

"Lord, love a duck," she grumbled.

It was one of her favorite sayings when she was frustrated, but like business formal, Lucian didn't have a clue what it meant.

"Your road will upset people because of the ground that would have to be cleared to build it," Karlee went on. "Plus, that would mean bringing in heavy equipment that you'd have to move over other ranchers' land. That's why the council's *farting around*. They don't want to tick anyone off."

"Well, they're ticking me off by delaying it," Lucian quickly pointed out. He started scrolling through the screen of missed calls. "How'd the garden guild even get involved anyway?"

"Because of the Hairy Corn Salad. It's a wild herb with a white flower," she added when Lucian just stared at her as if she'd sprouted an extra nose. "Apparently, one of the few places it thrives in this area is right where you want your road."

Lucian just kept staring at her. "Are you making this up?"

The corner of her mouth lifted a little. "Sorry, but I'm not. It's the same reason the historical society put in their two cents' worth. Apparently, your great-grandfather, who cofounded Wrangler's Creek, was especially fond of Hairy Corn Salad. He mentioned it in his letters that are now part of the town's archives."

"Shit." The historical society treated those letters like holy relics when they were just musings of a tobacco-chewing cowboy writing to the pen-pal girl that he was courting.

"My advice?" Karlee went on while she lifted the phone on his landline and started listening to the messages that'd been left for him. "Rethink the location for that road because you stand a better chance of winning the rodeo than you do of successfully convincing the Wrangler's Creek Garden Guild or the historical society to side with you on this. They don't like you, Lucian. You've upset them too many times to count."

Lucian wasn't going to rethink anything. First he was going to call his mother and make sure it wasn't just another salt-related emergency. Then he would start phoning every member of those whining groups who didn't like him.

"Before this, it'd been months since I pissed them off," Lucian argued. "There's no reason for them to keep calling me to complain and whine."

"Multiple months, multiple times of you pissing them off," Karlee reminded him. "If you want specifics, I can give them." But she didn't wait for him to refuse hearing those specifics. "Demanding more water rights from the creek. Pushing too hard for a resolution on the land dispute with your cousins. Building fences that cut off historic ranch trails—"

Karlee probably would have just kept going on and on if their visitor hadn't stopped her.

"Yoo-hoo? Lucian?" Megan Simpson called out. "Your housekeeper said you were in here."

Lucian grumbled another "shit."

That's when he noticed that one of the missed calls on his cell was from her. Megan was his current girl-friend, but he didn't have time for personal stuff today. Plus, that "current" label wasn't going to be there much longer. The relationship, if you could call it that, had run its course, and it was time to end it. Lucian just hadn't counted on that happening today.

Since Karlee was still listening to the messages on his landline, Lucian stepped out into the hall with Megan. As usual, she looked well put together with her blond hair tumbling on her shoulders and the red dress that hugged her body. Though she did look a lit-tle pale. Then he realized she didn't have on as much makeup as usual.

And she wasn't smiling.

"Uh, are you okay?" Megan asked.

Lucian followed her gaze to his dusty shirt. There was some blood on the sleeve, too, probably from a scrape he'd gotten when thrown from the Appaloosa. "I'm fine."

Megan didn't seem to believe that, and that's when Lucian noticed something else. She was suddenly look-ing everywhere but at him. The floor must have been riveting from the way she was staring at it. Crap. What was wrong now?

"Is this about the Hairy Corn Salad?" he asked.

Judging from the way her mouth pursed, that'd be a no. "You mean that flower that so many people are upset about?" She didn't wait for him to confirm it, and Megan added a head shake. "I'm not here for that. Well, not really."

Okay. But along with the gaze dodging and the vague "not really," Lucian could feel a whole lot of hesitation coming from her. Plus, he realized something else. Megan hadn't even kissed him when she'd seen him. Not that he wanted her to kiss him, but that would have been the norm. Before he could ask her what was wrong, though, Megan continued.

"Uh, Lucian, I know you're heading out for a trip, but I wanted to talk before you left. I'm sorry about the timing…what with everything else going on. I'm very sorry about that, too, by the way."

What with everything else going on? *I'm very sorry about that, too*?

Did Megan mean the road/Hairy Corn Salad/people being riled at him? Because usually she didn't even ask about his business, much less any local flora issues. Actually, she rarely asked about anything. That was one of the main reasons he liked her.

"Anyway," Megan went on, "I'm afraid I'm going to have to break things off. It's just not working out between us."

Lucian figured he shouldn't look relieved, but he was certain some of that particular emotion crossed his face before he could rein it in.

"I mean, I knew you weren't the commitment type,"

Megan went on, "but I thought I could change your mind. I thought you were over Amelia Carter by now. You're not. Everyone is right. You'll never be over her."

There were several times during Megan's breakup that Lucian nearly interrupted her. Yes, he was not a commitment type. No, Megan wouldn't be able to change his mind. And, yes, despite what *everyone* believed, he was over Amelia.

Most days, anyway.

Anytime anyone said Amelia's name, he got that feeling that he'd just been sucker punched in the gut by someone who knew just how to do that, but he'd had a lot of practice pushing that all away. Work helped. So did sex. But the best treatment was reminding himself that he would have to have shit for brains to let that happen to him again.

"Lucian, I'm sorry to interrupt," Karlee said, coming to the doorway, "but you really should listen to the voice mails your mother and father left on your cell."

Hell. It hadn't been a salt emergency after all. And as for his father, well, Lucian didn't know what the deal was with him because the only time he ever called was when he needed money or had found "true love" and was remarrying.

There'd been four such calls so far. Maybe five.

His father, Jeremiah, aka Jerry, had managed his personal life just as shoddily as he had everything else he'd ever touched. Not only had he repeatedly cheated on his wife and nearly driven the ranch into the ground, he'd run out on his family. In Lucian's eyes, that made the man lower than the crap beneath that ball-less Appaloosa's hooves.

Lucian thumbed through the calls, found his mom's

voice mail and hit the listen button. While he waited for it to start playing, he turned back to Megan, who was still not looking at him.

"It's okay," he told her. "I hope there won't be any hard feelings between us," Lucian added just as Megan blurted out, "I hope there won't be any hard feelings between us."

Now Megan looked at him, and he shook his head. "Why would there be hard feelings?" he asked.

She blinked. "Uh, because I wasn't able to stop my mom and dad from pushing for this to happen." And with that rather cryptic and gut-tightening comment, Megan skittered right out of there.

Her mom and dad? They owned the town's large-animal veterinarian practice. One that serviced a lot of the livestock at the ranch. What had they done that Megan hadn't been able to stop?

Lucian didn't go after Megan to ask her because at that exact moment, his mom's voice mail started. "Why aren't you answering your phone, Lucian Jeremiah Granger?" his mom had greeted.

Great. She used his full name. Even though he was thirty-seven, that wasn't a good sign, and Lucian wasn't immune to it, either. He suddenly felt like a kid who'd just gotten a D on his report card.

"You really messed up this time, and I'm not happy," the message went on. "I've been getting one call after another for the past two days, and everyone is complaining about you and your demands."

"It was a request," Lucian grumbled, obviously talking to himself since his mom couldn't hear him.

"I just got another call from Megan Simpson's folks, and they're so mad, they aren't going to do business with us anymore. They called your dad, too. So did plenty of other people, and he's fed up," his mom continued. "We both are, and we're on our way back home."

This time, Lucian did a double "hell," and he looked at Karlee to see if she knew about this. Apparently, she did, probably because his mom had left a similar message on his landline. But that was more than just a gloom and doom look that Karlee was giving him.

Whatever this was, it was *bad*.

"Listen to your dad's message," Karlee insisted.

Since that voice mail came right after his mom's, it wasn't hard to find. Dragging a long breath that he was certain he would need, Lucian stabbed the play button.

"You really should answer your phone," his dad snarled. "I'm on my way to the ranch to fix this shitstorm you started with the mayor and the rest of my old pals. Oh, and your mom's coming, too. I won't be saying thanks for involving her in this. Or me. But I do have something to say to you. Lucian. You're fired."

CHAPTER TWO

KARLEE DIDN'T NEED to hear Jerry Granger's message to his firstborn son because she'd just listened to the one that the man had left on Lucian's landline.

Lucian, you're fired.

This was one particular issue that she hadn't counted on having to deal with today, and Karlee was certain Lucian hadn't seen it coming, either.

"I've already tried to call your father," Karlee told him. That was huge for her since she despised the man. "He didn't answer. Ditto for your mother because they're on their way here."

Well, they were on their way if what they'd said in their messages was true. Regina was a frequent visitor to the ranch anyway, and Karlee had been expecting her back any day now to visit her four grandchildren.

But Jeremiah "Jerry" Granger was a different story.

He'd visited only once in the ten years she'd worked for Lucian and that was to bust Lucian's chops about some cattle deal with one of Jerry's friends that Lucian had nixed. That meant Jerry was likely returning for a second chop busting.

Too bad that Jerry could do that. Or rather, he could try it, anyway. Because despite his less-than-stellar track record, Jerry owned the majority shares of both the ranch and the family businesses. That meant Lucian did, in theory, work for him. In reality, Lucian did the work, and Jerry and Regina got richer and richer from all the hours that Dylan and Lucian put in.

Lucian stared at his cell even though his father's message had already finished playing. He was no doubt trying to process it.

Since this firing was a first, she wasn't sure how he'd react. Karlee suspected, though, that profanity would be involved. Or perhaps a soul-crushing revelation that his parents had just pulled a Texas-sized rug from beneath his feet. She steeled herself up for either reaction. But neither of those things actually happened.

Lucian shrugged.

Then he winced, but she didn't think the wincing was because of the *you're fired* but because the motion had messed with his shoulder.

"I need to change my shirt before my meeting," he said. "This one has blood on it."

And that was it. He headed down the hall and in the direction of his bedroom. Karlee followed him because she wasn't sure he was actually grasping the situation.

"Your parents sounded serious," she pointed out. "Should I reschedule your trip—"

"No. But you can arrange to have flowers sent to Megan. Yellow roses. Put the usual on the card."

The usual was just his name. Lucian. Nothing else. That was standard for his breakups, which were so frequent that Karlee had set up an account at the florist. It was akin to a form letter where she just provided the florist with the woman's name.

At least Megan didn't seem upset with the inevitable way things had turned out, but it made Karlee wonder what the discarded string of lovers thought of only having his name and no other greeting or message on the card. Maybe, depending on what they were feeling, they filled in the blank.

Wishing you the best. Lucian.

It was good while it lasted. Lucian.

Don't call me again. Lucian.

Karlee doubted he should go the vague/make your own interpretation when it came to this situation with his parents, and that's why she continued to follow him to his bedroom. But any words she was about to say died on her lips when she saw him.

He'd already peeled off his shirt, so she could see plenty of things to distract her. That toned and tight chest. The six-pack. Yep, he had one of those, too. Of course, she'd just seen some of those things in the corral when she'd reset his shoulder, but this seemed more intimate, because they were in his bedroom.

It was also intimate because he was unzipping his jeans.

Now, that part of him she hadn't seen, and while her nether regions encouraged her to let him continue with the peep show, Karlee cleared her throat to stop it. And to remind him that she was not only there but that she was also a woman who could be affected by such eye candy.

Yes, Lucian had to be reminded of that. Because he only saw her as his gender-neutral assistant. She saw him as a hot cowboy with an equally hot body.

A misunderstood hot-bodied cowboy.

Most people thought he was an SOB, and he could be, but Karlee knew there were other layers. Ones that she was certain were there, but Lucian kept them more zipped up than he ever did his jeans.

"Sorry." He tossed his phone on the bed and stopped undressing. Their eyes met for a moment. The same kind of moment they'd had dozens of times throughout their business day. His look was laced with that distracted annoyance that let her know he was trying to sort out the dozens of things that he always managed to sort out.

Maybe not this time though.

She drank in that look, holding on to it a moment longer than she usually would have because of the slippery slide of arousal that his shirt removal had caused.

Mercy, he had a gorgeous face. There was no other word for it. All those angles framed with the permanently tousled dark brown hair. And the eyes! Oh, the eyes. Sizzling blue like the edges of a really hot fire on a cold day. She wouldn't even get into mentally describing his mouth because if she did, if she thought about it too long, the slippery slide of arousal would be an avalanche.

Lucian glanced away from her, grabbed a clean pair of Wranglers from his closet and went into the adjoining bathroom. "I need to take a quick shower, but I can still hear you if you talk loud enough." And he turned on the water.

She could hear him as well—when he grunted. No doubt from his sore shoulder, but Karlee resisted the urge to go and check on him. She stayed put, anchoring her hands to the door frame along with telling her nether regions to calm down. Thankfully, she had a tasty topic to distract her.

"What are you going to do about your parents?" she asked. "Will you back off from the road request?"

"No. This is a bluff. My dad doesn't want to run the

family business or the ranch. That's why he left when I was eighteen. He only wants the profits from it."

There was always bitterness in his voice whenever he mentioned his father. Plenty of bitterness inside him, too, and Karlee could certainly sympathize.

Because their bitterness overlapped and had a common denominator.

Jerry Granger.

When Karlee was thirteen and Lucian was seventeen, her mother had run off with Jerry. To make matters even worse, her mom, Glenda, had drained most of their bank accounts and taken the money with her since Jerry had already blown through his annual trust-fund payout by then. Overnight, the O'Malleys had gone from being respectable and comfortable to being poor and the family that everyone gossiped about.

The town had taken sides, and most had sided with Jerry. Or rather, with Regina, who had been the wronged woman in all of this. Glenda had been labeled the husband-stealing hussy who'd tempted Jerry away from his loving wife. Their wild affair had lasted less than a year, but Glenda never came back to Wrangler's Creek.

Or to her children.

Her parents had gotten a divorce, Glenda remarried and moved heaven knew where, and Karlee's father drank himself to death. And all of that had started with Jerry.

Karlee didn't blame him to any greater extent than she did her mother, but she felt plenty enough blame to go around. Now Jerry was coming after Lucian.

Lucian was still in the shower when Karlee heard

the footsteps coming down the hall. Footsteps that belonged to Dylan.

"What the hell's going on?" Dylan asked. He had his
phone in his hand and a thunderstruck expression on his
face. "I just got a call from Mom, and she said that Dad
had fired Lucian and me, that we're no longer running
the ranch or the cattle broker company."

Thankfully, Dylan's three-year-old adopted son, Corbin,
wasn't with him—his wife, Jordan, had taken the boy to
preschool. Considering the circumstances, "hell" likely
wouldn't be the only profanity bantered around in the next
few hours. Karlee definitely didn't want Corbin around
for that since he was also her nephew. He was the bio-
logical son of her very irresponsible brother, Mack, who
had thankfully decided that Jordan and Dylan were better suited to raising the boy. And they were. Karlee loved
the boy too much to have him even on the fringes of what
was about to go down.

"I didn't know about you being caught up in this,"
Karlee said. "But Jerry left Lucian a message telling him
he was fired."

She'd been right about the abundant use of curse words,
and it took Dylan a moment to work his way through the
name-calling aimed at his dad. "He can't do this. Not to
me, not to Lucian. Is this about the ruckus over the road
and that stupid wildflower with the dumb name?"

"I think that was just a straw that broke the camel's
back. Jerry's still fuming over that cattle deal that he
wanted Lucian to make with his shady friend."

"Lucian was right to ax that," Dylan argued.

Karlee agreed. Jerry, however, hadn't. And that's
why they were about to have a blowup with his parents,
one that Lucian had dismissed with a shrug.

"By any chance, were you able to talk your mother out of coming?" Karlee asked him. "Because you know that having both her and Jerry together under the same roof will only make matters worse."

Dylan's mouth tightened. "She's coming. In fact, she'll be here any minute. Not sure when my dad will arrive, but he's on his way, too."

Well, there went her last-ditch hope that this had all been a temper tantrum that would blow over. That meant she had to do some damage control. She would have to call each member of the city council, the garden guild and historical society to try to smooth things over with them. They, in turn, might do some smoothing with Jerry and Regina.

Might.

Since things had never gone this far before, Karlee wasn't sure if her damage control would work. Lucian, however, still didn't seem concerned when he came out of his bathroom. Fully dressed, thank goodness, except for the shirt that he was still buttoning.

"Is Ian McClemore here for our meeting?" Lucian asked her.

"Not yet, but with everything else going on, I think you should reschedule."

Lucian shook his head and finally looked at Dylan. "Mom called you?"

"Yeah, and this sucks ass." Dylan volleyed glances at both of them. "It's been a while since I've done the math, but because of his inheritance from our grandfather J.L., Dad still owns fifty percent of the family holdings, right?"

Karlee nodded. "Your grandfather didn't want to give Jerry that much because he didn't trust him financially, but his hands were tied because of the terms of his own father's will. He had to leave at least fifty percent to the oldest male heir. Since Jerry was J.L.'s only son, he had no choice."

"That old will was the reason J.L. had to leave one percent share to the garden guild and another one percent to the historical society," Dylan pointed out.

For reasons she'd never understood, J.L.'s father had cofounded the town and wanted to make sure those two groups had a steady stream of funds. Well, a steady stream as long as Granger Enterprises continued to thrive. It was ironic that the very groups he'd funded were now the ones helping Jerry stage a coup against Lucian.

"J.L. divided up the other remaining forty-eight percent equally among Regina, you and your siblings," Karlee continued. "Lucian bought out your brothers' and sister's shares, but Regina and you still have yours."

Lucian didn't seem to be paying any attention whatsoever to the conversation. He stepped around her, heading back to his office, and Karlee and Dylan followed.

"So, if all of us team up against Dad, Lucian could get back control of Granger Enterprises," Dylan concluded.

"Yes. But for that to even be a possibility, both the historical society and the garden guild would have to throw in their support," Karlee explained. "If they did that, then it would be your fifty percent against Jerry's. It'd still take a legal battle, but I believe you could oust him."

"It'd be worth the fight," Dylan insisted.

Lucian glanced over his shoulder at his brother. "You

call me an asshole on a regular basis. Why would you want me to keep this *job* anyway?"

"Because this is a case where size matters a whole bunch. Dad's a bigger asshole than you. Besides, he wouldn't be just taking the business, he'd be taking over the ranch, too."

That had to cut deep because the ranch was Dylan's baby. He tended and nurtured it just as much as Lucian did the rest of the family holdings.

When Lucian went into his office, he immediately sat at his desk and started going over the agenda for his meeting with Ian. Again, no signs that the sky was falling. Which actually settled her stomach some. If Lucian wasn't worried, then maybe she shouldn't be.

"I'll go into town and talk to the mayor and anyone else who'll listen to me," Dylan volunteered.

That was probably the best solution since Dylan had inherited all the Granger charm. He was their best bet at trying to smooth this over. Even if it wasn't a necessity, if this really all did just blow over, it wouldn't hurt to have mended things with the bigwigs in town.

When Dylan left, Karlee turned to Lucian. "Since you're running a little late, do you want me to go ahead and finish packing for you?" she asked.

"Sure. And thanks."

She got the feeling he was thanking her for more than just the packing. He was probably glad that she hadn't gone into worry overload mode.

Just as Karlee walked out, she saw his appointment, Ian McClemore, making his way toward the office. She showed him in, shut the door and continued to Lucian's bedroom. She hadn't noticed it before because she'd gotten distracted with his dad's call and seeing Lucian's undressing, but everything that she'd laid out for him was all still on the bed. His clothes, the suit, toiletries.

And a jar of extra-chunky peanut butter.

It was something that didn't seem to go with the other items, but she knew it was his favorite, and since the jar usually came back at least half-eaten, it meant that it served its purpose when Lucian got too busy to grab something to eat.

All of those things were next to the open suitcase— that she'd also left.

But the suitcase wasn't empty.

She spotted the only thing he had packed. The rodeo buckle.

It wasn't his. He'd never won one. This one had belonged to his grandfather and his namesake, Jeremiah Lucian Granger, J.L., who'd started the charity rodeo back in his day and had been a four-time winner. He'd left one of the buckles to each of his grandsons, and Lucian carried his on every trip. Karlee had never discussed it with him, but she figured it was like a good-luck charm. If so, it'd worked because no one could dispute that Lucian had been a success. Just not at the rodeo.

She heard footsteps coming toward the room, and Karlee automatically went stiff. Because it wasn't Dylan. These belonged to someone wearing heels, and since the housekeepers and Jordan normally wore flats, she suspected it was Regina.

And it was.

"Lucian's in a meeting," Karlee told her right off.

"I figured as much since the door was closed, and that's why I came looking for you." Regina dragged in a weary breath. "Did you know that Lois Fay Merkle from the historical society is trying to make Hairy Corn Salad a protected species for the local area?"

Karlee had to shake her head. She'd gotten a lot of calls about this mess, but that hadn't come up.

"Lois Fay has too much time on her hands," Regina added in a grumble.

Karlee relaxed a little, enough so that it didn't feel as if her ribs were being crushed. Regina hadn't come in ranting, and that was good. It might mean she would be on Lucian's side in this.

"Is Jerry with you?" Karlee asked.

"No. Thank heaven." She came in and sank down on the foot of the bed. "I prefer to minimize my time around him."

Everyone with the surname of Granger seemed to feel that way.

"Jerry's not only a jerk, he's also a terrible business-man," Regina continued. "His father knew that, and that's why he set up Jerry's trust fund to be given to him in increments every year. He spends that and all the profits that Lucian sends him on his tart-of-the-month club. And, no, I don't mean pastries. Sorry," Regina quickly added.

The apology was because Karlee winced a little. It was an involuntary reflex since she'd spent the past twenty years of her life hearing her mother called that particular term of un-endearment.

Karlee waved it off. "If I've never said thank you for not holding that against me, then thank you."

Regina's forehead bunched up for a moment. "That was your mother's doing, not yours. But a word of cau-tion. My slimy ex-husband might try to hit on you be-cause you look so much like her."

That gave Karlee a big *ewww* moment. Yes, she was well aware of the resemblance, and it probably didn't help that she was now the same age Glenda had been when she'd run off with Jerry. It also didn't help that Lucian was the spitting image of his father. When the folks from Regina's generation saw Lucian and her together, Karlee figured it jogged memories about the scandal.

As for the hitting on her, if Jerry did indeed do that, Karlee would be hitting back. Perhaps with a knee to his groin.

"So, are you really quitting your job?" Regina asked.

Ah, that. Karlee wondered how long it was going to take for it to come up because by now, the gossip mill would have made sure everyone knew about it. "Yes, I've been saving my money, and I finally have enough to become a cattle broker. It's always been a dream of mine."

That was mostly true. Karlee had wanted a job that would give her some level of respect. And, yes, she still needed that. Plus, she needed to make a clean break with Lucian. As long as she was around him day in and day out, these feelings for him weren't going to cool off.

"My last day of work here should be in two weeks," Karlee added. "But Lucian hasn't hired a replacement yet. Of course, he won't need a replacement if Jerry actually ousts him. If that happens, then I'd leave immediately, too. No way would I work for Jerry."

"I suspected as much." Regina dragged in another of those weary breaths. "We have to do something. We have to fix this."

Karlee was all for that. "I don't have a clue how to do that."

"I do." Regina motioned for Karlee to sit down next to her. "I have a plan. One you're not going to like. One that Lucian is especially not going to like. That's why I need you to help me convince him that it's the right thing to do."

"I'm all ears," Karlee assured her despite Regina's warning about not liking this. "What's the plan?"

"Well, he'll have to back off on the notion of that road, of course, but that's just for starters. The mayor and those other groups have to see that Lucian's a changed man. That he's, well, likable. Only then will the garden guild and historical society give us their two percent vote from their shares."

Karlee's optimism about this idea was waning with every word Regina continued to say. She knew that Lucian had plenty of positive traits, but it was going to be hard to make anyone else believe them.

"If people like Lucian," Regina went on, "then no one will be upset with him any longer, and Jerry won't have any reason to fire him."

All right. Karlee supposed that could work if not for a major sticking point. "How exactly is Lucian supposed to make everyone believe he's a changed man?"

Regina looked her straight in the eyes. "You and me need to get started with some phone calls. But sweet talk alone isn't going to fix this. Drastic times call for drastic means."

Frustrated, Karlee shook her head. "What measures?"

"Ones that Lucian won't like much. Or you," Regina added. She patted Karlee's hand, and a minute later, Karlee got confirmation of what Regina had just warned her about.

And no, Karlee didn't like it much at all.

CHAPTER THREE

LUCIAN FORCED HIMSELF to focus on the meeting with Ian because it was an important one. Worth tens of thousands of dollars along with continuing to build the long-standing working relationship he had with the cattleman. But the forcing only worked for a couple of minutes before the thoughts came, causing his stomach to knot.

You're fired.

Those were words he'd thought he would never hear, especially not from a man who'd shown zero interest in dealing personally with the ranch, business or his kids. So something had to be up. Jerry's old cronies were in various key positions in the town and county, and Lucian could see advantages in getting him out of the CEO seat and replacing him with someone who could be manipulated.

Like Jerry.

But something must have happened to make Jerry want to accept. Lucian figured that *something* was money. His father was probably broke again and looking for a quick fix to whatever debt he had to pay before he got the next installment from his trust fund or his payout from the family businesses.

"Is this about Karlee?" Lucian heard Ian ask.

Lucian shook his head to clear it because he wasn't

sure what Ian meant. Lucian hadn't mentioned Karlee's name and she wasn't in the room.

"Because she's quitting," Ian clarified a moment later. "Your mind's not on business today, and I thought maybe it's because you're losing her."

Well, he wasn't happy about that, but Lucian hadn't given up that particular fight just yet. He would indeed need to figure out a way to keep her. However, the big distraction of the day was the stunt his dad was trying to pull.

"Sorry," Lucian told him, and he looked at Ian's proposal for the purchase and transfer for the cattle. "You have to come up with some better numbers before I can sign this."

The corner of Ian's mouth lifted. "Guess your mind's on business after all. This is the part where you and I go back and forth until we end up with figures that won't make me nearly as happy as they'll make you."

"Yep, this is the part all right." And normally Lucian was good at it, too. That's why he mentally cursed his father again for causing this unnecessary distraction.

Ian stared at him. Lucian knew this part, too. It was sort of a game of chicken, but Lucian wouldn't back down, and Ian knew that. Hell, everyone knew it.

"Okay," Ian finally said. He took the proposal, putting a line through the prices that were there and reducing them by enough so as not to be insulting before he handed it back to Lucian.

Lucian studied the numbers again. Or rather, he looked at them. He could do the cost analysis in his head and knew this was a good deal. He wanted better though. He gave the numbers his own adjustment, passed the proposal back to Ian and waited. But the waiting/chicken game was cut way short by a couple of rounds when his office door flew open.

And there was Jerry.

His whole life Lucian had heard how much he favored his father, and maybe that's why he felt a little as if he were disgusted with himself when he looked at him. Of course, Jerry's bad track record played into that, too. So did Lucian's own guilt at what he felt for his father. It certainly wasn't love. But then, Jerry hadn't done much to ensure that he was the apple of his family's eye.

"Ian McClemore," Jerry immediately greeted, and while ignoring Lucian, Jerry went to the man and gave him a beefy handshake. "It's damn good to see you."

Ian looked about as comfortable with the exchange as a steer with his rump on a hot branding iron. That's because before Lucian had taken over Granger Enterprises, Ian had had some business dealings with Jerry. And Jerry wasn't exactly favored by some of his former associates. Ian fell into that category because way back in the day, Jerry had supposedly slept with the woman Ian had been dating.

Apparently, his dad had had a quick zipper even back then.

"So, we're good on this deal?" Ian asked Lucian. He tipped his head to indicate the proposal.

Jerry tried to get a look at it, but as soon as Lucian nodded, Ian tucked the proposal under his arm. "I'll be going, then," Ian said, his tone suddenly crisp and cold, like an overly chilled salad. "It was good doing business with you, Lucian."

Since Jerry was still trying to peek at those papers, Ian wisely got out of there. Ian's speedy departure was also because he probably hadn't wanted to get caught up in the middle of a family squabble, which the cattle-man had no doubt sensed was coming. But Lucian had no intentions of squabbling. He was just going to spell this out.

"I made this company and the ranch what it is." Lucian reined in as much of his emotion as he could so his voice would remain steady. "When I took it over at eighteen, every part of it was in the red. *Every. Part.* Dylan and I have both worked hard to undo a lot of the mess you made."

Jerry flashed that cocky-ass smile that always made Lucian wish he had a different gene pool. In fact, it was the very reason that Lucian kept his smiling to a min-imum. He didn't want to do anything else that would make him look more like his dickwad of a father.

"That's a lot of old water under a really old bridge," Jerry drawled. He put his hands on his hips and glanced around the office. The kind of glancing someone would do if they were about to stake their claim on the place. "I'm a lot better at that sort of thing now."

Lucian's eyes automatically narrowed. "I'm not going to let you test out that theory by running Granger En-terprises into the ground."

At least that got the cocky smile off Jerry's face. "Can't see that you have a choice about that. I'm the majority shareholder, and what I say goes."

"Then it's time for us to fix that." Something Lucian should have done ages ago. "How much do you want to walk away from this?"

By giving his head an indignant little wobble, Jerry tried to look insulted. He failed. "This isn't about money."

"Bullshit. It's always about money when it comes to you."

"Not this time," Jerry added under his breath. And that breath was weary, too.

That put Lucian even more on edge because Jerry sounded desperate, and it had to be pretty damn bad if it was something money couldn't fix. Still, Lucian tried again. "Just give me a bottom line because I've got work to do."

His father jammed his thumb to his own chest. "No, I have work to do. And the only bottom line is that you'll be stepping aside so I can take over. There's no ifs, ands or buts about that."

Lucian was about to point out some *buts* and maybe an *if* or two, but he was interrupted by the busty blonde who stepped into the doorway. "Jerry, there you are." But her gaze went straight past Jerry to Lucian. "Whoa, you two could pass for twins. Well, except Jerry's got some age on him, of course."

No smile this time from Jerry. His mouth twisted a little. Probably because of the age reminder but also because the blonde was combing her hungry baby blues over Lucian as if undressing him.

The woman went to Lucian and extended her hand. "I'm Candy Burns, your dad's fiancée." She laughed and thrust her ring out for him to see. It was the standard issue for his dad's soon-to-be ex-wives. Big and flashy. It had no doubt cost a small fortune that Jerry didn't have. "And I guess that means I'm about to be your stepmother."

"There have been a few of those," Lucian said.

Candy laughed again as if it were a fine joke, and she kept it up until Regina and Karlee walked in. Regina took one look at Jerry, then at Candy, and judging from her eye roll, she knew exactly what was going on.

"Regina," Jerry growled. Definitely nowhere in the realm of a friendly greeting. "Karlee." That was friendly with a side order of lechery.

Shit. If Jerry made a play for Karlee, Lucian was going to have to wipe the floor with his randy ass.

"Regina?" Candy repeated. She obviously knew this was the original Mrs. Jeremiah Granger. She hurried to Jerry's side, her needle-thin heels making woodpecker clicks on the floor. Once she reached her man, she threaded her arm through his and staked her claim much as Jerry had tried to do when he'd made that sweeping glance of Lucian's office.

Candy thrust out her ring for Regina, too. "I'm Jerry's fiancée."

"Oh, it's gold," Regina remarked after pausing to do some sizing up of her own. "Did you know that people still dig for gold? Gold diggers, they call them. Or so I've heard."

Sheez, Louise.

"Hey, I'm not a gold digger," Candy howled. "I have my own money, thank you very much."

"She does," Jerry piped in. "Candy's the Hoo-Poo heiress."

That caused some blank stares, with Lucian's being the blankest of them all. For shit's sake, what was this about now?

"Hoo-Poo," Candy repeated as if that would help with the cluelessness. It didn't. She huffed. "My dad invented a feminine hygiene shampoo they sell on a shopping network on TV. It's made a fortune."

Lucian looked at Karlee to see if she had heard of this product or if it was even relevant to this conversation—

which he was certain it wasn't. But Karlee's blank look had morphed into a *please get me out of this level of hell*.

But the levels of hell just kept on coming.

"Your *dad* invented it?" Regina said with extreme emphasis on the word *dad*. "Not making any judgments here, but does he have a hoo to poo, or did this stem from a hobby of his?" She chuckled as if that were a fine joke.

Candy's eyes narrowed. "My father's a doctor. A gynecologist, and he saw an untapped need and filled it."

The only one who laughed at that was Regina, and apparently she was just getting started because she turned to Jerry and patted his belly that was sticking out over his enormous rodeo buckle. "I see that you quit doing Botox and liposuction. Good for you. A man your age should be able to sock on some belly fat and wrinkles without people judging you for looking like the senior citizen that you are."

Karlee closed her eyes a moment and groaned softly, but Jerry didn't waste even a second before he returned the insult. "You must have a good whetstone to keep your tongue that sharp."

Regina didn't hesitate a beat, either. "Well, I could buy good whetstones and plenty of other things from all that divorce money I got because you cheated on me. Remember? Of course you do because you have to send me an alimony check each month."

"I like knowing you have ready cash for all those witch's broomsticks you must go through," Jerry slung back at her.

Karlee groaned even louder and stepped between them. "Mr. Granger, could you give Regina a moment alone with Lucian? She just got here, hasn't seen him yet, and she wants to tell him about her latest cancer treatment. Regina's been through so much, and Lucian's really worried about her. We all are."

Lucian could practically hear the violins that came with that sob story. One that wasn't completely true. His mom had indeed had breast cancer, but she'd been in remission for a year and a half now. And there was no latest cancer treatment because Regina called him at least once a week just to let him know that she was okay.

The part about Lucian worrying was true though. When she'd first gotten the diagnosis, he'd been scared of losing her. Still was. Regina might not have been a perfect mom, or even one who'd been present in his life, but she'd never tried to run the family business into the ground with her irresponsible lifestyle.

Despite Karlee's sob story, Jerry didn't budge, and for a moment Lucian thought he was going to refuse to leave. And he might have, but it was Candy who got him moving. "Come on, Jerry. You can show me to our room so I can get my things unpacked."

"Our room?" Regina challenged. It sounded as if his mom was about to launch into a second wave of insults, but she stopped when Karlee looked back at her. Something passed between them. Something that seemed on the sneaky side.

Was his mother up to something?

If so, Lucian only hoped it didn't make matters worse. Of course, that was a very low bar since things were already somewhere deep in one of those levels of hell.

"Jerry and his bimbo are staying here?" Regina asked Lucian the moment her ex and Candy had walked out.

Lucian lifted his shoulder. "Apparently so." And he

stared at Regina. "Do you think it helped to exchange barbs like that with Dad?"

"No," Regina readily admitted. "It didn't help one bit, but it felt sooo good."

"Nothing about this feels good," Lucian assured her.

Regina smiled as if there was actually something to smile about. "Well, let's see what we can do to change that."

Some sons probably could have gotten comfort from a comment like that from their mother, but Lucian didn't think this was heading in a good direction. Apparently, neither did Karlee.

"By the way, I had nothing to do with this idea," Karlee said as she shut the door. "Regina came up with it on her own."

"It's not an idea," Regina corrected. "It's a plan. A good one."

Hell. He'd already had too many surprises for this day, and he wasn't sure his painkillers had kicked in enough to put up with whatever his mother had concocted.

"I told your mom for the plan to work that we'd have to drug you first," Karlee added. "Or perhaps do some brainwashing."

All right. So the plan sucked for sure, but apparently despite a high level of suckiness, Karlee still hadn't been able to nix it.

"I've already talked to Lois Fay Merkle from the historical society," his mother went on. "So, now that the bug's been planted in her ear, it'll get all over town—fast. Lois Fay is better than group texting or a national news alert when it comes to getting the word out."

"And what word would that be?" Lucian asked, though he wasn't sure he wanted to hear the answer.

"That you're a changed man. I didn't know about your fall from the bronc, but after I saw the bloody shirt, Karlee told me what happened. I knew that was the right angle to use."

So now she'd added angles to the plan. Lucian looked at Karlee to see if she could give him an explanation at a faster rate than his mom, but she just lifted her hands, palms up. It looked like an act of surrender.

"I told Lois Fay that when the horse threw you, that you had an epiphany," Regina said. "That your life flashed before your eyes."

"It did," he mumbled. No epiphany, though, unless it was that he needed to get a better horse to use for training. But his mom didn't respond to that. She just kept on talking.

"I explained to Lois Fay that when you had the close call, you decided to make some big changes in your life. No more demands for roads that would hurt the wildflowers. That you would donate even more money for the park you promised. And that you were going to be a nicer person."

Lucian stared at her. "You did what?"

Regina stared back. "I'm trying to do some damage control to get your dad and the queen of tarts out of your hair. FYI, Lois Fay was optimistic. She thought it was a good start and that she'd talk to her fellow board members."

"Lois Fay said she'd *think* about contacting her fellow board members," Karlee corrected.

Well, that wasn't as bad as Lucian knew it could be, and it could result in nothing. "I need that road."

"More than that, you need to get Jerry out of your business." Regina walked closer. "*Our* business," she amended. "You know I'm right. Jerry will bankrupt us and put us all in the poorhouse."

That was a whopper of an exaggeration. Lucian had his own personal assets that Jerry couldn't touch. So did his mother and his siblings. Still, he hated the thought of Granger Enterprises going down the tubes or being so poorly mismanaged that it might never recover.

"All right, I'll postpone the plan for the road," Lucian said. It was a huge concession because it would mean him backing down. That would chip away at his authority and make him look weak. Still, he'd rather look weak than put his father at the helm of this company and the ranch.

"And the park?" his mom pressed.

Lucian nodded. "I'll donate more money for that, too." Compared to the road concession, that didn't sting much at all. In fact, he'd never intended to withhold funding. That had been a bluff to give him some leverage. "But I don't think that's nearly enough to change the minds of the city council, historical society and the garden guild."

"It's not," Regina quickly admitted. "We've got to think big. I mean, something huge enough that everyone in Wrangler's Creek will know that you're no longer Lucifer. We also need to make sure they all believe that you're clean over Amelia. I mean like once and for all."

There it was again. The sucker punch. "I am over Amelia," he grumbled. "And why would she even be part of this anyway? Amelia and I ended things years ago."

"It wasn't a clean break, and you know it," his mom explained.

No. It hadn't been. But Lucian prided himself on being smart enough to recognize a break when his lover picked up and moved. Still, he couldn't connect why Amelia had anything to do with what was happening right now. That's why he looked at Karlee for an explanation.

"Remember, I had nothing to do with this," Karlee grumbled. As explanations went, it sucked.

"She's right. This is my brainchild," Regina bragged. "We need a celebration. Something to bring everyone back together. The biggest party this town has ever seen." His mother smiled even though Lucian hadn't heard or seen anything to warrant such a happy mood. "Lucian, that means you're getting engaged."

CHAPTER FOUR

LUCIAN HAD KNOWN right from the get-go that his mom's plan would be out there into what some folks would consider batshit crazy land. And it was.

"Engaged?" he challenged, and he would have argued with a lot more than just that one word if Regina hadn't interrupted him.

"Trust me, I've thought this through, and it's the best solution. The town will be shocked, yes, but they'll see this as proof that you've changed. It might take a month or two, but you'll have them on your side in no time because you won't be Lucifer any longer. You'll be Lucian Jeremiah Granger, the soon-to-be family man."

"It gets *better*," Karlee warned him when Lucian opened his mouth again.

Well, hell. That could move them even beyond batshit. "I'm guessing my mom has a solution for the teeny tiny problem that I'm currently not seeing anyone and that I have no plans whatsoever to get married? And perhaps she's even considered the pesky little fly in the ointment that even if I ever did say I do, it wouldn't be to hang on to what's rightfully mine?"

"Yeah, she's got a fix for that," Karlee grumbled, her voice as flat as her expression.

"Karlee is the solution." Regina then beamed a big ol'

smile suitable only for delusional people who thought they were doing something fabulous.

"You want me to marry Karlee?" Lucian asked, though he probably didn't need clarification.

Karlee's expression said it all. His mom had already presented her with this stupid notion. Karlee had shot it down with what Lucian figured was an ocean of logic. Logic that Regina had ignored.

"I want you to *get engaged* to her. You wouldn't actually have to get married. You could call things off once everything is back to normal with the business. And Karlee's perfect for you," Regina went on. "Folks in town love her—"

"They feel sorry for me," Karlee corrected.

"They *sympathize* with you because of what happened to you and your family. That sympathy will go a long way toward helping them see Lucian in a different light."

"Or folks could just realize this is a sham," Karlee countered, "that Lucian and I aren't really a couple, and they could end up despising him even more."

Clearly, Karlee had already argued this out with his mom, and she was making sense, too. Also clearly, that hadn't stopped Regina from proceeding.

Regina took both Karlee and him by the hand and moved them closer to each other. "You must see how Karlee reacts around you," Regina went on. "She just lights up—"

Karlee groaned and turned away. What she didn't do was dispute that whole "lights up" thing. Did she really do that around him? Had he missed something? Lucian admitted that it was possible. When it came to cattle and business proposals, he was at the top of his game, but he often missed the stuff that made people light up.

Their eyes met, the connection holding a little longer than usual. Just as it'd done earlier when she'd walked in on him undressing. He hadn't seen light then but maybe some kind of basic animal attraction. Something natural that happened between a man and a woman, but they'd quickly reined it in.

He wasn't doing a good job with that now.

That's because he was noticing the soft curves of her mouth and imagining what it would be like to have it slide right over various parts of him—starting with his own mouth. He was imagining her hands, too, and yes, they were sliding and gliding. And since he'd obviously lost his mind, he was also noticing the flush on her cheeks. An angel face, some would call it, but Lucian knew there was plenty of toughness beneath the surface.

"All right, so maybe you're both not sold on the notion," Regina concluded.

Obviously, his lustful thoughts hadn't made it to his expression. Thank God for that. This situation was complicated enough without Karlee—or his mother—knowing the fantasies going on inside his head. Fantasies that he mentally shoved aside.

"But do either of you have a better plan?" Regina pressed. "I doubt it because if you did, I would have already heard about it."

Nope. Lucian didn't have one. Since Karlee was still groaning and had turned away, he doubted that she did, either.

Regina huffed. "Look, you've got maybe ten minutes at most before your dad comes back in here and starts swinging his weight around. You can't stop him today, but you can have him out of here in a month or so if you just get engaged to Karlee so I can start planning a party."

"I'm not getting engaged." Karlee spoke up, and she finally faced them again. "I'm going to quit working here in two weeks and start my own business."

The reminder of her leaving stung. Lucian definitely didn't want her to go, but then, there were a lot of things he didn't want to happen here. And the biggest thing on that list was Jerry taking over.

"You could do this," Regina assured her. "For Lucian. For all of us. You've been his assistant for ten years, and I know you don't want to see what he's worked so hard for go under with Jerry's mismanagement."

Lucian wanted to hold out some hope that a) his father would change his mind, b) if there was no mind changing, that Jerry would do a stellar job or c) Lucian would wake up and learn this was all just a bad dream.

But he figured none of those things would happen.

So, he was facing a shitstorm with no paddle and no boat. The only thing he had was a half-baked plan concocted by his mother and a possible lighting up from Karlee—which had no bearing on this anyway.

That was hardly the basis for making a good decision.

However, as Lucian did with all his business proposals, he tried to look at it from the various angles. Especially the angles that could come back to bite him in the ass. The highest potential for an ass bite would come from Jerry, so that meant Lucian had to attempt to neutralize him. Short of locking him in the tack room and boarding up the door, he didn't have anything, so he did the unthinkable.

He considered Regina's plan.

His mom must have seen something in his eyes, too, to let her know what he was doing because she went into a full-court press.

"Just picture it," she said, fanning her hands out to indicate something big. "An engagement party where we invite everyone in town. Heck, you could ask Bernie Jessup from the city council to do the ceremony since he's an ordained minister."

"Wait—you said this was just an engagement," Lucian pointed out.

"It would be, but of course, we'd have to do wedding planning so that it all looks like the real deal. Wedding planning with the purpose to help fix things. Lois Fay Merkle from the historical society could do the music, and you know the garden guild would jump right on making the floral arrangements for both the party and the wedding. We could bring in pots and pots of Hairy Corn Salad to make everyone happy."

Well, it wouldn't make Lucian happy, but he was beginning to see that whatever he was feeling was on the very bottom rung of priorities here. Karlee's rung was significantly higher than his since there was no benefit whatsoever to her going through with an engagement to him.

Unless that light-up theory was true.

Lucian didn't consider himself an impulsive man, but he suddenly wanted to kiss her just to see if there was any truth to it. Actually, he'd always wanted to kiss her because she was an attractive woman. What had held him back was that he didn't want to ruin a top-notch working relationship. That relationship was on the brink of being ruined, though, because she was quitting.

And that was the logic Lucian used to move in for that test kiss.

Thankfully, he stopped himself at the last possible second, and he sort of froze there with his mouth hovering over hers. Yes, the very mouth he'd just imagined cruising over him. She smelled good, like that cream-heavy coffee that she favored. However, despite the good scent, it was a moment that should have had her stepping back. Or asking him if he'd lost his flipping mind.

That didn't happen.

A soft half breath left her mouth. It was as if she hadn't been able to gather enough air for a full one. Was he responsible for that?

Hell, maybe her bra was just too tight.

Either way, the moment was soon lost when his mom clapped her hands. "See? You two can make it work. You gave me tinglies." If she hadn't shown them her goose bumps, he wouldn't have had a clue what she was talking about. "An engagement, followed by an engagement party."

"No," Karlee said. She not only dragged in enough breath, she also moved back from him. "It wouldn't work. We need to come up with something else. Maybe you can buy out Jerry," she added to him.

Lucian shook his head. "Already tried, and he declined."

Of course, that didn't mean Lucian couldn't keep trying. The problem with that was Jerry would smell the desperation, and this could end up costing him not just the ranch and the business but his personal assets, too.

Maybe his mom had been right after all about him ending up in the poorhouse.

"Too bad that Jerry didn't jump on the buyout," Karlee said, obviously disappointed. "Can you at least toss him out of the house?"

Regina and Lucian shook their heads. "Jerry owns fifty percent of this house, too."

Another layer of disappointment crossed Karlee's face. "What about contacting all your business associates and asking them not to deal with Jerry. Would that work?"

Lucian wished that it would, but even if he'd had a pair of rose-colored glasses, he couldn't put them on for this. The people he dealt with wanted to make a profit, and some of them flat out didn't like him. They might feel they could strike a better deal with his more gullible father.

"See?" Regina concluded when Lucian didn't answer Karlee. "I told you that an engagement with attached wedding plans is the way to go. And you wouldn't even have to do anything, other than get engaged, that is. I'd take care of everything else and make sure the right people were there at the party to see how much you've changed."

Lucian had no doubts, *none*, that his mom would indeed "take care of everything" when it came to planning an engagement party/wedding.

Especially *his* engagement party/wedding.

He was the oldest of her five kids and the only one who wasn't married. Regina had been hinting for years that it was time for him to settle down. The problem was that any engagement party or wedding that she put together would likely be way over-the-top. And sadly, that was only a minor issue in this situation.

The bigger problem was Karlee.

She obviously wasn't convinced yet. Neither was Lucian, but he was bending in that direction. He leaned even more when the door flew open, and Jerry waltzed in without even asking if they were done with, well, whatever the heck it was they were supposed to be doing.

"Is Cindi all settled in?" Regina asked. And yes, it was a sharp-tongued tone. "I'll bet she was disappointed when she didn't find a stripper's pole in the master bedroom. No way for her to practice her craft."

"Candy," Jerry corrected, his eyes narrowing. "No disappointment of any kind. She's taking a little beauty nap—something you could probably use. I hope y'all are all talked out by now," Jerry said before Regina could return fire, "because I'd like to get to work." He went straight to Lucian's desk, sat down and leaned back in the chair. "Guess you'll need to box up this personal stuff you got in here so that it doesn't get in my way."

The only personal stuff was Lucian's laptop and his business cards. He didn't intend to move them just yet.

"Why are you really doing this?" Lucian came out and asked him. "And don't tell me it's because your old buddies are pissed off at me. It'd take more than that to bring you back here."

Butter wouldn't even come close to melting in that cool-mouthed expression. Which meant there was indeed something. Lucian needed to find out what so he could leverage it against Jerry, but that wouldn't stop the here and now from happening.

Hell.

He was going to have to walk out and let this piece of dung have a go at messing up something else. Something that Lucian loved.

"I can take these for you," Karlee said, gathering up

the laptop and the small holder with the business cards. "Should I put them in the office in the guesthouse?"

"Lucian won't be needing an office unless it's just for playing a game on his computer," Jerry jabbed. "I'd certainly better not find him sticking his nose in my business. But you are a different matter."

Karlee must have realized that Jerry was talking to her because she went stiff. "How am I a different matter?" Butter would definitely melt in her mouth because it had an anger-hot temp to it.

"Because I want you to stay on and work for me. Now, sweetie, I know you put in your notice and all," Jerry continued without giving her a chance to speak. Or address the fact he'd just risked eye daggers by calling her *sweetie*. "But I'm gonna need somebody who knows the ropes of Granger Enterprises."

Karlee stared at Jerry, the eye daggers flinging right at him. "No one knows the ropes better than Lucian."

"Maybe so, but he won't be here. Look at it this way—y'all think I'm gonna f-up. Well, what better way to keep an eye on me than to be right by my side when I'm doing all that wheeling and dealing?"

"Sonofabitch," Lucian growled. "You're blackmailing Karlee."

"I'm offering her a chance to keep her job. And yeah, I know all about her wanting to start her own business, but that can wait awhile so she can help me out. It wouldn't be for long. Just a couple of months. I figure by the New Year, this'll all be second hat to me."

Karlee's eye daggers stopped, and the breath she dragged in didn't seem to be going anywhere. It just sort of stalled there, making it look as if someone had hit the pause button on her.

"You don't have to do this," Lucian quickly assured her. He took her by the arm, turning her to switch off that pause, and she finally released that breath. "In fact, I don't want you to do it." No way did he want to put Karlee directly in Jerry's path on a daily basis.

Karlee stared at Lucian before looking first at Regina, then Jerry. Lucian could see the muscles working in her jaw, could see the discussion she was having with herself. Heck, he could practically envision the profanity going through her head.

It was a lot of very long moments before Karlee finally said anything, and then it was just one word. "Yes."

Jerry cackled with celebratory laughter and clapped his hands. Lucian sure as hell wasn't celebrating.

"Yes to you, too," Karlee added, snapping toward Lucian. She leaned in and went through with the kiss that'd nearly happened before Jerry came back in. It didn't taste or feel very good, though, because her mouth had tightened to iron. Instead of sweet coffee, it tasted like a whole lot of anger.

"Yes?" Jerry challenged. The hand clapping stopped, and some wariness started to creep into his eyes.

"Yes," Karlee verified. "Lucian and I just got engaged."

KARLEE FIGURED THAT she wouldn't be leaving alone when she walked out of the office after delivering the bombshell news to Jerry. It was also a bombshell for Lucian. Judging from his stunned expression, he certainly hadn't been expecting her to say yes.

Welcome to the club.

She hadn't expected to say yes, either, but Jerry had pushed her to the brink with his horse's-ass demand that she work for him. But that wasn't what had caused her to blurt out that yes. It'd been the realization that Jerry would indeed destroy everything that Lucian had worked for his whole adult life. She could put a stop to that.

Well, maybe.

If she worked for Jerry, she could at least keep an eye on things and do damage control as needed. Then, in a few months, maybe less, Lucian could oust his father and get on with his life. Of course, that would only take care of the business and the ranch. There was the other yes of that bombshell. She'd just agreed to get engaged to Lucian.

"You don't have to do this," Lucian repeated, following her.

Karlee had no idea where she was going, so she just kept walking. Away from his office, through the front of the house, then the sunroom and finally onto the back porch. It wasn't nearly enough steps to burn off all the jagged-edged emotions she was feeling. She didn't especially want any of those feelings—the anger, the uncertainty and the disappointment over having to delay her own plans for her business. But the craziest thing that zip-lined through her head?

She was engaged to Lucian.

That thought didn't come with anger or disappointment. It arrived with a full-blown heat wave over her body. One that she didn't want.

For years, she'd managed to corral the lust she had for her boss—or rather, her former boss—and she needed to keep it that way. She couldn't think of this as anything good. It was simply necessary to help Lucian and hopefully get back at the pond-scum father of his.

When Karlee started down the steps, Lucian moved in front of her, forcing eye contact between them. She knew what he was going to say, so she spoke before he could.

"You're going to tell me again that I don't have to do this. I know that. But I'm not going to let Jerry win." And because Karlee knew that wouldn't be enough to convince Lucian, she added, "This is for me, too. You won't be able to help me start my cattle broker business if you lose the company. Plus, your father could end up alienating any potential customers that either of us might have."

That stopped Lucian. For a few seconds, anyway. "If I lose this company, I can start another one. I have my own money. Hell, I have a trust fund that I haven't touched."

"Yes, you're rich, but you've worked hard to build your business. There's no reason to just chuck that in the trash without making the effort to save it."

She had no doubts that Lucian could build another company. Several of them, in fact, but there was also the other issue.

"You can't buy another family ranch," she pointed out. "Not one that your great-grandfather founded, anyway. It would crush Dylan to lose this place. This is his home."

It was Lucian's home, too, and even though he didn't live here full-time, he wouldn't want it run into the ground. And that's how Karlee presented the final piece of her argument.

"All of the hands will be affected by this," she said. "Heck, the entire town. Let's just think of this as a raging forest fire that you and I need to contain." But she stopped when she thought of something else.

Or rather, *someone* else.

The one-hundred-and-twenty-pound elephant that was always in the room when it came to Lucian and relationships.

"You could call Amelia and tell her what's going on," she suggested. "I mean, so that she'd know the truth."

Because Karlee was certain he wouldn't want Amelia to believe he was actually engaged. That would mean that one of them had moved on with their lives. Maybe Amelia wanted that. Heck, maybe Lucian even did. And that was what Karlee liked to let herself believe when she was struggling with that whole business of corralling her lust for him.

Since Lucian still wasn't arguing, that meant he was at least considering the valid points she'd just made. And then he made a valid point of his own. "You'd end up wanting to kill Jerry if you have to work for him," Lucian reminded her.

Karlee had to nod in agreement, and because she thought they could use some levity, she added, "I've wanted to kill you plenty of times, too."

The corner of his mouth twitched a little. Not a smile exactly, but close, and it caused that shallow dimple to flash in his cheek. "How'd you stop yourself?"

"By using an old speaker's tip. I pretend you're naked." Until the words left her mouth, she hadn't realized how that would sound.

No mouth twitching for him this time. Not at first, anyway. "Funny, that's exactly how I handle it when I'm pissed off at you," he said. And now it was an actual smile. A very short one though. "You don't have to do this," he tacked on, his voice a hoarse whisper. "Even if you work for Jerry, you don't have to go through with the engagement."

Karlee certainly wasn't smiling, either. "The two go hand in hand. Your image makeover and Jerry's ousting. As your mom said, we can call off the wedding when things cool down."

"And then the town will know it was a sham, and there would go my new nice-guy image."

She shook her head. "Not if we handle it right. Think of it as an agenda with many moving parts, and we're both very good at that sort of thing. Besides, Jerry will help because you know he'll end up riling people."

Lucian was obviously still trying to wrap his mind around that when Regina came out onto the porch. "So, it's all settled?"

"Yes," Karlee said just as Lucian said, "No."

But then Lucian cursed under his breath, groaned and then cursed some more. Because Karlee was watching him so closely, she saw the exact moment that Lucian did something that he didn't do very often.

He surrendered.

It wasn't a split-second kind of thing. By degrees, she saw his shoulders lower. Heard the rough, frustrated breath. But most of all she saw it in those flame-blue eyes. The heat didn't leave them completely, but they seemed to flicker with licks of sharp glass.

"All right," he grumbled. It definitely wasn't the tone of a happy soon-to-be bridegroom since he'd said it through clenched teeth.

Regina squealed with delight. "I have an engagement party and a wedding to plan. And I need to start calling people to let them know. A sort of personal Save the

Date message until I can send out the real ones." She whipped out her phone from her pocket and loaded her calendar. "I think I can pull together an engagement party in about two weeks. How does that sound?"

Terrifying. But Karlee kept that to herself. "The sooner, the better," she ended up saying. "The longer Jerry is here, the longer it'll be before I can start my own business."

"Totally agree. So, that'll be the first Saturday in December. I'll get started on those calls."

"Wait." Lucian spoke up. "I just thought of something. With the hasty engagement, people might believe Karlee's pregnant. I don't want her reputation ruined because she's trying to help me."

Regina dismissed that with the wave of her hand. "They'll suss that out soon enough when she doesn't start to show." She paused, eyed them with a little suspicion. "Uh, you won't start to show, will you?"

Lucian and Karlee both glared at her. "No," they said in unison.

"Then it won't be a problem. And that leads me to my next question. Should we go with a business formal engagement party?"

"No," Lucian and Karlee said in unison, again, though Lucian's was a lot louder than hers. "I'm not wearing a suit," he added in a grumble.

Regina's perky expression faded a little. "But you'll pick out a white dress for the wedding?" she asked Karlee.

Karlee shook her head. "There's no reason for a dress because there'll be no wedding."

"No, but we have to make everyone believe there'll be a big I-do. So, we need to set a date. I'm thinking the morning of the charity rodeo in June. No, wait. They've moved the rodeo to March this year because it conflicted with the town's centennial celebration."

Karlee knew that, of course, because it shortened Lucian's training time for the bronc-riding competition. Something that hadn't pleased him. Well, this conversation wasn't very pleasing, either.

"That's four months from now," Regina went on, "plenty enough time for us to deal with Jerry, and then call off things between you two. But in the meantime, we'll have to keep planning for the big day. That means you getting a dress. Maybe one fit for a princess wedding?"

Karlee wasn't sure how a princess wedding differed from a regular one. Yards and yards more lace, maybe. Perhaps a higher level of discomfort to the shoes. Still, it was only for a few hours. The ding to her bank account, though, would last for much, much longer since Karlee intended to pay for the dress herself.

"A dress it is," Karlee agreed.

Regina squealed again, turned as if to leave but then stopped. "I nearly forgot." She tugged at the canary diamond ring on her left hand, and once she had it off, she thrust it at Lucian. "It was my granny Bee's, but you can give it to Karlee for your engagement."

As with their unified response, Lucian and she did a head shake together, too. "I don't want a family heirloom," Karlee insisted.

Regina volleyed glances at them, obviously waiting for a firm decision on this. Well, firmer than the one Karlee had already given her.

"I'll buy Karlee a ring," Lucian finally said.

That sent Regina into yet another squeal, and she ran back inside, no doubt to set this big fat lie in motion.

Karlee and Lucian certainly weren't squealing, but she patted his arm. "It'll be okay."

She hoped.

The problem with a moving-parts agenda was that it could go south in a hurry. And speaking of going south, that happened, too, when Jerry came out of the house to join them.

"So, what's this so-called marriage proposal really about?" Jerry asked.

Lucian and she sprang right into action. He put his arm around her just as Karlee tried to do the same. They ended up doing some awkward bumping, but they finally managed an embrace.

"Nothing so-called about it," Lucian assured him. "Karlee and I are getting married. Your coming back here like this made me realize that life's too short to keep putting my personal life on hold."

It sounded convincing enough if you didn't think about it too hard or know either of them very well. Jerry certainly wasn't in the "know them" category, but he did have a marginally functioning brain, and that's probably why he squinted his right eye. It was too much to hope that a bug had flown into it.

When Jerry's eye squint deepened, she knew he wasn't buying it. But he wasn't the one they had to convince anyway. The convincing part would be for the town, and Regina was plenty confident that she could make that happen.

Jerry eased up on the skeptical eye expression and then shrugged. "All right, then. You ready to get some work done?" he asked Karlee. "Because I'd like to go over that deal that Lucian just made with Ian. You know, just to see if I could have made a better one."

To hold back her temper, Karlee had to bite her lip and imagine the whole world was naked. Thankfully, that gave her a jolt of disgust since Jerry was in the naked cesspool of the image. The disgust took care of what would have been a snapped, profanity-laced response. Instead, she just nodded.

"Good." Jerry grinned. "Well, come on, sweetie, and let's get started." He slung his arm around her shoulders to get her moving out of Lucian's embrace, but Karlee held her ground.

No naked imaginings could stop her from addressing what Jerry had just said. She threw off his grip with far more force than necessary. "Yes, we can get started, but if you call me *sweetie* again, I'll put a virus on your computer and cow shit in your coffee. Have I made myself clear?"

Jerry laughed. Karlee didn't. And he finally seemed to get the point because he quit laughing, too. In fact, she got a crystal clear glimpse of the asshole who was now her boss.

God, what had she done?

CHAPTER FIVE

WHEN LUCIAN STEPPED into the doorway of the guest-house, he immediately asked himself one important question: What happened when you mixed together a gift fairy, a moving company and a florist with bad taste?

The answer was *this*, the mess that was sprawled out in front of him.

He wished that was part of a joke, but it wasn't. All of that—gifts, the moving boxes, flowers—and so much more had apparently converged in the ranch guesthouse that Karlee and he were about to call home now that they were a week into their "engagement." Apparently, nothing said engagement celebration like a shitload of stuff.

While he tried to take it all in, Lucian reminded himself that it'd been his idea for them to move into the guesthouse for their fake engagement. He'd reasoned that it would stop some of the too-frequent encounters where he would have to see Jerry. It would also complete the facade of Karlee and him being a happily engaged couple who couldn't keep their hands off each other.

Plus, there was the issue that the main house was getting pretty crowded since Dylan, his wife and son lived there with their current houseguests, Regina, Jerry and

Candy. *Crowded* was an exaggeration, of course, since the place had something like thirty rooms, but Jerry had a way of making it seem as if it'd been whittled down to the size of an efficiency apartment. His booming voice thundered through halls and stairways, and it didn't pair well with Regina's thundering zingers, which in turn didn't pair well with Candy's nasal complaints and constant splattering of heel taps as she followed Jerry around.

Another part of Lucian's reasoning to move to the guesthouse had been that it would give Karlee a reprieve. As Jerry's assistant, she'd been working and staying in the main house. Even though the guest cottage was only a stone's throw off the back porch, it would still give them some privacy so they didn't have to keep up with the engagement pretense 24/7.

In hindsight, all of the reasons he'd had for this move had been stupid.

The guesthouse was small. A combined living, dining and kitchen area and two bedrooms with their own baths. Lucian estimated it was about twelve hundred square feet. Enough for a guest or two. Or it could be used as office space—which was how Karlee had been using it for the past couple of years. Her desk was still there, shoved to the corner behind the sofa, and seemingly every other inch of it and the rest of the place were covered with stuff. It looked like a TV set for an episode of extreme hoarding.

The boxes with Karlee's clothes and such were stacked nearly to the ceiling. What space they weren't taking up had been crammed with engagement/early wedding gifts that had been arriving at an alarming rate. And now there was a new form of clutter.

Weeds.

There were about a dozen silver pots scabbed with

what he supposed were intended to be artistically placed swaths of rust and green paint smears, and they were filled with weedy-looking white flowers. Several of the pots were sitting on top of the wrapped gifts that were in turn sitting on top of boxes marked as Karlee's stuff.

Yes, indeed. A gift fairy, a moving company and a florist with bad taste.

Lucian was still standing in the doorway and trying to figure out a path to the bedroom where he'd set up a makeshift office when he heard the footsteps. Thank God it wasn't someone else bringing in more boxes or gifts, though the visitor was carrying a small brown paper bag. It was Abe Weiser, the cook who'd worked at the ranch for over twenty years.

Despite the chilly temp, Abe wasn't wearing a coat. He was dressed in one of his many old concert T-shirts that he'd collected over the years. This despite that, to the best of Lucian's knowledge, Abe had never actually attended a concert. He just liked to wear them, and this one had what appeared to be a mustard stain over Ringo's left ear.

Abe took his time coming up the steps. Actually, Abe took his time with pretty much everything he did in life. Even though the man was only in his fifties and nowhere near feeble, no one would ever accuse him of being in a hurry. Or of being a good cook. Or being especially friendly. In fact, everyone wondered what he actually did at the ranch to earn his paycheck.

Everyone but Lucian.

Abe had layers. Well, one layer, anyway. Unlike an onion, he was more like a banana about to go bad. The kind of bad where you were trying to decide if you wanted to just toss it or try to use it in a recipe that no one would end up eating anyway.

Lucian suspected he'd been one of the few people who'd actually gotten a look at the fruit beneath the cook's thick, somewhat-spotted layer. Abe had the face of an old boxer with his flat nose, flabby jowls and muscles gone soft. He wasn't one for long heart-to-heart chats, or even short ones, but he could say plenty with his weathered gray eyes. Eyes that spared Lucian a glance before looking inside at the crammed-in clutter.

Abe snorted, and despite it being such a simple sound, Lucian didn't miss the disapproval, frustration and the sympathy. Or at least Lucian thought that was a reasonable interpretation.

"I know," Lucian said. "Bad idea."

Abe snorted again, adding a grunt of agreement. He nudged the back of Lucian's hand so that he'd take the brown bag. "Show Jerry who you are and kick his tiny wrinkled balls into his eye sockets," Abe muttered once Lucian had hold of the bag, and he strolled away.

It was Abe-style sage advice, and while plenty of folks wanted Jerry's balls relocated to various parts of his anatomy, it was the first part of what Abe had said that would stay with him.

Show Jerry who you are.

Lucian hadn't especially needed that reminder, but it was good to hear it. Good to get the bag, too. It wasn't something that Lucian figured anyone would understand, but Abe's bags always grounded him and told him that someone knew that his own Lucifer layer wasn't such a bad thing.

He went in and had to search for a place for the bag. Since every inch of counter space was covered, he put it inside the dishwasher—where there was yet more stuff, including what appeared to be more weeds.

Lucian was just heading to his bedroom/office when the front door opened and smacked him in the back. Hell. That motion sent his knee ramming into a coffee table that had not only been moved from its usual spot, but it had also seemingly changed its composition from wood to galvanized steel.

The pain shot through him, causing him to curse. It coordinated well with the mumbled profanity from Karlee. She was the one who'd smacked him with the door, but it wasn't exactly her fault. She had a stack of presents piled up so high in her arms that there's no way she could have seen him.

"Are you all right?" she asked, and as soon as Lucian managed a not-very-convincing nod, she glanced around the room and muttered more of that PG-rated profanity. "Good God, what happened here?"

"I think we got some deliveries while we were in San Antonio." Lucian had been there to get some things from his house, and Karlee had likely done the same to her place.

She put the presents she'd been balancing on the small porch and came back in to survey the damage. And make a call. "Skeeter," she said when the ranch hand apparently answered. "Could you get some guys to the guesthouse to move some things for Lucian and me?"

Lucian was sure he would have thought of that soon enough, but he was still in shock. And feeling a little claustrophobic and overwhelmed. He was usually so organized, a reminder that the only reason for his good organization skills was because Karlee kept track of everything.

"I was supposed to give you this days ago," he said when she was done with her call. He took out the small jewelry box from his pocket. "It's your engagement ring." He didn't put *engagement* in air quotes because he would have banged his funny bone on something.

She blinked, and there was plenty of uncertainty in her eyes when she took the box from him. Was Karlee having second thoughts?

If so, that was yet more proof that she was as smart as he knew she was.

She flipped open the box lid and stared at the ring. Lucian had no intention of admitting that it had taken him six hours to pick it out. He didn't want her to think that he was feeling any pressure from what was supposed to be an engagement of convenience. But there was nothing but pressure and no convenience right now.

"It's beautiful." She slipped the solitaire onto her finger. It wasn't yellow, overly big or embellished. "Perfect," she mumbled.

That's when Lucian released the breath that he didn't even know he'd been holding. That's when Karlee noticed he'd been holding, then releasing his breath. And shortly thereafter, she got her attention on something else. Something that wasn't perfect or an influence on his oxygen intake.

"That looks like Hairy Corn Salad," Karlee said, tipping her head to the plants. "Heaven knows how your mom managed to get it since it's not in season."

Witchcraft might have been involved. He was having a hard time believing that mere motherhood and social connections could allow Regina to completely dismantle and rearrange his life in two weeks, but this clutter and the out-of-the-season weeds were proof of it.

The only silver lining in this otherwise-putrid cloud was that so far his father hadn't interfered in the daily operation of the ranch. That wasn't just good for Dylan, it was also good for all of them since the ranch was successful. And it would almost certainly stay that way if Jerry kept his fingers out of it.

"Is that Hairy Corn Salad, too?" he asked. He motioned toward little plates of what appeared to be food on the kitchen counter.

Karlee shook her head, moving past him. Or rather, attempting to move past him. There was only about a foot of space in between the furniture, boxes and gifts, so that resulted in a whole lot of body bumping.

"Sorry," she mumbled.

Yeah, he was sorry, too, because he was in a crappy mood, and those body bumps were a reminder that sex would help lighten him up a little. It would also complicate things even more than they already were, and that's why Lucian backed into the kitchen so that she could reach the counter without further touching.

There were about twenty of those plastic plates. Saucers, really. And each one had something different perched on them. Some of them appeared to be actual edible food. Others looked like sprigs of stuff from old Easter bonnets he'd once found in his grandma's cedar chest. There was a note card next to each saucer to let them know what the items were. Or rather, what the items were *named*.

Potato coins with chipotle crème. Blue-cheese bacon boats. Crushed crostini. Filet bobs.

There was an additional note with instructions for them to rate them ASAP because the caterer—the daughter of a city council member—needed a final decision before noon so she could get the food started for the engagement party. Since it was already 3:00 p.m., they'd missed that particular blue-cheese bacon boat.

"This explains the six calls from your mom that I let go to voice mail," Karlee said. She glanced at him. "Sorry, but Regina was driving me nuts, so I quit answering."

"Same here. I have eight missed calls from her." But Lucian didn't see this as a great calamity. Regina had almost certainly done the final food selection since the engagement party was now only twenty-four hours away.

Twenty-four more hours where he'd continue to ask himself—*what the hell are you doing?*

Lucian suspected he wouldn't have a better answer tomorrow than he did now, and it was entirely possible the question would just continue. But at least there seemed to be progress. More folks were smiling at him whenever he was in town. Of course, there were some scowls, too, but the smile to scowl ratio was evening out some.

Karlee grabbed a spoon that was next to one of the saucers and took a bite of the chipotle crème. "Mmmm," she said, "and now I can tell your mother that I sampled the stuff." Almost absently, she offered him the rest of what was on the spoon, but then shook her head. "Sorry, I guess that'd be a little like kissing."

Yeah, it would be only one degree of separation from her mouth, and that's probably why Lucian leaned in and licked the spoon while Karlee was still holding it. It didn't taste like Karlee, but his overly aroused body could imagine that it did.

She smiled. Then frowned, no doubt remembering they should be cooling this off rather than revving it up, and she yanked open the dishwasher to put in the spoon. She had a similar reaction as he had when she saw the weeds. A frustrated huff. But then her attention landed on the bag.

"Abe was here," she said.

Lucian nodded, knowing that she wouldn't ask what was in it. She hadn't in the ten years she'd worked for him. Maybe because she knew. Karlee had ESP about that sort of thing. But if her special insights had clued her in, she'd never pushed to find out why a crusty, lazy cook would give him such a thing—and why a cowboy called Lucifer would take it.

Layers, Lucian thought to himself. Something that Karlee had plenty of, as well.

Easing the dishwasher shut, Karlee gave him one more glance. The kind of glance to make sure he was okay. He licked his lips to remind her that deep glances and concern could lead to deep kisses and sex. With a shrug and a smile, she moved on to the rusty tubs of weeds and to the note that was next to them, as well.

"Aren't these beautiful?" his mother had written. "Chic rustic, like the engagement party and the wedding. Let me know by noon if these are okay to put on the bridal path because it'll take some time to get enough going in a greenhouse."

"There's a bridal path, as in some place for the bride to walk?" Lucian asked. "Or does she mean bridle, like headgear for a horse?"

Karlee shrugged. "She booked the rodeo grounds for both the engagement party and the wedding." *Wedding* went in air quotes. "I suppose it could be either."

Lucian had to do his own shrug. It didn't matter. The deadline had passed for that particular decision, too. But it hadn't passed for what could be a last-ditch effort at some common sense. However, Karlee spoke before he could say anything.

"Maybe we should have stayed in your house in San Antonio after all?" she threw out there.

That had indeed come up as a possible place for their den of lies. So had Karlee's apartment, which was also in San Antonio. But in the end, they'd decided it was best to stay close to Jerry in case the man tried to pull something stupid.

"Once some of the stuff is out of here, it'll be okay," he assured her. "I'll have the hands move the gifts to one of the spare rooms in the main house." But that didn't address his concerns about common sense. "Should we just call this off?"

The surprise flashed through her eyes. "Is that what you want?"

And there was the million-dollar question. If he said yes, Karlee might be disappointed. Hell, he might be disappointed because there would go his best shot at ridding the ranch of Jerry. But if he said no, then it would look as if he wanted her to say yes, and confusion would ensue.

There was no time for confusion ensuing, though, because there was a tap on the still-open door. It took a moment for Lucian to make his way back there. Not Skeeter or the hands though. It was Alice May Merkle. She was Lois Fay's sister, but more important, she was a longtime member of the garden guild.

"I took a chance that you'd be here," Alice May said. She was carrying a huge present, and even though there clearly wasn't room for it, she brought it in anyway and handed it to Karlee. "I can't come to the engagement party because my nephew's got a recital in Austin."

"Oh, we're so sorry you can't make it," Karlee said. "We'll miss you."

Alice May wasn't a smiler. In fact, Lucian always thought her face looked like an apricot right before it went bad. Wrinkled but still round. Her mouth just sort of curved in a downward turn, and the turn increased when she looked at Lucian.

"I have to say I was surprised when I heard you'd asked Karlee to marry you." It sounded like an accusation coming from Alice May. "I mean, Karlee's such a sweetheart."

And you're an asshole. Of course, Alice May didn't come out and say that, but it was strongly implied.

"My first thought was that I didn't want to see Karlee hurt," Alice May went on. "I mean she's been through so much, bless her heart."

Karlee didn't have any outward reaction other than a syrupy smile, but he figured she was biting the inside of her lip. She hated it when people felt sorry for her.

"I'll be fine," Karlee assured the woman. "Lucian and I make a great pair."

But when Karlee's gaze drifted to his, he saw the doubt there. Some deep concern, too. Probably because of that question he'd asked her before Alice May showed up.

Should we just call this off?

Lucian suspected he'd be getting an answer to that after their visitor left.

"A great pair," Alice May repeated, still not sounding convinced. Her eyes narrowed some when she turned back to Lucian. "There'd be a lot of folks plenty upset if you hurt her. Just remember that."

It seemed like a threat, and coming from a longtime

garden guild member, it seemed like a threat with some teeth. The woman knew how to use a hoe and shovel.

Alice May's eyes suddenly brightened a little, though, and when Lucian followed her gaze, he saw that she'd noticed the weeds in the rust pots. "You have Valerianella Amarella. Hairy Corn Salad," she clarified when Lucian gave her what had to be a blank look.

"Oh yeah. *Yes*," he amended, remembering to stay polite. "It'll be on the bridal path at the wedding." Thankfully, he didn't have to spell out what type of path since he didn't know, and it didn't matter since they'd never make it to a wedding ceremony anyway.

Alice May put her hand over her heart as if to steady it. "This is so touching. And it's the right thing to do since it was your great-grandfather's favorite. It's as if a little part of him will be there for the ceremony. I knew him. And your grandfather, too, of course. Everyone called him J.L. He was a good man, and he loved riding in the charity rodeo."

He hadn't known his great-grandfather, but Lucian could agree with what she'd said about his grandfather. "J.L. left me one of his rodeo buckles. The one he got for winning both the bronc- and bull-riding events in the same year."

She nodded. "That was the only time anyone's ever done that in the entire history of the rodeo. He left you a real treasure."

That was true on many levels. J.L. had shown him what family was supposed to do. How they were supposed to support each other. Sometimes Lucian had forgotten those lessons, though, and that's how he'd ended up with the nickname Lucifer.

"Such sweet memories of your grandfather," Alice

May said, and she did something that obviously Karlee hadn't been expecting. The woman hugged her. Alice May followed it up by hugging Lucian. He hadn't expected it, either.

"Well, I'll just be going, then," Alice May said a moment later. She looked at them and smiled. "Have a happy engagement and a happy life." She paused, her attention settling on Lucian. "I'll see what I can do about smoothing things over between you and the members of the garden guild."

Dumbfounded, Lucian stood there as the woman threaded her way out of the clutter. "Well, shit," he mumbled. "My mom's plan is working."

Karlee made a sound of agreement. "But you want to call it off," she reminded him.

Lucian tried to figure out how to word this and hoped it sounded better out of his mouth than in his head. "I don't want to ruin things between us." The memory of those body bumps flashed before his eyes. "Business things," he added.

Nope, it wasn't sounding any better as actual words. It made it seem as if he was perfectly fine with touching, which would almost certainly lead to sex.

"I mean I want us to still be friends when this is over," Lucian tried again. Hell, that was even worse. That seemed like a line better suited for breaking up with a girlfriend.

"You want us to be friendly business associates," Karlee phrased for him. "Which is good. I'll need an ally when I start my new company, and you'll want me to step in occasionally when you're dealing with a buyer or seller who works more favorably with me than you. Like Elgin Smith and Hank Myers."

Yes! No wonder she'd been his assistant for so long. Those two cattlemen were prime examples where Karlee could work her personable magic to smooth the deals along.

"So, since your mom's plan seems to be working," she went on, "we just have to be careful about things. No more body bumping because that gave certain parts of me bad ideas."

She chuckled, and Lucian attempted a smile, too, but certain parts of him latched on to the bad ideas. Actually, only one part of him did the latching, and it was the brainless part of him that rarely made good decisions.

"Did you work on the business proposals you mentioned?" she asked when she quit chuckling.

Lucian appreciated the change of subject, but it took him a moment to push it aside. His dick really wanted to know what Karlee would consider bad.

"I worked up two of them," he answered. "One is for some quarter horses. The other for rodeo bulls."

Both were out of his usual realm of buying and selling. He normally just dealt with bulk herds of cattle, but he didn't have the fenced acreage for bulk.

His dad did since he controlled the ranch.

But Lucian was working on getting more fencing on the land he owned outright. Of course, that meant spending lots of money, which in turn meant cashing in some of his investments.

"If you want, I can look over the proposals," Karlee offered.

It was tempting, but he knew Karlee was already burning the candle at both ends. "Isn't Jerry keeping you busy enough?"

"He's trying. By the way, I emailed you a copy of

the latest deal he's trying to negotiate. I thought you could use the laugh."

Lucian could indeed. He'd known his dad would screw up. Had also known that Karlee would do what she could to minimize their losses. But it cut him to the core that this was going on right under his nose.

"So, do you still want to call it off?" she asked.

Despite the great argument Karlee had just given him, there was the personal side of this. Those *bad ideas*. That's the kind of stuff that could lead to her getting hurt. Before he could attempt another answer, there was another interruption. A knock on the door. It wasn't any of the hands, but it was a familiar face.

Joe O'Malley. Karlee's brother.

She hurried to him and pulled him into her arms. Or rather, Joe did the pulling. He was a big guy, towering over his sister.

Since Karlee and her brothers had been raised in Wrangler's Creek, Lucian had known him his entire life. Of course, most of that time there'd been the tension between their families because Jerry had run off with their mom. Tension on Karlee's family's part, anyway. Lucian had never held that against her, and he would have liked for her brother to do the same for him.

So far, though, that hadn't happened.

What happened was that, unlike Karlee, her brothers had all moved off. Joe lived near Kerrville, where he had a horse ranch.

"I wasn't expecting you until tomorrow," Karlee told Joe after they finished a long, hard hug.

"That's the nice thing about being the boss. You can cut out when you want. You'll see when you have your own business."

Joe was smiling when he looked at his sister, but that smile dissolved when he looked at Lucian. It was similar to the reaction he'd first gotten from Alice May. He doubted, though, that Joe would make a quick turnaround like Alice May had.

"Lucian," Joe greeted, and it was as frosty as his expression.

Karlee, however, was the opposite of frost, but she did look a little panicked when she glanced around the room. "Sorry that I can't offer you a place to sit. Or stay. Were you able to get something at the inn?"

He shook his head. "I'm staying with Lawson and Eve. It'll give us some time to catch up."

That made sense. Lawson was Lucian's brother. Eve was his wife. And they'd been friends with Joe back in high school.

There was yet another knock on the door, but this time it was the person they'd been expecting. Skeeter. And he had three ranch hands with him.

"Oh, excuse me for a minute," Karlee said to her brother. "I need to give them instructions on where to move the gifts and some of these boxes."

She went onto the porch with them, leaving Joe and Lucian alone. Joe came toward him. Not easily. His shoulders bumped the box stacks, but Lucian could tell that no amount of cardboard was going to stop him.

"What kind of shit are you trying to pull?" Joe demanded.

Lucian wasn't surprised at all by the question. Joe was very protective of his sister, and it'd caused a few run-ins when Joe had thought Lucian had been working Karlee too hard. However, what stumped Lucian was figuring out how to answer that. It turned out, though, that answering wasn't a problem because Joe didn't wait for Lucian to say anything. But he did lean in even closer.

Normally, Lucian would have put a stop to any personal-space violations by an angry man with a beef against him. But in this case, he just held what little ground he had left and waited for the rest of what would no doubt be a brotherly rant.

"Karlee's always had feelings for you," Joe tossed out there. He glanced back at his sister, probably to make sure she wasn't listening. She wasn't. Karlee was talking to someone on the phone. "For reasons I'll never understand, she just lights up whenever you're around."

There it was again. The whole "light up" thing. Man, Lucian figured he was either stupid or blind because he'd sure as hell never seen it. But he didn't have to comment on that, either, because Joe just kept on.

"I know you never thought of her that way. And that you'll never get over Amelia."

Lucian stopped him with some cursing. "Amelia isn't part of this."

"She kicked you in the teeth, so, yeah, she is part of it. But your so-called baggage and my sister's feelings for you won't give you a free pass," Joe warned him. "Just hear this." Joe's finger landed against Lucian's chest. "You'd better not be pulling some kind of stunt. You'd better go through with this wedding and make her happy. Because if you hurt my sister, I'll kick more than just your teeth."

Lucian stayed put as Joe went back to the porch, where Karlee was finishing up her phone call. Joe's exit was a little harder, though, because the hands had already started to move the boxes, and he had to step around them. He didn't hear what Joe said to Karlee, but as soon as her brother left, Karlee came back in. As Joe had done, she maneuvered her way to him.

Lucian had to tell her that he was calling off the wedding. And no, it didn't have anything to do with Joe's threat. Besides, Lucian was reasonably sure if any ass got kicked that it would be Joe's and not his.

"I don't want you hurt…" Lucian started.

She nodded, then huffed, and her mind clearly wasn't on what he'd just said or what he wanted to say to her. "That was Delbert Sweeny on the phone."

That got Lucian's attention off the wedding-nixing. Because Delbert was the chief financial officer for Granger Enterprises.

"Delbert called me because Jerry gave him specific orders not to speak to you," Karlee went on. "It's not good, Lucian." Her forehead bunched up. "Your father just started the paperwork to sell off about a fourth of the company assets."

Hell. A fourth was well over a million dollars.

"Please tell me that doesn't include land." Money he could earn back, but land needed to run the business and the ranch was hard to come by.

"It does." Karlee blew out a rough breath. "God, Lucian. We have to stop him."

CHAPTER SIX

"It's missing something," Regina mumbled as she eyed Karlee and the getup she was wearing.

There was no chance it was missing anything. The simple mint-colored sheath dress that Karlee had chosen for the engagement party was no longer simple thanks to Regina's "family" embellishments.

Karlee was now wearing a massive heart-shaped emerald brooch that had belonged to Lucian's great-grandmother. It had company in the form of the equally massive multijeweled hair comb that had also belonged to his great-grandmother. And then there were the white cowboy boots. They were new, a gift from Regina, but the woman had added silver spur charms to complete the "look." Regina just kept on completing, too, because she stuffed some sprigs of Hairy Corn Salad into Karlee's hair.

"There now. That's perfect," Regina announced.

No. It wasn't. With her Celtic red hair and pale skin, she looked like some kind of shabby chic cowgirl pagan creature who was ready for a ritual dance. Karlee sighed. If a ritual dance had a shot at making this better, she would have already gone for it.

Regina stood behind her, looking at Karlee in the full-length mirror. There were tears in her eyes. "You're a walking advertisement for everything that can fix Lucian's image. Of course, you're the best fix there is."

Karlee wanted to believe that. Wanted to believe, too, that things could indeed be fixed, but with Jerry attempting to sell off parts of the family holdings, it wasn't looking good. Of course, he'd have to give Regina, his kids, the guild and historical society their cuts of the money he got, but that wouldn't help with the losses.

That was why Lucian had marched right into his office—or rather, Jerry's office—and offered to buy the land and holdings. Jerry had refused, saying he already had a buyer lined up and that the deal was final. Jerry had also refused to tell Lucian the name of the buyer.

Somehow, Lucian had held his temper after that, but she suspected he'd punched a wall or two after he'd stormed out to go call his lawyers to stop the sale. And he'd managed it. The lawyers had filed some kind of motion to stop the sale until it could be evaluated, but it was only temporary. The sale would almost certainly go through unless they could convince the other half of the owners to fight Jerry. Even that might not be enough since Jerry was the majority shareholder.

Karlee hadn't seen Lucian after the chat with his attorneys because once that conversation had finished, Dylan had whisked him away for beers at the Longhorn Bar. Maybe also to try to talk him out of going through with this engagement party.

And the engagement itself.

Karlee would have talked herself out of it days ago if it didn't seem to be working. The chill was definitely less chilly for Lucian, and maybe this engagement party would mend all those broken fences. Then they could oust Jerry and she could get on with her life.

Without Lucian.

Unfortunately, that thought kept going through her head, too. It had always been a fantasy of hers to be with him. Not as his fiancée, though, but as his lover. She'd wondered what it would be like to have one of those monthlong relationships that dotted his life since his breakup with Amelia. She was betting it would be pretty darn amazing. Too bad, though, that it would come with strings longer than the miles and miles of west Texas. Because thirty days of sex with Lucian might make it impossible for her to walk away with her heart still in the unbroken mode.

"Remember to smile a lot," Regina said, pulling Karlee out of her fantasies. It was a shame because imagining a naked Lucian was far more fun than getting another glimpse of the party dress or remembering that she was about to put on a show. One that could determine Lucian's fate.

Hers, too.

Because if they could do all their fence mending tonight, then she wouldn't be tempted to become Lucian's temporary bedmate.

"Will you be able to smile *a lot* if Jerry shows up?" Karlee asked.

"Oh, he'll show up all right and will try to make himself the center of attention. I have a few things in mind when that happens."

That didn't sound promising for helping to repair Lucian's reputation. Then again, if folks got focused on Jerry and Regina, then Lucian and she wouldn't be under such close scrutiny.

"I suspect Jerry will be riled that Lucian's lawyer put a stop to that sale," Regina went on. "Have you had any luck finding out who that mystery buyer is?"

"None." And that was troubling. The Texas cattle broker business was actually a fairly small community, and no one was fessing up to wanting to purchase a slice of the Granger assets. Of course, the person might be staying mum so as not to get on Lucian's bad side. After all, it wasn't a sure thing that Jerry was going to remain at the helm for long.

"I'll keep poking around to see what I can find," Regina said. "Say, you don't think Jerry's trying to sell to the mob, do you?"

Mercy, she hoped not, but Karlee couldn't imagine organized crime being interested in assets in rural Texas. Still, something was fishy.

Regina and she started toward the door of the makeshift dressing room. It was actually a converted storage area with creepy rodeo clown costumes and floats from the previous years. One was an enormous papier-mâché bull that had toppled off and someone had put deflated balloons where his balls should be. Regina had wanted her to get dressed there so she could make a "grand entrance" directly into the huge barn where most of the indoor rodeo competition took place.

It was also where Lucian would be waiting for her.

Karlee was reasonably sure that her idea of grand entrances was not the same as Regina's.

The door opened before they even reached it, and Dylan's wife, Jordan, stuck her head in. She wasn't just married to Dylan though. She was also Karlee's best friend. And Karlee needed her right now to help steady her nerves.

Jordan looked at her, and it seemed as if she forgot all about the greeting she'd been about to give. "Oh," she said.

That reaction pretty much summed it up.

Jordan, who was a former military officer, was obviously cool under pressure because she turned to Regina. "Could you give Karlee and me a little girl time? Alone," she added. "I just want to talk to her before she goes out there."

"Of course. In fact, you two should walk out together since you're a war hero. That'll really get the crowd cheering."

The *war hero* had Jordan rolling her eyes, but thankfully Regina didn't see it. Also thankfully, the woman left them alone.

"You know this outfit looks bad, right?" Jordan asked her.

"Yes. Other than the green dress, it was all Regina's idea."

"Well, the dress is great. It skims all the right places, so let's do some fashion editing." She started plucking the flowering weeds from Karlee's hair and rearranging them so that they weren't haloing around her. "How about the boots? Did you plan on wearing those?"

"No." And Karlee led her back to the mirror where she'd left the silver heels she'd bought to go with the dress.

Jordan eyed the boots, the family adornments that Regina had put on her and the weeds she was holding. "Put on the heels." Jordan plucked off the brooch and the comb. "I can put them on the boots to use them as a centerpiece."

It was tempting, but she didn't want to offend Regina. Plus, this might earn her points with the historical society, who would likely recognize the heirlooms. Karlee moved the brooch to the center top of the dress so that it seemed less like a sparkly corsage and more like a necklace.

Jordan tucked the comb into the back of Karlee's hair. "I'll tell Regina it was my idea," Jordan said as if reading her mind. The look she gave Karlee also seemed to have some mind-reading abilities to go along with it. "Having second thoughts?"

"No. The second thoughts came and went days ago. I'm on the fiftieth round of thoughts right now." Karlee paused and gathered her breath. "It's all a lie."

Jordan made a quick sound of agreement. "But being in that guesthouse with Lucian will be real. I'm guessing you've considered that a pretend engagement can lead to real sex. Are you ready for that?"

Mercy, was she ready. Well, her body was, anyway. But there was all that trouble with the strings. Besides, their living arrangement might not even last more than a couple of days if Regina's plan succeeded tonight. Even if it did last, there was still the barrier of separate bedrooms.

"Much better," Jordan said once Karlee had on the heels.

"Thanks." It was exactly how she looked before Regina had had a go at her. "Have you heard any talk? Are people really buying the engagement?"

"There's talk." Jordan paused. "Not all good. Some people think Lucian's playing on your feelings for him so he can improve his image."

"My feelings for him?" Karlee said that a whole lot louder than she'd planned. "People know about that?"

Jordan gave her a flat look. "Everybody except Lucian knows that. You're the only one who cheers for him during the bronc ride at the rodeo. And don't say you do that because he's your boss—or rather, your former boss—because you were also cheering for him when you were still a teenager."

It was true. It was both a blessing and a curse that Lucian hadn't noticed. She hadn't wanted him to see that lustful look in her eyes because it would have sent him running. That four-year age difference between them made her jailbait in those days. By the time she'd been "legal," Lucian was running the family business and had been in love with Amelia.

"Just because we're under the same roof, it doesn't mean sex will happen," Karlee assured her. "Lucian doesn't think of me that way."

Jordan huffed and patted her arm. "Honey, you're beautiful. All men think of you that way. Well, everyone but my husband."

That last part was true, as well. Dylan only had eyes for Jordan and vice versa. But Jordan was wrong about the other.

"Okay, are you ready to do this?" Jordan asked her.

She wasn't, but the sooner she got out there, the sooner this night could end. "How many people are here?"

"Loads. More came to this than even the rodeo. I think it was the lure of free food and booze. Of course, the single women might be here to throw daggers at you for snagging Wrangler's Creek's most eligible bachelor."

They could save their daggers because Lucian would soon be back on the market.

The moment they were out of the storage area, Karlee heard the music. A country band playing a Garth

Brooks song. There was chatter and laughter. And that all stopped when Karlee walked into the barn. Seriously, it got so quiet that she heard her heels sinking into the dirt. And everyone was looking at her.

Everyone.

There wasn't a single unfilled seat in the stands, and people lined all sides of the barn. In contrast, the center of the massive barn was practically empty. Only Lucian, Regina, Dylan were in there, and they were clearly waiting for her.

"And here's the bride-to-be," Regina announced, her voice booming through the microphone she was holding. "As you can see, she's wearing the family jewels." No one except Regina laughed at her joke.

Karlee walked out on the ground of the barn where Lucian had busted his butt eighteen times while competing in the rodeo. Perhaps he saw this party as a metaphorical toss from a bronc, but if so, there was no trace of that in his expression. He smiled, his gaze sliding over her, making her thankful she'd opted for a curve-hugging dress and the shoes.

Lucian walked toward her, and the moment he reached her, he curved his arm around her waist, pulled her to him.

And he kissed her.

The world dissolved. That included the ground beneath her feet and every bone in her body. This wasn't like the other stiff kiss in his office. Heck, this wasn't like any other kiss that'd happened—ever.

The feel of him raced through Karlee, and what damage the lip-lock didn't do, his scent finished off. Leather and cowboy. A heady mix when paired with his mouth that she was certain could be classified as one of the deadly sins.

She heard the crowd erupt into pockets of cheers, but all of that noise faded. The only thing was the soft sound of pleasure she made. Lucian made a sound, too. A manly grunt. It went well with that manly grip he had on her and his manly taste. Jameson whiskey and sex. Of course, that sex taste might be speculation on her part since the kiss immediately gave her many, many sexual thoughts.

Lucian eased back from her. "You did good," he whispered.

That dashed the sex thoughts. It dashed a lot of things because it was a reminder that this was all for show. But Lucian didn't move away from her after saying that. He just stood there, looking down at her with those scorcher blue eyes.

"You did good, too," Karlee told him because she didn't know what else to say.

He still didn't back away despite the fact the applause and cheers had died down and the crowd was clearly waiting for something else to happen. Karlee was waiting, as well. Then it happened.

Lucian kissed her again.

This time, though, it wasn't that intense smooch. He just brushed his mouth over hers. Barely a touch but somehow making it the most memorable kiss in the history of kisses. Ditto for the long, lingering look he gave her afterward.

"That was from me," he said as if that clarified things. It didn't. It left Karlee feeling even more aroused. And confused.

What the heck did that mean?

This wasn't the time for her to ask. Maybe there'd never be a good time for it because Lucian's forehead bunched up as if he instantly regretted kissing her. Karlee knew how he felt because she knew what it was like to be kissed by someone who knew exactly how to do it.

Talk about a benchmark.

Just as the ground had earlier, the moment dissolved when Regina came back on the microphone. "Lucian, Karlee and I want everyone to have a good time. Just enjoy yourselves, eat some good food catered by Bess Harkins."

The daughter of one of the most influential city council members, Deke Harkins.

"Have yourself something to drink, too. The bartender is none other than Dewey Chase," Regina added.

The mayor's nephew.

"And take the time to Smell the Roses." Regina ended that with a chuckle since it was a play on words along with being the name of the florist. "Floral decorations are from Wendy Kay Merkle and her staff. Aren't they beautiful?" Regina asked the crowd, and they applauded the efforts of the niece of two ladies from the historical society and garden guild.

Regina had covered a lot of bases. She opened her mouth, maybe to add a base that Karlee hadn't noticed yet, but she stopped and scowled when Jerry walked out into the barn.

Jerry waved and smiled like a politician pandering for votes. Candy was right behind him, and she was teetering on heels much too high for walking in dirt. She wobbled to get her balance, causing her large breasts to jiggle. That, in turn, caused a lot of behind-the-hand whispers and not-so-whispered comments from some of the guys.

"Hi, y'all," Jerry called out. "I just wanted to thank everybody for coming to this shindig."

He said something else, something that no one heard, because Regina motioned for the band to start playing. The woman had probably arranged the maneuver in advance just in case Jerry tried anything because it was the loudest version of "Friends in Low Places" that Karlee had ever heard. It was so loud that people quit using their hands to shield their whispers and instead put them over their ears.

Leaving Candy and Jerry behind, Dylan and Lucian led Regina and her out of the center of the barn/arena so the mingling could start. Something that Karlee knew was definitely out of Lucian's comfort zone. He tolerated dinners and parties only because it helped his business, and this fell into exactly that category.

Except for that second kiss.

Karlee didn't have time to dwell on that though. She immediately got swept into a sea of hugs, handshakes and congrats. It was hard to actually hear the congrats because of the music blare, but she suspected only a fraction of them were genuine anyway.

Regina finally gave the band the signal to lower the volume on the song. It was in the nick of time to prevent permanent hearing loss. However, it meant Candy would have no trouble complaining about Regina's musical diss, and Karlee figured that was exactly what was on the woman's mind when she made a beeline toward them. Well, as much of a beeline as she could make since the high-heel teetering and breast jiggling were still going on.

"That was rude," Candy told Regina. "Jerry was about to introduce me so everyone would know I was his fiancée."

"Honey, everyone already knows who you are," Regina assured her. Her voice was too sappy sweet, and it must have sent a big red-flag warning that an argument was about to break out because Lucian quickly took his mom by the arm, mumbled something about her needing to meet someone, and he got Regina out of there, heading in the direction of the dessert table.

Karlee prevented Candy from following them by stepping in front of her. And lying. "You look fantastic. People can't take their eyes off you."

Candy blushed a little. "You think so? Jerry was worried my dress wasn't right for this crowd."

It wasn't. The cut was too low, both in front and back, and the lipstick-red color seemed more suitable for a Vegas cocktail party than a gathering at the rodeo grounds. But despite the lack of wardrobe suitability, it was something Karlee wished she could wear. She could go for semisexy with a dash of inappropriateness. However, she'd learned the hard way that anything that was out there would trigger gossip about her mother.

Yes, even all these years later.

Candy snagged two glasses of champagne from a waiter who was making his way through the crowd. Karlee thought one was for her, but Candy downed both and got a third glass.

"It's so hard being here in this town," Candy said. "No one likes me, and Regina is always so nasty to me. It doesn't help that she's right there on the ranch. I asked Jerry to tell her to leave, but he says he can't make her go."

"He can't," Karlee assured her. That was because Regina owned a Victorian house on the grounds of the ranch. She'd once sold it to Lawson's wife, Eve, but with Eve and Lawson living in his place, Eve had sold it back to her. It practically put Regina right on Candy's doorstep. Of course, it was a doorstep that Regina co-owned since the house was part of the family holdings.

"Well, I wish he'd try harder." Candy glanced around, her nose turned up as if she'd gotten a whiff of some cow that was probably somewhere around. "I want to be back in Houston, where there are shops. And friends. I don't want to be here." Candy's gaze froze for a moment as if she'd said too much. However, she hadn't said anything that Karlee didn't already know. Candy wasn't fond of Wrangler's Creek. Maybe that lack of fondness would get her to bug Jerry into leaving.

And that brought Karlee to an angle she should latch on to.

"I'll talk to Regina for you," Karlee said. "Maybe I can get her to back off. Or at least get her to take a vacation." After all, it would better suit her to have Candy as an ally rather than the fiancée of Lucian's pond-scum father.

The offer caused Candy to do a sort of double take, maybe to see if she was serious. Candy must have thought she was because she smiled. "Thank you. That's sweet. And if there's anything I can ever do for you…" Her words trailed off when she helped herself to another glass of champagne.

Karlee wanted to jump right on that offer so she could try to find out what Jerry was up to, but this wasn't the time or place. Instead, Karlee stepped away to continue with the damage control. Lucian seemed to be doing the same. She spotted him chatting to Don Byrner, who was on the city council. She also saw Lois Fay, who was coming straight toward her.

This was yet another woman whom Karlee needed as an ally, so she turned from Candy to greet her. But it turned out that Lois Fay wasn't interested in a greeting. She was staring at the brooch.

"There are photos in the archives of Sarah Granger wearing that," Lois Fay told her. "And she wore it just as you're doing. Right in the center neckline of her dress. Of course, her neckline was higher than yours."

That last bit came with some disapproval, but then, Lois Fay only wore turtlenecks even in the summer, so Karlee didn't hold her fashion opinion in high regard.

"Maybe we can talk Lucian into allowing the historical society to put the brooch on display next to the picture," Karlee suggested.

Lois Fay smiled. Not disapproval but reverence. It didn't last. The woman's forehead soon bunched up. "If you're trying to sway me in Lucian's favor, it won't work. I can't be swayed like that."

"Of course not." Karlee patted her arm. "I just thought it was a shame that a brooch this beautiful—and this important to the town's history—will soon be shut away in a safe. This comb, too." She turned her head a moment so that Lois Fay could get a look at that, too.

The woman's forehead loosened up a little. "I like you, Karlee. I always have. Ever since…" But Lois Fay thankfully didn't finish that. "I wish you the best," she added before she walked away.

Coming from Lois Fay, that qualified as a full-fledged gushing, which meant this party was already a success.

"You know if Lucian hurts you, I'll kick his ass," she heard someone say.

Karlee recognized the voice. Her brother Judd. He was Joe's twin, and he was sporting the same sour expression that Joe had when he'd visited the day before. Karlee suspected that Joe had issued an ass-kicking threat to Lucian.

"Thanks for coming," Karlee whispered when he hugged her.

"I thought you could use the support. Is that what this engagement is all about, you supporting Lucian so he can fight Jerry?" Judd came out and asked.

There were way too many people close enough to hear every word she said. "Of course not. You know I've always had a thing for Lucian. Well, he finally got a thing for me."

She hated lying to Judd. Actually, she hated lying, period, but maybe they wouldn't have to continue it much longer. Karlee saw possible hope of that when she noticed Jerry talking to a man. A stranger. And it didn't seem to be a pleasant conversation. They'd moved off to the side of the barn, away from everyone else.

"Excuse me a second," Karlee told her brother, and she would have started through the crush of people to get closer if Judd hadn't taken hold of her hand.

"Best not to interrupt that," Judd said.

Karlee snapped back toward him. "Why?" And what the heck did her brother know about this?

Judd brushed a kiss on her cheek. "Tell Lucian to call off his lawyers who are trying to block the sale that Jerry wants to make," he whispered with his mouth right against her ear. "It'll work in Lucian's and your favor."

She pulled away from him. "What are you talking about?"

"I'm talking about fixing this so that you don't have

to wear that." He tipped his head to her engagement ring. "Someone other than Lucian and you is working to bring Jerry down."

"Who?" she asked as fast as she could.

Judd gave her another of those cheek kisses. "You wouldn't believe me if I told you," her brother said as he strolled away.

CHAPTER SEVEN

IT WAS LUCIAN's version of *High Noon*, an Old West show-down. One that he intended to win this time.

Lucian looked at Outlaw, the rodeo gelding, and he tried to channel a little horse whispering. Basically, he needed to convince this hellhound Appaloosa that eight seconds wasn't that long to have a saddle and cowboy on your back.

He tried to put out some positive energy. Even that positive-energy attempt was a little dignity reducing to his cowboy mind-set. He was the one in charge. He was the one with the reins. And he would stay on this shit-kicker for the whole time.

Lucian took his phone out of his pocket to put it aside for the ride, but it rang before he could do that. The name on the screen practically jumped right out at him.

Amelia.

And just like that, the memories came, both good and bad. Hell. There was no dignity in being a cowboy with a broken heart, either.

He debated letting it go to voice mail but knew that if he didn't answer it, he'd just be thinking about it during the ride. Best not to give the Appaloosa any more advantages than it already had.

"Amelia," he greeted after he cleared his throat.

"Please tell me you were up and that I didn't wake

you." Her voice had a way of melting away the years. Both good and bad.

"I was up." Since mentioning the rodeo training would only lead to a conversation about how that was going, Lucian just waited for her to continue.

"Good. It's early afternoon here in London, and I'm about to head to a business lunch, so I thought I'd take the chance that you'd answer."

"London, huh? You get around."

She made a sound of agreement, and he got a too-clear picture of her face and the expression she'd have when making that sound. A slight shrug. A smile. But there would be plenty of weariness in her eyes. Yes, she did get around, running her father's investment business, a responsibility she had inherited when her dad had had a stroke. Amelia had been just twenty-five, and she'd stepped up to the plate even though it meant leaving Wrangler's Creek.

And him.

But Lucian had understood because he, too, knew a thing or two about the sacrifices that it took to run a business. Of course, Amelia's sacrifices seemed to take her anywhere but here. It'd been nearly a year since she'd come back, and then it'd been for sex and dinner. In that order. The following morning, she'd kissed him, told him that nobody was as good in the sack as he was and left.

"I heard about what Jerry did…and your engagement," Amelia went on a moment later. "I'm sorry about Jerry. He always was an ass. Guess that hasn't changed." She paused. "But an engagement. Wow."

Again, he got a too-clear picture of that expression as well because that wasn't congratulations she was gushing. She sounded, well, down about it. Not crushed though.

"Karlee's wonderful," she added. "I just wanted to tell you that I hope you'll be very happy."

So, Amelia hadn't picked up on the gossip that the engagement was fake. Or maybe she had heard of the suspected pretense and was feeling him out. "I need to get back in charge of Granger Enterprises," he settled for saying.

"Oh" was her response.

For such a little word, it conveyed a whole bunch. Amelia got it. Well, she got the big picture, anyway. She probably didn't have a clue about the fine print—that while the engagement wasn't real, the kick he'd felt from that kiss with Karlee sure had been. Of course, now the kick was tempered somewhat by the memory that attraction and relationships led to a Sunday-morning call from London from a woman he'd once loved. A woman who'd crushed him when she'd left.

"Then I'll think good thoughts for you," Amelia said. She groaned. And he could see that expression, too. She hated this chitchat tone as much as he did. Maybe because she still had feelings for him or maybe because they both knew it was way too formal, considering she was the only woman he'd ever said those three little words to.

I need you.

At the time he'd said it, Amelia had seemed disappointed that it wasn't *I love you.* But love was easy. He loved lots of people in different ways and for various reasons. But since he'd been eighteen, he'd only needed one person—her. She'd likely known that as well, but it hadn't stopped her from pushing his need aside and putting her family's business first. Of course, Amelia might see it that he'd done the same thing by staying behind to work a gazillion hours a year.

"I will think good thoughts," she amended, and he knew this time it wasn't lip service. "Gotta go. My car is here. I'll be in touch."

And just like that, she was gone. The staying in touch wasn't just blowing smoke, either. She would. Amelia would call, text and occasionally show up to remind him that needing someone came with a damn high price tag. Even when you didn't need them anymore.

"I'm ready, boss, to start timing ya," Skeeter called out to him, pulling Lucian's thoughts back to where they should be.

As usual, the ranch hand was on the corral fence, looking pretty chipper considering it was 7:00 a.m. on a Sunday morning. Also considering that Skeeter, like nearly everyone else in town, had spent most of the night before drinking and eating at the engagement party.

That party was the reason Lucian was out so early to practice for the rodeo. Well, Karlee was the actual reason. The reason that conversation with Amelia had been even more uncomfortable than usual.

He'd kissed Karlee in what should have been all for show, and now his dick thought sex was going to happen. That's why he'd gotten up too early and come out to the barn so that he wouldn't be tempted to go into her room. Which was only six steps from his. Five if he lengthened his stride a bit more. And he knew this because he'd tested that out before forcing himself out the front door and to the barn.

Where he would now face a different obstacle.

At least if Outlaw managed to throw him again, it might injure him enough to cool down any sexual urges that he had for his pretend fiancée.

Lucian put his phone aside and climbed into the saddle, taking a moment to steady both Outlaw and himself, though the horse definitely required steadying less than Lucian. Many folks thought the horse bucked because it was in pain from the spurs or scared, but nope, that wasn't true. Outlaw, like other rodeo broncs, had just been trained to buck. Some horses took to it better than others.

Outlaw had taken to it very, very well.

At Lucian's nod, Skeeter leaned over, threw open the gate, and Outlaw bolted out and immediately tried to get Lucian on the ground. Lucian cooperated with that, too, but it wasn't something he'd planned. It was because the moment Outlaw did the first buck, that was when Lucian spotted Karlee. She was at the corral fence, and she was smiling.

And the next thing Lucian knew, he was in the air.

Thankfully, this time his shoulder didn't hit, but the landing on his balls would definitely keep sex off his mind for an hour or two.

"Boss man, that was only two seconds," Skeeter called out. Outlaw went straight back into the gate, and Skeeter shut it. "You're gonna need to stay on a mite longer than that."

Lucian was so riled at himself for allowing the Karlee distraction that he didn't even want to smother Skeeter for that unnecessary commentary. However, a ball busting apparently wasn't enough of a cooldown because he got those notions of sex again when Karlee came into the corral and put out her hand to help him up. Of course, those sex notions were heightened somewhat because Karlee was wearing a dress. It wasn't particularly short, but since he was on the ground, looking up at her, he saw probably more than he should have.

"No dislocated shoulder this time," she remarked. "That's an improvement."

Yeah, for pain levels, it was, but a lot of people were going to be laughing at him if he only managed two seconds. Maybe he could start wearing blinders so he wouldn't get a glimpse of Karlee.

"You're up early on your day off," he said, trying to make the conversation sound as normal as a strained/sexually charged conversation could sound.

She nodded. "It's my father's birthday, and I want to go to the cemetery to put some flowers on his grave. It's sort of an annual pilgrimage for me."

Well, hell. That gave him a good cooling off. "Are you okay?"

"Sure."

She answered so fast that it made it seem as if there was no sure to it. Of course, it wouldn't be. After Karlee's mom had run out on them, her father had started drinking too much, and it'd killed him. That had set Karlee on a hard path that Lucian understood. Of having to raise her younger siblings. At least he'd had a part-time mom around, but Karlee hadn't had anyone.

"Your dad died when you were eighteen?" he asked.

She nodded. Again, it was a fast response. "Almost. I was just a few months shy of my birthday. A long time ago," she added.

He was betting it didn't feel that long to her. Lucian wasn't good at picking up on feelings, but he sensed something there, just beneath the surface. Or maybe he was just picking up on his own crappy baggage that went with his equally crappy childhood. Besides, when it came to less-than-stellar childhoods, Karlee had him beat hands down.

"We didn't get a chance to talk after the party last night," she added as they walked back to the guest-house.

That'd been intentional on his part and had been his way of avoiding the temptation of continuing the *that was from me* kiss that he'd started in the corral at the party. Talk about stupid.

The first thing Lucian smelled when they got inside was the coffee. Karlee had a pot of it already brewed, and there were some muffins on a plate on the counter. Apparently, her efficiency didn't just apply to work.

"They're blueberry. I went to the diner when I heard you in the shower," she explained.

He hadn't heard her. In fact, Lucian had thought she had still been asleep when he'd gone out to the barn.

"Judd said something odd last night," she went on, pouring them both cups of coffee. She sat at the table with Lucian.

"He told you to get my lawyers to back off from trying to block the deal Jerry put together," Lucian finished for her. "He talked to me, too." And it had fallen under the definition of a confusing conversation. "He wouldn't tell me who this so-called ally is that wants to bring Jerry down."

"He didn't tell me, either." She paused, sipped her coffee. "When I pressed him, he said he couldn't betray a confidence. I trust Judd, but this secrecy doesn't sit well with me."

"Me, either. I'm guessing you didn't find anything on Jerry's computer about this proposed sale?"

She shook her head. "His computer is password protected, and he hasn't left any notes on his desk or in the trash can."

Lucian had the same reaction he always did when Karlee talked about snooping on Jerry. He threw up a little in his mouth. He hated that Karlee had to resort to such things. Hated even more that the situation existed that needed such resorting. Now he hoped he didn't come to hate the decision he was about to make.

"I'm going to have my lawyers back off but only a little," Lucian explained. "Before I give up completely, I want to find out the specifics of the deal. Delbert only knew it was about a fourth of the holdings and a hundred acres of land on the back part of the property. I want to make sure it doesn't include something else."

So, there. He'd laid out his game plan for her. In the meantime, he would continue to work on his own business deal. Karlee would work on hers. And he would continue to pretend that this lust wasn't a problem between them. At least Karlee wasn't bringing it up.

"About that kiss last night…" she said. He doubted that she had developed sudden mind-reading skills and hoped that there hadn't been something lustful in his expression to give him away.

That was from me.

Lucian debated which way to go on this. He could blow it off and say it was just him getting caught up in the moment, but he wasn't a *getting caught up in the moment* kind of guy. So he went with the truth, something he was certain he was going to regret as much as the *that was from me*.

"There are six steps between our bedrooms," he told her, "and you taste like coffee and strawberries even when you haven't had either of those things."

All right. So that was a piss-poor attempt at the truth. And yeah, Lucian regretted it.

She studied him as if trying to figure out how to respond to that. *Good luck with it* because he'd sure as hell screwed it up.

"There are five steps between the bedrooms if you go for a long stride," Karlee corrected. "Four if you bunny hop." Her mouth quivered a little, threatening to smile.

That quivering smile made him want to kiss her. Of course, her breathing was doing the same thing.

"Trust me, I've thought about this," Karlee went on. "Last night it took a lot of willpower not to shuck off my clothes and go climb between the sheets with you."

Instant erection. His fastest ever, and that included his teenage years.

"That probably would have been more like three steps," she added with a chuckle.

Nope. Less than that. Because if he'd seen her naked, he would have gotten to her even faster than he'd just gotten this hard-on.

She kept staring at him. "Thankfully, we're both sensible people, so I took a shower instead."

There was nothing sensible about him at the moment, and Lucian was certain he would have carried that insensibility straight to the bedroom. Or the table since it was closer. But the knock at the door gave him some forced willpower.

Temporary willpower.

Because he was hoping Karlee could get rid of their

early morning visitor. Lucian couldn't do it himself because he wasn't sure he could walk yet.

Karlee walked after she gave him a "this conversation isn't over" look. At least he hoped that's what her look was all about. But that soon became a moot point since Jerry was their visitor.

"I figured y'all were up," Jerry greeted. "Didn't figure I'd be interrupting anything, either."

Jerry was so wrong about that, but it wasn't a point that Lucian cared to stand up and prove. "What do you want?" Lucian snarled. That was the one good thing about the small living space. He could stay seated and still manage to get his scowl noticed.

"It's business," Jerry declared. And he did indeed have a laptop tucked under his arm.

"It's too early for that. Karlee and I were having breakfast."

"This won't take long." His father stepped in, and he didn't come in alone, either. He had a woman with him. Not Candy. But it was someone Lucian knew. Darlene Sullivan, the mayor's daughter.

Even though Lucian was still trying to sway the mayor and city council in his favor, it was hard to look even a little polite with the interruption. Karlee, however, was right on form.

"Would either of you like some coffee?" Karlee asked.

"No, thanks. Like I said, it's business." Jerry wasn't going for polite, either, when he looked at Lucian, but as usual, his expression softened when he turned to Karlee. "I've got some news that I think will please you. I've hired Darlene as your replacement."

There was a flash of surprise in Karlee's eyes. Maybe some slight disappointment, too. She hadn't wanted to continue working for Jerry, but she'd likely reasoned that by being around him day in and day out, she would have been able to keep an eye on him.

"That's wonderful," Karlee said, and she sounded genuine about that. Maybe because she knew this meant she could get on with her own business plans. "But what about your job at the library?" she asked Darlene. "Did you quit?"

The woman nodded. "I was just a volunteer there. When Mr. Granger offered me this, my dad said he thought it was a good thing."

What wasn't good was that Darlene was in her twenties, and her father was still calling the shots. Still, Darlene was engaged to a guy in the air force. Once he returned from his deployment and got out of the service, they'd be getting married. Which meant Darlene probably wouldn't be working for Jerry for very long.

"So, you're not mad?" Darlene asked Karlee. "I don't want you to be mad."

Lucian didn't know Darlene very well, but she was the mayor's youngest daughter and only in her early twenties. From what he'd seen, she wasn't big on social skills. Not on office skills, either, which meant this was some kind of deal worked out between Jerry and the mayor.

A deal that would continue to sway the city council in Jerry's favor.

That wouldn't matter, though, if Lucian could sway the historical society and garden guild. Jerry would do anything to prevent that, though, and hiring Darlene was probably part of his plan. Plus, Jerry had to be wary about Karlee since her loyalties were to Lucian, *her fiancé*. The very fiancé she'd just given a hard-on.

"Of course I'm not angry," Karlee assured the woman.

"Told you she wouldn't be." Jerry handed Darlene the laptop and gave his enormous belt and the waist of his pants an adjustment.

"But Miss Regina is," Darlene muttered under her breath.

"All that masking tape's not about you, Darlene," Jerry piped up. He spared Lucian a glance just to let him know that he was now the recipient of his father's conversation. "Your mother's decided to divide up the house into everybody's shares. She's using masking tape to mark off areas in every room, and she's writing names on who owns each particular marked-off spot."

Hell in a big-assed handbasket. "What caused that?"

"Candy and Regina got into it about who hadn't changed a roll on the toilet-paper holder, and that's when Regina got out the yardstick and tape. She's as mad as a hornet and doesn't want Candy and me in her space." Jerry's mouth twisted. "FYI, if you need to take a leak in the powder room off the foyer, then you'll have to stand in the corner and aim because Regina's marked off the area by the john as belonging to Dylan and her."

Lucian's first instinct was to intervene. Or at least roll his eyes at his mom's childish behavior, but this was one of the exact reasons he was now staying in the guesthouse. This was obviously some kind of power play on his mom's part. Something designed to remind Jerry that the place wasn't all his, and he'd get that reminder with every step he took.

Jerry stared at him several moments, maybe waiting

for Lucian to say he would fix it, but he soon figured out that his firstborn son was off fixing duty for a while.

"Anyway," Jerry finally continued after he turned his attention back to Karlee. "I know it's Sunday and all, but I was hoping you could start training Darlene today. I'd like her to go on a business trip with me tomorrow, and she needs to be up to speed. Maybe you could show her how you create those agendas and such."

Lucian had to force himself to drink some coffee rather than ask about that trip. Or press why it was so important that Jerry take an assistant. Lucian hoped to hell that this wasn't a sex trip because Darlene was young enough to be Jerry's granddaughter.

"Karlee's going out to the cemetery today," Lucian said to let Jerry know that she had plans. One that didn't involve something that would almost certainly take more than a couple of hours.

Karlee nodded and took the laptop from Darlene. "But I can go through some things with Darlene while you grab your shower. Then we can go to the cemetery together as planned."

That hadn't been the plan at all, which meant Karlee was up to something. Good. Lucian hoped it was something that would make Jerry's trip a permanent exit from the ranch. At least his exit from the guesthouse was a speedy one, and Lucian got up from the table so he could pour himself another cup of coffee before heading off to that shower he was supposed to be taking.

"This is one of the laptops Jerry keeps on his desk," Karlee remarked, placing the computer on the table and opening it. "I hope he gave you the password."

"He did." Darlene's gaze darted from Karlee to Lucian. "But Mr. Granger said for me to make sure no one else got it."

"Of course. I'll look away while you put it in."

Karlee did indeed look away. Lucian didn't, and he saw the woman type in three-five-two-one. He mentally repeated it, stirred his coffee and generally tried to look as if he weren't spying.

"Okay, here's an agenda for a meeting that Mr. Granger had last week," Darlene said, pulling up a file. "I was looking for examples of what's included on them and such. Is this what I should be doing?"

"Yes, the idea is to give your boss everything he'll need to make a meeting go smoothly, so you start with the details of what Jerry wants to accomplish." Karlee took over the keyboard and began to scroll through the files. "Here you go. Here are Jerry's notes for the meeting. It's in San Antonio with a company named Melcor." Karlee shook her head. "I'm not familiar with them."

Neither was Lucian, and that was a red flag. Of course, there were plenty of those whenever it came to his father, but Lucian especially didn't like Jerry dealing with a company that might not even be reputable.

"Mr. Granger said that Melcor was headquartered in another state," Darlene offered.

Karlee made a sound of agreement and kept reading. Lucian wanted to lean in, too, and have a look, but he didn't want to spook Darlene enough to have her take the laptop and run. She was still giving him those wary glances.

"Did Jerry do a background check on Melcor?" Karlee asked.

Judging from the blank stare Darlene gave her, she didn't have a clue.

"Okay," Karlee went on after clicking some buttons. "You'll need to involve Legal, then. And the CFO, Delbert Sweeny."

Darlene shook her head. "Jerry said not to copy them on the agenda."

That was past the red-flag stage, though Karlee didn't show any signs of that. She just kept on typing, kept on scrolling through the folders.

"You know, maybe I should ask Mr. Granger before we go any further on this," Darlene said, and she took the laptop. "I'm sorry, but he said he didn't want anyone other than him and me in the files."

Of course he didn't because he was about to pull something shady.

"Oh, all right." Karlee stepped back. "Then maybe you need to try to figure out how to do the agenda on your own, then? Just be careful because if you make a mistake, it could end up costing your boss a fortune. That wouldn't be a good way to start your workweek."

Most of the color blanched from Darlene's already-pale face, and he could see the debate going on in her eyes. A debate that didn't end well for Karlee and him.

"I'll be going now," Darlene said, heading to the door. "If I have any questions, I'll call you."

"Hell, I was hoping you'd get a look at the file for that meeting," Lucian grumbled once Darlene was out of the guesthouse.

"I will." Karlee hurried to the corner desk where she kept her laptop and turned it on. "I copied the files and sent them to me."

Damn, Lucian had known she was good, but this was a couple of steps beyond that. Of course, it was possible that Jerry hadn't put anything in those files that let them know what was going on.

But he had.

Lucian gathered that from the moment Karlee opened the Melcor file because she made a soft sound of surprise. Not rah-rah, happy birthday, either. This was more of an oh-crap.

"We need to find out everything we can about Melcor," Karlee said. "Because Jerry's about to sell them one percent of all the family holdings."

One percent didn't sound like much, but it was huge. Because it added yet another player into what could turn into a big legal battle.

Hell. What was Jerry trying to pull?

CHAPTER EIGHT

JERRY STOOD AT the window of the office and watched his family. Dylan and Jordan were playing with their adopted son, Corbin, in the yard. Karlee and Lucian were there, too, all of the adults enjoying a beer while Corbin chased Regina's squirrel-looking dog around.

Everyone was smiling, even Lucian, and while Jerry would have liked being part of that, he knew the smiles and fun would end if he stepped out there with them.

Because they hated him.

They probably didn't know, though, that he hated himself even more.

He could pinpoint the exact moment when the hatred started. It'd been when he'd fallen in love with Karlee's mom, Glenda. He'd known it was wrong. So had she. But they'd gotten so caught up in the fire and sex that they hadn't been able to turn back. Or rather, they hadn't wanted to. He didn't mind giving a different version of the truth to others, but he tried to make a point of not lying to himself.

He'd wanted Glenda, and he'd taken her. And she'd let him take her, period.

In the end, it had cost them both their families. Their self-respect, too. There was no way to undo it, no way to atone, so his solution had been to put up this wall.

Oh, and to keep making mistakes.

When he'd been trying to salvage marriage number three, or maybe it was four, he'd been suckered into going to a marriage counselor who'd told him that all the bad choices he was making was a way of punishing himself. That was a depressing realization because it meant it was going to go on forever.

Like now.

He was in debt all the way to the roots of his seriously thinning hair, and the only way to recover had been to come back here. Which, in turn, only made him more of an asshole. But maybe he could still salvage things and leave the ranch and company. If not, Lucian would just add another level of hate to what he already felt, along with fixing whatever it was that Jerry ended up botching.

And speaking of hate, Regina opened the door of his office. He'd known it wasn't Candy because she was in Houston on a shopping trip. Darlene had already left work for the day, and with the others outside, that meant Regina was the only one left in the house. Other than the maids and Abe Weiser—and they avoided him, too.

She didn't wait for him to invite her in, probably because she knew that a sizable amount of hell would have to freeze over for that to happen. She came right in as if he'd issued a sweet invitation. No beeline to his desk though. Regina did a little hopscotch to avoid stepping on the area that she'd marked off as his. He wasn't exactly sure when Regina had made the tape lines. They'd just been there one afternoon after he'd come back from a business trip to San Antonio.

At first the tape had royally pissed him off along with reminding him why Regina and he were no longer married.

Which was probably her intent.

But he'd ended up leaving them and ignoring them. Unfortunately, Candy and Regina didn't ignore them. Anytime Regina accidentally stepped in his designated area and Candy stepped in Regina's, both Regina and his beloved fiancée let him know all about it. He'd been caught in the middle so much that he felt like the squished filling of a cookie.

Regina dodged his taped-off areas, staying only on hers, Dylan's and Lucian's until she made it to his desk, where she deposited a double shot glass filled with what smelled like Glenlivet. Of course, the scotch could be used to mask the poison that she no doubt wanted to give him.

"Drink up and let's talk," she insisted. She had a second glass of some kind of liquor in her hand, and she took a sip from it.

Jerry debated his options here. He could go into asshole mode and try to get her to leave by saying something rude and ugly to her, but Regina had a mode higher than asshole. He'd learned over the years that if he tried to match wits with her, he was going to lose. That's why he drank a good amount of what was in the shot glass and hoped if it was truly poison that it didn't hurt too much.

While she continued drinking, she went to the window next to him—dodging his designated area for that trip, too. The small crowd in the yard had grown in the past couple of minutes. Lawson and his wife, Eve, were out there, and their son, Aiden, had gotten in on the chase game with Corbin.

"When did Lucian and Lawson mend fences?" Jerry

asked. "Last time I was here, they weren't even on speaking terms."

"They mended fences...about eight weeks or so ago."

That was when he'd arrived at the ranch. So, his return had accomplished something. Of course, now Lawson had a new layer of hate for him, too.

"Is this visit for a reason other than to tell me how wrong I am?" he came out and asked.

"Yes. There's a reason." Now she sat down and dragged in a long breath. "A little bird told me that you'd sold one percent of your shares of the family holdings. Any reason you didn't come to me or Lucian so we could buy it?"

He looked at her from over the rim of his glass. "Because then you and Lucian would have had enough shares to take me to court."

"True," she readily admitted. "But it would have stayed in the family. This way, it's in the hands of strangers, and I suspect that's causing your daddy to turn in his grave."

If grave turning was indeed a real thing, then, yes, that was happening. Because this ranch and the cattle broker company had meant everything to his dad. Well, those two things and Lucian had. Jerry had never felt he had to give his son much love because his dad took that role over almost immediately. It had driven a wedge between Jerry and his own dad and then between Jerry and Lucian, and the wedge just kept getting bigger and bigger.

"Melcor," Regina continued, sipping her drink. "That's who now has the one percent."

Well, shit. That didn't stay secret for long. "Did Karlee tell you that? Because someone copied my files, and I suspect it was her."

"I didn't hear it from Karlee, but good for her if she copied them. She's trying to protect the man she loves."

A burst of air left his mouth. Definitely not from humor. "You can't BS me, Regina. Their engagement's as fake as that rosy glow on your cheeks."

She made a sound that could have meant anything. It certainly wasn't a denial, and she got up so she could stand next to him again. "Karlee's been in love with Lucian since she was old enough to notice that he has man parts. Nothing fake about that."

Now Jerry made one of those noncommittal sounds. Karlee did have feelings for Lucian, but that didn't mean their engagement was real. Ditto for Karlee helping Darlene transition in the job. The only reason Karlee was helping was to spy on him for Lucian. That would make his daddy smile in the grave—if that were even possible.

"The ruse isn't working," Jerry assured her. "Just as everyone knows Karlee has feelings for him, folks also know that Lucian is still hung up on Amelia." Again, she didn't deny it. "So, you can tell Lucian to cut the bull, that it's not going to hurry things along like he wants. I only need one more big sale, and I'll have enough—"

He stopped, but it was already too late. Regina was no dummy and could fill in the blanks. He'd have enough to pay off his sizable debts to the wrong people. Investment advisers, which was code for loan sharks. Of course, he hadn't known that's what they were when he'd taken their money for one of his business deals.

And he still owed them.

The payout was just to get some heat off him, but it wouldn't cancel out his debts, especially since they kept skyrocketing with the interest rate. That meant he'd have to hang on to control of Granger Enterprises awhile longer so he could figure out a way to collect the cash without bankrupting them.

Since Regina had known about Melcor, that meant she likely knew plenty of other things. Like the fact that he'd tapped into Candy's accounts. Everyone thought she was the gold digger, but that couldn't be further from the truth.

"For the past two years someone's been sabotaging me," Jerry admitted. "Someone's set up business deals that I was certain were a sure thing only to have those deals crumble into huge losses for me." He paused. "Are you the one who's doing that?"

"Me?" She seemed flattered rather than alarmed by the accusation. And she certainly didn't deny it. But she did smile. "Who would do something that low to the father of her children?"

Regina was the most likely candidate to try to screw him over, and she would say she was doing that since he was the one who'd screwed her over in the first place.

And she'd be right.

She stood and finished her drink. "Karlee didn't tell me about Melcor, and I'm not the one sabotaging your business deals."

He wasn't sure he believed her on either count. But he immediately rethought that. Regina had faults, but she wasn't usually a liar. That said, she was the one who'd almost certainly orchestrated Lucian and Karlee's fake engagement.

"Then who is?" Jerry demanded.

Regina smiled. Definitely not a good response. She didn't attempt a better one, either. She took an envelope from her pocket and handed it to him. "It's an invitation to Christmas dinner. I really hope you and your fiancée will come."

It sounded like a threat. A creepy one because Regina smiled, and with that creepy smile on her face, she hopscotched her way out of the office.

"REGINA'S UP TO something," Jordan concluded. "Dylan and I got ours about an hour ago." She was sitting on the corner of Karlee's desk, where both of them were staring at the invitation that one of the Granger housekeepers had just delivered to the guesthouse.

Karlee hadn't just stared at it though. She'd cursed it. Most people probably didn't have that reaction to a Christmas dinner invitation, especially when they didn't have other plans, but Karlee muttered some profanity over this one. It was from Regina, and she wanted to have a big family "to-do" at the ranch. One that included Jerry and Candy.

There wouldn't be much fa-la-la-ing going on during that feast.

Of course, even without this meal, it would be a hard day for her. It always was. A day she usually avoided by taking a vacation where she crammed her agenda with as much "fun" as possible. It had never quite worked. She always remembered *that day* when she was seventeen, but it would likely be much, much worse if she was here in Wrangler's Creek.

Lord, she didn't want that on top of dealing with Jerry. And Lucian.

More than that, though, it meant Jordan was 100 percent right: Regina was up to something. Something that as a minimum would lead to Jerry and her swapping barbs and insults throughout the meal. Because there was no chance whatsoever that Regina actually wanted to celebrate the holiday with her ex and his fiancée.

"You don't think Regina's going to give Jerry food poisoning, do you?" Jordan asked.

"No." At least probably not. "But there'll be something else on the menu other than turkey and pumpkin pie."

Jordan nodded. "Maybe Regina's come up with another way to get Jerry to leave, and she wants to do it in front of the whole family. Regina likes grandstanding that way."

She did. And Karlee would love if that happened, but if Regina had that kind of workable plan, she couldn't imagine the woman hanging on to it for another week. All of them wanted Jerry out but no one more so than Regina and Lucian, but here it was nearly Christmas, and unless Regina had come up with a mini miracle, they were no closer to ousting Jerry. Which, in turn, meant they were no closer to ending their engagement and living arrangements.

"Wonder if Lucian knows what's going on," Jordan remarked. But it wasn't just a remark. She raised her eyebrow, asking for an update.

But the update about that was just as puzzling and frustrating as the Christmas dinner invitation.

"Lucian's been spending some time at his house in San Antonio," Karlee settled for saying.

That only caused Jordan's eyebrow to raise even more.

"All right." Karlee huffed. "He's been spending *most* of his time there."

He'd called her, of course. A time or two. But he'd been busy working on his own new business, and the only time he'd come back to the ranch was for the parties and get-togethers that Regina had organized so that folks could "see" that Lucian was a changed man. It did seem to be working. Well, people were friendlier toward him, anyway, but no one had budged on giving Lucian the support he needed to send Jerry packing.

"Lucian's avoiding you because he's attracted to you," Jordan concluded.

Only a best friend could come up with that spin on things. "It's also possible—likely, even—that he's avoiding me because he's tired of all of this and wants to get on with his life." Possibly by seeing someone else. Lucian rarely went long without a girlfriend, and Karlee certainly hadn't been heating up his bed.

Though that's what she wanted to do.

In her case, out of sight was definitely not out of mind.

"I think you're missing a great opportunity here," Jordan went on. "You've always wanted to have a fling with Lucian, and the timing is right for that."

No, it wasn't. Because of his family's turmoil, the timing was awful. There were also other problems with a fling.

"An affair could end my friendship with Lucian," Karlee reminded her. "Plus, he's still hung up on Amelia."

"Forget Amelia. If Lucian was really still hung up on her, he'd be with her now that he doesn't have the family business forcing him to stay put."

That was true. Well, maybe it was. Lucian was trying to build his own business, so he'd need to be in the area where he had contacts. The last Karlee had heard, Amelia was in London.

Jordan looked her straight in the eyes. "Do you want to still be avoiding sex with Lucian when you're sixty because you're moving at a snail's pace? My advice— just go for it because I think in the long run, you'd regret it more if you didn't try than if you tried and failed."

Karlee gave that some thought. Actually, what she thought of was that kiss at the party and the not-so-innocent flirting she'd done with Lucian the day that Jerry had interrupted them. That'd been weeks ago, and, yes, she had regretted not carrying things further. Regretted even more that she might not get another chance like that with Lucian distancing himself from her.

She got so swept up in the whole regret/fantasy thing that Karlee gasped when there was a knock. She had to shake her head to bring herself back from Lucian-land, and when she opened the door, she nearly did another gasp. This time for a completely different reason.

Because her visitor was Lucian's cousin Roman.

To say that Roman was a heartthrob was a little like saying that Texas was somewhat big-ish. He'd throbbed many hearts all over the state and continued to do that even though he was now married. Karlee wasn't immune to all that manly hotness, and apparently neither was Jordan because they both stood there gawking at him before Karlee got her mouth working again.

"Roman," she managed to say.

All right, not her best effort, but sadly, it wasn't her worst, either. She'd always gotten a little tongue-tied around Roman, and it hadn't helped that Lucian and he were practically enemies. And always had been. It stemmed from a land dispute that'd started between their great-grandfathers who'd cofounded the town. Lucian and Roman had carried that dispute into the current decade.

Old feuds aside, she wasn't blind and all her parts were functioning, so she'd had a sexual fantasy or two about Roman. They were never as hot, though, as the ones she'd had for Lucian.

"Karlee," he greeted. "Jordan." He was either oblivious to their gawking or else he was so used to it that he didn't even react. "I was driving by the ranch and wanted to drop off the contract."

"Contract?" Jordan questioned.

Karlee nodded while she motioned for Roman to come inside. "Yes, I bought my first lot of Angus, and I'm leasing some land from Roman." Karlee said that last part very quickly, hoping it would be too fast for Jordan to catch it, but her friend caught it all right.

"I needed land," Karlee added.

What she hadn't expected was for Roman to personally deliver it since he had plenty of people who worked for him to do things like this. Especially since this thing was small potatoes.

Jordan didn't respond to what Karlee had said—not verbally, anyway—but her silence and expression said loads and was laced with questions. For example—did Lucian know about this?

Not yet. Karlee had every intention of telling him, but she wanted to do that face-to-face so she could explain why she hadn't gone to him for this. There were just too many unknowns with Jerry, and she didn't want to put the Angus into a winter pasture only to have to move them if Jerry actually managed to sell any of the land.

"I'll sign this now and give you a check," Karlee told him.

"No hurry. Just look it over and bring it by when the Angus are delivered on Monday. I suspect you'll want to be out at the ranch for that shipment."

"Definitely." This was the first step in her business. "Thank you again for making this happen."

He shrugged. "We have some land we won't be using this winter."

Maybe, but she figured if Lucian had made a lease request like this, it would have been immediately axed. Of course, Lucian wouldn't have made a request like that in the first place.

Roman tipped his head to her hand. "That's the big reason I stopped by." It took her a moment to realize he meant her engagement ring. "Is it real?"

She didn't think he meant the ring itself. "Yes," she lied.

Karlee had a good BS meter, but she suspected Roman had a better one. "You know what you're doing?" he asked.

No. Not even close, but she lied again with another nod and a smile. Roman smiled, too, several moments later after he studied her face.

"All right. Suit yourself," he said. It seemed he was about to add something else, but his phone rang. "Excuse me for a second. I have to take this." And he stepped into the kitchen to do that.

"I should be going," Jordan whispered to her, but she kept her eyes on Roman. "I think I'll find my husband and see if he wants to take a shower or something."

Karlee chuckled, and she walked Jordan to the door, but when she opened it, the chilly December air wasn't the only thing that she felt. Lucian was there, reaching for the knob. Karlee immediately tried to mask all the heat that came flooding through her. No way did she want him to see just how happy she was that he was there. But like the lies she'd just told Roman, she probably failed at that, too, because Lucian scowled.

Narrowed eyes, tight jaw, and his forehead was bunched up.

Jordan gave them a quick wave and hurried off. Maybe because she was indeed anxious to find Dylan, but it might have had more to do with Lucian's intense expression. Karlee would have asked him about that expression, but she didn't get a chance.

That's because Lucian hauled her to him, and he kissed her.

Karlee's first thought was that someone was watching, someone Lucian wanted to convince they were truly engaged. But the fire quickly took over. Probably because she'd just been thinking about having sex with him, and that scalding heat soon clouded her mind enough that she didn't care about his motive for the kiss. She only wanted it to keep on going.

And it did.

When he broke for air, Lucian gutted out some profanity and went back for seconds. Karlee got her own share of seconds in because she slipped her arms around the back of his neck, the movement bringing their bodies directly against each other. All in all, it was a good way to feel all those incredible muscles in his chest and stomach.

Like the other kiss, this one was thorough. A sort of "I'm schooling you on the right way to do this." And it worked just fine. The pressure was there. The touch of his tongue to hers. He'd told her once that she tasted like strawberries and coffee, but Lucian's taste was like his touch.

Sex.

Just sex.

Everything he did made her want him even more, and Karlee had started backing him inside when she heard a sound she didn't especially want to hear. A throat clearing.

Roman.

Good grief. How could she have forgotten that he was there? Because Lucian's kiss had drained her brain of any thoughts or logic, that's why.

"What are you doing here?" Lucian asked his cousin. Normally, his mean voice wasn't quite so raspy, but he was probably as oxygen-deprived as she was.

Roman looked at her, maybe because he wanted her to be the one to tell Lucian about their business deal. And that's what she wanted as well, but her breath was gusting like an asthmatic. Plus, she had seemingly lost her ability to speak. That's why she did some throat clearing.

"Roman leased me some land for my cattle," she finally managed to say.

"And that's my cue to head out." Roman tipped his Stetson and smiled—a kind of smile he'd practiced from the *Mona Lisa*—and he stepped around them to go outside.

"I'm sorry I didn't tell you he was here," Karlee told Lucian. Of course, that was just the beginning of what he probably wanted her to explain.

"Roman leased you some land." He kept his eyes on his cousin until Roman got into his truck that he'd parked next to the row of vehicles that belonged to the ranch hands. That's probably why Lucian hadn't noticed it when he arrived.

It wasn't exactly a question, but Karlee nodded anyway. "He worked out permission with his siblings and Lawson." He'd included Lucian's brother Lawson in that because even though Roman owned his family's ranch, Lawson and Roman's brother, Garrett, actually ran it.

"Are you going to get pissed off about that, too?" Roman came out and asked him.

Lucian didn't exactly jump to answer. "No," he said after a long pause. "I want Karlee's business to succeed. In fact, when I regain control of what I should be controlling, I'd like to sit down and talk to you about the land that's in dispute."

Roman gave him a blank stare, as if waiting for the punch line, but Lucian seemed serious. *Seemed.* But she had to wonder if this was his way of convincing Roman that he'd indeed had a personality makeover. Of course, there really was no need for him to get Roman to believe that.

However, there was a reason to settle the land dispute.

It'd gone on for decades with both sides of the family claiming they owned it, and in the meantime, the acres weren't being used. Since it wasn't a haven for that blasted Hairy Corn Salad, it would make great pasture.

"You have something specific in mind?" Roman asked. That was a surprise, too, and she knew for a fact that Roman wasn't in the process of trying to make people think he was a nice guy.

"An even split right down the middle." No pause

that time, which would have meant Lucian was in the "seem" mode here. He was serious.

Roman looked at Karlee as if to ask her if she was somehow responsible for this change of heart. She wasn't. But maybe Lucian was so tired of battling Jerry that he didn't want to battle anyone else.

"I'll talk it over with Garrett and Lawson and get back to you." With that, Roman started down the porch steps, but Lucian stopped him.

"Do you know anything about the investment company Melcor?" Lucian asked.

Roman shook his head. "Is that the company your dad's been dealing with?"

"Yeah. The sonofabitch sold them a share of the family holdings, and I want it back even if I have to bust some balls to do it."

The corner of Roman's mouth lifted. "There's the Lucian we all know," he said from over his shoulder as he made his exit.

Things weren't exactly warm and friendly between them, but they were a lot better than they had once been, and while Karlee wanted to know why the change of heart/attitude, it could wait. For now, her priority was that kiss.

"You really didn't know Roman was here when you arrived?" she asked.

He shook his head.

Okay. So, she moved to her second option. "Did you just see your father or something before you came out here?"

Lucian stared at her. "You think I kissed you because I was pissed off at Jerry?"

"I considered it."

He made a fair-enough grunt, but there seemed to be some anger in his eyes. "I'm pissed off—at you, not Jerry."

Karlee was certain she looked confused. "So, you kissed me to…punish me?" And because she thought they could use some levity, she added, "That's not very BDSM if that's what you were going for."

No smile whatsoever. Not even a mouth quiver as Roman had done. "What I'm going to do is bad. I mean, permanent shit list bad."

Karlee was no longer smiling, either, because that sounded serious. Maybe serious in that he was breaking off their fake engagement. Or murdering her. But no murder, either.

In fact, speech wasn't even involved because he kissed her again.

It was just as steamy with a layer of smuttiness as the other one, but Lucian added some touching to it. Specifically, he slid his hand over her butt and started maneuvering her inside.

Where sex would happen.

There was no chance that Karlee was going to try to talk herself out of this, though it seemed as if Lucian had attempted just that because of what he'd said.

What I'm going to do is bad. I mean, permanent shit list bad.

He'd apparently had some kind of argument with himself and had lost. Good. They could be on that bad list together.

Karlee was already inside, already reaching out so she could get Lucian in there with her and then shut the door. However, before she could manage the last step of this raging foreplay, she heard someone.

"I'm sorry to interrupt," the woman said.

Lucian stopped the kiss, but he didn't let go of her. With Karlee still in his arms, he turned toward their visitor. Karlee turned, too. Then blinked. Because at first, she thought she was seeing things.

But she wasn't.

Well, shit.

What was *she* doing here?

CHAPTER NINE

GLENDA O'MALLEY.

Or whatever the heck her name was these days.

If someone had given Lucian a list of possible visitors to the ranch, Karlee's mom wouldn't have been anywhere on it. Yet here she was, walking toward the guesthouse.

Karlee reacted to her mom's arrival, and it wasn't a good kind of reaction. Lucian saw plenty of muscles in her body go stiff, and she snapped back her shoulders as if she'd just spotted a coiled rattler that was about to strike.

"Karlee, Lucian," Glenda greeted.

Neither of them did any greeting back, that's for sure. Lucian because he didn't know what the hell to say and Karlee because she was likely still trying to get her tongue untied over the shock of seeing this particular blast from her past.

Lucian had no idea why the woman was there, but the only silver lining he was seeing in this was that Glenda's arrival had delayed him with that whole *permanent shit list bad*. He wasn't going to have sex with Karlee after all and ruin things forever between them.

Well, not right now, anyway.

The next hour or two were in question though.

Glenda's arrival would also give Karlee some time to

think about the inevitable destruction of her friendship with Lucian. But for now, she had to deal with the inevitable anger that had to be there. After all, her mother had run off and left her family high and dry.

"What do you want?" Karlee snapped. There was nothing friendly about her tone. "Why are you here?"

Lucian figured she could have easily added a whole other boatload of questions. Along with some cussing. Plus, she was shivering a little now. It wasn't exactly freezing, but Karlee only had on a thin sweater, so Lucian kept his arm around her. Of course, he hoped his arm—along with the rest of him—wasn't just giving Karlee warmth but some support, as well.

"*You*. You're the reason I'm here," Glenda said to Karlee. She finally stopped coming closer when she got to the bottom step.

"Then it'll be a short visit," Karlee quickly assured her. "Because I don't want to see you."

Glenda nodded as if that was the exact answer she'd expected, and she took a business card from her jacket pocket. Still not coming closer, she stretched out her arm for Karlee to take it, but when she didn't, Glenda tried to hand it to Lucian. He didn't take it, either, so Glenda gently laid it on the porch railing.

"I know you'll never forgive me—" Glenda started.

"I won't," Karlee quickly assured her. "And neither will my brothers."

Glenda didn't nod that time, and something went through the woman's eyes that made Lucian believe that Glenda didn't agree with Karlee on that last part. Maybe that meant Glenda had already visited the O'Malley boys and had managed to mend a fence or two. Mack, the youngest, was her best bet for that since he was so young when Glenda left that he didn't even remember her. It wouldn't be exactly like her starting with a clean slate with him, but she would have had to fight through the bad memories the older boys and Karlee had of her.

"I've been keeping up with what goes on in your life," Glenda continued. "Best wishes on your engagement."

Other than a glare, Karlee didn't respond to that. "Do you have any idea how much pain you caused?" She didn't wait, though, for Glenda to speculate about that. "I had to drop my plans for college because there was no money. And when Dad died…"

Her voice broke, and Lucian tightened his grip on her. He also added his own glare at Glenda, and he was pretty damn sure that his was a lot meaner than the one Karlee was giving her.

"After Dad was gone," Karlee continued several moments later, "my brothers ended up in foster care until I could petition for custody to get them out. I was eighteen years old. *Eighteen.* So, you don't have the right to come here and say anything to me. In fact, you don't have a right to be here at all."

Lucian had known Karlee her entire life, and he saw something he'd never seen. Tears in her eyes, and in that moment he hated Glenda more than he hated his own father. Because, yeah, Jerry had left, but Lucian and his siblings hadn't ended up in foster care since they'd still had family money.

There were no tears in Glenda's eyes, but judging from her slightly swollen face, there'd been some crying earlier. She turned to leave, but she only made it a few steps before the back door of the main house flew open, and Candy stormed out into the yard. Jerry was right behind her. Regina as well, though she stayed back. Maybe his own mom was just trying to get a good "seat" to the little drama that started to play out.

"Candy, I told you that there's nothing going on between Glenda and me," Jerry called out to his fiancée. "I didn't even know she was coming here."

"You kissed her!" Candy shouted.

Lucian wasn't surprised by either the kiss or Candy's reaction.

"I hugged her because she was upset and crying," Jerry protested. "Big difference."

Apparently, Candy didn't see things that way, and Lucian was betting this argument had been going on for at least the couple of minutes since Glenda's arrival at the guesthouse. It meant that Glenda had stopped in the main house first, where that hug and the tears had happened.

Lucian glanced at his mom to see if she had a take on this. Regina merely lifted her hands. She was showing the least amount of emotion of the group, but she might be enjoying this. Lucian certainly wasn't. Karlee had been through enough, and that's why he led her back inside.

"There's nothing going on between Jerry and me," Glenda tried to say to Candy, but the woman just kept yelling out her accusations. Some were clever, too, and involved Jerry dicking around with Glenda in his taped-off area of the foyer. From what Lucian had seen, any kind of dicking around in that space would have required the skills of a very limber gymnast—something his father didn't have.

Lucian got Karlee into the guesthouse and was going to suggest a strong drink or a shower to drown out the noise, but those were piss-poor Band-Aids for something that couldn't be fixed.

"Wait here," he told her, sitting her on the sofa.

The least he could do was move this quickly escalating shouting match away from the guesthouse so that Karlee wouldn't have to hear it. However, by the time he made it back outside, Candy was already storming off. So was Glenda. And Jerry was standing in the center of the backyard looking up at the sky as if hoping for divine intervention or maybe a sudden lightning strike.

Regina was still there as well, and she was making her way to the guesthouse. "Candy broke off the engagement, and she went upstairs to pack her things," his mom explained. "I hope she stays in Jerry's space and doesn't step in anybody else's."

In the grand scheme of things, taped space violations didn't seem important, but apparently Regina was going to stick to that divvying system even if all hell was breaking loose.

"Is Karlee okay?" Regina asked. The slight smirk that had been on her face vanished.

Lucian glanced back at Karlee, and their gazes met. She didn't say anything, but he figured it wouldn't be a good time to have his mother come in for a long chat.

"I'll make sure Karlee's okay," he assured Regina, though he didn't have a clue how to do that. Sex and kisses weren't going to fix this. "Did you know Glenda was coming?"

Regina didn't hesitate. "No way. She just showed up, rang the doorbell, and Jerry let her in. I couldn't hear what they said because Jerry took her in his office. It's too hard to listen at the door because I only have a little part of a square of taped space in there. Bad planning on my part."

Again, this wasn't relevant. Well, it would have been if Regina had actually learned why Glenda had shown up out of the blue after seventeen years.

"I don't think she came here looking for money," Regina went on. "She came in a Bentley, and she has a driver all dressed up in a suit."

That could all be for show because he was betting that Jerry had gone through all or most of Glenda's money before they'd parted ways. Of course, she could have married into money or had a sugar daddy. Even after all these years, the woman was still attractive. And that might have been the real reason Jerry had let her into the house.

Hell.

He hoped Jerry and Glenda weren't about to start up their affair again because it would only stir the old shit memories for Karlee. It wouldn't do much good for Lucian's family, either, though his mom didn't seem overly concerned about that. Unlike Candy. That hug Jerry gave Glenda must have been a doozy for her to react that way.

Maybe similar to the hug Lucian had given Karlee. Of course, there'd been some kissing that'd gone along with that particular embrace.

"I know the timing is bad, but could we talk a moment?" Regina asked him.

Lucian glanced at Karlee again. She hadn't moved, but he wanted to sit with her to make sure she was okay. Which she probably wasn't. He was about to ask his mom if their talk could wait, but she launched right into it.

"I think I have a way to cut off your dad's testicles," Regina blurted out.

That got Lucian's attention—because it could be literal. "Is that why you invited him to Christmas dinner?" Lucian got instant images of scenarios involving malfunctioning carving knives or rigged chairs.

"No. Maybe," Regina amended after he kept staring at her.

"What are you planning?" he snapped.

Regina glanced around, too, but not at Karlee. The glances went all around her as if making sure no one was listening. "I set up a dummy company, and I'm going to try to get Jerry to sell me the one percent or more that you need to take back the ranch and business."

Lucian had not been expecting that, and this time there was only one scenario that he could see. "It won't work. Jerry just got a lot of money from Melcor." He paused. Frowned. "You aren't Melcor, are you?"

"No. But that's what gave me the idea. I mean, none of us except Jerry seems to know much about Melcor, so I thought if I set up something like that and offered him enough, that he'd take the bait." She put her hand on his arm. "This is our chance to get back our lives."

Yes, it could be. And it was very tempting.

But it was also wrong.

Possibly even illegal. Yes, they could get back the ranch and business, but it would come with a soiled reputation. Jerry was already smearing that up enough without adding more.

"Nix the dummy company," he said, and it wasn't a suggestion. "And rethink your plan of having Dad and you at the same dinner table."

She scowled, opened her mouth as if to argue that,

but Lucian put on his SOB face. It'd been a while since he'd had to use it, but it was as effective as usual.

"Fine," his mother said in a tone to let him know that it was in no way *fine*. She whirled around to leave but then whirled back just as fast. "Were you really making out with Karlee on the front porch while Roman was here?"

Frickin' hell. "Did Roman tell you that?"

"No. One of the ranch hands saw it and called Delphine, the new housekeeper, and she told me."

Lucian checked his watch. All of that happened fast, proving yet again that Wrangler's Creek didn't need an emergency response system or an updated tornado siren. Technology paled when it came to the speed of communications by folks hell-bent on gossip.

"So, you did kiss her," Regina concluded, and she smiled. No doubt because this had been a matchmaking scheme right from the beginning and now she thought it was working.

And it sort of was.

Except it probably wasn't a falling-in-love plan that his mother had envisioned. This was about sex.

He said goodbye to Regina and warned her again to nix her dummy company. Whether she would was anyone's guess. But he'd already spent enough time trying to put out that particular fire. Right now, the priority fire was Karlee.

Lucian shut the door, hoping that was the last of the interruptions, and he sat down on the sofa next to her. Only then did he realize that something was missing. Christmas was only a couple of days away, and there wasn't a single decoration in the guesthouse. He wasn't big on tinsel and lights, but Karlee had always decorated his office. Maybe her mood had been so bleak over their situation that she wasn't in the holiday spirit. If so, Glenda's arrival certainly wasn't going to help with that.

"I just texted Joe to see if he knew that Glenda was back," she said. "No response yet. My guess is he doesn't know or he would have already called me."

Yeah, that's what Lucian had figured, too. It was his guess as well that Karlee wasn't going to want him to give her a lot of questions about this, so he just sat there and waited for her to continue.

"I haven't gotten as much as a card from her over the years." When she dropped her head on his shoulder, Lucian slipped his arm around her. "And now this. Do you think Jerry sent for her?"

"It's possible. Regina seems to think your mom has some money now, so maybe Jerry's after that." Though he would have thought that Glenda would have already learned her lesson about that particular financial sinkhole.

"Money, huh?" She groaned softly. "She had a trust fund, but she took all of it with her when she left. Her parents were killed when she was just a child, so I don't think there was another inheritance. And I'd heard that she had remarried, but she wasn't wearing a wedding ring."

Lucian hadn't even noticed that. Probably because he'd been too busy glaring at her. He hated her for hurting Karlee all those years ago and for freshening up that hurt by coming today.

As for the lack of a wedding ring, it was possible that Glenda had remarried and then divorced. If so, she could have gotten a settlement that allowed her to have that pricey car and a driver.

"I'll put her business card in the trash," Karlee added. "I don't want any contact with her." She paused. "But my brothers might not feel the same way. I'm not sure how to handle that if they want her back in their lives."

Yeah, that wouldn't make family gatherings pleasant, but then, his weren't exactly a basket of golden sunshine, either. "Glenda might not even stay long enough to see them," he pointed out. "This might all blow over, and you could never have to deal with her again."

She turned to him, and there were definitely no signs of tears. But he thought he saw a little anger. Anger directed at him.

"You're being nice to me," she said.

Was he? Hell, yes, he was, and in this case, nice was code for feeling sorry for her. He did. However, he also knew that was one particular sentiment she didn't want. So Lucian did something about that.

"Why didn't you tell me sooner about your deal with Roman?" Lucian made sure there was some snarl in his voice. Not too much though. "And why aren't there any Christmas decorations up?"

That earned him a little smile, one that made him want to kiss her again. Bad timing though. Her nerves were already right there at the surface, and she didn't need him to add to that.

Her smile didn't last anyway. "The only place I ever decorate is your office, and since we're short on office space these days, I decided to skip it."

It was true about the office space, though he still had the one in his house in San Antonio. A couple of times she'd put up Christmas stuff there when his schedule was going to be so tight that he wasn't going to be around much at the ranch. However, he hadn't known that she didn't add all those holiday touches to her own place. And that's when it hit him.

Her father had died on Christmas Day.

Shit. No wonder people called him an asshole. That was one of the worst days of Karlee's life, and here he hadn't considered that it would continue to be a tough anniversary for her.

"I'm sorry," he said, and that encompassed a lot of things. Including an apology for that earlier kissing and groping on the porch.

She shook her head and looked at him as if waiting for him to explain. Or waiting for another kiss. But Lucian didn't get a chance to do either because his phone rang.

"It's Alice May Merkle from the garden guild," he said when he saw the name on the screen.

"Oh, I forgot to tell you that I sent a proposal to the garden guild to show them your plans for making a protected area around the creek for Hairy Corn Salad. It won't affect any of the operation of the ranch since it's on a spot by the creek that Dylan and you don't use for livestock."

Lucian certainly wasn't opposed to something like that, so maybe the call was just to thank him and not fuss at him for something else that he might have done wrong. After all, there were likely other weeds by the creek that someone cared about.

"Miss Merkle," Lucian greeted. He put the call on Speaker so that Karlee could hear. "How can I help you?"

"I won't keep you. I just heard that Karlee's mom was back in town, so I suspect things are a little hectic there."

Karlee groaned softly. She probably knew that news of Glenda's arrival would spread like wildfire, but there was no chance she wanted to discuss that with anyone, especially the garden guild.

"Is Karlee all right?" Alice May asked.

"She's fine. How can I help you?" Lucian repeated. He tried to sound busy rather than just impatient.

"Well, I'm calling about the sanctuary land you set up for the Hairy Corn Salad. I wanted to thank you. Actually, the entire Wrangler's Creek Garden Guild wants to thank you."

Lucian relaxed enough so that the grip on his phone wasn't hurting his hand. "You're welcome. By the way, that was Karlee's idea, so I'll pass along your thanks to her."

"Yes, please do that," Alice May said. He was about to end the call, but the woman continued. "The garden guild just had our monthly meeting, and you were on the agenda. Specifically, whether or not to give you power of attorney to represent our one percent share of the Granger's holdings."

His grip tightened again. "And?"

"And we voted to do just that. It wasn't unanimous," Alice May quickly added, "but there were enough votes to throw our support your way."

Those words plowed through his head like a tornado. It meant his father and he were now on equal footing and neither of them had control. Not perfect. But it was exactly the start he'd needed because he could stop Jerry from making any solo business decisions.

"Thank you," Lucian managed to say to the woman.

"You're welcome. Oh, and merry Christmas," Alice May added before she hung up.

Well, it certainly had a better chance of being merry now that he had this news. He could get back the company. He could stop Jerry from running it into the ground. Things could be the way they had been before he'd been fired.

Lucian had never doubted this moment would come, but it surprised him that he wasn't as relieved as he'd thought he would be. Or particularly happy. That was because of Karlee. He needed to start the avalanche of paperwork to undo the past weeks, but that would mean not staying put. Not being with her. Not trying to help her.

Finally, there was something that had gotten his mind off kissing her.

Ironic that it would be his leaving.

"Go," Karlee insisted as if she was homed into every thought he was having right now. Every emotion. Of course, she was. She knew him better than anyone else.

When he didn't budge, she stood, pulled him to his feet. "Go," she repeated, leading him across the room and to the door. "Reconquer the world."

With that, she nudged him onto the porch, brushed her mouth over his. And then shut the door in his face.

CHAPTER TEN

THE ANGUS HERD stared at Karlee as if demanding that she explain her presence at the pasture fence on such a chilly morning. She was shivering, her breath fogging around her when it met the cold air, but she stayed put with her foot propped on the bottom fence railing.

Along with the spooky staring, the cows also smelled. Of course, she'd known that a herd could throw off some unsavory scents, but maybe she noticed it more because these were special.

Because they were *hers*.

Many people probably wouldn't have felt so much pride at the ownership of smelly, staring animals, but they were proof of a dream that she'd waited a long time to come true.

She already had a buyer for part of this first herd, so they wouldn't be here on Roman's land much longer, but it was possible some of the others might stay until spring. If so, there'd be repeat trips over here to check on them. Trips that she might need for more than just the welfare of her investment. It could be necessary for her sanity.

She'd needed to escape, and that's why she'd gotten up early and sneaked out of the guesthouse. Not that she had to "sneak" too hard. Lucian was back in San Antonio, where he'd been since the garden guild had given them their support. For the past couple of days, he'd been having emergency meetings with his lawyers so he could put a halt to Jerry's business operations. She was certain he'd be back later for the family dinner, but he hadn't spent a night in the guesthouse since the legal fight had started. He had called and texted her, though, to make sure she was okay.

She wasn't.

But there was no way she would let him know that. No way, either, that she would tell him how much everything was closing in on her. And Regina certainly hadn't helped with that.

It was as if the Christmas elves had puked decorations all over the place. Regina had lined the entire road with thousands of lights and wreaths, and she'd continued her quest for overillumination in and around the house. And that included lights on the six trees—yes, six—that she'd stashed in the living and dining areas.

Since Regina normally didn't show up at the ranch until a day or two before Christmas, this decorating mania was a first, and the timing for it sucked. With so much of Karlee's life in transition, she could have used a little of the "same ol', same ol'," but Regina hadn't cooperated with that. Lucian's mom was obviously trying to make a point, but Karlee wasn't sure exactly what it was.

In Regina's defense, she didn't know just how hard Christmas was for her. Of course, Lucian's mom and anyone else in Wrangler's Creek would remember that Whitt O'Malley had died on Christmas Day. But what they didn't know was all the things that'd gone on that morning.

The devil was in those details.

So was Karlee's childhood. Maybe even a piece of her damaged soul was in those details, too.

Because that was the day the lie began.

Even now remembering that caused her heart to feel as if someone had clamped a squeezing fist around it. Some wounds didn't heal, and this was one of them. Hard to heal when she'd found her father's suicide note lying beside the chair where he was slumped and cold.

A note that she'd hidden while waiting for the ambulance to arrive.

She still had it, tucked beneath the bottom drawer of her jewelry box. A clichéd hiding spot normally reserved for naughty boyfriend photos and letters, but she hadn't been able to bring herself to throw it away.

There'd been no need to hide or throw away the bottle with the sleeping pills her father had taken. Whitt had left the remainder of those in the medicine cabinet, but the bottle of whiskey that he'd used to chase the meds was next to the note. The pills had shown up when the autopsy had been done. So had the whiskey. But without any indications of suicide, the ME had ruled it an accidental death, saying that Whitt had been so drunk that he hadn't realized how many pills he was taking.

That'd been so much better than the truth.

She'd only been seventeen, but she'd known what a suicide note like that could do. Her brothers were barely hanging on by a thread. Heck, Joe had already been arrested for underage drinking. Judd was flunking out of school. Knowing that their father had taken his own life would have ended them as a family. Especially if any of them had ever read it.

The words were burned into her mind, and there was

no way she wanted that kind of hurt in her brothers' minds, too.

She heard the sound of the approaching vehicle and figured it would be Roman or one of his siblings. But no. It was Lucian. He pulled his truck to a stop behind her car, and he was frowning when he stepped out.

"Isn't this enemy territory for you?" she asked, only partly joking.

It didn't soothe his expression any. "I came looking for you when you didn't answer your phone."

"I turned it off because I didn't want to spook the herd." Overkill, yes, but she'd also wanted some quiet time. Karlee pulled her cell from her pocket and saw the two missed calls from him. That was enough to send some alarm through her. "Is something wrong?"

He shook his head and went to her, putting his foot on the fence next to hers. "I was just worried when I got to the guesthouse and you weren't there."

Ah, she got it then. This was about Glenda showing up.

The last time Lucian had seen her, she had been on the verge of crying—which she had indeed done after Lucian had left for San Antonio. His leaving had happened only after she had insisted that he go, and she'd had to repeat that insistence multiple times. That told her just how troubled she must have looked for him to consider delaying something so important like the legal paperwork to oust Jerry.

There'd been a second reason Karlee had pressed to have Lucian leave. It would give her some thinking time, not just about him but Glenda, as well. But in Glenda's case, out of sight/out of mind had helped. Her mother hadn't returned to the ranch, nor had she made any appearances in town. If she had, Karlee was certain she would have heard about it. She'd told her brothers, of course, but they hadn't seen Glenda, either. Karlee was hoping it would stay that way.

That out of sight/out of mind, however, hadn't applied to Lucian. He'd been on her mind almost constantly, and that wasn't good because now she had her own business to run. Plus, there were all the social obligations that Regina kept piling on. It was hard to argue with those, though, now that they were so close to permanently getting Jerry out of their lives. All it was going to take was getting that share vote from the historical society or Melcor.

"Is everything moving on the legal action to stop your father?" she asked.

He nodded. "Nothing will get done today because it's Christmas, but I told everyone I expected the motions to go in full swing first thing in the morning."

And there was the Lucian that everyone feared and respected. But because she knew him so well, she could tell there was something missing. She just couldn't put her finger on exactly what.

"So, how does it feel to be a business owner?" he asked.

She nearly said it was better than sex, but that would only be true of sex with someone who didn't happen to be Lucian. Karlee was betting that sex with him would be a list topper. And something that she didn't want to bring up. All that flirting they'd been doing was heating her up, and she didn't have an outlet for burning any of that off.

Well, not an outlet she'd pursued yet, anyway.

"It feels good," she settled for saying. "How does your new business venture feel?"

"Better than sex." He smiled. "Well, almost. Better than some sex, anyway."

Karlee sure wasn't smiling. She went still, and she was glad that Lucian continued to keep his attention on the Angus or he would have seen that "come-hither" look in her eyes. She didn't mind him seeing it but only when and if he was ready to take all of this flirting to the bedroom.

"Don't get me wrong," he went on. "I enjoyed building the family business. But it felt like a huge responsibility, too. Something I owed my grandfather for putting so much faith in me. The new company is all mine."

She totally got that even though the herd was the first big thing she'd ever owned other than a car.

"I'm sorry I couldn't do this for you." He tipped his head to the herd. "I should have been able to let you use the land at the ranch so you could get started."

Karlee shrugged. "It all worked out, and Roman gave me a good deal on the land lease."

Though that probably didn't help Lucian's feelings about this. Roman and he had reached a sort of truce that day at the guesthouse, but there was still a lot of old bad blood between them.

"So what will you do when Jerry finally backs off?" she asked. "Will you try to keep both businesses going?"

"I'm not sure."

Karlee thought maybe a little part of hell had just frozen over. Never had she imagined Lucian turning over the reins or even being undecided about something that important.

"One thing for certain—Jerry won't be running things,"

he added a moment later. "Maybe my mom will want to help out more. It'd be a better use of her time than what she's doing now. There are Christmas lights on the barns and balls of mistletoe hanging from the hayloft."

Karlee had missed that, and she wondered what the hands thought of all of that. The barn certainly wasn't a mistletoe hot spot for them. Which made Karlee wonder if Regina had put it there for Lucian's and her benefit. The woman had made it crystal clear that she wanted the fake engagement to be a real one. That was asking a lot, though, of mere mistletoe.

"All those decorations are one of the reasons I escaped and came here," Karlee admitted.

Now he looked at her, but thankfully she'd recovered from his "better than sex" remark. "I thought you enjoyed getting ready for Christmas," he said. "You always put up a tree and stuff."

"Only in your office. And that's because I thought it would remind you to be your nicer self."

"I don't have a nice self." He smiled again, then paused. "I don't suppose you've figured out a way to get out of this Christmas family dinner?"

She shook her head. "Unless we come down with a sudden case of Ebola, we're stuck. You do know Regina invited the mayor, his daughter and a member of the historical society."

Lucian's mumbled profanity told her that he hadn't known that. "And Jerry will be there, of course. Since I got that one percent share to tie up things, Mom's tapping off the house fifty-fifty now. Jerry's fighting back by boarding up some of the rooms so she can't get in them. If you need to use the bathroom, go to my room because Jerry superglued the door shut in the hall powder room."

That should make things interesting for guests. Though if things got even more tense between them—or if more bathroom doors got glued—maybe Regina would cancel this dinner.

Lucian reached in his coat pocket, took out a small box and handed it to her. "Your Christmas present," he said.

Surprised, Karlee stared at it a moment mainly because Lucian had never given her an actual Christmas present. His gift to her had always been a bonus check. Of course, she was no longer working for him, so he must have decided to go with something more, well, personal.

"Thank you." She took the box and stared at it a moment. "I have a gift for you, but it's back at the guesthouse. I'll wait to open this when I give you yours."

That seemed personal, too. Intimate, even. Of course, with Lucian standing so close to her, anything she said or did was going to feel that way.

"Or we could just skip the gifts and have sex," he said.

She laughed, but it was all from nerves, not because she was overly surprised by it. They'd been skirting around this for days. Or in her case, years. And that's why Karlee leaned in and brushed her mouth over his. But the kiss never got past the brushing-lips stage because Lucian's phone rang, the sound shooting through the silence, and it sent the Angus moving away from the fence.

He cursed, glanced at the screen. "It's my mom." And he let it go to voice mail.

However, another call came in right behind it. This

one from Dylan. Something was obviously going on. Lucian cursed again and took the call.

"This had better not be a call about glued doors," Lucian growled to his brother.

"It's not." Even though Lucian hadn't put the call on Speaker, Karlee was standing close enough to hear Dylan's response. And the rest of what he said. "You need to come to the jail. Mom and Jerry have been arrested."

"JERRY DUMPED COFFEE in the stuffing," Regina explained to Lucian. She'd already explained it to Dylan and Chief of Police Clay McKinnon, but Lucian was glaring, so she thought he needed to hear it, too.

"It was an accident," Jerry growled from the cell next to hers. "I spilled my coffee, and it went in the stuffing pan. But what wasn't an accident was you hiding all the toilet paper."

"I was merely rearranging things." And this was only the first leg of the explanations where she had to defend herself, but judging from Lucian's increased glare, he didn't want to hear it.

"Does this mean dinner is canceled?" Karlee asked, sounding way too hopeful for Regina's liking. She was doing this dinner for Lucian, for their engagement. It wasn't her fault that Jerry had tried to sabotage it.

"The dinner will go on as planned," Regina insisted. "Only without the stuffing."

"And what about the toilet paper?" Jerry snapped.

Regina ignored him and came out of the cell when Chief McKinnon unlocked it. Obviously, Dylan had managed to post her bond. "Putting me in there wasn't necessary, you know," she reminded him.

"It was when you both resisted arrest," the chief reminded her right back.

She could have continued the *reminding* by telling him that since he was a cousin by marriage that he should have cut her some slack, but she was wasting her breath. This was the last straw. And it was all Jerry's fault—as most of her problems had been in the past two decades.

"Who called the cops?" Lucian asked, his glare volleying between Jerry, who was also getting out of lockup, and her.

"Abe," Jerry spit out. "He thought I was going to hit Regina, but I wasn't. I was just getting my point across."

"Then how did you end up here?" Lucian pressed when he shifted his attention back to her.

It was the chief who answered that. "When the deputy showed up and told your mom to get back in the house so he could talk to your dad and calm him down, Regina refused, and she kept getting in Jerry's face. The deputy arrested her after she refused to go inside."

That was pretty much it in a nutshell. And in hindsight and with a now-cooler head, it made her sound like an idiot.

"I'll be firing Abe as soon as I get home," Jerry grumbled. "He had no right to call the cops."

"You're not firing anyone," Lucian quickly assured him. "In fact, you're not doing anything that involves the ranch, the house or the business."

Regina wanted to cheer for Lucian putting Jerry in his place, but Lucian turned that frosty look back on her. "And you'll stop these childish games. Was Corbin in the house when all of this happened?" He didn't wait for the answer because he knew that the boy was. "What kind of example did this set for him?" Again, no waiting for them to respond. "A shitty example, that's what."

That was true, and it had the effect that Lucian had no doubt intended. She felt horrible. She'd let her temper get the best of her, and it'd led to this.

"I'm sorry," Regina said, extending that apology to Karlee.

"I'm sorry, too," Jerry grumbled a moment later, and he sounded about as sincere as a crooked politician.

"I'll give Mom a ride home," Dylan offered, and he turned to Lucian, no doubt waiting for him to say that he'd drive Jerry.

"Lucian and I came here in separate vehicles, so Jerry can ride with me," Karlee quickly offered. "And you'd better behave," she warned him.

Lucian and she exchanged a glance before she headed out with Jerry trailing along after her. Lucian wasn't far behind. He left only seconds later, probably because he didn't trust his father to actually behave.

"You want me to lecture you?" Dylan asked her once the others were out of earshot.

The answer to this was easy. "No. I just want to get back home and finish cooking." Maybe she could even scrounge up the makings for stuffing, though she'd already used the fresh herbs in the batch that Jerry had ruined.

Dylan had brought her a coat when he'd come to the police station to bail her out, and she was thankful for it when she stepped out into the chilly air. She hadn't noticed the cold when she'd been brought in because the anger had heated her up.

"Wait inside," Dylan instructed. "I'll bring the truck around."

He headed toward the parking lot, but just as Regina was turning around to go back in, she saw Glenda making her way toward her. If she'd been a cussing sort, she would have used some of those words right about now, and it bothered her that she felt that punch of anger.

Then hurt.

She was long over the love she'd once felt for Jerry. In fact, she was glad to be rid of him, so if she looked at it that way, Glenda O'Malley had done her a favor. Of course, it sure hadn't felt that way at the time.

"I thought you'd left," Regina said, but it wasn't very loud because her throat was suddenly a little tight.

"No. I'm staying in the area until I can see all of my kids. May we talk?" Glenda added.

Regina motioned toward the Wrangler's Creek Police Station sign. "It's not a good time."

Glenda nodded as if that was the exact answer she'd expected, and she didn't seem to make any judgments about the location. The woman certainly didn't ask if something had gone wrong. Of course, it was possible that it was already around town by now.

"Call me when you get a chance." Glenda handed her a business card. *"Please."*

Until she'd added that *please*, Regina had been about to say something snarky like they had nothing to discuss, that she didn't have another husband for Glenda to steal. Instead, Regina went for as civil as she could manage. "Look, if it's forgiveness you want, you've got it. I just wish you'd managed to keep Jerry with you, and then he wouldn't be here."

"That's what I want to talk to you about," Glenda insisted.

Now, that wasn't an answer Regina had expected. "What do you mean?"

Glenda looked her straight in the eyes. "I mean, I'm here to see my kids, but I'm also in town to bring Jerry to his knees. *Permanently.* If you want to know what I'm planning, then call me."

CHAPTER ELEVEN

LUCIAN TOOK COMFORT in the fact that in homes all over America this same sort of hell was going on. Regina and Jerry were glaring at each other, and the glaring put a thick blanket of tension over the dry turkey and lumpy gravy.

Their guests didn't seem to be having much fun, either. The mayor, Bennie Sullivan—who was extremely hard of hearing. His daughter, Darlene. And Myrtle Carmichael from the historical society.

All were giving each other nervous glances while taking tiny bites of food. Darlene wasn't really even eating. She was just scraping her fork over her servings, moving things around while she blurted out the occasional compliment.

Other than Dylan, Lucian's siblings had all managed to get out of this fiasco by saying they wanted to have Christmas dinner in their own homes with their families. Dylan was stuck because he lived at the ranch. Ditto for his wife and son, Corbin, but Jordan had lucked out when Corbin had gotten fussy and she'd taken him to his room. Most parents probably wouldn't have called it lucking out to have to deal with a fussy toddler, but the alternative was far, far worse.

Karlee managed a smile or two, but Lucian figured that was for Myrtle's benefit. If they could just sway the historical society, there'd be no need for a legal battle. Unless, of course, Jerry got pissed enough to file a lawsuit that he could never win. But at the moment, getting Myrtle's seal of approval didn't seem to be on the horizon. She hadn't smiled at anyone, not even Corbin, which gave her the title of the sourest person at the dinner table.

"The gravy is yummy," Darlene said while making little swirls in the puddle of the gluey stuff that she'd scooped onto her plate.

"Thank you. I'm sorry about the dry turkey," his mom remarked. Again. This time she aimed it at Myrtle, who was attempting to chew it. The woman would have had better luck getting her incisors through the leather of Lucian's boot. "It was left in the oven too long because of the…altercation that happened right in the middle of my cooking schedule."

Altercation was yet another repeated word, and it was apparently what she was calling her and Jerry's arrest. Jerry hadn't said a thing about it. In fact, his only conversation had been with the mayor. Probably because Jerry knew that was his best shot at having any moral support whatsoever. But even then it'd been more of a shouting match because of the mayor's malfunctioning hearing aid. When the mayor had been able to follow along, Jerry had kept the topics shallow, mentioning the weather and the charity rodeo.

"The turkey's fine," Karlee assured his mom. "In fact, everything's delicious, even the coffee-flavored stuffing."

That was BS and everyone knew it, but at least she'd made the attempt to be civil. No one else other than Darlene had even tried, including him. He was still so riled about the bickering games that his mom and dad were playing that he had no intentions of cutting either of them any slack.

Hell. Even the dining room was still marked off in fifty-fifty squared areas, and Jerry's square hadn't been at the head of the table. That's apparently what had prompted the now-infamous coffee dump in the stuffing. He'd retaliated against squares on the floor that he could have simply ignored.

Their arrest had spoiled not only a nice morning he was having with Karlee, it had also added a newer level of crap to all of this because word would soon get around that Jerry, the acting CEO of Granger Enterprises, had been arrested in a domestic dispute.

It would hurt the business.

Of course, Jerry had already done that with some of the stunts he'd been pulling, but this could cost them future deals long after Jerry's ousting. Lucian hadn't lied when he'd told Karlee that he wasn't sure what he was going to do about the family business, but he didn't want it to go under.

"I saw your mother in town this morning," Myrtle said, drawing everyone's attention to her. Partly because it was the woman's first full sentence since she'd arrived. Mainly, though, it was because of the topic itself. Myrtle had addressed the comment to Karlee, and now she was staring at her, waiting for a response.

Karlee took a sip of wine first. "Yes. Glenda's in the area so she can visit with my brothers."

"These rolls are yummy," Darlene said. Obviously, she knew this was nowhere in the thread of the conversation, but she was trying to keep them off sensitive topics.

Good luck with that. The whole shitstorm was sensitive.

Like everyone else at the table, Myrtle ignored Darlene and kept her focus on Karlee. "Oh, and how did Glenda's visits with your brothers go?"

Karlee gulped down some more wine. "I'm not sure. I was going to call Joe and Judd after dinner."

This was the first Lucian was hearing about Glenda seeing her sons and Karlee following it up with a call. Karlee had managed not to show much emotion with her response, but he knew this had to be eating away at her. Of course, there were plenty of things doing that to both of them right now.

"I do hope the visits went well," Myrtle remarked. "If there's any way I can help with that situation, let me know."

On the surface it was a nice offer, but Lucian figured it was Myrtle's way of trying to keep in the gossip loop. And he figured Myrtle would continue to pump Karlee for info and that's why he moved the conversation in a different direction. One that would put a smile on Karlee's face. Because right now he thought they could all use something of a happy nature.

"Karlee and I went to see the Angus she bought," Lucian threw out there. "She's a bona fide business owner."

That didn't interest Myrtle nearly as much as the Glenda topic, and she gave only a mild *hmmm*. The mayor nodded. No smile but that was probably because he hadn't heard a word they'd said. Jerry grunted or possibly that was a belch or fart.

"It's good that you have your own company. This way you won't be working for your husband-to-be when he's back in charge of everything," Regina added. "That's for the best. Might cause some tension in the marriage."

Her comment sure caused some tension. It set off another round of glares from Jerry, who clearly wasn't pleased that Regina had just assumed Jerry would soon be out. But it was the marriage remark that had Dylan, Karlee and Lucian tensing up. Because there'd be no marriage. Heck, it wouldn't be long before there'd be no more fake engagement.

Which caused Lucian to feel an even-grouchier mood coming on.

"This butter tastes fresh churned." Darlene again. And everyone ignored her.

Lucian wanted to stop the pretense of this engagement right this second, but he didn't want to put an end to what had been stirring between Karlee and him. Even though he should. His change in job titles didn't give him a decent résumé in the relationship department, and he was back to that old mantra of not wanting to hurt her. Too bad, though, that he couldn't see a way around that.

"So, how did your visit with Glenda go?" Myrtle asked. Again, she got all eyes on her—especially when Myrtle's own eyes were on Regina. "My mouth fell open when I saw you two talking outside the police department because I was certain if you two crossed paths again that the fur would be flying."

Speaking of mouths, Karlee's fell open, too. And Jerry's. Lucian was sure his jaw dropped some, as well.

"Glenda and I didn't really talk," Regina was quick to say. "She just happened to be passing by when I stepped out of the building."

That sounded like a lie. Apparently, Myrtle also

thought so. "Oh, it looked as if you two were having an intense discussion," the woman commented. "And she handed you something. It looked like a business card. I just figured you two would be staying in touch if she gave you her card."

"Well, we won't be," Regina practically snapped, but she added a smile and tipped her head to Karlee. "Perhaps we should change the subject." The head tip was meant to remind Myrtle that this was probably an unpleasant subject for Karlee, but the most uncomfortable person in the room right now was Regina.

"I'm okay with it," Karlee insisted just as Darlene said, "And this wine is scrumptious!"

"Good." Jerry didn't even spare Darlene a glance, and he didn't give Karlee a chance to change her mind about her not minding, either. With his fork just inches from his mouth, Jerry turned to Regina. He'd skewered some green beans on the fork tines, and they looked like big green spider legs. "Because I want to know exactly what Glenda said to you."

"Nothing that concerns you." If Regina's tone had gotten any frostier, they'd all have to be reaching for jackets. "And no fur flew," she added to Myrtle.

"I must have your recipe for these mashed potatoes," Darlene gushed. "They're the best I've ever eaten."

Even Regina glared at Darlene that time.

"Well, good," Myrtle answered, but Lucian was almost positive the woman wasn't buying any of what Regina had told her. "After the falling-out you had with Jerry's new fiancée, I thought maybe it would be just as bad with the old mistress."

Lucian was betting his mom hadn't thought she'd be served up as a tasty gossip morsel at her own dinner table. Payback was a bitch since Regina had been the one who'd insisted on this stupid gathering.

Now that Myrtle had exhausted the Glenda topic, it was apparently Lucian's turn because the woman looked at him. "I was thinking about having some new displays at the historical society. You know, something to keep folks coming in. That's how we get the bulk of our donations."

After the wringer that Myrtle had just put Regina through, Lucian considered himself lucky that she was only hitting him up for money. "I'd be happy to make a donation," he said.

Myrtle smiled. "I knew I could count on you. I mean, what with the epiphany and all that you went through. And when my sister and I were talking about this, I told her that you wouldn't mind giving us your grandfather's rodeo buckle."

Lucian nearly choked on the sip of water he took at the exact moment Myrtle said that. "Rodeo buckle?" he challenged, hoping that he'd misheard her.

"Yes, the one he got for winning the two events at the charity rodeo. It really should be on display for the town to see."

No. It should be with him since his grandfather had given it to him. It was literally the possession that he valued most. And he wasn't going to hand it over to anyone—even if it meant he could win this war with his dad.

"I think I'll hang on to it," Lucian said. While he was at it, he was going to quit kissing butt in this town. Along with putting an end to this meal.

Myrtle's eyes nearly matched the size of the turkey platter. "I was so sure you'd say yes that I went ahead and ordered the display case." She looked at Regina as if prompting her to plead her case.

Which Regina would have almost certainly done. But Lucian was fed up with that, too.

"If you'll excuse me..." He stood, ready to add something that people usually added when they were about to leave, but he couldn't think of anything that he hadn't already said. So he just walked out.

Lucian didn't head out back to the guesthouse. Right now, he just needed to walk and level his head, and that's why he went to the front. Maybe he could walk down to Lawson's house and have his brother pour him a triple shot of whiskey. Shots that Lucian realized he needed a lot more than he thought when he opened the door and he saw the person on the porch.

Amelia.

She had her hand out as if she'd been about to ring the doorbell, and she sort of froze there. Lucian thought maybe he did some freezing, too. Yes, it was Amelia all right. Smiling and looking nervous at the same time.

"Hi," she greeted. "Wait right there," she added.

He didn't have a choice about waiting because Lucian wasn't sure he could move yet. Worse, he didn't know what he was supposed to feel. He got that gut-punch feeling that he always did when he saw Amelia, but this time it was tempered a bit because he immediately wondered what she wanted.

And how Karlee was going to react to this.

"I saw this in a movie," Amelia said, taking some large cards from the bag she'd set on the porch. "Since I was having trouble figuring out what to say, I decided to do it this way."

She lifted the first card so he could see the bold

print that she'd written: "I know you must be surprised to see me, but I hope you're happy, too." She'd drawn smiley faces on it.

Yeah, he was surprised all right, and happy—more or less. Probably not as happy as he would have been a couple of months ago.

Amelia pulled out the second card. "I took the chance that you might want to spend some of your Christmas Day with me," it read. "For old times' sake." She'd drawn stick figures holding hands on it.

She took out the third and what appeared to be the final card. "So, what do you say, Lucian? Do you want to make this Christmas a merry one for both of us." She'd drawn kissing stick figures on it.

Smiling and with the card held up in front of her, Amelia looked at him. "Well?" she prompted.

And that's how Karlee found them when she stepped into the doorway beside Lucian.

CHAPTER TWELVE

AFTER LUCIAN HAD practically stormed out of the dining room, Karlee had given him just a couple of minutes before she had gone after him. She'd seen that "I'm done with this" look in his eyes.

Not just done with the awful dinner, either, but also the engagement.

She had wanted to tell him that if he was ready to nix this plan, then she was ready, too, even if it meant not keeping Jerry in control. Something that might happen no matter what they did. The last thing that Karlee had expected to see was...whatever it was she was seeing.

Amelia. Here. And holding a sign covered in red lipstick kisses.

So, what do you say, Lucian? Do you want to make this Christmas a merry one for both of us.

Judging from Lucian's stunned look, he was as surprised by the visit, and the card, as Karlee was. No, wait. She rethought that. No one could be more stupefied than her. Not even Amelia, who clearly hadn't been expecting Karlee to come out of the house. Which told Karlee loads. Amelia knew the engagement was fake, and she'd come here expecting Lucian to fall into bed with her as they usually did.

And he just might.

"Karlee," Amelia said on a rise of breath.

"Amelia." She kept her voice as flat and void of emotion as possible, but Karlee did tip her head to the sign. "There should be a question mark instead of a period after *both of us*."

Amelia tore her stare from Karlee, looked at the sign. "You're right." And she laughed. It was smoky and thick, a laugh that could make people feel good. Actually, that applied to Amelia, too. She was not only stunning with her honey-blond hair, sapphire-blue eyes and perfect body, she was also a nice person. Someone whom Karlee found it hard to hate.

But she hated Amelia now.

Because Lucian was fed up with the engagement plan, then he would go back to Amelia. No surprise, really. He always went back to her. Though Amelia's being here would make the going back to her so much easier.

Karlee didn't look at Lucian. That's because she knew what she would see. Along with the surprise, there'd be confusion and concern that this was hurting her. That's why he'd held back. Well, other than when he'd kissed her. But even then that kiss had come with a warning label—that he didn't do relationships. However, what the label should have actually said was that he didn't do relationships with any woman whose name wasn't Amelia.

"It's safe for you two to go inside," Karlee said. Thankfully, her voice didn't crack. "Jerry left the table and went to his room. Myrtle's getting her things to leave, too." She took out her phone. "And if you'll excuse me, I need to call my brothers."

"Karlee," both Amelia and Lucian said when she went down the steps.

Instead of going back in where someone could see her,

she'd walk around to the guesthouse. Without looking back, she fluttered a wave, muttered a "Merry Christmas" and kept on walking. But she didn't get far enough because she heard what Amelia said to Lucian.

"I thought you said the engagement wasn't real."

Karlee quickened her pace enough that she didn't catch Lucian's response. No need for that. If he'd told Amelia about the fakery, then they'd talked. Maybe even laughed about it.

No, Lucian wouldn't have laughed.

But he'd certainly kissed her while still hung up on his ex, who might not even be his ex. And that made Karlee a fool. Jordan had been right. She should have just gone for sex, for a scorching-hot one-night stand. It wouldn't have helped with what she was feeling, but at least she would have some orgasmic memories to get her through the next couple of hours.

Somehow, she made it to the guesthouse despite the fact that her legs weren't steady. Heck, no part of her was steady, and that's why she wouldn't call her brothers. They'd hear the emotion in her voice and come running. Or rather, come punching, because they would go after Lucian for hurting her.

The first thing Karlee saw when she stepped into the guesthouse was the gift Lucian had given her when they'd been looking at the Angus. She had put it on the kitchen counter next to the gift she'd gotten for Lucian. The plan had been to open them together.

Her plan had been to finish off the present unwrapping with sex.

That wasn't going to happen now. Seeing Amelia was a reminder that there'd been a reason she had decided to quit working for Lucian and start a new life.

She had spent a decade lusting after a man whose heart had already been claimed.

She blinked back the tears, but there was no way to blink away the hurt she was feeling. Karlee refused, though, to hurry to the bedroom, pack her things and leave. Though that's what she would do very soon, maybe in an hour or two. She just didn't want it to be done out of hurt and anger with her storming away from the ranch. No reason to put that on Lucian's shoulders since she'd known what she was getting into before she'd ever started these sexual fantasies about him.

The knock at the door helped her dry up those tears along with sending her stomach to her knees. She wasn't ready to face Lucian yet—or for that matter, anyone else checking on her—and she considered hiding out in her bathroom. Briefly considered it, but she decided to do the brave thing and assure Lucian that she was okay.

However, it wasn't Lucian.

Her stomach went south again when she saw Glenda on the doorstep. Of course, she had known that her mother was still in town because Myrtle had mentioned seeing Glenda with Regina outside the police department. But Karlee certainly hadn't expected her mother to show up here.

"This isn't a good time." And she would have shut the door in Glenda's face if the woman hadn't taken hold of it.

"Please," her mother said. "I just need to talk to you for a few minutes."

Karlee huffed. "This really isn't a good time." Of course, there really wasn't any good time when it came to seeing Glenda. "If you need forgiveness, you got it.

Not because you deserve it, but because I needed to get on with my life and forgiving you was a start."

Glenda glanced away. "Save your forgiveness. You're right—I don't deserve it, and you have every right to hang on to the hatred and the pain."

If her mom was trying to pull some kind of reverse-psychology crap, Karlee did not want to hear it. Though there was nothing about this conversation she actually wanted to hear. Still, Glenda wasn't budging, and she still had her hand on the door.

"You've got two minutes," Karlee warned her. "Say your piece and then leave. And I don't mean leave for a day or two. I want you gone from my life."

Glenda nodded, but she used up those first few seconds of those two minutes just trying to steady her breath. "I know about your father. I know what he wrote in that note he left."

Everything inside Karlee felt as if it got sucked into a vacuum. For a moment she was certain she had misunderstood. Because Glenda couldn't have known about the note. She hadn't been there. Karlee had.

"Please," Glenda repeated. "Just let me come in so I can tell you what happened."

"I know what happened!" Karlee snapped.

"No. You found his body. You found the note he left, too, but you don't know that your father called me right before he killed himself. I'm the last person who spoke to him."

Karlee actually dropped back a step. It was the first time she'd ever heard someone say those words aloud. *Killed himself.* She'd certainly never said them. And she was absolutely sure she hadn't known about any call her father had made.

But why would Glenda lie about something like that?

One look at her face, and Karlee knew it was the truth. And that's why she moved out of the doorway to allow Glenda to come inside.

"You might want to get a drink to steady your nerves," Glenda warned her.

Karlee was certain that no drink could do that. "Just start talking."

Glenda nodded again, went to the sofa and sat down. She seemed as unsteady as Karlee felt, and that's why Karlee took the chair across from her.

"Whitt called me about six hours before I got word that he was dead," Glenda said. And yes, her voice was shaky. "He was depressed and had been drinking. And he said he was going to kill himself."

Her heart tripped over a few beats. "You should have told me. You should have gotten in touch with me immediately."

Glenda acknowledged that with a weary sound of agreement. "It wasn't the first time he'd called me to say that. It was the third or fourth. I considered changing my number or blocking him, but I didn't want to cut off contact with him in case there was some kind of emergency."

"That was an emergency," Karlee quickly pointed out, but that was her frustration and grief talking. Frustration and grief that were bubbling beneath her skin, clawing their way to the surface.

"I didn't know that night was different from the other times he'd called," Glenda went on. Then she paused. "At least that's what I tell myself. I know I should have hung up and dialed nine-one-one. I should have gotten someone out to the house."

"Yes, you should have." But Karlee knew she should

have done more, too. She'd seen her father's slide into depression, knew he had a drinking problem, and she hadn't forced him to get help.

Glenda glanced away again but not before Karlee saw that she, too, was battling tears. "Whitt read me the suicide note he planned to leave. I'm guessing you took that since the cops didn't mention it when they came to tell me he was dead."

Karlee nodded. She hadn't known about the cops informing Glenda, either, but maybe her father hadn't changed his emergency contact information at the hospital or at his job.

"I didn't want my brothers to see the note," Karlee added. "It would have only made things worse."

"Yes." Glenda lost the fight with the tears and she wiped away one that slid down her cheek. "Well, unless he wrote a different note. The one he read to me said that he—" she stopped, cleared her throat "—would always love me. That he couldn't go on any longer without me."

Her father's note had indeed said that. The ramblings of a drunk man who obviously thought there was no other way to do this.

"He was right," her dad had written. "I'll always love Glenda. She'll never be mine again, and I can't go on living without her."

No mention of his kids and his love for them. Nothing that would tell them that they mattered to either of their parents. Because both had left of their own free will. The only thing that was unclear was the "he" in the "he was right," but even that hadn't mattered in the end. As drunk as her father was, the "he" could have been some voice from God.

"FYI, there was no insurance money," Karlee explained. "If there had been, I would have had to produce the note or at least explain why I couldn't collect on it since most policies don't pay out for suicide."

It still wasn't easy for her to say it. *Suicide.* Hearing it only made everything seem more real. It felt as if she were reliving those horrible moments. Of course, the days that followed were no picnic.

"Insurance money would have made things easier though," Karlee added under her breath. The next part she didn't even try to muffle. She wanted her mother to hear it. "If it hadn't been for Dad's aunt sending us some cash, we wouldn't have made it."

Glenda stayed quiet a moment. "The money came from me. I knew you wouldn't take it if you'd known who it was actually from, so I had your great-aunt Bessie send it."

Karlee figured that was probably meant to soften her feelings for Glenda, but it only caused another ripple of anger. "You're right. I wouldn't have taken it." And she couldn't stop the anger from going past the ripple stage. "Did you know that Mack, Joe and Judd ended up in foster care until I could get them out?"

Glenda didn't answer. Not with words, but judging from the volume of tears that began to spill, she had known. "I went to the foster-care home, but Joe said they wouldn't leave with me."

That was something Joe had kept from Karlee, but it didn't surprise her. Even though Karlee was the oldest, Joe had always tried to be the big brother. He'd tried to shoulder some of the responsibility for himself to take pressure off her. Pressure that wouldn't have been there had it not been for Glenda's leaving.

Karlee stood. "I'm pretty sure your two minutes are up."

Glenda didn't argue. She stood, her gaze finally meeting Karlee's. "I know I can't make up for what I did. I know I can't fix things. But I can help with Jerry if you want."

She stared at her mother a moment. "Help how?"

"I have lots of resources and connections to people in the cattle business. I don't want to go behind your back, or Lucian's, but if you want me to help you oust Jerry, just let me know." She took a business card from her purse and handed it to Karlee.

This time Karlee took it. Not for herself but for Lucian. She wasn't sure if Glenda could indeed help him, but she wasn't about to close a door that wasn't hers to close. But when Karlee took the card, it did remind her of the conversation that'd gone on at the dinner table.

"Did you tell Regina about your *resources and connections*? Was that what you two were talking about outside the police station?"

"Yes," Glenda readily admitted. "I believe Regina is still thinking over my proposition."

Karlee could definitely understand Regina's need to mull that over. After all, Glenda had destroyed her marriage, so it would be hard for Lucian's mom to trust this woman. Heck, Glenda might not even be able to do whatever it was she wanted to make them believe she could do. This could all be a ruse to regain Karlee's trust.

But it didn't feel like that.

Glenda went to the door and opened it. "What will happen between Lucian and you now that Amelia is back?" she asked. Her gaze drifted down to the engagement ring that Karlee was still wearing.

Glenda waved that off though. Maybe because it wasn't necessary for Karlee to voice aloud what they both already knew. For years Karlee had watched Amelia breeze back into town, and only one thing happened when she returned.

They got back together.

Even though it never lasted, it never ended, either. And that's why Karlee had to be the one to do something different. She had two clear choices here. She could take off the ring, pack her bags and leave.

Or she could go out there and fight for the only man she'd ever wanted.

"Lucian, did you hear me?" Amelia asked. "I said that I thought this so-called engagement with Karlee wasn't real."

He'd heard her just fine, but he didn't answer because he was watching as Karlee walked away. He needed to go to her and talk things out, but the talking out needed to begin with Amelia. And for it to start, he had to figure out what to say.

"Should I just leave?" Amelia pressed, drawing his attention back to her. Not that it had strayed too far from her. Hard to keep his attention off the very woman who had been pulling his heartstrings for years.

And maybe she was still pulling at them.

Lucian wasn't sure any longer what kind of hold she had on him—which made this crazier than it already was. Amelia had always been in his life.

The woman he'd trusted with that "I need you."

Now, though, he was wondering about that need. It existed, had been as real as the heat in a Texas summer. That's because Amelia had always been the perfect woman for him. No strings. No pressure to ease back on his seventy-hour workweek and spend more time with her. He was certain that he would never see the hurt in Amelia's eyes that had just been in Karlee's.

And he was responsible for it.

No, he hadn't asked Amelia to come. But she was here, and seeing her had no doubt made Karlee remember why they'd never flirted, kissed or come close to having sex before.

"Are you going to say anything?" Amelia begged.

Lucian answered Amelia's question with one of his own. "Why did you come?"

It got the exact reaction he expected. Clearly surprised, Amelia pulled back her shoulders. "Wow," she muttered. "I didn't expect that."

Probably because it was a first. Every single time she'd come back into his life, no matter how inconvenient, he'd dropped everything—including the women he'd been seeing at the time—to be with her. He was her "I need you" man.

But not this time.

"Karlee and I aren't together," he explained, "but she has feelings for me."

Her shoulders relaxed a little. "Of course she has feelings for you. She always has." Amelia stopped, studied his expression. "Oh."

That "oh" was a mouthful. Because Amelia got it. Karlee's caring wasn't one-sided. Heck, he cared for Amelia, too, but Amelia wasn't the one who was going to get burned in this.

She muttered another "oh," managed a smile and looked as if she was about to turn and leave, but the sound of an approaching car stopped her. It gave Lucian somewhat of a stop, too, because it was Glenda.

The woman headed in the direction of the guesthouse. Obviously, Glenda had something she needed to say to her daughter, but Lucian didn't want her upsetting Karlee any more than she already was.

"When did Glenda O'Malley come back?" Amelia asked.

"Long story." It wasn't, not really, but he didn't want to discuss Glenda or play catch-up with Amelia. He wanted to end this conversation and check on Karlee.

"I'm sorry you came all this way," Lucian started.

He didn't get very far, though, because Amelia leaned in and brushed a quick kiss on his mouth. "I got it. I can figure out what's going on here. No worries, really," she added when she studied his expression. An expression that likely had some surprise that she was taking this so well.

"I'm not sure what's going on between Karlee and me," he admitted. It was the truth.

Amelia nodded, smiled. "Then why don't I give you some space so you can figure that out?"

In that moment he remembered another layer of why he'd told her that he needed her. She really held up to that "no pressure." She didn't make him feel like shit when he bulldozed over someone else's feelings. She didn't hold him accountable for anything. That was both good and bad. Good, because he hadn't wanted pressure from her. Bad, because it meant this shallow level of need was as far as things would ever go between them.

"Next time, I'll call," she added, still smiling. Amelia touched her hand to his cheek and kept it there a moment. "Though I got to tell you, I was looking forward to the sex. Lucian, you're my sex benchmark. If you change your mind and want to see me, I'll be at the inn for the rest of the day." Amelia smiled, headed to her rental car. "Merry Christmas," she added, and waved as she got inside.

Now he felt like shit. Not because he'd hurt Amelia. He hadn't. But because she had been so much a part of his adult life, and he'd just sent her packing with only five minutes or so of conversation. That felt wrong, but then, it felt even more wrong to have Karlee thinking that he…

Well, he didn't know what Karlee would be thinking, but he doubted it was good. She was likely in the mindset that he'd slipped right back into his old ways. Which meant stepping back into Amelia's arms. Until this moment he'd been so sure that if he ever settled down, then Amelia would be the one for him. And now that certainty had turned as sour as the dinner he'd just had.

Lucian risked going back through the house, hoping he didn't run into anyone. He heard his mom in the dining room still chatting with their dinner guests that she'd obviously convinced to stay awhile longer. Good. Maybe she could salvage some part of Christmas now that Jerry and she weren't exchanging barbs and eyeball daggers over the coffee stuffing.

When he made it to the sunroom, he saw Abe, sitting in front of a tray table. No turkey for him. He had a cheeseburger on his plate, but he wasn't eating. Instead, he had his attention on the guesthouse.

"Glenda's in there," Abe said. He reached down, picked up a brown paper bag from the floor next to his chair, and he handed it to Lucian.

Lucian sent the man an unspoken thanks. "Don't tell me, though, to kick Glenda's balls into her eye sockets."

"No." Abe sounded disappointed that Lucian wouldn't

be able to do that. "But do right by Karlee. It's okay to
fuck her, but don't fuck with her."

Despite the stampede of emotions going through him
and the urgency to check on Karlee, Lucian lifted his
eyebrow. "The others have said they'd kick my ass if
I hurt her."

Abe gave a rare chuckle that was barely audible, and
he signaled an end to the conversation by taking a King
Kong–size bite off the burger.

Lucian stuffed the bag into his pocket and went out
onto the back porch. The moment he was in the backyard, he immediately saw Glenda coming out of the
guesthouse, and Lucian cursed. Because she was crying. She quickly wiped away the tears, but he knew that
if Glenda was this upset, then so was Karlee.

"What'd you say to her?" Lucian snapped.

Glenda opened her mouth as if she might answer,
but then shook her head. "If Karlee wants you to know,
then she'll be the one to tell you."

That made him feel about as comfortable as a pop-
corn kernel in a fire. Because it meant there was something to tell. Something that extended beyond the usual
crap that involved Karlee's mother.

"If you hurt her—" Lucian warned Glenda. He didn't
get to finish since Glenda interrupted him.

"I've hurt her for years. You and your family, too. I
can't fix that, and I'm sorry." She stared at him. "But
you can hurt her, as well."

Hell, he hoped this wasn't going to turn into a Karlee lighting up around him discussion.

Glenda stepped around him to leave, but then she
stopped and looked back at him. "You do know that

you don't actually love Amelia, right? That you're with her because she's safe?"

Since he'd only come to that realization minutes earlier, Lucian didn't want to give Glenda the satisfaction of him telling her she was right. Even agreeing with the woman felt like some kind of camaraderie that he didn't want to have with her. Not after what she'd done to Karlee and her sons.

"If you're planning on being with Amelia," Glenda went on, "let Karlee down gently. She's a little fragile right now."

Lucian cursed and got to walking. *Fragile* even coupled with the word *little* wasn't good. He didn't know what the heck Glenda had told her, but paired with Amelia's arrival, Karlee might be inside falling apart.

Thankfully, when he got to the door of the guesthouse, he found it unlocked. Lucian had considered that she might do anything to give herself some time alone, and a locked door would have done it. For a short while, anyway. But he wouldn't have let too much time go by before he would have used his key to check on her.

He eased open the door, glanced around. No Karlee. However, he did see something that told him how this visit was likely about to go.

Her "engagement" ring was on the kitchen counter next to a small wrapped Christmas present with his name on it. Since she'd worn the ring the entire time since he'd given it to her, it was a clear signal to him that the pretense was over.

He heard her moving around in her bedroom, so that's where Lucian headed next. Not that he needed it, but he saw yet more proof of the finished pretense. Karlee was packing. Or rather, she'd just finished packing because she was zipping up her suitcase.

She looked up at him, their gazes connecting. Her eyes were red as if she'd been crying, but there were no fresh tears, thank God. Lucian wasn't sure he could have handled that right now.

Karlee hoisted her suitcase off the bed and onto the floor before he could get to her to help. "I had two choices," she said. "To pack and leave or do this. I decided to do both."

Lucian was plenty confused about the *do this*. Until she slid her hand around the back of his neck and kissed him. It wasn't one of those little bitty pecks, either. This was the real deal. Hot, deep and French. Just the way he liked his kisses.

Well, he would have liked it if it hadn't been damn confusing.

Her choice had been to leave or kiss him. He was pretty sure that's what she'd said, though his thoughts were getting muddled in his head because of what was going on with the other parts of their bodies.

Specifically, Karlee's breasts.

They were mashed against his chest, the fit so good that he could feel her nipples. He'd never been sure why nipples had always done it for him, but they did, and Karlee's did it to him in the worst kind of way.

Hooking his arm around her waist, he tried to yank her even closer despite it not really being possible. They were already body to body, her leg between his, and the only way he was going to get more contact was to be inside her. Something his muddled head was already considering—though it was getting egged on by his quickly hardening erection.

Karlee didn't let his hard-on get to the full-blown stage though. With every inch of him begging for every inch of her, she moved back, taking her inches with her. In the same motion, she pulled up the handle on her suitcase and got moving.

Toward the door.

"Work out your feelings for Amelia," she said, throwing him a glance from over her shoulder.

"Amelia's leaving." He hurried to try to get ahead of her, but it wasn't easy to do much darting with a hard-on.

"But she'll be back. She always comes back."

No way could he argue since there had indeed been a lot of coming, and going, when it came to Amelia.

"Work out your feelings for her," Karlee repeated. "After that, if you still want to kiss me, then you know where to find me."

The moment she finished saying that, Karlee walked out.

CHAPTER THIRTEEN

KARLEE WALKED INTO her apartment, and what she saw waiting for her nearly had her turning around and leaving. That's because her brothers Judd and Joe were there. Oh, and Mack was, too. She'd missed him at first because he was in the kitchen, drinking a beer.

In addition to the three immediate members of her gene pool, there was someone in the bathroom because she heard the toilet flush. Maybe Mack's current girlfriend since neither Judd nor Joe would have other witnesses to this, well, whatever this was.

An intervention, maybe?

Or perhaps the start of what would turn into an attempted ass-kicking for Lucian dallying around with their sister's feelings? She seriously doubted they were here to share tidings of comfort and joy.

All of her brothers had keys to her place. Something she'd given them years ago when she'd first leased it. But to the best of her knowledge, this was the first time anyone other than Mack had actually let themselves in.

"Who called you and what did they tell you?" she immediately asked. Huffing, she set her suitcase on the floor and shut the door. Hopefully, she'd be opening it right back up again when she convinced her sibling posse that she was okay.

Of course, first she had to convince herself of that,

but she'd gotten a head start on it since she'd been driving around for the past couple of hours.

"Regina called," Joe told her. He stood, towering over her. With those wide shoulders, he could have blocked out a sun or two, and he gave her a look that had no trace of sympathy. That's because he'd never approved of her feelings for Lucian. "Regina said you stormed off from the ranch when first Amelia and then Glenda showed up."

Karlee lifted her shoulder. "No storming. I merely left."

After she'd kissed Lucian, that was. And delivered her ultimatum about no more kissing until he'd sorted out his feelings for Amelia. Regina hadn't seen the kissing, but she'd obviously seen the leaving and interpreted it as Karlee departing because she was crushed.

Judd stood, too, blocking out any other remaining solar objects, and he gave her that same unsympathetic look as Joe had. His had a smidge more ass-kicking, though, than Joe's. "You didn't answer your phone."

That was brother code for *we were worried about you, but instead of hugging you right now and asking if you're okay, we're going to pester you with an annoying conversation that you don't want to have. In addition, we're going to cast off dangerous vibes that will be aimed at kicking Lucian's ass since that's our preferred method of conflict resolution when it comes to our sister.*

She huffed again. "I turned off my phone because I wanted some quiet time to think."

"You could have turned it off after you called one of us," Judd grumbled. His hands went on his hips. "What the fuck did Glenda want?"

Karlee didn't know where to start. Nor did she even want to tell them. She got a reprieve—one that would no doubt be short—because Mack came out of the kitchen, and with the beer still in his hand, he hooked his arm around her neck and brushed a kiss on her cheek.

"Did Lucian knock you up?" he whispered.

Karlee sure didn't whisper. "No! Where did you hear that?"

He tipped his head to the bathroom just as the door opened, and she saw her fourth visitor. Amelia.

"She told you that Lucian got me pregnant?" This time, Karlee lowered her voice. Not a whisper exactly. More like a really throaty, angry growl.

"She thought maybe it was something like that."

In other words, Amelia needed justification as to why Lucian hadn't dragged her off to bed when she'd come breezing onto the ranch.

Amelia immediately held up her hands as if under arrest. "Hey, I was just going to leave a note on your door since you weren't answering your phone, but then Mack let me in."

Later, Karlee would ask Mack why he'd done that—especially since it was going to be very difficult to have a discussion about any of their three current Yuletide topics: Lucian, a false knocking up and Glenda.

"I won't stay," Amelia went on. "I just wanted to check and make sure you were all right. You seemed upset when you stormed off the ranch."

Karlee nearly did another autocorrect on the "storming" word choice, but she waved it off. "I'm fine. Lucian didn't send you, did he?"

But Karlee knew the answer to that. Nope. That kind of attempted comfort wasn't in Lucian's wheelhouse of responses. He would have just called Karlee himself. Which he had done, she realized after she glanced at her phone. Sixteen missed calls from her brothers, Glenda, Regina, Jordan, Dylan and Lucian.

"I'm fine," Karlee repeated. "There's no reason to check on me." She aimed that comment solely at Amelia. No way would that get her brothers to budge, but it had a slight "don't let the door kick you in the butt on your way out" tone that might cause Amelia to leave.

Amelia stayed put, though, and she stared at Karlee. "Lucian doesn't want you hurt. Neither do I. So, this is me giving you an official *I'm sorry*. Consider the apology from both of us."

Karlee opened her mouth. Closed it. And tried to figure out what the heck that meant. Was this Amelia's way of telling her that Lucian and she were back together? It was possible. After the high-broil-heat kiss Lucian and she had shared in the guesthouse, he could have waltzed right out and gone back to Amelia. If so, then why wasn't Amelia with him right now?

Maybe Amelia liked a little downtime between orgasms.

Amelia glanced back at Karlee's brothers, then gave Karlee another stare as if she, too, was trying to sort all of this out.

"I'm not pregnant," Karlee assured her.

Amelia didn't seem convinced. Perhaps because she thought the brothers were there to discuss the impending arrival of their niece or nephew.

"All right," Amelia finally said. "I'll just be going, then." She did pick up her purse from the kitchen counter and started toward the door, but she paused again. She also did another quick look at Karlee and muttered something that Karlee didn't catch before she finally left.

One down, three to go. But the three who were left weren't going to be an easy fix.

Karlee went to the cabinet, took out a bottle of Irish whiskey and four shot glasses. While she poured, she motioned for them all to sit. She sank down into the chair across from them, tossed back a shot and opened Pandora's box.

"Dad's death wasn't an accident," Karlee said. "It was suicide, and that's why Glenda came to see me."

She braced herself for the inevitable fallout because Pandora's box could be a bitch to deal with. She waited while they tried to absorb it, and it took her several moments to realize there was no absorbing going on at all. Her brothers were giving her blank stares. The kind of stares that came when someone had just stated the really, really obvious.

"So, Lucian didn't knock you up and dump you for Amelia?" Joe asked.

"No! I've never even had sex with Lucian." She hadn't meant to blurt out that last part, but it earned her approving nods from Joe and Mack. Judd cursed, though, took out his wallet and handed both Joe and Mack some twenties.

"Told you she wasn't stupid enough to bed down with Lucifer," Mack gloated.

Karlee didn't gloat. She glared. "You bet on my sex life? And don't call him Lucifer," she added in warning to Mack.

All three of the O'Malley males shrugged in unison. "It came up in discussion and bets were made," Judd said as if that explained everything. It didn't explain squat. And it sure didn't address why they'd glossed over the supposed bombshell she'd just delivered.

"Did you hear what I said about Dad?" she asked.

Another trio of shrugs. It was Joe, the oldest of the three, who became their self-appointed spokesman because he was the one who continued. "Dad was depressed. He talked about ending things."

He had, when he'd been in a drunken stupor, but Karlee thought he'd only mentioned that around her.

"When he died, we figured out what had happened," Joe added. "Well, all but Mack, but he sussed it all out later when he found the suicide note. Dad killed himself, and you wanted to protect us from that."

When this conversation had started, Karlee hadn't figured she'd be the one who needed multiple shots of whiskey, but she had another one. "How'd you find the note?" she asked Mack.

He grinned that cocky boyish grin that usually got him out of hot water. Karlee glared her mom-sister glare to let him know that grin wasn't going to work.

"I was looking in your jewelry box to see if you had a cheap ring or something I could give to Allie Carver so that she'd be my girlfriend," Mack explained. "Found the note instead and took a picture of it with my phone so I could show it to Joe and Judd."

So they knew that their father's last thoughts hadn't been about them, that they'd been about the wife who'd run off and left him.

"Dad called Glenda that night," Karlee continued after another shot. "She feels guilty because she didn't do anything to try to stop him."

Again, she thought that would be a revelation or at least a mild surprise. It was neither. "Dad called Glenda nearly every night," Joe told her. "Or rather, he tried to call her. She didn't answer very often."

It might be the effect of the three quick shots of Jameson, but that pissed her off. All of this was going on while she was busting her butt to keep the rest of the family together.

"Is there anything else about Dad or that night that I don't know?" she demanded.

That got her three more shrugs. "Do you know about Lucian?" Joe asked.

Karlee was betting she was about to learn even more, and here she thought she was the only one keeping secrets. She just motioned for Joe to continue.

"While you were at your study group at the school library, Lucian called Dad that night," Joe explained. "I believe Lucian's the one who sent Dad over the edge."

Oh. God.

Lucian was the "he" in her father's suicide note. Well, maybe. Karlee hated to leap to that conclusion because she might not ever be able to jump back from it.

"What did Lucian say to him?" Karlee pressed.

But again, she only got the shrugs. "My advice?" Joe looked right into her eyes when he spoke. "If you really want to know, ask Lucian."

And she watched as her brothers took bets as to whether or not that confrontation would actually happen. Two out of three were pretty darn sure she wasn't going to do it.

CHAPTER FOURTEEN

LUCIAN WAS ABSOLUTELY certain this wasn't going to happen, so he slid the so-called invitation right back across his desk toward his new assistant, Sunny Adler, who'd just slid it to him.

Even though Sunny had worked for him now for well over a month, since a few days after Christmas, she still had a lot to learn. Karlee had helped with that by giving Sunny some detailed notes and exchanging emails with her. However, Sunny still had a ways to go. Not just learning about him but also the job at his new cattle broker company. However, Lucian was about to give her one very important lesson.

"No." He stretched that out a few syllables just so she'd get it.

"No?" she questioned, but it was really more of a challenge. She gave her wad of pink gum a crack and stared at him, somehow managing to keep her eyelids open despite the quarter pound of makeup on them. "But the invite says if you don't go to the party, Miss Stapleton won't buy those cows you're trying to sell her."

"Cattle, not cows," he corrected. "And it's Mrs., not Miss."

What the invite didn't say was that this was a party for two—specifically for him and Carrie Stapleton—

where she would be expecting him to pony up with his dick to get the cattle. Even if Carrie had been single, it wouldn't have happened. He didn't mix business with pleasure, which was why he'd kept his hands off of Karlee for over a decade.

"Karlee?" Sunny asked, making him wonder why she'd said it.

Hell, had he mumbled Karlee's name out loud—*again*? He'd been doing that a lot in the six weeks since Christmas when she'd ended their fake engagement and moved back to her apartment. Actually, he'd been doing a lot of thinking about her, too, which was why he'd called her at least a dozen times. She'd answered each of those dozen times, but the conversations had been as shallow as a stream during a drought. Ironic, since they seemed to discuss the weather a lot these days.

When the topic of discussion wasn't weather, Karlee's fallback was the charity rodeo, specifically how the training was going. Lucian's answers had been fairly short in that department, mainly because he was getting his butt busted whenever he climbed into the saddle. Most riders actually improved their time with training, but Lucian was definitely going in a different direction.

Sunny slid another paper on his desk. Not a booty call this time but a copy of a proposal for some cattle Karlee was apparently trying to buy. "You said you wanted any updates on this," Sunny reminded him.

He did. Because it was the same cattle that Lucian was about to bid on. And his bid was going to be bigger.

Lucian mentally repeated that part about not mixing business with pleasure and made the keystrokes on his computer to delete his bid. Karlee could have the cattle, and maybe the next time he called her there'd be a little more depth in that proverbial stream.

God, he missed her.

Not just her easy way of running things and keeping his life in order. He missed *her*. Her smile. That sweet drawl in her voice. And yes, he missed her nipples. That last one probably put him in the horndog category, but that particular part of her had made an impression on him when she'd been kissing his lights out. Then, just like that, they'd gone from nipples to cool conversations that only made him ache for her even more.

"Amelia," Sunny said, drawing his attention back to her. That gum got another crack when she handed him the message. "She phoned when you were in that meeting and asked you to call her. She just wants to chat."

No, it was going to turn into a conversation about going back to their old ways. Specifically, no-commitment sex. In the past month, Amelia had let him know through repeated phone calls that she was his for life. Well, if all he wanted was sex without the hassles. While that sounded good on the surface, he was beginning to think that some hassles might be worth it.

Lucian glanced up to make sure a lightning bolt wasn't about to hit him. Never had he had a thought like that, and it was best to keep that notion in his head—until he figured out what to do about it, anyway.

"And finally Lois Fay Merkle from the Wrangler's Creek Historical Society called." Sunny slid him another message. "She asked if you'd reconsidered giving them the rodeo belt."

"Buckle," he automatically corrected. The answer to this was easy, too. "No."

It was stupid for him to dig in his heels like this.

After all, he was in a legal stalemate with his father, one that would end if the historical society threw their 1 percent support his way. Still, this felt like that dick-invite from Mrs. Stapleton. If he let the historical society screw him, then he'd win. But it wouldn't feel much like a win to him.

"That's the buckle they want, isn't it?" Sunny asked, tipping her head to the case on his desk. It was right next to his copper-etched nameplate.

"It is." And thanks to Karlee's Christmas gift to him, it was now in a nice display box, one that he could easily pack for his overnight trips. The case would stop it from getting scratched. Leave it to Karlee to think of something like that, and it sure beat the business-card holder that he'd gotten for her. Still, he hoped that she saw his gift as an endorsement for her new company.

Sunny was only holding one more piece of paper, and she put it on his desk. "That's your itinerary for the week." She eyed him over the top of her red sparkle glasses. "Karlee said it wouldn't do any good to remind you that you should wear a suit for the dinner party you've got on Saturday."

"No, it won't do any good."

But it made him wonder just how much contact Karlee had had with Sunny. Probably a lot since Karlee had offered to help Sunny during this transition. Lucian was betting their conversation hadn't been as shallow as the ones Karlee had had with him.

When Sunny finally left, Lucian got up, walked to the window and stared out at the San Antonio skyline. To go with his fresh start, he'd left his office at Granger Enterprises and moved downtown. He had the right office, a prime corner one, and it was in the right building. It was expensive enough to go with the image he wanted for his new company, Lucian Granger Cattle. And he'd structured the business so that it wasn't something his father or anyone else in his family could ever touch. It was his and only his.

Something that should have sent him back to his desk to work instead of staring out a window. But instead of feeling excited about possible new deals, he felt as if he'd burned too many candles at both ends.

Shit.

Enough of this.

"Send Karlee flowers to congratulate her for the cattle deal," Lucian instructed Sunny.

"Is that deal final?" she asked.

"It will be after I send out a few texts."

"Oh, okay. And should I use the florist Karlee mentioned in the notes she gave me?"

Lucian nodded, though he didn't care where the flowers came from. "Reschedule my appointments for the day," he called out to her as he grabbed his Stetson.

Sunny immediately scurried into his office, and he saw her confused expression. That's because he wasn't an appointment-rescheduling kind of boss. But he was today. "Uh, is there some kind of emergency?"

Lucian didn't answer, but yeah, there was an emergency. A big-assed personal one. He needed to fix this shallow shit between Karlee and him, and he thought he knew the fastest way to do that.

He grabbed some condoms from his desk drawer and shoved them into his pocket.

KARLEE HAD ALWAYS thought herself good at multitasking, but clearly that didn't apply to getting ready for a date while making notes for the counterbid she would almost certainly have to make. She had presented a decent first bid. However, there would no doubt be a lot of competition.

Likely from Lucian.

She tried not to think about that though. Actually, she tried not to think about Lucian himself, but she was failing at that. Not just now, either. She'd been failing at it for the past month. Karlee could blame Joe's revelation for that. Lucian had called her father on the night he'd died, had perhaps even unknowingly given the suicide a nudge, and Karlee didn't know how to deal with that.

Or rather, she didn't know how to deal with it *well*.

And that's why she'd limited the contact she'd had with Lucian. A conversation about that night couldn't result in anything good. If something that Lucian had said had indeed triggered the suicide, he'd never forgive himself once he learned it hadn't been an accidental death. And while Karlee would be able to get past it, eventually, it wouldn't be easy.

Of course, none of what she was doing was easy. With so much of her money tied up in her cattle investments and with no cash coming in yet, she could barely afford the rent on her apartment and her office—such that it was. It was in such a sketchy section of town that she'd been meeting clients at restaurants. Or else out at the Granger Ranch, where Roman was still leasing her some land.

She finished smoothing on the lipstick that she immediately decided was too red. She wiped it off, discarding the tissue in the trash can next to her desk. The Kleenex landed on top of the other two colors she'd tried and dismissed. Now her lips were slightly swollen from all the rubbing, making it look as if she'd just been kissed. A lot. That wasn't a good image to have for a first date.

Digging through her makeup bag, she located some simply tinted lip gloss and went with that. She also managed to get on her shoes, which she second-guessed, as well. They were red heels, footwear more suited for Amelia or Candy, but when Karlee had bought them, she'd wanted something different in the hopes that it would rub off on her attitude.

So far, it hadn't.

Even the date itself fell into the same general category of wanting something different. It'd been nearly a year since she'd had a date, and while she wasn't exactly tingly with anticipation about seeing Simon Metcalf, the rancher Jordan had set her up with, she was going through with the dinner and movie. Going through with rebuilding her life, too. She'd spent too much time lusting over Lucian, and she was ready to test out lust on other guys.

When Karlee heard the knock at her office door, she silently cursed. Simon was early. And she'd asked him to meet her in the lobby rather than her office. That was in part because she hadn't wanted him to see that her office consisted of a desk, chair and trash can. She had her eye on a filing cabinet that she'd be buying once she sold off the first herd she'd bought.

She grabbed her purse to cut down on the time they'd actually be in the office, threw open the door, and this time her cursing wasn't silent.

"Shit," she spit out, and her hand went over her heart to steady it. That's because it wasn't Simon but rather Lucian.

"I don't want to discuss the weather with you," Lucian growled. That sounded like some kind of complaint or declaration of war. The tone coordinated with the tight muscles in his face. "And I can't stop thinking about your nipples."

All right. Karlee certainly hadn't seen that coming, and she automatically checked the front of her top to make sure those particular parts of her weren't visible against the fabric. They weren't.

Now Lucian cursed, shook his head as if disgusted with himself for saying that. Karlee wasn't disgusted, but she was confused. She was about to tell him that they could talk—not about the weather, either—when she was back from her dinner date, but Lucian didn't give her a chance to say anything.

He snapped her to him and kissed her.

And it wasn't an ordinary kiss. Nothing weather-ish about this. It was all animal attraction, lust and his incredible body landing against hers. Lucian might have had nipples on his mind, but her thoughts had gone in a slightly lower direction. Specifically, a couple of inches below his belt.

The heat, his body and his below-the-belt inches swept her right away, but Karlee held on to her common sense long enough to wonder if she should bring up the call he'd made to her father. Common sense, though, didn't last long. It was no match for Lucian's inches and touches.

Yes, he touched.

Specifically, his hand slid from the back of her neck all the way down her body until he reached her butt. Then the cupping started. The moving, too, because he backed her into the room, and without even pausing the kiss, he kicked the door shut and locked it.

So, apparently he wanted some privacy.

Considering that he already had an erection, Karlee didn't think it was much of a stretch for her to believe that he was here for sex. She wanted to feel a little conflicted about that. Or at least slightly hesitant. But there wasn't a shred of anything she could remotely consider as hesitation. She was just as ready for this as Lucian and his mouth apparently were.

Lucian took those scorcher kisses to her neck, a move she greatly appreciated. It was a hot spot for her, and Lucian must have quickly figured that out from the whimpering moans she was making because he kept it up, using his tongue to get his point across. His point being that he was going to make this an orgasm to remember.

And speaking of orgasms, Karlee nearly had one when Lucian slid up her top. In the same motion, he pushed down the cups of her bra, and he showed her what he could do with tongue kisses.

Yes, he really did like nipples, and when he was done kissing her there, Karlee had to admit she had a thing for them, too. Well, she did when Lucian was doing the kissing.

He went lower with the kisses, to her belly, which he made bare by pushing her skirt down to her hips. But then he stopped and looked up at her as if waiting for something.

"We aren't going to discuss the weather, are we?" she asked.

"Hell, I hope not. But I should give you a chance to stop or at least catch your breath."

She wasn't even sure if she had breath any longer,

much less if it needed catching, but she had to know. "What brought this on?"

He kissed his way back up her body so they were face-to-face, and she waited for what might be some deep response to her "what brought this on?"

"You" was all he said.

Not a bad answer. Nope. And she didn't think it was a dose of Texas malarkey, either, since that wasn't the way Lucian did things. Of course, she'd never gotten this far with him to know if malarkey or sweet nothings came into play when his erection was calling the shots.

"Good," she managed to say, and this time she was the one who did the pulling and kissing. She dragged Lucian back to her. Not that it took a whole lot of effort. He came back to her with the same heat and enthusiasm as he had when this had first started.

That seemed to be the only green light that Lucian needed. He maneuvered her to her desk and pushed aside the papers and such that were there. Business cards and ink pens pinged to the floor, and that's when she realized sex was going to happen right here. Definitely not the moonlight-and-roses fantasy she'd always had, but then, just getting to this point was fantasy enough.

The moment her back was on the desk, Lucian pushed up her skirt and rid her of her panties. The kisses and touches stopped for just a few moments while he fumbled in his pocket. For a condom, she realized. In fact, multiple condoms since she saw several of the foil-wrapped ones fall to the floor amid the office supplies.

Apparently, he'd been thinking about her nipples *a lot*.

Karlee would have smiled about that if Lucian hadn't

finished with the condom and moved back to her. Not on top of her exactly but close enough that his chest brushed against her breasts. It took a moment for her to realize why the sensation of that caused her to make more of the moaning sounds of pleasure. That's because her top was still up, her bra still down, and her breasts were touching his shirt. She quickly did something to make that sensation even better. She unbuttoned him so that bare skin was against bare skin.

Now, this was part of the fantasy.

So was the look he gave her. It was a cowboy warrior look as if he'd just conquered herds of wild cattle and won a range war or two. The air was heavy with testosterone. Probably heavy as well with all the heat generated in her body. A heat that would make this all end too soon for her. Of course, holding off didn't stand a chance against a fantasy.

She was having sex with Lucian Granger.

Finally!

And those deep, hard thrusts inside her were swirling her around and around until Karlee only had one place to go. The place where pleasure moans peaked and turned to whatever sound was now coming from her throat. She was lost, willingly lost, and she kept on losing, losing, losing until she got the best part of the fantasy.

The orgasm that Lucian gave her.

CHAPTER FIFTEEN

LUCIAN WAS ABSOLUTELY certain that sex on a desk with Karlee didn't qualify as shallow. However, it was about to become one of his biggest regrets. At least it would when the pleasure from the climax quit slamming through him.

Karlee was clearly experiencing some of those pleasure slams, too, because her eyes were glazed, and she had a dreamy but surprised look on her face.

"Did the earth just move?" she asked, and she sounded serious.

Lucian glanced down to find the cause. "No. The stack of folders shifted under your butt."

She actually seemed a little relieved about that. Maybe that meant she was putting this all into perspective. Exactly what that perspective might be, he didn't know yet, but when she'd wrapped her head around it, maybe she'd clue him in. For now, Lucian settled for getting off her so he could go into the small bathroom. He didn't look for anything to use to hit himself on the head, though he probably should have.

Not hurting Karlee had been a high priority of his. Not just because of his relationship with Amelia but because of that whole fact about him sucking at relationships. She needed someone a lot better than him.

Lucian frowned.

Too bad he hadn't had this pep talk with himself before he'd gotten her on that desk. Now she was probably out there either a) planning their future together or b) upset because she knew there was no future. Either way, he'd screwed her over while actually screwing her.

Lucian cleaned up, splashing some water on his face and trying to steel himself up for whatever he'd find when he went back into the office. But he hadn't expected to see what he was seeing.

Karlee wasn't alone.

There was a tall, dark-haired guy with her, and he was hugging her. Both of them were smiling as if there was something to smile and hug about.

"Oh," Karlee said when she saw Lucian. It was as if she'd forgotten he was there. Well, that sure as hell didn't do anything for his ego. "Lucian, this is Simon Metcalf. Simon, this is Lucian Granger."

An awkward silence followed, and it got even more awkward when Simon thrust out his hand for Lucian to shake. "It's good to meet you. I'm Karlee's date."

"I forgot to mention Simon when you came in," Karlee mumbled.

Yeah, she had, but then, Lucian hadn't given her much of a chance to say anything. He'd swooped right in and started kissing her. It would have been hard for her to talk with his tongue in her mouth.

"I understand Karlee used to work for you," Simon went on. The man obviously didn't know that Karlee and he had also just had sex.

Lucian settled for a nod and then turned to Karlee for some kind of explanation. Was she literally about to go on a date only minutes after having sex with him?

If so, then it was obvious she wasn't as upset about this as he'd thought she would be.

"I was just telling Simon that I need a rain check on our date." She fluttered her fingers toward her desk, which was in surprisingly good order. Lucian hadn't been in the bathroom that long, so Karlee must have scrambled to get everything back in place—including shoving her breasts back in her bra and putting on her panties. "I need to finalize the paperwork for that cattle deal."

At first Lucian thought that was a BS excuse, but he could see some giddiness between the awkwardness.

"The seller accepted my bid," she said. Definitely giddy, though he hoped some of that was from the orgasm. "I was certain you would outbid me—" She stopped, and just like that, any and all traces of celebration vanished.

Karlee managed a thin smile when she turned back to Simon. "As I was saying, I hate to ask you to postpone, but I really need to get the contract printed out and signed so I can arrange for a delivery date of the cattle."

"No problem. I deal in livestock myself, so I know these things happen." The guy leaned in to kiss Karlee, but she moved at the last second, and Simon's mouth swiped across her cheek.

Simon definitely didn't seem pleased about that, but he headed for the door. He stopped, though, as he reached for the knob and looked back at Lucian. "I guess you're here to help walk Karlee through that contract?"

Lucian hadn't meant to hesitate, but he wanted to make sure whatever he said meshed with what Karlee had told this guy. So Lucian just went with another nod. Thankfully, it was enough to send Simon on his way.

However, when Karlee snapped toward him, Lucian knew this wasn't going to be some postsex cuddling.

"Did you rig things so I'd get the cattle deal?" she asked. Her body language confirmed her snappish tone. She had her arms folded over her chest, and her eyes were narrowed.

Lucian knew there was only one way to go with this. The truth. "Yes. But before you get mad—" Which, of course, was a moot point because she was already mad. "Withholding a bid is something I do every now and then for a friend."

That was a half lie. He'd never done it before today, but the reasoning still stood. There were people—i.e., Karlee—whom he would do it for.

"Friends?" she questioned.

But before Lucian could think of a way to explain himself on that, the breath rushed out of Karlee's mouth. He was pretty sure it was a breath of relief, too.

"I'm so glad you feel that way." She stopped and shook her head. "I don't mean about the deal. I don't want you doing me favors like that. But I'm glad we're still friends. I was afraid that the sex had messed that up. I don't want anything to ruin our friendship."

Wait… What? Friendship?

Since when had Karlee and he been friends? They'd worked together and then pretended to be engaged. They'd kissed. Hell, they'd had *damn good* sex. All of that started to churn inside Lucian until he realized this was, well, the way it should be. Karlee wasn't hurt. In fact, she didn't seem on the verge of anything related to hurt.

She chuckled, brushed a very chaste kiss on his cheek. "You should see your face. I'm betting you thought you'd crushed me, but it's all fine, I swear. Sex with you was very high on my bucket list."

So he was a number on her bucket list. It made him sound like a destination or a rodeo buckle. "Glad I could help," he grumbled.

He was well aware that he sounded a little sour. And he shouldn't have been. This was exactly the kind of relationship he'd had with Amelia. No hurt, no strings. Hell, there'd even been some postsex cheek kisses. He didn't want another relationship like that. Heck, he didn't want another relationship, period, but this was better than the alternative of Karlee being hurt.

Lucian repeated that to himself.

Karlee took a step toward her desk but then stopped again. Maybe because she was trying to figure out how to tell him to get out of there so she could get to work on that contract. Lucian made it easy for her. He gave her a cheek kiss, too.

"Call me when you have time to celebrate the deal," he said, and he headed out the door.

With each step away from her office, the knot in his stomach tightened, and Lucian was certain that he couldn't feel any worse than he already did.

But he was wrong.

His phone dinged with a text message from Dylan.

You'll want to come home now. We've got an interesting problem.

KARLEE DIDN'T RELEASE the breath she'd been holding until Lucian was out of her office. Only then did she allow the emotions to sweep over her. The trouble was she didn't know which of the feelings to latch on to so she could deal with it.

Sex won the latching battle.

Okay. So it'd finally happened. She'd had sex with Lucian, and it didn't matter that it'd happened on top of a potential client file folder. It was still amazing, exactly as she'd known it would be. Of course, the amazingness was a given because Lucian was her dream sex partner.

It didn't take long, though, for her to remember the look on Lucian's face. Regret. Maybe because he thought he was going to hurt her, but it was just as possible he was worried about tangling himself up in a relationship with her. On Christmas Day she'd told him not to kiss her again until he'd dealt with his feelings for Amelia. But it was entirely possible that Amelia was someone who was always going to be there, which meant there'd be no room for anyone else for long.

That thought brought on the next emotion in the queue of what she was apparently going to experience today.

The tight ache in her chest.

Before she'd actually had sex with Lucian, the possibility of being with him had been on the horizon. Something to fantasize about. But now that the particular horizon was right there in her face, maybe there'd be the one and only time for desk sex. Or any other sex, for that matter.

Karlee immediately shook her head. Lucian wasn't a one-night-stand kind of guy. So, there'd be other times. Well, maybe. But even if there wasn't, Karlee refused to regret what'd just happened. Or rather, she tried not to have any regrets. Tried, too, not to think of possible outcomes. She just needed to take this one day at a time.

Thankfully, she had work to do, and that helped with the next wave of emotions. She had something to celebrate. Except her victory did have a massive asterisk next to it. That's because this was more Lucian's win than hers. She'd need to do something in the future to stop that from happening again. She wanted to succeed, but she wanted to do it on her own.

Now that she'd canceled her date, there was no reason for her not to work late into the night. Once she was done with the contract, she could make that call to Roman to let him know about the new shipment of cattle. Then she could...

Cry.

That hadn't been on her agenda, but it was definitely tears that sprang into her eyes. Tears that she cursed and quickly wiped away. The interruption helped with that because there was a knock at the door.

"Lucian," she said on a rise of breath.

Karlee hurried but tried to make it look as if she weren't hurrying when she threw open the door. Definitely not Lucian, unless he'd managed to sprout a bouquet of yellow roses on his head.

"Delivery for Ms. Karlee O'Malley." The young woman behind the flowers thrust them at Karlee. "The tip's already covered," she added before she walked away.

It wasn't her birthday, but Valentine's Day was coming up, so maybe... But she stopped when she pulled the card from the tiny envelope and saw the one word written there.

Lucian.

Just Lucian.

And Karlee got the sickening feeling that she'd just been dumped.

THE MOMENT LUCIAN walked into the house at the ranch, he knew why Dylan had qualified their problem as "interesting." He'd expected to see Jerry and maybe Regina embroiled in some kind of domestic dispute in the making. Maybe even a new argument about masking-tape boundaries.

But what he saw were bare walls.

The oil paintings that'd once hung in the foyer were no longer there. Ditto for the vase that normally sat on the table near the door. Heck, even the table was gone.

"Were we robbed?" Lucian immediately asked when Dylan came out of the adjacent living room.

"Jerry," Dylan corrected. He motioned for Lucian to follow him. "While everyone was out of the house, Dad took everything of value in his taped-off areas, and we believe he's trying to sell it."

Lucian cursed. He didn't have any sentimental attachment to the paintings and such, but it showed just how low, and desperate, Jerry was.

"Please tell me he didn't sell any family heirlooms," Lucian grumbled.

Dylan shrugged. "Mom's trying to figure that out now. Oh, and she changed the locks, so you'll need to get a new key. And don't ask if it's legal for her to do that because she's not exactly in a rational mood."

Neither was Lucian. He'd managed to stop Jerry from selling off any of the company assets, but the house and its contents didn't fall under Granger Enterprises. Plus, if Jerry would stoop this low, he might try to figure out a way to get around the freeze on the business accounts.

"Did you call me so I could try to track down Dad?" Lucian pressed. Because if so, he was wondering why Dylan wasn't doing that himself.

"The missing stuff isn't the interesting part." He glanced over his shoulder at him as he led Lucian into Dylan's office.

Where Candy and Glenda appeared to be waiting for him. Both of Jerry's ex-lovers got to their feet, but it was Candy who spoke.

"Glenda and I are here to stop Jerry," the woman insisted.

Lucian looked at his brother to see if Dylan was going to offer up an explanation for what appeared to be an unholy alliance. Except maybe it made sense. Both women were probably pissed off at Jerry for their soured relationship, but it was, well, *interesting* that they'd seemingly teamed up.

"Candy brought pictures," Dylan said to him like a warning.

Lucian hoped they were photos related to her being the Hoo-Poo heiress, but he soon realized this was a different kind of feminine issue. Because when Candy opened the folder she'd been holding, he saw the picture of Jerry kissing a woman. It was only after Candy fanned out the photos that Lucian realized the woman was none other than Jerry's assistant and the mayor's daughter, Darlene.

"Darlene's twenty-four," Candy quickly pointed out. "And I don't think Bennie Sullivan is going to approve of his daughter being with a man forty years older than she is."

Lucian glanced at the photos, which appeared to have been taken in Jerry's office, and with each one that Candy uncovered, Darlene was wearing fewer and fewer items of clothing. He stopped Candy when Darlene was down to her underwear. He didn't need any further proof of what had gone on. However, Lucian did have some questions.

"Who took these pictures?" he asked.

For such a simple question, no one jumped to give him a simple answer. Glenda and Candy volleyed a few glances at each other, and it was Glenda who finally answered. "I hired a PI, and he took some photos of Darlene and Jerry in a car parked on one of the old ranch trails. I've got those if you'd like to see them."

"I'll pass." Lucian turned to Candy. "Did you hire a PI, too, who snapped these particular shots?"

Bingo. He knew he'd gotten it right when Candy gave an indignant huff. "Jerry treated me like dirt, and I'm not going to let him get away with it."

Lucian hoped that revenge streak didn't extend to his mom because Regina hadn't exactly been kind to the woman. Of course, Regina wasn't doing things to harm the family. He hoped.

"I'm guessing your PIs saw each other and let you two know that you had tails on the same person," Lucian continued.

Glenda nodded. Candy followed suit. "As I said, Bennie Sullivan isn't going to like Jerry playing bump and grind with his daughter," Candy added.

It didn't take Lucian long to piece the rest of this together. Once the mayor saw the pictures, then he'd be pissed off enough to throw his support Lucian's way and could convince the historical society to do the same.

"So, why didn't the two of you just take the pictures to Bennie?" Lucian asked.

Dylan lifted his hand. "I stopped them. I saw them parked outside the mayor's office and decided to see what was up. I convinced them to come here and talk things over before they charged in with naked pictures of his daughter."

Good. Lucian nodded in approval, and then he groaned while he scrubbed his hand over his face. "As much as I'd love to turn public opinion against Jerry, this isn't the way to do it. Darlene's reputation would be ruined. I'm sure you remember what that's like." He aimed that comment at Glenda. "Plus, her fiancé's overseas. This isn't a good time for him to get news of Darlene's cheating."

Candy's mouth tightened. "That's what Glenda said. And Dylan. But if we just give the pictures to Bennie—"

"It'd be all over town within a matter of hours," Glenda interrupted. "I thought the way to handle this would be to tell Bennie directly. No pictures. No one else around. If you go to him," she added to Lucian, "you could convince Bennie to talk to Darlene."

"Along with convincing him to put pressure on the historical society without telling them why he was applying pressure," Lucian finished for her.

Glenda made a sound of agreement. "I want Jerry out of your life."

Lucian followed that train of thought, too, and he silently groaned. This was about Karlee. About that whole lighting-up thing whenever she was around him. Glenda was trying to save the business because she believed that one day Karlee and he would be together.

"You know that Karlee and I aren't engaged?" Lucian threw out there.

Before Glenda could answer, Candy stepped in front of him. "I don't see how your engagement or lack thereof has anything to do with those pictures. You can talk to Bennie. You can ruin Jerry."

It was tempting. God, was it. "I can be a dick when

it comes to business, but I'm not ruining two lives, Darlene's and her fiancé's, because she made a bad choice."

Even though if Jerry and Darlene were being so careless about their trysts, then someone would discover it soon enough. Lucian just didn't want to be the messenger on this.

"Well, if you won't do it, I will," Candy snapped.

Glenda shook her head. "Please reconsider that."

Candy's hands went on her hips. "Hey, you hired a PI, too. You want to destroy Jerry as much as I do."

"I don't want him in charge of his family's business," Glenda corrected. "And if you go to Bennie with these pictures, I'll tell him they're photoshopped, that you're a scorned woman who would stop at nothing to hurt Jerry. If Bennie believes me, and I think he will, then it could cause him to take an even stronger stance to support Jerry."

Candy's mouth dropped open, and she snapped to Lucian, then Dylan, as if she expected them to do something. Lucian just shrugged, causing Candy to grumble something he didn't catch before she gathered up her pictures and stormed out.

"I'll try to calm her down," Dylan volunteered, heading after her.

Glenda stayed put, and so did Lucian. That's because something about this wasn't adding up.

"Why are you doing this?" Lucian came out and asked her. "Karlee no longer works for me. You don't owe me and my family anything."

She smiled but it wasn't from humor. "I owe your family plenty." Glenda paused. "I've done things. Bad things. The *wrong* things," she corrected. "And it's been very costly for not just your family but for mine. Whitt wouldn't have killed himself if it hadn't been for me."

He shook his head. "Whitt drank because of you, but he's the one who drank so much that it killed him."

Glenda stared at him. "I thought you knew. I thought Karlee had told you."

Lucian did some staring, too. "Told me what?"

She made a sound of frustration and squeezed her eyes shut a moment. "Whitt committed suicide. I talked to him that night, and he even read me the note he was leaving behind."

"There was no note—" But he stopped. "I spoke to Whitt that night, too."

"Yes, Whitt told me. He'd seen you earlier in town that day and said some things to you."

"Actually, Whitt had cussed me out and accused me of not doing enough to stop Jerry from running off with you. Don't apologize," he said when she opened her mouth. "That all happened a long time ago. Whitt staggered off, but I was young and hotheaded, so I called him later to continue the argument."

Glenda nodded again. "Whitt mentioned that when he talked to me later that night."

So, all of that had happened on the day Whitt had killed himself. And that gave Lucian an uneasy feeling in the pit of his stomach. "Does Karlee know that I called her dad?"

"Yes. Joe told her on Christmas Day."

Hell. That was when the shallow weather discussions started. Of course, they'd moved past that when he'd barged into her office and had sex with her, but there was still some air that needed to be cleared.

Shit, did she blame him for her father's death?

"Excuse me," Lucian mumbled, taking out his phone.

He stepped outside the office and pressed Karlee's number. It rang, rang and rang, causing that bad feeling to go up a notch. Finally, though, she answered, but she started talking before Lucian could get a word in edgewise.

"Sorry, but I don't have time to chat." Her words were rushed together. "I'm leaving right now for a trip to meet with some prospective buyers for that first herd. I might be gone for a day or two. Gotta go."

And she hung up.

Lucian stared at the phone for several long moments, and he considered calling her right back. However, he was afraid that he would get the same shallow response. It wasn't her discussing-the-weather tone, but it was close enough for him to back off. He put his phone away, ready to go out and see how Dylan had fared. Before he could do that, though, Glenda stepped out of the office and into the hall with him.

She handed him an envelope. "I hope you'll be able to forgive me for what I've done," she said.

Lucian groaned because he figured it was more of the sex pictures of Darlene and Jerry. He had already seen enough of those to last a lifetime or two, and he would have handed them right back to Glenda if she hadn't stepped away from him.

"Keep it," she insisted as she started leaving. "If things get really bad with Jerry, there's something inside that you might be able to use."

CHAPTER SIXTEEN

THE FIRST THING Karlee spotted when she rolled her suit-case to the door of her apartment were the flowers that were sitting on her welcome mat. Since it was Valentine's Day, that would have pleased most women, but these were yellow roses, which meant they were almost certainly from Lucian since those were his usual fare.

Yep.

When she pulled out the card, she saw his name, but at least this time there was a message. "Call me." It wasn't all in caps and didn't have an exclamation mark, but the fact that he hadn't included anything else other than his name made it feel like somewhat of an order.

Lucian might be worried that her overnight trip had turned into a week, but she'd decided to go ahead and personally visit many of the prospective buyers and sell-ers on her list. Not only was it good business, it had given her a chance to clear her head. She wasn't going to cry over spilled milk—or in this case, cry over Lu-cian. She'd felt him pull away almost immediately after they'd had sex, and she was just going to let that take its natural "pulling away" course.

Still, it would hurt.

And she wasn't going to read anything into the flow-ers or the message. The bottom line was that Lucian did care for her, and he was likely feeling crappy for what'd happened. In his eyes, this could ruin their friendship.

Scooping up the vase of flowers, she unlocked her apartment door and got another surprise. Like the flowers, this wasn't a good thing, either. Because Joe was there. She'd texted her brothers to let them know she'd be home today, but Joe wasn't the sort to wait around to welcome her back.

Which meant something was wrong.

Or maybe this was another intervention about her feelings for Lucian. The last time that'd happened, Amelia had been there, and Karlee was about to express some kind of relief that she wasn't, but then she spotted Amelia at her breakfast table. Not alone. She was sitting there with Glenda.

Yes, something was wrong.

Most of her baggage was now under the same roof. All that was missing was Lucian and Ellen Carmichael—someone that Karlee had punched in third grade because she'd thought Ellen was telling lies about her. Turned out, though, that it'd been someone telling lies about Ellen, and Karlee had been too ashamed to apologize.

"Who wants to start?" Karlee asked, setting both her suitcase and the flowers aside. "And then maybe one of you can convince me not to change the locks so that I won't walk in on another surprise like this."

Amelia stood. Apparently, she was the designated "go first" person. "Your mother called me, so I made a quick trip in. I can't stay," she added.

That was the only good thing Karlee had seen and heard so far. "So, this is about Lucian?"

All three of them nodded. Well, Glenda and Amelia did. Joe grunted.

"Glenda called me," Joe growled. He didn't sound any happier about this visit than Karlee was. "I used my key to let them in. And yes, you should change the locks. That way, I won't get roped into meetings like this."

So Joe hadn't wanted this. Not a good sign.

"After hearing what your mother said, I'm worried about Lucian," Amelia went on. "Jerry has sold everything of value in the house, and now he's trying to start selling the land."

"But the lawsuit should stop that," Karlee reminded them.

"Jerry's legal team is pressing for a way around it," Glenda explained.

Karlee was certain that Lucian's lawyer would continue to block it. Still, this stalemate coupled with the legal fees had to be costing a fortune. Added to that was the emotional toll it was taking on the family.

"I suspect things aren't great between Lucian and you or you wouldn't have left on that long trip," Glenda went on, "but I figured you'd still want to help him."

"This involves you," Joe said before Karlee could respond. Not that she knew how to answer that anyway. Yes, she did want to help Lucian, but she wasn't keen on admitting that "things aren't great" part.

"How?" Karlee asked.

"Jerry is apparently going for the title of asshole king because he's been calling his old pals and telling them not to do business with Lucian or you."

Karlee shook her head, not understanding why Jerry would include her in his vendetta, but she quickly got the big picture. If he could hurt her, then Lucian might be faster to settle. That also explained why Joe was here. He wouldn't have come if this had solely been about Lucian.

"There's more," Joe said, giving Glenda more stink-eye than usual.

Apparently, Glenda was to provide the *more*, but she took a moment, gathering her breath. "You're not going to like this," she warned Karlee. "And FYI, I put all of what I'm about to tell you in an envelope and gave it to Lucian, but I'm not sure he's even read it."

Okay, that got Karlee's full attention, and she motioned for Glenda to continue.

"I own Melcor," Glenda finally said.

Karlee immediately recognized the name. That's because Jerry had sold 1 percent of the family holdings to Melcor. But it took Karlee a couple of seconds for her to process what her mother said.

"You own the company that could settle this legal stalemate between Lucian and Jerry," Karlee spelled out as she sank down onto the sofa. "I think you'd better give me an explanation about that."

Glenda came closer and took the seat across from Karlee. Since neither Amelia nor Joe looked very surprised about this, Glenda had already told them. Maybe they'd gotten envelopes as Lucian had. An envelope that Karlee was certain he hadn't opened. Because if he had, Jerry would already be out.

Maybe.

Or maybe there was some weird angle to this that Karlee wasn't seeing.

"After my second husband died, I went through a horrible depression," Glenda continued. "I kept thinking about how Jerry had ruined so many lives."

Karlee had to stop her. "You're not putting all the blame on him for you leaving, are you?"

"No," Glenda quickly answered. "I know I was just as responsible, but I learned my lesson. Jerry didn't. When I found out he'd left a string of brokenhearted women after me, I decided to do something about it." She paused. "Using my business contacts, I lured him into deals that failed. I'm the one who caused him to go broke."

Karlee had no idea how she was supposed to feel about that. After everything Jerry had done to Lucian, she seriously despised the man, but she didn't like that someone had manipulated his financial failures. Especially when that someone was her own mother.

"I'm very sorry about this," Glenda went on. "I never thought this would hurt Lucian and his family. And I'm not sure how to fix it."

"What do you mean you don't know how to fix it?" Karlee huffed. "You fix it by giving Lucian control of your one percent."

"I'd gladly do that, but it might not make this right. My so-called business contacts aren't willing to back off from the debts that Jerry owes. I've stalled them, but they're after a majority share of Granger Enterprises."

Oh God. That would mean Lucian would lose the company he'd worked so hard to build. Of course, that could have happened anyway under Jerry's mismanagement, but still, it stung to know her mother had had some part in this.

Joe turned to Glenda. "Tell Karlee about these *business contacts*," he insisted.

Judging from the way Glenda's gaze darted away, Karlee wasn't going to like this. "They were friends of my late husband. I swear, I didn't know they were loan sharks."

Great. Loan sharks. This whole mess was tangled enough without adding that. However, it meant that Lucian's reputation had nothing to do with Jerry's return to oust him as CEO. Jerry had merely seized an opportunity so he could bleed the business and pay off his debts.

"I own the one percent that Jerry sold Melcor," Glenda added. "No one else has a part of that. And I'll gladly give it to Lucian. What concerns me, though, is that when Lucian takes control, Jerry might sell his portion to the people he owes money."

That wasn't just a possibility, it was a likelihood—especially if the loan sharks threatened violence. Then Lucian would be in charge with a majority share, but he'd be doing daily dealings with criminals. That only confirmed that Lucian hadn't read what Glenda had given him. But there was still a big question here, and Karlee looked at Joe to answer it.

"Judd and you knew that Glenda was Melcor. That's why you said I wouldn't believe it if I found out who was trying to help Lucian."

Joe nodded.

"Then why didn't you tell me?" Karlee demanded.

"Because I asked him to hold off telling anyone," Glenda volunteered. "I was trying to fix things."

"So was I," Amelia chimed in. "I've been trying to get the creditors to back off and have even offered them money. They refused. And now we've got a new player in all of this."

Good grief. What now—the mafia? Satan?

"Candy," Amelia and Glenda said in unison.

If they'd made this multiple choice, Karlee would

have gotten it wrong. She would have thought they'd seen and heard the last from the Hoo-Poo heiress.

"She's outraged at the way Jerry treated her," Glenda explained. "And now there's that whole problem with the pictures."

Karlee wasn't sure she could give another surprised reaction even though it would be genuine. This conversation continued to be full of revelations. "Pictures?" she asked.

"Of Jerry and the mayor's daughter, Darlene," Amelia explained. "They're having an affair, and Candy managed to get pictures of them. She took them to the mayor, thinking he'd turn against Jerry, but it backfired. Jerry convinced the mayor that the pictures were photoshopped, and that Candy was out to ruin him because she's jealous. Now the mayor got a restraining order against Candy."

Hearing all of this made Karlee want to pick up her suitcase and go on another long business trip. And she might just do that. First, though, she needed to find out one key piece of info that had yet to be dropped like a bombshell onto her.

"How much of this does Lucian know?" Karlee asked.

Amelia, Joe and Glenda volleyed glances at each other. "He knows about the restraining-order mess," Glenda said. "He also knows about Jerry's affair with Darlene. But again, unless he read the letter I gave him, he doesn't know about the loan sharks or me being Melcor."

That put her mother at the center of what could be a huge moral dilemma for Lucian. He might not want to accept help from someone who'd helped tear his family apart. Karlee wouldn't have if she'd been in his shoes, but then, it might come down to just how much he despised Jerry and what he was doing. Of course, even with Glenda's 1 percent, Lucian still wouldn't actually have control of Granger Enterprises.

"And Lucian doesn't know I'm in love with him," Amelia added when the room got quiet. That caused all of them to snap toward the woman, and Amelia lifted her shoulder. "I'm sorry. That's probably not what you want to hear, but it's true, and one of the reasons I'm here is so I can tell him."

No, it wasn't something Karlee wanted to hear, but like the other stuff, it wasn't much of a surprise. For all of her adult life, Amelia had always come back to Lucian and vice versa. Even really good sex probably couldn't have that kind of hold on a couple for such a long period of time.

"I'm sorry," Glenda echoed. She apparently thought it was a done deal that Lucian would welcome Amelia back with open arms.

"If he hurt you, I'm going to kick his ass," Joe griped.

Best not to mention that Lucian and she had had sex. That wouldn't make anyone in the room happy.

And speaking of happy, Karlee wanted them all gone so she could try to absorb everything she'd just learned and come to terms with it. Not that their leaving would actually make her happy, but they wouldn't be around to see her stewing. It was ironic that what troubled her most was Amelia's declaration of love.

Before she could come up with a polite way to tell them to scram, her doorbell rang. Great. Maybe Ellen Carmichael from third grade had shown up after all to demand that apology and add another level of old baggage to the room. But it wasn't Ellen. It was the topic of multiple facets of the conversation she'd just had.

Lucian.

He stepped in. Then stopped. Whatever he'd been about to say stopped, too, and his gaze fired from Joe. Then to Glenda. Then Amelia.

"Uh, am I interrupting something?" he asked.

"Yes." Karlee huffed. "And thank you for doing it. Glenda is here to confess to being head of Melcor and other assorted things that are going to rile you. They certainly riled me," she added. "Joe wants to do some ass-kicking, and Amelia wants to tell you something personal."

That was a lot to dump on him, but Karlee figured Lucian would prefer just to put everything out there. That way, he could pick and choose which one he wanted to deal with first. Apparently, though, he didn't want to tackle any of those options right now. That's because Lucian took hold of the back of her head, angling her and moving her.

And then he kissed her.

LUCIAN FIGURED HE should have at least acknowledged all the things that Karlee had just told him. However, he'd mentally prioritized and had put the kiss at the top of his to-do list.

Kissing her was risky because he hadn't been sure how Karlee would react, but the fact that she didn't push him away was a good sign. It was also good that she leaned into him while she slipped her arm around his waist.

It wasn't all positive though.

Despite all the signals that she was enjoying the lip-lock, she also went a little stiff. He was pretty sure that had more to do with their audience than what he hoped would be a thoroughly satisfying make-out session/air clearing. Best not to launch into either of those things until he'd addressed the three eight-hundred-pound gorillas in the room.

Lucian pulled back, running his tongue on his bottom lip so he could get the jolt of Karlee's taste there. All in all, it was a good place for her taste to be, and it gave him a little nudge to hurry this conversation along so that he could continue what he'd already started.

"Can the ass-kicking wait?" Lucian asked Joe. Unlike Amelia and Glenda, Karlee's brother didn't look surprised by what had just happened. But he did look ready to tear Lucian limb from limb.

With his gaze locked with Lucian's, Joe stood and studied him. The kiss must have earned Lucian some brownie points with him because Joe gave a crisp nod and looked back at Glenda.

"Don't involve me in anything else you've done or plan to do," Joe warned her. "You're my mother, so I'll give you some level of respect for giving birth to me. *Some*," he emphasized. "But find a way to fix this shit you've created with Jerry and Lucian."

Glenda swallowed hard, nodded as Joe walked out.

Since Joe had put the spotlight on Glenda, that's where Lucian looked next—though it appeared he was about to have powder-keg conversations with both Amelia and her.

"You're head of Melcor?" he asked, wondering if he'd misheard that.

Glenda nodded. Not a firm, yes-sir kind of nod, either. It had a shakiness to it that let Lucian know he'd heard the other part of that correctly, too. That what she'd done was going to piss him off.

"I didn't know it was going to come to this," Glenda explained, "but I wanted to hurt Jerry, so I connected him with the wrong people when he needed to borrow some money."

Well, shit. Yeah, that definitely fell into the category of things to rile the hell out of him. Lucian did some filling in the blanks and quickly figured out where this was going. "These *wrong people* want Granger Enterprises?"

Glenda nodded again, but it was Karlee who did some blank-filling of her own. "Glenda will give you her one percent so you'll have majority control, but it could trigger Jerry into selling to these guys."

"He'll probably sell anyway. No choice about that. Judging from the paintings and family heirlooms he's unloaded, he's getting desperate."

"What can I do to fix this?" Glenda came out and asked.

It was an important question, and Lucian wanted to give it an important answer. Too bad part of his brain was only half listening to this conversation. It was still thinking about kissing Karlee. Of course, his dick had more of a say in this than his brain did.

"For now, don't do anything," Lucian told her. "And give me the names of all of those bad business contacts you hooked Jerry up with. I want to know who I'm dealing with before I decide what to do."

Glenda's nod was firmer that time. "I'll email them to you as soon as I'm on my computer. What about the one percent? Do you want me to go ahead and sign it over to you?"

"Wait on that, too."

He needed to figure out the best way to approach that, and this in no way qualified as the best time. It didn't help when Karlee tried to move away from him. Probably because she knew that Amelia would be next up in the conversation queue. Even after that scalding kiss Karlee and he had just shared, he could feel her trying to go into the wallflower mode.

"I really am sorry," Glenda added.

Since Joe had just given the woman a dressing-down, Lucian didn't feel the need to add to it. It didn't mean that he approved of what she had done, but he didn't see the need to spell that out. Especially since Glenda seemed to be doing a good job of punishing herself.

Glenda repeated the apology to Karlee, and Karlee did something that surprised him. She didn't scowl at her mother. Didn't snap out any criticisms. Maybe because Karlee also thought Joe had done enough for all of them.

"I've got enough unresolved issues without heaping on another layer," Karlee muttered in a near whisper.

Glenda must have heard it because her expression softened. It wasn't the warm and fuzziest of mother-daughter moments, but Lucian figured that Glenda appreciated it anyway. The woman walked away with a lot less of the "the sky is falling" expression she'd had when Lucian had first walked in.

And that left Amelia.

Before Lucian could even say anything, Karlee blew out a long breath, picked up her suitcase and headed toward her bedroom. "I'll give you two some time alone while I grab a shower," she added. "If you leave before

I'm finished, lock up behind you." With that, she closed the bedroom door.

It riled him that she would even consider that he'd leave with Amelia, much less without telling her, but then, there wasn't much about this that hadn't riled him. He'd come over to do that whole kissing thing with Karlee, and he'd gotten embroiled in way more than he'd wanted.

"You're surprised to see me," Amelia remarked. She slid her hands along the sides of her skirt. She was nervous, he realized. A first. "Well, I was surprised when you greeted Karlee like that."

Lucian had no idea how to respond to that. He wasn't one to kiss and tell, so he just stayed quiet and let Amelia continue.

"I've been thinking," Amelia went on, "and I decided I should speak up. I don't want to go through life regretting things left unsaid. Lucian, I'm in love with you, and I want to see if we can try again. Not go back to the way things were, but try for something, well, deeper."

Sonofabitch. When had this happened? And better yet, how could he stop it?

He still didn't know what to say, but it turned out that Amelia had no trouble keeping up the conversation. However, what she added next was troublesome.

"I need you, Lucian."

Sonofabitch times two. There it was, all in a nutshell. The handful of words that he'd hung on to all these years. The very ones he'd said to Amelia when he'd been asking for that same *deeper* that she apparently wanted now.

"It's true," she went on. "This isn't a knee-jerk reaction to possibly losing you. I love you and want to spend the rest of my life with you."

A few months ago, that might have been music to his ears. *Might*. But with hindsight being a whole lot better than regular sight, Lucian had to admit that it would have been just as likely to send him running. Amelia and the no-strings relationship were his fantasy. Amelia with strings would have felt, well, like strings. Also, in hindsight Lucian could see that stringless sex didn't cause nearly as many complications as sex had with Karlee.

Because here he was.

Wanting more and feeling caught in the middle of something he should have been way ahead of.

"Amelia," he finally managed to say. Not his best effort at complex communication, but he sounded surprisingly calm, considering the tornado going on in his mind. Not because he intended to take Amelia up on her offer.

He didn't.

But Lucian realized that he was about to hurt the only woman who actually needed him. Because he believed everything she'd just told him. Amelia needed him and wanted this to work.

He went to her, gently taking hold of her shoulders. "I can't do this."

And the hurt came just as fast as he'd thought it would. It was in her eyes, in the slight tremble of her mouth. However, she quickly covered it up by stepping away from him and dodging his gaze. "I waited too long," she whispered. "You're in love with Karlee."

"I'm not in love with anyone," he assured her.

She probably didn't believe him, but it was true. However, he did feel drawn to Karlee. And confused. Hell, *drawn* was beginning to feel like a whole bunch of strings, too.

"Well," Amelia said. He could practically see her steeling herself up by pulling back her shoulders and lifting her chin. "I never thought I'd have to do this."

He did some steeling up of his own. Maybe she'd curse him or slap him. He might be on the verge of hearing a lecture as to how she'd wasted all those years on him. But Amelia merely leaned in and brushed a kiss on his mouth.

"Goodbye, Lucian. I hope you have a wonderful life."

And that was it. Lucian figured it would be a long time, if ever, before Amelia said anything else to him. Even then, it would be casual conversation. Nothing nearly as personal as the moment they'd just shared.

"Have a wonderful life, too," he echoed, causing her to give him a brief, tight smile that he knew would fade the second she turned away from him.

The turning away happened pretty fast. Amelia walked out, easing the door shut behind her. Lucian locked it, not because he thought she'd be coming back, but in case Glenda came back for round two of surprises.

Or Joe.

Though Karlee's brother wanting to kick his ass wasn't much of a surprise. Joe was just looking out for his sister. Since there was a strong possibility that Lucian had already hurt her or would do that in the near future, then Joe would want to keep that ass-kicking on the table.

Lucian didn't hear the shower going, so he knocked. And waited. And waited some more. Finally, Karlee opened the door. She was in her bathrobe, and she was toweling her wet hair.

"Amelia's gone," he let her know right off.

If that pleased her, he couldn't tell because her mouth

was a little tight. Well, he was sure there was some tightness in his expression, too.

"*If you leave before I'm finished, lock up behind you*?" he repeated. "What kind of dumbass thing is that to say?"

He expected her to give him some kind of explanation that involved her feeling uncertain about where she stood with him, but that was not an explaining look in her eyes. "You sent me flowers. Not those." She flung her hand in the direction of the living room. "The ones you sent me last month had only your name on the card."

"What?" And Lucian followed that with a blank stare.

Apparently, that wasn't the response she wanted because Karlee huffed. "That's the same flowers and the same cards you send to your sweet things of the month."

Oh.

Shit.

He got it then. Lucian opened his mouth to say that was the standard order at the florist, an order that Karlee herself had set up years ago, and that Sunny was just following suit when he'd told her to send a bouquet. But he doubted that explanation was going to soothe anything. Besides, he had his own beef with Karlee, one that would hopefully cancel out the flower f-up.

"You talked about the weather," he reminded her.

She gave him the same blank stare he'd given her just moments earlier. She said the same thing, too. "What?"

"The weather," he clarified, which, of course, didn't clarify squat. "You went all casual and shallow on me when you should have told me what was bugging you. And FYI, I didn't find out the source of the bugging until Glenda told me that Joe had told you that I called your dad."

He hoped she could work her way through the repeated "tolds" and make some sense of that. And it appeared to work. She quit staring, anyway, and released a very frustrated-sounding breath.

"Another FYI," Lucian went on. "When I spoke to your dad that night, he didn't say anything about killing himself. If he had, I would have gone right over there and tried to stop him."

Karlee gave another of those frustrated breaths, paused and tossed the towel onto the vanity. In the same motion, she grabbed a handful of his shirt, and she yanked him to her. Finally, Lucian got that second kiss that he'd come here to get. But it was a little different than he'd expected.

Because this felt like anger foreplay.

He'd experienced it before, mainly after an argument with one of his exes. Not quite makeup foreplay because of the still-sour feelings lingering around. And judging from what she said next, Karlee apparently had some sour stuff to get out there.

"Don't ever send me flowers like that again," she grumbled. This time, she latched on to his hair, pulling him even harder to her.

He didn't mind hard. In fact, it coordinated well with the erection he got. Plus, it was a relief to know that Karlee wasn't going to stay pissed at him. Well, maybe she wasn't. He hoped this wasn't a case of anger foreplay leading to anger sex leading to yet more anger after an orgasm.

"No more flowers," he assured her. Or rather, he tried, but it came out garbled because she kissed him again.

All in all, he liked her taking control like this even though there was some pain involved when she pushed him against the vanity, and the glass drawer knob hit him on the butt. He made a sound of pain. Then pleasure when Karlee pulled open her robe, and he discovered that she was bare-assed naked.

Exactly the way he preferred his anger foreplay.

Seeing her in her birthday suit revved him up. Not that he needed anything else to do that, but it was a sweet reminder that she'd be a lot easier to kiss and touch without pesky underwear. Lucian lowered his head and started sampling.

That involved some pain, too, since she still had hold of his hair, but it was worth it. Now he wanted to make it worth it to Karlee, too. Shoving her robe off her shoulders, he whirled her around so that it was her backside against the vanity. He kissed his way down to her neck. Then her breasts.

Of course, he lingered a bit there, but today the grand prize was much lower. Still, he took his time getting there. Kissing her stomach. The inside of her thigh. To reach the good part, he lifted her knee, sliding it onto his shoulder, and then he licked and nipped his way to the best part of all best parts.

Karlee cursed him, calling him a dirty name—one that he liked very much. He didn't even mind the hair pulling now, either, because it gave him an urgency. He put all of that urgency into giving Karlee a kiss that he hoped she would remember for a long time. He certainly would.

More cursing, all from her, and then she caught onto the vanity with her free hand, the one that wasn't making him bald from the hair pulling. His mouth was still on her when she shattered, but Lucian didn't give her any time to recover. He made his way back up, unzipping his jeans and getting on a condom while he pinned her against the vanity.

She shook her head when he pushed into her. "You'll have to have this one on your own. I never had two orgasms."

That sounded like some kind of challenge to him. Good thing he was hard and ready.

"I'm going to have to prove you wrong," he drawled.

And he did just that.

CHAPTER SEVENTEEN

KARLEE COULDN'T FEEL her feet. Or her butt. Both were numb, but thankfully the other parts of her body were working just fine. She had managed to feel every quiver, tremble, pulse and slam of the second orgasm that she was certain she wouldn't be able to have.

But she had. Thanks to Lucian.

It had taken a while for Lucian to get her there—hence the numb feet and butt. But Lucian seemed to be operating just fine. He carried her to her bed, eased her onto the mattress and then disappeared into the bathroom, giving her time to catch her breath.

Along with that, she also needed to "catch" her thoughts. After Amelia had spilled the beans about her declaration of love, Karlee hadn't figured that sex between Lucian and her would be on the table. Or rather, on the vanity. But he'd obviously sent Amelia and Glenda on their merry ways, and he must have worked out things enough with them or he probably wouldn't have ended up in her bathroom.

Karlee glanced down at her body and realized she didn't have on a stitch of clothes. Somewhere along the orgasm-giving process, she'd lost her bathrobe. Since she was too spent to get up and locate it or a gown, she just threw the covers over her and continued to mull her situation.

However, the mulling didn't even have time to get started because Lucian walked back into her bedroom. This time, though, he was stark naked, giving her a really nice eye-candy view before he dropped down on the bed beside her. He also pushed the covers off her—yes, the very ones she'd just pulled over her—and he gathered her against him for a hip-to-hip snuggle. Strange. She had never thought of Lucian as the snuggle type.

"Want to talk about the weather?" he asked, causing her to smile.

"Only if we can then have a long and meaningful discussion about flower choices."

He smiled, too, but it didn't last, and he turned on his side to face her. It was such a simple move, but the sight of him caused her heart to flutter. Yes, an actual flutter.

She nearly blurted out that no man had a right to look as good as he did. Nearly told him that he had always done things to her that felt close to magic. It was as if he set off sparks just beneath the surface of her skin.

Karlee figured all these romantic thoughts were causing her to have a dreamy expression, but she couldn't say the same for Lucian. His forehead bunched up.

"Shit," he growled. Obviously, he hadn't been thinking about sparks or romance. "You do light up."

Color her confused, but Karlee didn't think this was a good thing. She shook her head and waited for an explanation. And she got one. Sort of.

"Karlee, I'm bad news. I don't deserve a lighting up."

Since he seemed to be talking about her expression/a reaction she was having to him, Karlee quickly tried to fix it. She scowled, which wasn't that hard to do because she thought this might be "the" conversation. The one he had with his sweet things right before he left and sent them flowers.

She quickly weighed her options and was just as quick to realize that she didn't have any that would give her back that lovely after-the-orgasm buzz. Lucian wasn't the commitment sort, apparently not even to Amelia, the woman that everyone thought was the love of his life. If he couldn't handle Amelia's "I love you," then she stood no chance. Which meant she had nothing to lose that she hadn't already lost.

"A blow job or a waffle?" she asked. In her mind, the options made sense—mainly because they didn't want to address the lighting-up problem. But she probably shouldn't have just sprung those choices on him like that, either.

She huffed, not a huff for his totally blank stare but because she needed to explain herself. "You're out of condoms, I don't have any here, so if you want a second orgasm before you leave, it'll be the blow job. But if you're hungry, which I am, then I'll make you a waffle. It'll be frozen because I'm a lousy cook."

The blank stare continued, and since she doubted a healthy red-blooded man—even one who'd just had sex—would turn down a blow job, she decided on both. But she'd start with the waffle.

Leaving Lucian there with his gobsmacked expression, she got up, threw on the first T-shirt she located in the dresser drawer. It wasn't one of the oversize ones, so Karlee felt a draft on her bare butt when she headed for the kitchen.

By the time she made it to the freezer, Lucian was coming out of the bedroom. Unlike her, he hadn't opted for even minimal clothing. He was in all his naked glory, which meant she had to look away rather than risk a different kind of look. A heated one that might make her want to take a quick condom-shopping trip.

He opened his mouth, closed it and frowned. Probably because he didn't know where to start with the conversation they were about to have. Since she wasn't sure how long a talk like that would take, she went ahead and put two frozen waffles in the toaster. She also took out the peanut butter in the hopes of making the frozen circle slightly more palatable to Lucian, and she scooped out a spoonful.

The silence dragged on and on, and she wondered if he made all his sweet things wait this long before ending things.

"You don't cook?" he finally said.

She hadn't intended to eat the peanut butter that she'd gotten for him, but as if the spoon were on an autopilot mission, it went in her mouth to give her time to think of something clever to say.

Nothing clever came to mind.

"No. I suck at it," she settled for saying.

"And blow jobs?" The corner of his mouth lifted in a sly smile, which meant he was already thinking of the play-on-words punch line she'd just intentionally handed him.

"Fair to middling," Karlee settled for saying.

For such a short exchange of conversation, it worked miracles. She felt the tension in her body evaporate, and she saw things in a new light.

"Yes, this relationship will end." With the peanut-butter spoon still in her hand, Karlee walked closer to him. "Yes, I'll probably get hurt. But there's no way to avoid it now. So, I say you just give me the same thirty days as your other lovers."

He caught onto the bottom of her T-shirt and pulled her closer so he could kiss her. "You're not just another lover," he pointed out.

That heated her up more than the next kiss. "Then give me six weeks because of my premium status." Best to keep things light. "By then, the rodeo will be over, and we can have breakup sex while you're wearing your championship buckle. Just the buckle," she added, causing him to smile again.

"And if I lose?" he asked.

She thought about that a second and decided to assume that he was still talking about the buckle. Best not to consider that he could be talking about letting go of whatever this was between them. "Then sex while you're wearing your grandfather's buckle."

He didn't get a chance to respond because her phone rang, and from the ringtone she knew it was Roman, which meant it could be important. The only time he called was when it was about her cattle. Karlee hurried into the living room, where she'd left her purse, and fished out her phone.

"Sorry, but there's a problem," Roman said, confirming that this was indeed important. "We're going to have to quarantine one of our herds, and we need to use the pasture where you were going to put the new cattle you bought. I'm looking around for other options for you, but so far, nothing."

Karlee groaned. Yes, this was a problem, and she was about to tell him that she'd already looked for other places as well, but Roman continued before she could say anything. "Is Lucian there? If so, let him know it's time to move to the backup plan. Talk it over with him and get back to me."

Roman said a quick goodbye, and she turned to see if Lucian had any clue about what she'd just learned. Judging from his expression, she was guessing he did.

"What's the backup plan?" she asked. "And why did Roman go to you with this first and not me?"

He lifted his shoulder. "Roman and I are working out the land dispute, and we were at the lawyer's office when the quarantine problem came up."

All right. That sounded plausible and didn't feel as if they were combining forces to give her a safety net. A net she might indeed need. But there was no way in Hades she would ask one of them for it.

"What's the backup plan?" she repeated when Lucian didn't add anything else.

"It's something that you're probably not going to like." With that vague answer, he glanced down at his naked body. "And it'll require pants."

Lucian turned and headed in the direction of her bedroom. Of course, Karlee followed. "Why do you need pants, and where are you going?"

"I'd rather have my loins girded when I see Jerry." He pulled on his boxers, then his jeans. "Jerry's part of the backup plan. Or rather, he's an obstacle—not just to you but to a lot of us."

Karlee could totally agree with that, but Lucian still hadn't told her what he intended to do. Apparently, he didn't intend to tell her, either, because the moment he had on his shirt and boots, he headed for the door.

She caught up with him, and Lucian brushed a kiss

on her mouth. "After today, you'll have all the pasture you need for your cattle."

After delivering that second vague answer, Lucian walked out.

IT'D BEEN A while since Lucian had played the Lucifer card, but he was sure as hell about to play it now. He'd had Jerry dick around with him and the family long enough, and it was time to put a stop to it. Then once Lucian had his business life sorted out, he could figure out the rest of it.

Of course, the rest involved Karlee. In fact, after ousting Jerry, she was at the top of his to-do list. Or rather, she would be once he figured out exactly what to do. One thing was for certain: he couldn't continue having sex with her. Yes, she'd said she would already get hurt from this, but there were degrees of hurt. Degrees of being an asshole, too, and Lucian couldn't push his asshole status beyond what he'd already done to her.

For now, he pushed the Karlee problem aside and braced himself for the fight as he pulled into the driveway of the ranch house. His bracing took a bit of a hit, though, when he saw the two women in the doorway. One was Lois Fay Merkle from the historical society. Not totally unexpected since she socialized with his mother, but the other woman wasn't the socializing type.

Vita Banchini.

She was the town's resident fortune-teller, who was considered weird even by other weird people. On a good day, Lucian wouldn't have looked forward to seeing her, and this was nowhere near a good day. Well, except for

246 THE LAST RODEO

sex with Karlee, but everything else about it had fallen in the "shit on a stick" category.

"Lucian," Lois Fay greeted once he was out of his truck.

Her mouth was tighter than usual, and he wanted to tell her it made it look as if she had a butthole on her face, but he doubted that would do much to help this conversation along. And "along" was a high priority because he wanted to have that showdown with Jerry.

Lucian glanced behind the women and saw Abe, who was apparently trying to shut the door. To get rid of them, no doubt. "Your mom's not here," Abe told him.

Lucian knew that because he'd called ahead and asked Dylan who was there. According to his brother, it was only Jerry and Abe. Dylan obviously hadn't known about their visitors.

"I came to talk to Regina," Lois Fay volunteered. "I didn't know *she'd* be here." She motioned toward Vita, something that was totally unnecessary. Ditto for the stinkeye that Lois Fay gave the woman.

The stinkeye was not only rude, it was playing with fire since Vita wasn't the sort you wanted to piss off. Not that Vita could actually do the spells and curses that were her claim to fame, but she often left smelly potions and such for those who'd crossed her. For those she wanted to help, too.

Sometimes, though, it was hard to tell the difference.

"I wanted to have Regina talk to you again about your grandfather's rodeo buckle," Lois Fay added to him.

"There's good juju in that buckle," Vita declared, causing Lois Fay to huff and dole out more stinkeye.

Lucian never thought he'd say it, but he was with Vita

on this one. It sure felt lucky to him. And he might indeed wear it for sex with Karlee if he didn't win one of his own. Which gave him an idea. Juju probably didn't have defined boundaries, and it wouldn't matter the location of the buckle for it still to be his.

"I'll donate it to the historical society the day after the charity rodeo," Lucian said. He wasn't sure who was surprised the most by that: Abe, Vita, Lois Fay or him. Lucian thought he might take that particular prize.

Lois Fay's hand landed on her chest as if to steady her heart. "My word. I never thought I'd see this day. Thank you."

Lucian got another surprise when Lois Fay flung herself into his arms. For a skinny little woman she had the art of bear-hugging down pat, and when she pulled back, she seemed downright giddy. It was actually a little spooky. Like one of those demon-possessed dolls from the movies.

"Of course, this means the historical society will consider throwing our support your way," Lois Fay assured him.

A couple of months ago that would have caused him to go giddy as well, but now it was just overkill. He already had what he needed to give Jerry a change in not only his job title but also his residence. Still, Lucian thanked the woman, hoping it would send her on her merry way. It did.

And then there was one.

Abe didn't stick around for Lucian's chat with Vita. The cook headed back inside, leaving him to face Vita alone. Even though she was half his size, and her face was layered with wrinkles, she still felt a lot more formidable than demon-possessed movie dolls.

"I'm here about Karlee," Vita said. She wagged her index finger at him, causing her yards of gold and silver bracelets to jangle. "I know she's crying over you."

Lucian hadn't expected this to be the topic of conversation. "Did you have a vision or something?"

Vita huffed as if he'd just said the dumbest thing ever. "No. Her mailman texted me. He's a friend, and he delivered a package to her at her apartment about thirty minutes ago. He said when she opened the door, he could tell that she had been crying, so he let me know in case I wanted to do something about it."

That sounded a little like a threat, especially if Vita believed the tears were because of him. And they almost certainly were. Shit. He hated the thought of being the reason that Karlee was crying.

"Do you plan to do something about it?" Lucian asked, though he wasn't sure he wanted to hear the answer. A moment later, he got confirmation about not wanting that because Vita took something from her pocket and handed it to him.

An egg.

She took something else from her other pocket and put it in his palm next to the egg. A condom.

Lucian eyed both of them. "Is this some kind of metaphor? Because if so, I'm not getting the connection."

That earned him another huff and an eye roll from Vita. "The condom is a no-brainer. You can use it to stop Karlee from crying when you have sex with her. At least it should stop her from crying if you're any good at it." She paused. "Are you good at it?"

He had no intentions of discussing that with anyone, especially Vita. "What about the egg?" And he hoped like hell Vita wasn't going to give him a sexual suggestion about that, too, like maybe scrambling it after for a postsex meal.

Vita stared at him as if she might not let it pass that he hadn't actually answered her, but then she shrugged. "The egg is from the Fates. I had a dream that I should bring it to you to help you ward off bad luck."

He wasn't even going to consider anything connected with Fates and dreams, so he dismissed it. But those tears were a big red flag that he should just put the condom in his pocket and leave it there. Along with leaving his dick in his boxers.

"That's it?" Lucian asked Vita when she started off the porch. "You're not going to put a curse on me or anything?"

"Boy, you already got enough troubles without me addin' to it," Vita grumbled.

Yeah, he did have enough. And now that he'd cleared out the visitors, it was time to start whittling down some of those troubles to a more manageable size. He shoved the condom in his pocket, and with plans to toss the egg, he headed straight for what would be his office again—passing the still-taped-off areas and bare walls along the way. The office door was open, and he could hear someone mumbling.

Jerry.

Lucian didn't have to do any more steeling up or bracing. He was primed for this fight—which he figured would be a short one since he now had the law on his side. In fact, he could get the chief of police to drag Jerry out, but Lucian didn't like handing off his dirty work to others.

He stepped into the doorway and stopped in his tracks. Along with his stomach going to his knees, he had some other reactions. All bad. Because what he saw was Jerry, seated, and he had a gun on the desk. His hand was on the gun, too, but his finger wasn't on the trigger, and it wasn't aimed at Lucian. Jerry had it turned toward himself.

Lucian didn't think—something he probably should have done. He hurled the egg right at Jerry, and it smacked him right in the face. Of course, the egg broke, the yellow and white goo oozing down Jerry's face. It clearly stunned him. Distracted him, too, because it gave Lucian enough time to get to the desk and snatch the gun away from him.

"Have you lost your fucking mind?" Lucian shouted. It wasn't actually a question because obviously Jerry had indeed done that for him to be considering suicide.

Or maybe that's what he'd been doing.

Without wiping his face, Jerry just stared at him. And that's when Lucian spotted something else. All the other things on the desk. Office supplies, a bottle of whiskey, files. Things that normally would have been in the drawers.

"I was just cleaning out the desk and took out the gun to put it in my briefcase," Jerry said. Now he swiped his hand over his face to clear away the egg. He didn't get it all though. Bits of shell were still on his head. "You really thought I was going to kill myself?"

Lucian had. He blamed it on the earlier conversation he'd had with Karlee about her own father. In hindsight, he should have known that Jerry was too egotistical to consider ending his own life.

This wasn't exactly how Lucian had pictured a show-down. Not quite a *High Noon* feel to it. Not with the egg debris and the fact that Jerry was already in the emptying-the-desk mode.

Well, hopefully he was.

Just in case his father had some skewed expectations in that area, Lucian spelled it out for him. "Glenda is Melcor. Since she hates your guts, she's handed me her one percent on a silver platter. And that means you leave."

None of that seemed to surprise Jerry, and a moment later Lucian knew why. Jerry nodded. "Glenda called me about an hour ago. She said you'd likely be on the way over to send me packing." He paused. "Truth is, I expected you sooner."

Sex with Karlee had slowed him down some, but Lucian didn't intend to mention that. "I don't want you in the house or on the ranch. Find some other place to stay."

Jerry's passive nod diluted some of the ire in Lucian. He was primed and ready for a fight that apparently wasn't going to take place. But this was good. It meant Jerry understood that he'd lost, and Lucian would immediately start working on the paperwork to ensure that his father never tried to pull a stunt like this again.

"I know it's worth a thimbleful of spit, but I'm sorry." Jerry raked all the items on top of the desk into his briefcase. Everything but the folders.

"You're right. It's not worth much. You screwed us over six ways to Sunday and all because of your bad business dealings. And don't blame Glenda for that," he added when Jerry opened his mouth.

Considering how fast Jerry shut up, he had been indeed about to pin some blame on Karlee's mom. Lucian hated what Glenda had done, but she'd only dangled bait in front of Jerry. His father had been the one to take it.

"Just how much damage did you do?" Lucian came out and asked him.

A weary breath left Jerry's mouth. "A lot." He tipped his head to the folders. "It's all in there. I'm sorry," he repeated. "But because of me, you might end up losing Granger Enterprises."

WHEN KARLEE HEARD the knock on her apartment door, her first thought was that Lucian had returned to explain his parting remark about the pasture. He'd only been gone fifteen minutes, so there was no way he'd had time to get to the ranch and return. It would take him nearly an hour just to get there. But it wasn't Lucian.

It was Joe and Judd.

Great. This had all the makings of another intervention, one that she intended to nip in the bud. At least she was dressed for the bud nipping. She'd put on her clothes and makeup as soon as Lucian had left. Good thing, too, since she wouldn't have wanted to greet her brothers while wearing only a T-shirt.

"There'll be no ass-kicking and no Lucian bashing," she spelled out for them. "Yes, I had sex with him. Twice. With three orgasms. But I'm a grown woman and can choose my own bed partners without interference from either of you."

Their reactions fell into the blank looks/couldn't care less categories. "We're here about Dad," Joe said. "Glenda gave us some letters that Dad sent her, one that he wrote the day he offed himself."

Oh. So she'd unnecessarily confessed her sex life to two people who shouldn't have an inkling about that since she was more mother to them than big sister. But she pushed that particular embarrassment to the back burner since she was sure it could come back later to haunt her, and she stepped aside so they could come in.

Joe immediately took a letter from his pocket and handed it to her. "We thought we should be here when you read it."

That definitely didn't sound good. In her brothers' eyes, she was tough, and the letter had to be bad for them to give her this sort of moral support.

"Why is Glenda just now giving you this?" Karlee asked.

"Because it's not going to make things better." That came from Judd, who went into the kitchen and poured himself a cup of coffee that she'd just made. "Apparently, after Glenda's Melcor confession, she's decided to come clean about everything."

Karlee reminded herself that all of this was water under a very old bridge. There was nothing in the letter that would go back and change things. Still, she opened it, and she felt the immediate jolt of emotions at seeing her father's familiar handwriting. It was an in-her-face reminder of the suicide note.

It all came back. The stunned grief of finding him. The realization that their lives had just gone from bad to worse.

When her hands started to tremble, she handed the letter back to Joe. "Just give me the condensed version, and don't hold back the way that Glenda did. I want it all out in the open. Does he blame me for not doing enough? Am I the final straw that made him kill himself?"

She waited, hoping they would jump to assure her

that it wasn't the case. But they didn't. They just stayed put, as silent as the grave. And that caused her to curse.

Oh God.

Had her father really blamed her?

"I did everything I possibly could," Karlee insisted, talking to herself more than Joe or Judd. "I took over running the house after Glenda ran off. I gave up dating, college. Heck, I gave up my life to do the right thing."

Karlee cursed again when the tears came, and there was more profanity when there was a knock at her door. She threw it open, expecting to find Glenda there with some kind of follow-up comments about the blasted letter that she'd held on to all these years. But it wasn't her mother. It was the mailman, David Carson, who handed her a package.

David obviously noticed the tears in her eyes and was no doubt about to ask her what was wrong. Karlee nipped that in the bud, too. She thanked him and shut the door. In the same motion, she turned back around to face her brothers. She was reasonably sure she didn't want to hear the rest of what they were going to tell her, but she had to hear it. Even though it meant reopening a wound that just never seemed to heal.

Joe went to her and pulled her into his arms. "We know everything you did for us. Mack does, too. Without you, we would have stayed in foster care a lot longer than we did."

That helped. Not with the tears. They were coming pretty hard now and so was the ache in her heart. Because her brothers might know the sacrifices she made, but obviously their father hadn't.

"What does the letter say?" she asked, though her voice was a hoarse whisper.

Joe didn't let go of her, but Judd moved closer until he was right by their sides. "Dad told Glenda that now you were taking care of things that he could leave, too," Judd explained.

Karlee winced because each word felt like a punch. It'd be laughable if it weren't so sick. She'd already had too much weight on her shoulders, but her father had seen her barely passable balancing act as his excuse to kill himself.

"Glenda told us that she got the letter around the same time Dad called her and read the suicide note to her," Judd added.

A note that Glenda hadn't taken seriously enough to do anything about it. Of course, even if she believed something tragic was about to happen, she might not have been able to stop it.

"I'm sorry," Joe muttered. "You don't deserve this shit."

"None of us deserve this shit," she reminded him.

But she appreciated the sentiment and brushed a kiss on his cheek. She gave Judd one, too. And it was when she pulled back that she saw the pain in their eyes.

Pain that would always be there.

"Maybe we just have to suck this up," she said. It was lousy advice, but it was sadly the truth. "There are no do-overs, and I can't go back and fix it."

Joe and Judd exchanged a glance. "But you did fix it," Joe pointed out. He outstretched his arms. "We're all here. All doing well. With the exception of Mack, of course, but he's got that whole baby syndrome fuckup thing going on. He'll get his act together, but he might not have had much of an act if you'd left him in foster care."

Oh, that didn't help the tears, but these were different. There was some happiness in this particular set of waterworks.

"Of course, if you had left Mack in foster care, we wouldn't have all those wrinkles and gray hair," Joe joked. He made a show of looking at her grays. "Man, you got a lot of them."

That earned him an obligatory jab to the ribs, but the light moment didn't last.

"You really had sex with Lucian twice?" Judd asked. "And with three orgasms?"

There it was—already coming back to haunt her. She nodded and waited for the judgment to follow.

"Is he like, well, human when he's with you?" Judd pressed. She nodded again, wondering where the heck this was going. "Then why don't you go see him?" her brother suggested. "Sex can cure a lot of ills. For a little while, anyway."

Yes, it could. Especially sex with Lucian, and her brother had just given her an endorsement rather than a judgment.

"Lucian's still a dickhead," Joe declared.

So, some judgment after all, but it was small considering the other insults they'd doled out about Lucian.

"You want me to drive you to Lucian's place?" Judd asked.

"No, thanks." But she would go to him at the ranch, and she would let him work his magic on the crappy pain she was feeling.

Of course, Lucian could be confronting his father right about now. If so, then it was entirely possible that he would need the magic a whole lot more than she did.

CHAPTER EIGHTEEN

LUCIAN STARED THE Appaloosa gelding right in the eyes. He'd renamed him. The horse formerly known as Outlaw was now Poopy Pants.

Since training and horse whispering wasn't improving his riding time one iota, Lucian had resorted to kindergarten tactics. The Appaloosa probably didn't care diddly about what he was called, but it made Lucian feel better to make fun of him any way that he could.

That *feeling better* probably wouldn't last long though. A shit-kicking horse by any other name was still a shit-kicker. But that still didn't stop Lucian from climbing in the saddle.

"Boss man, you're sure you want to do this?" Skeeter called out to him. "Your mood's a little more sour than usual. Poopy Pants might pick up on that and give you some trouble."

The Appaloosa wouldn't change his behavior even if Lucian showed up carrying a kilo of sugar cubes or a nuke, and giving Lucian some trouble was exactly what the horse had on the agenda.

However, Skeeter was right about Lucian's sour mood. Was probably confused by it, too. Now that Jerry had finally left the ranch and Lucian was back in control, Skeeter likely thought there was nothing to be sour about. But Lucian was back in control of a company that needed plenty of financial attention. Plus, there were the loan sharks.

Lucian doubted they were just going to go away simply because Jerry wasn't here. They might come after Lucian to try to recoup their losses. And that's why he'd called the chief of police before he'd come out for his training ride. He'd also called Glenda so she could give him not only names of the creditors but any details to help him win this fight.

And it was winnable. He refused to believe otherwise.

After all the debts and bad deals that he'd seen in those files Jerry had left on the desk, Lucian knew that he had his work cut out for him. That's why he'd made another call to their chief financial officer. Then to his lawyers. Soon, he'd have a much-clearer picture of what he was up against. He'd also called Sunny so she could start working at the ranch rather than in his San Antonio office. There was a crapload of paperwork to get started, and he'd need Sunny for that.

The one person he hadn't called before heading out to the corral was Karlee. That was despite hearing that she'd cried. It made him sick to his stomach to think those tears were for him, but he wanted her to have as much time as she needed. Time that she might use to tell him to get out of her life once she'd figured out what everyone else knew—that he wasn't good for her.

"Ready, boss?" Skeeter asked.

Lucian nodded, and Skeeter released the gate. As usual, Poopy Pants bolted as if giant bees with eight-foot stingers had popped him on the ass. It took no nudging from Lucian, no prompts. The gelding just started bucking the hell out of him.

That sour mood probably contributed to his and the gelding's attitudes, giving them both more stubbornness than usual, but Lucian just went with the slings, jolts and jounces. With all the recent turmoil in his life, this actually felt a little normal—which wasn't exactly a stomach-settling thought.

Lucian didn't count. No prayers, either. He didn't do anything other than hold on for dear life, and he kept holding on until he heard Skeeter let out a loud whoop.

"Eight seconds, boss man!" Skeeter yelled, and he added more whoops.

Lucian would have done some whooping on his own if at that exact moment, Poopy Pants hadn't managed to throw him. Hard. Of course, all of the throws were hard, and Lucian just tried not to land on his shoulder.

Shit.

He landed on his shoulder.

And he could have sworn he saw big-assed stars as the pain shot through him. God almighty, it was bad. Like a kick-in-the-nuts bad.

As usual, Poopy Pants just sauntered away, leaving him to sit there, grunting and groaning. Thankfully, his unmanly sounds were drowned out by Skeeter's equally unmanly cheers. Lucian suspected the man wouldn't celebrate this much if he'd won the Olympics.

"You want me to get an ambulance out here?" Sunny called out. Lucian hadn't even known she'd made it to the ranch yet, much less to the corral, but she'd clearly seen enough to alarm her.

"No ambulance," he started to say, but someone else said it ahead of him.

Karlee.

At first Lucian thought she was a pain-induced mirage, but she was the real deal. Wearing a slim skirt and heels, she walked past Sunny, greeting his assistant with a smile, but Lucian got no smile from her. Thankfully, no tears, either. However, she did give him a concerned, disapproving look.

"Congrats on the ride." And in the same breath, she added, "Your chin is bleeding."

He hadn't known about the blood, so he swiped at it with the sleeve of his shirt. Yeah, blood all right, but since his chin was the least painful point on his body right now, it wasn't much of a concern.

"You need stitches, which I'm sure you're not going to get. Did you dislocate your shoulder again?" Karlee asked.

He shook his head, giving himself a new jolt of pain. At least it was true though. No dislocation. And it was true about his not getting stitches.

Lucian somehow managed to get to his feet before Karlee reached him. It didn't lessen the pain at all, but at least now he could face her while they talked. It was dignity reducing enough for her to have seen him on his ass like that. He had won, though, so that was something. Not much since it was only practice, but for Lucian it was still a first.

Of course, it wasn't a first for her. This was like déjà vu when she'd had to set his shoulder a couple of months back. Today, though, he noticed all the parts of her that he hadn't allowed himself to notice before. Her eyes. That mouth. Those legs. The way that skirt hugged her butt. He didn't touch her, but that was only because Skeeter had gotten new glasses and might have actually been able to see them.

"You're sure about that ambulance?" Sunny called out.

"We're sure," Karlee and Skeeter answered at the same time Lucian added his "I'm sure."

Skeeter and Karlee knew him well. Sunny huffed as if she didn't care to get to know him that well at all, and she headed back toward the house. Skeeter got off the fence to go take care of the Appaloosa, leaving Karlee and Lucian alone.

"Though it wouldn't hurt for you to see a doctor," Karlee mumbled as she unbuttoned his shirt. It didn't have the same intimate vibe as when they'd had sex, and she seemed to look past his naked chest to examine the shoulder that was still throbbing a mile a minute.

"You're right," she agreed. "It's not dislocated. That makes you a lucky man because it'll save you a trip to the hospital. No, I wasn't going to set it for you again. You would have had to see a doctor for that." She looked up at him. "Now that you've managed to stay on eight seconds, I don't suppose it'd do any good to tell you not to ride Outlaw again?"

"I renamed him Poopy Pants," he corrected.

She lifted her eyebrow, and it seemed as if they had an entire conversation without saying a word. Of course, Lucian didn't need actual words for Karlee to remind him that he was taking his obsession with winning in a bad direction. No way could he argue with that because it was the truth.

"Once I've ridden in the rodeo, and won," he said, "then I'll stop and put Poopy Pants out to pasture."

That wasn't anything she hadn't heard way too many times to count. Well, other than the Poopy Pants part. That was definitely new info for her.

Karlee didn't even respond. She just hooked her arm around his waist to get him moving. Sadly, he needed the help, too, because the pain was zinging through his butt and legs. Still, maybe she'd think he simply wanted her to put her hands on him rather than realize he was hurting more than he intended her to know. Of course, she was maybe hurting more than she wanted to let him know, as well.

"Vita Banchini was here earlier, and she told me you'd been crying," he threw out there.

Karlee practically snapped toward him. "Did she have a vision or something?"

"That's what I asked, too, but apparently no. She knows your mailman."

"Oh" was all she said when she got them moving again. Not toward the house but rather in the direction of the barn.

As far as he was concerned, he didn't care where she was taking him. He just wanted answers, but Lucian had to wait a couple of gut-tightening moments for her to add anything else to that noncommittal response.

"Glenda gave my brothers an old letter from my dad." She dodged his gaze, causing him to curse, since it could mean she was crying again. If so, then he wanted to kick himself for bringing this up. "He thought it would be okay to kill himself since I'd be around to pick up the pieces."

Shit. What a jackass. Of course, that probably wasn't the right way to think of this since Whitt was depressed and all. But what a load of crap to dump on Karlee. From the grave, no less.

"I'm sorry," he told her.

She waved off his apology and led him into the tack room, where she took out the first-aid kit. "The house-keepers are mopping the floors to get rid of the tape residue," she explained. "Best for you not to bleed all over the place. Plus, your mom called in some extra cleaning help, and the place is packed right now."

He agreed but not just because of the blood. Lucian didn't want to interrupt any mopping chores since he wanted that tape gone so they could start returning to normal. Well, the new normal, anyway.

"Regina's letting her dog pee on the clothes Jerry left behind," Karlee went on. "But on the bright side, she no longer seems upset."

Yeah, he'd noticed that as he was coming out to the corral. Regina was giddy with the notion that Jerry had finally been bested.

Karlee pressed a gauze pad to his chin, but her little finger grazed against his lower jaw. For such a little touch, it felt like a whole lot more. Then again, he could be reading into that, what with his body always primed and ready whenever he was around Karlee.

Being this close to her didn't help with the primed and ready. She was close enough that it was possible more than her little finger would brush against him. They were practically body to body with just a sliver of space between them.

"Did you bring me here to have sex with me?" he asked.

She blinked and seemed a lot more stunned than he'd hoped she would be. "No."

"Good. Because barns suck for that sort of thing. Horseshit, splinters, hay poking into your knees and back."

Her smile was as small as that space-sliver between them. "It sounds as if you have some experience with that."

He shrugged. "Having sex in places other than a bed was my specialty years ago, but I ended such shenanigans around the time I graduated from high school. Then my preferred location became trucks."

That had its intended effect. Her smile got a bit bigger. His didn't, though, because she dabbed his chin cut with what felt like battery acid. The grunt he made didn't sound very manly, and he actually checked the bottle to make sure it was indeed alcohol. It was. But hellfire, it burned.

"So, if you didn't come here for barn sex," he managed to continue—after his eyes quit watering from the pain, "then are you here for some TLC because of the letter?"

TLC could lead to sex. He had some experience with that, too, but he wanted to make sure first that Karlee was truly okay. Of course, then he'd need to consider that whole issue about why TLC with her shouldn't be anything more than just that.

She nodded. "I was feeling…raw. And Joe and Judd gave me their blessing to come even though they knew we'd likely end up in bed."

There was a lot for Lucian to consider in those two sentences. He definitely didn't care for the raw part, and it confirmed that he needed to tread slowly. But Karlee had just given him an invitation to tread slowly to the bedroom. Later, he might do just that, too, but for now, that rawness needed some attention. So did what she'd said about her brothers.

"Joe and Judd actually approve of you having sex with me?" Lucian asked.

She rolled her eyes. "Not a chance, but they gave me a free pass because they wanted me to stop crying. Apparently, they believe you're some kind of wizard when it comes to tear stoppage, though they still think you're a dickhead and other assorted things."

That was him in a nutshell, but Lucian liked the part about being able to dry up her tears, and that's why he didn't go in for the kiss when she got the bandage on him. Instead, he just brushed his mouth over her cheek and got them walking out of the tack room. Despite his objections to barn sex, staying put was risky. After all, there was a door that could be shut to give them a false sense of privacy, but the truth was, a hand could come walking in at any time.

"How bad are things?" she asked.

That didn't eliminate the nudging and tugging his body was doing, but Lucian could almost feel the dark cloud forming over his head.

"There's good news," he said. "You can use the back pasture for your herd."

"Thank you. But how bad?" she repeated.

"It could be worse. That's the truth," he added when she huffed. "I should be able to use the half of the assets that Jerry couldn't touch to pay off the debts, and I'm hoping I can convince Glenda's business associates to quit hounding me through Jerry."

Karlee stayed quiet a moment while they walked up the steps of the back porch. "But Jerry still owns forty-nine percent of Granger Enterprises. That means when you pay off the debts and the company is viable again, then the loan sharks might force Jerry to sell to them. They wouldn't have majority share, but they could make your life miserable."

They would indeed. "But they can't touch the ranch. That's protected from being folded into Granger Enterprise assets."

Though Jerry did own a good chunk of the ranch. And the house. Lucian was going to see what he could do about that because as far as he was concerned, Jerry was never coming back.

They made it into the sunroom when he spotted Dylan coming toward them. One look at his brother's face, and Lucian knew something was wrong.

"Hell, what now?" Lucian snarled.

Dylan handed him some papers that he'd been holding. "They're from Candy," he explained. "She's suing us."

Lucian had had so much rough news lately that he didn't even bother cursing. "Hasn't she heard that Jerry is no longer in control?"

"Yep. But apparently she's riled at you for the blowup with the pictures of Jerry and Darlene."

Great. Now his dad's ex-fiancée was blaming the messenger. "I told her not to go to Bennie with those pictures."

Dylan lifted his shoulder. "Well, she's blaming you for it anyway. Candy's lawyers are working to put a freeze on all assets connected to Granger Enterprises."

Now Lucian cursed. He'd just gotten the freeze lifted after he'd ousted Jerry. "On what grounds?" he asked.

"Apparently, Jerry used a lot of Candy's money to hold off his creditors, and she has the signed papers to prove it." Dylan growled out some of his curse words. "Hoo-Poo is gunning for a takeover of Granger Enterprises."

CHAPTER NINETEEN

WHILE KARLEE SAT at the kitchen table, she jotted down some notes, and since Sunny was already reading them from over her shoulder, Karlee handed them to her.

"You really think gourmet chocolate, Irish whiskey and hydrogen peroxide will be necessary for the meeting tomorrow morning?" Sunny asked.

"Maybe not, but you should have those things on hand."

Karlee had come to that conclusion after learning who'd be at the meeting that Lucian had scheduled for 8:00 a.m. Candy, Glenda and Eddie Smith, aka the lawyer representing the loan sharks that Jerry owed so much money.

"In nearly every picture that Mr. Smith posted on social media, he has a shot of whiskey in his hand. So either he's an alcoholic or he merely likes his booze. Also, his mother is an O'Neill from Dublin, so that's why I suggested Irish whiskey. If he doesn't want a shot, he can put it in his coffee. Just keep the bottle visible."

Sunny nodded, but there was still some skepticism in her expression. "And the chocolate?"

"For Candy. Yes, I know it sounds like a cliché, what with her name, but according to the housekeepers, she had chocolate delivered from that site I listed in the notes. Call them and have them overnight a box of her favorites."

A nod, a deep breath and more skepticism from Sunny's bunched-up forehead. "And the hydrogen peroxide?"

"For Lucian. He'll tighten his jaw so much that it'll likely open up the cut on his chin. Put the hydrogen peroxide and some gauze pads in his top right drawer. Also, make sure there's tea for Candy and Glenda."

Not that Karlee particularly wanted either woman to feel welcome or catered to, but she wanted this meeting to go as smoothly as possible. Even though it was highly unlikely they could reach a solution that would satisfy all of them.

"Should I have Abe make pastries or something?" Sunny asked.

"God, no. He's a horrible cook, and he won't be up that early anyway. Just order something from the diner."

Sunny stared at her. "If Abe's such a bad cook, then why is he, well, the cook?"

Karlee only shrugged, but she figured the reason Lucian kept him around was because Abe had looked after Lucian and his brothers when all hell had broken loose with Jerry running off with her mother. Of course, the *looking after* hadn't included any edible cooking, but in his own minimal-communication sort of way, Abe had made sure they didn't do anything reckless enough to get killed.

"Lucian always takes those brown paper bags that Abe gives him, too," Karlee muttered, but she was talking to herself. That might be another reason Lucian kept the cook around. She didn't know what was in those bags, and when she'd found them in the trash a couple of times, they'd been empty.

"Okay, I'll get these things," Sunny said, going through the list again. "And then I need to get some sleep. I'll be in the guesthouse if anybody asks." She headed for the door, but then stopped. "Are you sure you don't want your job back? You're obviously a lot better at it than I am."

Karlee shook her head to the question. She definitely didn't want to work for Lucian again. "You'll figure it all out."

Sunny made a sound to indicate that might never happen, and she walked away, still studying her notes.

Karlee checked the time—already after ten, which meant she'd be staying the night, too, rather than driving back to her apartment. The question was—which bed would she be in? Since she wanted the answer to that to be Lucian's, she headed toward his office, where she'd last seen him. And he was still there, poring over the files that Jerry had left him. She doubted there was anything in them that he hadn't already discovered, but prepping and reprepping were Lucian's way of managing stress.

He looked up at her, their gazes connecting. Other than fatigue and worry, she didn't see much else in his eyes, but she figured there were other things simmering beneath the surface. All that flirting and sex talk in the tack room hopefully meant her time wasn't up with him just yet. That's why she shut the door and locked it.

She went to the bar, poured him a drink and set it on the desk. He still didn't take his eyes off her when she swiveled his chair around and eased down onto his lap. Straddling him. The motion automatically pushed up her skirt to her thighs.

"I know barn sex is out, but how do you feel about another round of office sex?" she asked. She draped her hands, first one and then the other, around his neck.

His intense stare didn't get any less intense, and for several heart-stopping moments she thought he might reject her and send her on her way.

But he didn't.

With a firm push on her back, Lucian brought her right against him, and he kissed her. The relief flooded through her, but it quickly got replaced by the heat the kiss generated.

"Don't move your chin too much," she reminded him.

If he heard her, Lucian ignored the advice because he continued the kiss the way he did everything else in his life. He left no stone unturned. That was especially true when he ran his hand up her top and into her bra.

Of course, he lowered his head and kissed her there, too, and soon, very soon, Karlee forgot all about hurt chins, meetings with loan sharks and the dire mess of the business. Heck, it was possible that she forgot how to breathe, but she was certain of one thing.

She could feel every inch of her body.

Could feel some inches of his body, too, because he already had an erection. Good. She enjoyed foreplay, but tonight it was the orgasm she was after. Not just for herself but for him. She was betting that would work faster and better than the bourbon she'd just poured him.

The fire in her body got hotter with each lick of his tongue, each nip and each bit of pressure from his clever fingers. It hadn't taken much time at all to send her from the "I want you" stage to the "I need you now," and she tried to let him know that by touching him, too. Specifically, she slid her hand over the front of his jeans and cupped him.

Lucian got the message all right. He made a grunt of pleasure, and while still kissing her breasts, he lowered his grip so he could pull down her panties. That meant her standing up for a couple of seconds so he could rid her of them, but when she dropped back onto his lap, Karlee made sure her skirt was up enough not to get in their way.

But what was in their way were his jeans. It would have been fun to get him naked again, but then he touched her in just the right spot. Her spot was pretty easy to find, too, now that the panties were gone. He touched and kissed until Karlee knew if she didn't do something fast that she'd be having a solo orgasm.

She unzipped him. Not easily. He was huge and hard, his erection straining against his jeans, but she finally managed to free him from his boxers.

"Condom," he growled.

It was an exercise in frustration that he had to stop and retrieve the condom from his wallet in his back pocket. All the shifting and moving around nearly gave Karlee that premature orgasm after all. But finally he got the darn thing on, and he didn't waste even a second pushing into her.

Wow. There it was. That shot of pleasure so undiluted that she had to fight just to hold on for the big finale. Lucian was very good at all parts of sex, but he was especially good at the end. He moved inside, guiding her hips with his firm grip, all the while he watched her face.

Actually, he watched as he pushed her right over the edge.

The corner of his mouth lifted, the smile of victory, and he kissed her, dragging her right against him when he pushed into her one last time.

Oh yes. This was much better than the bourbon.

LUCIAN WAS READY for this meeting. He'd collected all the information he needed, and he'd tanked up on enough coffee to give him that wired and dangerous look. He was also still pissed off enough at what'd happened with Jerry that he knew he had an edge.

An edge that most people liked to avoid.

Maybe that meant this meeting would be short and sweet. Or at least short. Because he took one look at Candy and realized she was going to be anything but sweet this morning. Teetering on heels so high and thin that they could have been used for drill bits, she scowled at him when she came into his office. She gave another scowl at the opened box of chocolates that Sunny had put out, but Candy's surly facial expression didn't stop her from helping herself to several pieces.

Three guys in suits came in behind Candy, and even though they didn't introduce themselves, Lucian knew who they were. Candy's lawyers, who were on retainer from Hoo-Poo. Lucian had purposely made sure there weren't enough seats for them. Maybe if their legs got tired, then they'd encourage Candy to back off on the lawsuit.

Well, a cowboy could dream, anyway.

"I want a cup of tea with milk to cool it down," Candy snarled to Sunny, who hurried to the other side of the room to pour the woman a cup. Later, Lucian would commend Sunny for being so prepared. He'd thank Karlee, too, since she had no doubt coached his new assistant.

When Sunny handed Candy the tea, the woman gulped it down as if it were the cure for all ills. Lucian wished that it did indeed have that capability. If so, he would have guzzled several pots of it.

He heard the footsteps, and several moments later, Eddie Smith, his second visitor, appeared, and Lucian saw that Karlee had escorted him in. The two were chatting, and Eddie must have liked the conversation because he was smiling.

Karlee made eye contact with Lucian. *Brief* eye contact. Maybe to give him some moral support. Lucian's eye contact probably had a lot more heat in it than hers. After all, he'd had sex with her right here in this office just the night before. But that was a sweet memory best pushed aside to savor later. For now, he had to deal with a dick, one that wasn't located behind the zipper of his own jeans.

Lucian hadn't really given a lot of thought as to how Eddie Smith would look, but after seeing the lawyer when he stepped into the office, Lucian was certain he hadn't been expecting *this*. No snake-oil salesman look. No Godfather jowls or black suit. Eddie was wearing jeans and a Green Day T-shirt. Lucian also didn't miss the hound-dog look the slimeball gave Karlee as she turned around and went back up the hall. Slimeball gave the same treatment to Sunny. Then Candy, who scowled at him.

Candy knew who Eddie was, and when Lucian had set up the meeting, he'd told Candy that Eddie would be there. Apparently, she didn't approve of that, or maybe, like Lucian, she was just pissed off in general about a lot of things.

"Thanks for setting up this meeting, Lucian," Eddie

greeted, and he grinned a big toothy grin better suited for a sitcom than this meeting.

If Lucian hadn't had other reasons to distrust the guy, that would have done it. For one thing, there was zilch to smile about, and he figured the casual attire was meant to put him at ease. It didn't work, but then, that would have been asking a lot of mere clothes.

"You didn't give me a choice about this meeting," Lucian countered. "Things are fucked-up, and we need to unfuck them."

"My clients agree," Eddie quickly said. He took a paper from his briefcase and slid it across Lucian's desk. "And here are the terms."

There wasn't much on the paper, just a summary of Jerry's debts, which were in the two-million-dollar ballpark. Lucian figured most of that was interest. Beneath that figure were the so-called terms.

Shit.

"You want Jerry's forty-nine percent of Granger Enterprises to cancel out the debt," Lucian summarized. "Any reason you didn't just go to my father with this?"

Eddie nodded. "We did, and he said he'd leave it up to you." And Eddie gave Lucian another paper verifying that.

Well, that was a surprise. Not that Lucian especially wanted this particular "gift." It was a damned if he did, damned if he didn't kind of situation. If he gave up Jerry's shares, Granger Enterprises would be joined at the hip with the likes of Eddie and his equally slimy clients. If Lucian said no, he'd have to pony up from his own personal assets to cover the debts. It would stretch him very thin, but it was doable. Still, he wasn't sure if more of the debts weren't going to come to light. There was no telling what kind of stupid deals Jerry had made when he was trying to recover his losses.

"Wait a doggone minute," Candy howled before Lucian could even respond to Eddie. "I want Jerry's forty-nine percent to cover the money he borrowed from me. You're not giving it to those thugs."

Eddie sure didn't smile about that. "My clients aren't thugs. They're businessmen who provide a valuable service to other businessmen in need of quick cash."

"They're thugs, and they're not getting what's rightfully mine," Candy argued, whipping around to face Lucian. She aimed her Pepto-Bismol-pink-painted index finger at him. "Jerry took money from my family's estate, and I intend to be compensated for that."

"Money would compensate you," Lucian pointed out.

Though it was another damned if he did, damned if he didn't situation, and Lucian hadn't wanted to wrangle with one of them, much less two. He couldn't pay off both Candy and the loan sharks without wiping out the company and some of his personal assets, but he could ask his brothers to chip in. Which they would do the second they heard of this problem. Then the whole family could be in financial hot water. Despite what everyone thought, the Grangers didn't just have an extra four million lying around.

Candy gave her head an indignant wobble. "I've decided I don't want money. I want Jerry's shares."

The trio of lawyers all voiced varying words of agreement.

Eddie didn't do the head wobble, but he gave Candy a look that could have frozen El Paso in August. "My clients have a right to those shares since their loan to Jerry Granger happened months before yours."

"Neither of you has a right to the shares unless I say so," Lucian reminded them. He held up the paper Eddie had given him to remind him of that. "For now, I'm not selling anything."

Candy huffed, her breath making it all the way across the desk to Lucian's nose. Those chocolate and tea scents came through loud and clear. "Hear this, Lucian Granger. Either you sign over Jerry's shares right now, or I'll tie up Granger Enterprises in litigation for years. And then I'll go after the ranch, since Jerry owns half of that, too."

With that threat, Candy spun on her teetering heels and strutted out, her legal team right behind her.

"She can't touch the ranch," Eddie grumbled. "The terms of your great-grandfather's will won't allow it."

Lucian knew that. The assets weren't shared between the ranch and the business. Still, Candy was right about being able to put Granger Enterprises in a legal circus that could go on, well, much longer than Lucian wanted it to.

"You've got a lot to think about," Eddie added when he stood and picked up his briefcase. "Just remember this. My clients are powerful men. Would you rather go up against them or the Hoo-Poo heiress?"

Lucian didn't want either of them with their fingers in his business, and no matter which way he went, that would happen. And that meant he needed to find another angle on this.

"You can let yourself out," Lucian told Eddie, and he gave Eddie a Lucifer glare when the man tried to continue his argument. "I'll be in touch," Lucian added, and he waited until Eddie was out of the office before he took out his phone to make a call.

A call he didn't want to make.

But he needed another angle on this, one that wasn't necessarily going to appeal to anyone. Still, it might be his last-ditch option.

Lucian pressed in the number, and he didn't have to wait long before Glenda answered.

"Come to the ranch tomorrow morning at ten o'clock," Lucian told her, and he made sure it sounded like the order that it was. "We've got things to discuss."

The moment that Glenda gave him an "okay," he made his next call. To Jerry. Like Glenda, his father answered on the first ring.

"I don't want to hear another apology," Lucian warned him right off. "Just listen and do exactly what I tell you. Meet me at our lawyer's office in San Antonio at eight in the morning. For once in your miserable life, you're going to do the right thing."

CHAPTER TWENTY

KARLEE HATED PACING and fidgeting. It was such a waste of time, but she couldn't make herself stop. Added to the paces and fidgets, she was also checking the window every few seconds, keeping watch for Lucian's return from San Antonio.

Since it'd been nearly three hours since he left, she was beginning to worry. Or rather, the worrying was starting to escalate. Karlee had been in the high anxiety/anxious zone since Lucian's meeting the day before with Eddie and Candy. The outcome of that hadn't been good, and now she had to hope that it went better with Jerry. Even though Jerry had a horrible track record when it came to Lucian and the rest of his family.

She hadn't pressed Lucian on the details of what he actually wanted to accomplish by seeing his father. That was mainly because Lucian hadn't given her a chance to ask. He'd stayed busy, working in his office while fielding multiple calls from his lawyers. Judging from Lucian's growly attitude, nothing had gone right. And he hadn't come to her in the guest room, either. Karlee tried not to take that personally, but of course, she did.

When it came to Lucian, everything was personal.

Regina walked by the living room and stopped when she saw Karlee. "Any chance you could pace over here in this spot?" She pointed to the area behind the sofa.

"There are still some tape residue marks that could use a little wear."

Regina smiled to let her know that was a bad attempt at a joke, and she went to her, pulling Karlee into her arms for a hug. "Lucian's messing with your head, huh?"

She opened her mouth to answer a firm no, but Regina would know it was a lie. Yeah, there was some head messing going on, and Karlee had given Lucian an engraved invitation to do just that.

"I'm sorry this didn't all work out for you," Regina went on when she eased back from her. "I mean, you got your own company. That's good. But the rest seems to have gone to pot."

Yes. Well, maybe. She was having sex with Lucian, and that certainly wasn't pot related.

"He's always been a hard kid to figure out," Regina added. "Always carrying stuff on his back as if there were no other backs around to carry stuff. Still, it's getting better for him."

Karlee just stared at her. "You do know that both Candy and the loan sharks want Jerry's chunk of Granger Enterprises?"

Regina shrugged. "Yes, that's a problem, but if there's a fix to it, then Lucian will find it." She chuckled. "Hey, I guess that's why he puts so much on his back, huh?"

Yes, because it was expected. Not just by Regina but also by Lucian.

"The one thing I hate most about this is that the engagement didn't work out between Lucian and you," Regina continued. "Any chance it'll happen for real?"

Karlee was trying to figure out how not to answer that while staying polite, but she got a reprieve. The sound of a vehicle approaching the house. Without even glancing out the window, she hurried into the foyer and threw open the front door. No Lucian though.

It was the florist.

"Good. You're here," the teenager said when he got out of the Smell the Roses van. Karlee knew him. He was Eric, one of the Busby boys who were known more for their troublemaking than their floral delivery abilities. Still, he took out not one but three bouquets.

They were the dreaded yellow roses.

"These are for me?" Karlee backed up a step, but Eric practically dumped one in each of her arms. Regina got the third.

"Yeah," Eric verified. "Since they're from Lucian, I guess that means you two are breaking up again?"

Of course, he knew the meaning of yellow roses. Everyone in town probably did because there'd been so many of the bouquets dispatched over the years.

"The tip's already taken care of," Eric said, "but you can add more if you want."

Karlee shut the door in his face, and she immediately checked the card on one of the bouquets. "Lucian"—that was all it said. Ditto for the other one.

"Lucian," Regina confirmed when she read the one on the flowers she was holding. "I'm thinking these must be a mistake. You should talk to Sunny about it."

Regina was right, and Karlee decided before she dropped down deep into a pit of despair, she would indeed talk to Lucian's assistant. She went to put the flowers on the foyer table, but when she remembered it was one of the things that Jerry had sold, she set them on the floor instead.

And she heard the sound of an approaching vehicle. She threw open the door, figuring that this time it had to be Lucian, but again she was wrong. The visitor was Glenda. It wasn't a total surprise that her mother was there. After all, it was getting close to the 10:00 a.m. meeting that Lucian had set up with her, but Karlee hadn't especially wanted to have this face-to-face. Glenda seemed to pick up on that, too.

"If Lucian's not ready to see me, I can wait in my car," Glenda offered.

"He's not back from San Antonio yet." Karlee cleared her throat to continue and hated that this woman could still jangle her nerves. "But you can go to his office. His assistant should be in there."

Glenda nodded, stepped into the foyer, and that's when her attention landed on Regina. "Oh, I didn't know that you'd be here… I'm sorry." And Glenda hurried off in the direction of Lucian's office.

Regina didn't have nearly as strong a reaction. She merely shrugged. "If you talk to her, let her know that I'm over what happened."

Karlee doubted that. Glenda and Jerry had created wounds that would never completely heal. Regina had likely made the comment for Karlee's sake, and she showed her appreciation by giving Regina a hug.

And then Karlee went after Glenda.

She caught up with her mother just outside Lucian's door, and Glenda immediately turned around to face her. "I know Joe and Judd gave you the letter from your father," Glenda said before Karlee could even bring it up. "I know it hurt."

Karlee couldn't gloss this over as Regina had just done. "It did. I just want to make sure there's nothing else. No more letters. No more phone conversations that you happen to remember. I want it all out in the open so I can finish this once and for all."

"You can do that, *finish it*?" Glenda asked. There was no snark but rather the tone of a woman in search of answers.

"Yes."

She didn't elaborate, didn't tell her mother that she didn't want to spend another moment of time in that dark place that Jerry, Whitt and Glenda had created. She wasn't that scared kid anymore and had enough current fears and concerns to keep her occupied.

At the exact second Karlee had that thought, her biggest concern came walking up the hall. Lucian. She didn't run to him and jump into his arms, though that's what Karlee wanted to do. Nor did she batter him with questions—like the meeting with Jerry or the flowers. But she did go to him and ran her fingers over the back of his hand.

Mercy, he looked exhausted, but she doubted he would want her to make a fuss about that. Especially in front of Glenda.

"Wait in my office," Lucian told Glenda. "I'll be there in a minute."

He waited until Glenda was out of sight before he brushed a kiss on Karlee's forehead. Definitely not the scorcher foreplay kiss like the night before. "I need a little time before I see Glenda," he whispered with his mouth still against her skin.

She nodded, looped her arm around his waist and got him moving up the hall. Karlee just stayed quiet and waited until they were in his bedroom. Lucian immediately sank down onto the foot of his bed and scrubbed his hand over his face. She doubted that meant the meeting had been positive.

"Jerry signed over his portion of both the ranch and the house to Dylan and me," Lucian finally said after some long moments. "He also did the paperwork to give me power of attorney to handle his shares in Granger Enterprises. That includes selling them if I see fit."

That certainly wasn't the bad news that Karlee had steeled herself up to hear. "Uh, that's good, right?"

"Good news about the house and ranch," he clarified. "It won't do anything to solve the problems with the business. Still, it's a start. This way, Jerry can't come back here months or years from now and try to ruin everything that I'm going to have to fix."

Karlee didn't ask if it was fixable, and she figured even Lucian didn't know if it was. Still, he would try.

"Jerry did ask that I help him get rid of the loan sharks," Lucian went on. "In fact, he wanted to make it a condition before signing over everything to me, but I told him the time for conditions was over."

She agreed. Jerry wasn't in any position to ask favors from Lucian. It wasn't only the damage he'd done to the business, either. It was the family heirlooms he'd sold from the house. The Grangers might never be able to recover all of that.

"I want you to come to the meeting with Glenda," he added. "Unless it'll be too uncomfortable for you."

It'd be uncomfortable all right, but there's no way she'd skip it now that Lucian had asked.

She nodded, went to him, put her arms around him and kissed him. She didn't make it one of those pecks, either. This was a real kiss, and Lucian slipped right into it. He pulled her down on his lap and took her mouth as if he'd declared war on it. Lots of pressure and intensity.

Karlee didn't mind. She just let him kiss this out, the way a runner would when pushing every muscle in his body toward the finish line. Except in their case, this was as far as things could go. For now, anyway. Best not to initiate full-blown sex when he needed to go to the meeting.

When he pulled back from the kiss, he looked at her. "I'm using you," he said.

She was sure she flinched a little. "I think that only applies if I'm not getting anything out of this. And I am."

"I fail at shit like this," he added.

"You've never failed at shit like this with me." Karlee tried to add a smile to that, but it wasn't a joke, and she didn't want to soothe this over by trying to keep it light. She needed Lucian to see that this could be good between them.

And maybe he did.

But if so, he dismissed it when he eased her off his lap and stood.

"By the way, I didn't intend to send the flowers that I saw in the foyer," Lucian said.

She tried to push away the ache at Lucian changing the subject. Especially since what they'd been talking about was important. Well, to her, anyway. To Lucian, maybe it was just another item on his agenda that he felt he'd need to deal with.

"Sunny must have screwed up," he continued a moment later. He went to the door but continued explaining the snafu while his back was to her. "She probably put in some kind of repeating order when she did the last ones I sent you. When we end this, it won't be with flowers."

Before the last words could even register in Karlee's mind, Lucian had already opened the door and was heading to his office. She followed him, somehow managing to get her feet moving, though it wasn't easy. And all because of that "when."

Not *if.*

So in Lucian's mind, their relationship was just like all his other ones. Temporary. However, she was pretty sure he'd feel worse about theirs than the rest because in addition to being lovers, they were also friends.

Yes, losing that would hurt.

Which was why he'd likely resisted this in the first place, but Karlee didn't regret it. Even temporary was better than not ever having him. And with that heart-breaking thought still running through her head, she mentally put on her big-girl panties so she could face her mother.

Maybe this meeting would produce results to fix the nightmare Jerry had started. Along with Glenda's help, of course. After all, it'd been her mother who had partly caused Jerry's financial troubles, and then Glenda had made things worse by introducing him to the loan sharks.

Glenda was seated, but she immediately stood when Lucian and Karlee walked into his office. She spared Lucian a glance, but her attention stayed on Karlee.

"You're upset," Glenda said, her breath uneven and the concern in her eyes. "I'm so sorry about that letter."

Ironically, the letter was no longer on the top ten things that were bothering her, but Karlee had no intention of telling Glenda what was actually wrong. Besides, this meeting wasn't about her. It was about Lucian and his family's business.

Sunny was in the room near the bar where she'd just made coffee, but after Lucian gave her a glance, the assistant excused herself and closed the door behind her.

Glenda took out some papers and handed them to Lucian. "That's Melcor's one percent. I'm giving it to you."

Lucian mumbled a thanks, but it didn't exactly sound heartfelt. With reason. Glenda shouldn't have meddled in this in the first place.

"Were you able to use the info I sent you about the loan sharks?" Glenda asked Lucian.

"In a way. It let me know who I was dealing with." Dragging in a long breath, he sat behind his desk, and Karlee took the chair next to Glenda. "I won't remind you that it was stupid and reckless to unleash those men on Jerry, and now they're coming after Granger Enterprises."

Glenda took a loud breath, too. A short and choppy one. "I was afraid of that. I'm so sorry."

Lucian didn't even acknowledge her apology. "You're not the only one of Jerry's lovers to cause trouble. Candy's also suing for Jerry's shares. Yes, the very shares the loan sharks want." He leaned in. "So, you can see my problem."

Glenda nodded. "I can call Eddie Smith and try to fix this. I'll see if I can get him to back off."

"You've already called him, already asked him to back off, and it hasn't worked," Lucian quickly pointed out.

"I can try again," Glenda insisted. But she stopped, shook her head and then stayed quiet a moment. "I can buy Jerry's shares, and you can use the money to pay off the loan sharks."

Karlee felt an instant jolt of relief. Lucian, however,

didn't look relieved in the least. In fact, he huffed, and he was almost certainly about to decline, though Karlee didn't know why.

Glenda must have realized what he was about to do as well because she shook her head. "There's more. Honestly, Lucian, I can fix this. When the dust has settled after I buy Jerry's shares, then I'll sign over my shares to you."

CHAPTER TWENTY-ONE

LUCIAN STOOD AT the window and watched the sun come up. He'd been on both sides of seeing plenty of sunrises. Those when he'd woken up early to get started on work. Others, in his younger days, when he was coming home late and hadn't gotten to bed yet. But this sunrise viewing was thanks to a restless night.

Everything kept circling in his head. Too many moving parts in what used to be his business and his life. He glanced back at one of those moving parts.

Karlee, who was asleep in his bed.

He hadn't turned her away when he'd seen the "look" she'd given him the night before. Hell, he hadn't even hesitated a second before he'd kissed her and taken her to his room for sex. And just like the other times they'd been together, it'd been great. But Lucian knew each time he was with her, he was just chipping away at her heart. Karlee deserved better than that.

His family deserved better, too. He was the fixer, the one they could rely on, but he wasn't sure he could make this work. That ate away at him, and Lucian figured the eating away would continue for a long time.

"You're thinking so loud I can hear you in my sleep," Karlee mumbled.

Lucian glanced back at her. She was on her stomach, naked, with the sheet draped across her butt and lower back. That'd been his doing as he'd eased out of bed about an hour earlier.

One thing he'd learned from sharing a bed with her was that she was the exact opposite of a cover hog. Instead, she kicked off quilts and even pillows, and a great portion of that bedding had ended up on Lucian's face. He had put the sheet back over her so she wouldn't get cold, but she had whittled down the coverage to only about a foot of her body.

She lifted her head, yawned and gave him a sleepy smile. "So, what's worrying you most?" she asked. "The rodeo, the business, Glenda's offer or me?"

"All of the above," he admitted. Though the rodeo was the least of his concerns. Ironic since it'd been such a big dream all his life.

Karlee sat up, dragging the covers over her breasts. Even though he was enjoying the view, that was probably a good thing. If he saw too much of her, it might entice him to crawl back in that bed for some morning sex. Best not to add another level of complication to those whirling thoughts in his head.

"You're not going to take Glenda up on her offer?" she asked.

It was tempting. God, was it. But one of those repeating thoughts was the financials he'd read on Karlee's mother. "This could wipe Glenda out. She has rental properties and gets income from that, but it wouldn't be enough for her to keep up the lifestyle she has now."

Of course, if he pointed that out to her, Glenda would just say she could change her lifestyle. And she would. Lucian could smell bullshit, and Glenda wasn't BSing him about her offer. She would indeed buy the shares, give them to him and then try to cobble her life back together. In other words, she'd do exactly what Lucian was trying to do now.

"What Glenda's offering is generous," Lucian said a moment later, "but if she did this, then the loan sharks would come after her. Judging from my dealings with Eddie, he'd apply lots of pressure for her to sell to them. Maybe even more than pressure. And she'd be without the ample finances to block him."

He glanced at Karlee to see how she reacted to that, and he didn't think it was his imagination that she'd gone a little pale. Lucian didn't know if Eddie's bosses would resort to violence, but they were loan sharks. That alone meant Glenda shouldn't be dealing with them.

"This isn't Glenda's fight," he clarified.

"But she is Melcor, and she was the one who introduced Jerry to those men," Karlee quickly pointed out, but then she shook her head. "Still, you're right. She shouldn't have to go up against loan sharks. Too bad there's not a way to hold Jerry's feet to the fire on this."

Yeah, too bad. Even though Jerry had lost everything, it didn't feel as if he'd been punished quite enough. He'd swooped in on Granger Enterprises at the first sign of trouble. All starting with that blasted Hairy Corn Salad. And Jerry had used it as an excuse to take over and bleed the family's funds.

"I've arranged a meeting with my mother, Lawson and Dylan this morning," Lucian told her. "Our sister, Lily Rose, will be coming, too."

She got up from the bed, winding the sheet around her as she walked toward him. "You'll still have time to get ready for the rodeo?"

It was a legit question. Normally, he spent the morning of the rodeo at the fairgrounds where the event was held. It was a ritual for him to mull over every angle that the bronc could possibly buck. Obviously, it was a shitty ritual since he'd never won anyway. Still, he would have stuck to it if his life hadn't been going to hell in a crap-lined handbasket.

Karlee went to his side, and since he was wearing only his boxers, they stood there, naked arm to naked arm.

"We'll be discussing Glenda's offer at the meeting," Lucian went on. "So, you're welcome to be there if you want."

She looked up at him, studying his eyes. It definitely wasn't her "take me to bed now" silent invitation. Instead, she seemed to be trying to suss out what he was thinking.

Good luck with that.

Lucian was still mulling things over. Not some things, either. *Everything.*

A slight smile crossed her lips, and he didn't think it was a smile of happiness. Now he was the one trying to figure out what was going on in her head, but she dodged his gaze before he could even come close to doing that.

"Thanks for including me, but I'll pass on the meeting. I just hope it all works out the way you want it to." Karlee brushed a quick kiss on his mouth. A strange kiss because it felt different from any other kiss she'd ever given him.

She went back across the room and put on her clothes as she gathered them up from the floor. "I've got a few things to do before the rodeo," she said, still not looking at him. "But maybe this is a good time for us to tie up a loose end."

"Which one?" he asked.

She did that little smile again. *"Us,"* she said. "I

think this is the day for both of us to move on. I promise I won't send you flowers."

While he stood there, speechless, Karlee gave him another quick kiss and walked out.

KARLEE WAS THANKFUL she made it all the way from Lucian to the upstairs guest room before the tears came. She cursed them—again. Then she cursed herself. She'd cried more in the past couple of months over Lucian than she had in the past decade. And it had to stop.

Now.

Of course the angry pep talk didn't work, and she ended up crying through her shower and while she dressed. She'd brought a pair of jeans with her, but the only top was her green silk business shirt. The only shoes, a pair of black heels. The outfit didn't exactly scream rodeo wear and the top was slightly wrinkled since it had lain the night away on Lucian's bedroom floor, but it wasn't stinky and would have to do.

Thankfully, she had makeup with her, and she slapped on enough of the stuff to cover up the worst of her splotchy face. Nothing she could do about her red eyes, but maybe she'd get lucky and no one would notice before she got out to her car. That way she could drive around, check on her cattle and figure out how to get past this sickening knot in the pit of her stomach.

Despite the knot, she knew this was the right thing to do. Like pulling off a dirty bandage from a still-sore wound. It hurt like the devil but it was necessary for healing.

She'd seen the look in Lucian's eyes. Had known that he was trying to wrap his mind around how to end things with her so that she wouldn't be hurt, and she had made it easy for him. Now he'd have a better chance of focusing on the meeting with his siblings.

And she stood a better chance of, well, she wasn't sure what yet.

But she'd had a life before Lucian, and she would have one afterward. She still had goals, still wanted a family and her own business, and she could have all those things. She just couldn't have them with Lucian.

Gathering her purse and overnight bag, Karlee threw open the door to find Jordan there, her hand lifted and ready to knock. Jordan wasn't alone, either. She had Corbin with her. Her friend was smiling until her attention landed on Karlee's face.

"You've been crying," Jordan blurted out.

So much for the notion of no one noticing. "I'm all right." But the moment she said it, Karlee frowned. Jordan did, too, because she knew it was a lie. "Okay, I'm not actually all right, yet, but I will be."

She hoped that was true. At the moment it felt as if a gorilla was squeezing her heart and chest. Despite that, Karlee forced a smile, picked up Corbin and gave him a noisy, sloppy kiss along with goosing his belly. Corbin's laughter was like magic. It didn't cure her ills, but it instantly made her feel a little better.

"Lucian broke up with you," Jordan concluded, pulling Karlee into her arms the moment Karlee put Corbin down.

Since little ears were right there, and so was one of the housekeepers, Karlee kept her answer profanity free along with tugging Jordan into the guest room with her. "No, actually I broke up with him. A preemptive strike," she added when Jordan pulled back to stare at her. "In hindsight, maybe the timing sucks a little because of the rodeo, but I didn't want him worrying about me during the family meeting."

Jordan made a face. "How do you know Lucian wanted to end things? Because I'm not even sure Lucian knows what he wants right now."

Oh, Karlee was sure of it. He wanted his life back, with all the pieces in place. The only piece he likely wouldn't have was Amelia. That particular ship had sailed, but she figured it would be a long time before he told another woman he loved her. If he'd indeed said that to Amelia. More likely, though, it had been a different kind of term of endearment.

I need you.

Yes, that would have been Lucian's way of throwing his heart at Amelia's feet. In the end, that hadn't worked, though, even after Amelia had realized he was the best thing since rosemary-garlic cheese-crusted bread.

Jordan glanced at the stairs. "The family meeting starts in a few minutes, and Dylan wants me there, but I don't want to leave you like this."

"Go," Karlee insisted. "Do you have someone to watch Corbin?"

Jordan shook her head. "I was going to take him with me."

"Bad idea." Unlike this conversation, that one would likely be riddled with a whole bunch of cussing. "Why don't I take Corbin out to see my cattle, and then you can meet us at the rodeo?"

That would accomplish not only Corbin not being in the meeting, but Karlee was far less likely to cry around her nephew. Plus, she'd be away from the ranch where she could easily run into Lucian. She wasn't ready to see him just yet. Actually, she wasn't sure she'd be ready to see him in a week or two, but she was going to force herself to be there for his bronc ride.

"You're sure?" Jordan asked.

"Positive." That was more wishful thinking than anything. Another crying jag still might happen.

Jordan nodded, muttered a thanks. "So that you don't have to move the booster seat for Corbin, take my car. It's in the side driveway, and the keys are in the ignition."

The only problem with that was the side driveway was next to Lucian's office. But maybe he was so engrossed in the details of the meeting that he wouldn't even look out. Besides, other than this morning, she'd never known him to be much for staring out windows.

Karlee took Corbin by the hand and headed downstairs. She lucked out, too. No Grangers crossed her path before she made it out the door. However, Karlee found a much-bigger obstacle outside. Before she made it to Jordan's car, Joe pulled up in his truck.

"Uncle Joe!" Corbin squealed, and he ran to him so that Joe could scoop him up.

There were fist bumps, noogies, grunts and other manly exchanges of affection. However, that affection didn't last long when Joe's attention landed on her.

"You've been crying," he growled. Joe didn't curse, not verbally, but she could practically hear the words flying out of his mouth, and some of those words would be Joe's repeated threat to kick Lucian's ass.

Karlee went to him and brushed what she hoped would be a soothing kiss on his cheek along with giving him a "don't do anything stupid" warning glare. "If you have to say anything related to *L-u-c-i-a-n*, then use pig latin the way we did when we were kids and we didn't want Mack to know what we were talking about."

She would have suggested spelling out everything, but Corbin was learning to read.

"Grown cowboys don't use pig latin," Joe grumbled, causing Corbin to giggle. She doubted Corbin actually knew what pig latin was, but it was a reminder to Joe that the boy was listening. That's probably the only reason he cooperated with the dignity-reducing request. "Ucian-lay umped-day ou-yay."

Her pig latin was a little rusty, so it took her a moment to do the translation: *Lucian dumped you.*

She huffed.

First Jordan, now Joe. Karlee shook her head. Was there anyone out there who'd assume she'd been the one who'd ended things with Lucian? Apparently not. For good reason, too. Half the world knew that she'd been hung up on Lucian since about the time she'd put on her first bra.

Karlee repeated the lie she'd first told Jordan. *I'm okay.* Or rather, "I'm all-way ight-ray."

Of course, like Jordan, Joe didn't believe it, either, but he loved his nephew and wouldn't press things. Not right now at this exact moment, anyway. Karlee suspected she'd get an earful later on. Joe's jaw muscles were at war with each other, and that was never a good sign.

"We're gonna see Aunt Karlee's cows," Corbin announced. "When you're done talkin' funny."

They were done. No more Lucian or breakup talk. "And then I'm taking him to the rodeo," she added to Joe. "I'll see you there?" Karlee made sure that sounded like a goodbye. As long as she lingered around, there was the possibility of a Lucian sighting.

Joe huffed and grumbled "uck-fay" before he got back in his truck and drove off. Karlee hurried toward

Jordan's car, hoping this time she could make her get-away, but no such luck.

Jerry came driving up.

Hell's bells. What now?

"Grandpa!" Corbin greeted. It wasn't nearly as enthusiastic as the one he'd given Joe, but Corbin went to him and hugged Jerry's legs. Jerry hugged him back, lingering a bit because he was likely well aware that it might be a while before he got another one from anyone in the Granger family.

"I won't be here long," Jerry said when he looked at her.

"Good. Because I don't think anyone wants you around while they're trying to clean up things."

Jerry nodded, and Karlee saw something she'd never seen before. Jerry looked thoroughly broken and defeated. She wasn't going to make any attempts to cheer him up, but she did drop back a notch on her glare. Not just for Jerry's sake but for Corbin's.

"For what it's worth, I loved your mother," he said. "Still do. But I stink at relationships."

"That seems to be going around," Karlee mumbled. "I warn you, though—if you're about to say anything else that little ears shouldn't hear, then use pig latin, sign language or some other form of conversation that isn't English."

Jerry pulled back his shoulder, and she thought maybe he was trying to come up with something. But then he shook his head and took something from his pocket. A small box. He took out a pen, too, and wrote something on it.

"Give this to Lucian," the note said, "and tell him something for me. Tell him, Goodbye, Son."

CHAPTER TWENTY-TWO

LUCIAN WAS SORRY that one of the windows in his office had a view of the side driveway. That meant he'd seen Karlee, not only when she'd had a brief conversation with Joe but also when she'd chatted with Jerry.

Neither encounter had seemed especially comfortable for her. However, at least Karlee wasn't crying. That was good. But he hated that her lack of tears didn't feel so good for him. It made things seem, well, final.

Which made him feel like shit.

He'd hurt her. Hell, he'd hurt himself by pushing to be with her, and now he'd made a mess of his personal life at a time when he sure as heck didn't need any more messes.

"Uh, Lucian?" he heard his mother say. "If you need more time…"

Lawson got up, went to the window and cursed. "All done now with watching Karlee?" he snarled.

That got Jordan; Lawson's wife, Eve; his sister and Dylan coming to the window, too. They got a view of Karlee just as she was putting Corbin into his booster seat, and when she turned around, there was just a split second, one unguarded moment, when he saw that she was hunched over a little and that she had her teeth clamped over her bottom lip, probably to stop it from trembling. Lucian knew those were signs that she was upset, but he doubted his family would pick up on it.

He was wrong about that.

"Shit," from Dylan.

"You dickhead," from Lawson.

"You didn't," from Lily Rose.

"Lucifer," from Jordan.

"Uh, what's going on?" from his mother.

Oh, to be clueless like his mother. There was something to be said for not knowing. It had only been a few months ago that Lucian hadn't been able to see the whole lighting-up thing with Karlee. Only a few months when he could look at her and only imagine how she tasted, or how she felt beneath him in his bed.

All right, best not to linger on those last two.

Besides, in addition to getting through this meeting, he apparently had some explaining to do.

"Karlee broke up with me," Lucian said. That was a first, too. A couple of months ago he wouldn't have felt the need to explain his sex life to anyone other than his sex partner. Hell, he still didn't, but he wanted to hurry this along and get them back in their seats.

They didn't budge.

"And you really think it was Karlee's idea to end things?" from Dylan.

Well, it sure as hell hadn't been his. Not to end it today, anyway. Lucian had planned on waiting a few more weeks. Maybe after he'd had a chance to take her to the cabin he owned in the Hill Country.

"Dickhead." Lawson, again. Obviously, he had a limited vocabulary.

And Jordan and Eve had no vocabulary at all because they just glared at him.

His mother only sighed. "Karlee's a smart girl. Sweet and beautiful, too. I'm betting she'll find someone else in no time at all."

With that comment hanging in the air, they all went back to their seats. But it made Lucian wonder if Regina was the least clueless of all of them. Because that was the right thing to say if she wanted Lucian to go running after Karlee.

He didn't.

His mother was right about her being smart, sweet and beautiful. And she had great breasts and legs. Again, best not to dwell on those last two. However, it was the fact that she was so special that made him see that she needed someone who could give her that life she wanted. Marriage and kids. Normal stuff.

Stuff that he sucked at.

With that reminder fresh in his mind, he went to his desk and handed them each a copy of the business proposals he'd had Sunny print out.

"First of all, we're going to lose Granger Enterprises," Lucian spelled out for them, and then he had to clear his throat. He also gave them a few moments to absorb it.

They absorbed it a lot better than he thought they would.

"Yeah," from Dylan as he read through it. "Figured as much."

"Dickhead Jerry," from Lawson. He was reading the proposal, too.

"It's not your fault. We know how hard you've worked. Don't take this too hard," from Eve, Jordan and Lily Rose, who were also reading.

"Dickhead Jerry," from his mom.

They could all agree on that, but Lucian was betting

that he'd get some raised eyebrows when they got to what he was advising. And yep, the eyebrows came up.

"You want to sell Dad's shares to the loan sharks and your shares to Hoo-Poo?" Dylan asked, but then he had a surprising reaction—he chuckled. "Candy will do just fine handling the loan sharks."

Candy did indeed seem to think she could, and she was especially thrilled that she would be the majority shareholder.

"What about the historical society and garden guild?" his mother asked.

"It shouldn't affect them financially since they aren't actually involved in the business decisions, but I called Lois Fay to let her know this sale was a strong possibility."

And she'd had a surprising reaction, as well. Giving Lucian info he'd never wanted to know, Lois Fay had admitted to being a huge fan and user of Hoo-Poo and was excited to have Candy in charge.

"Holy shit," Lawson said when he looked at the numbers from each of the two groups. "That's a lot of money."

Lucian made a sound of agreement. "About thirty million. I'm combining the money for my shares with Jerry's to come up with that total. If you agree with this, all you each have to do is sign, and then I'll close the deal. We'll divide it evenly among Mom and the families, and then each of you can start fresh."

They gave him blank looks.

"I'll just keep running the ranch," from Dylan as he signed.

"I'll just keep raising my horses," from Lily Rose as she signed.

"I never wanted anything to do with this shit anyway," from Lawson as he signed.

"Uh, you're the only one who was tied to Granger Enterprises," his mom pointed out as she signed, too. "I'll just keep going to yoga retreats and playing with my grandbabies."

Okay, so this hadn't been the gut-wrenching meeting he'd anticipated. In fact, the only gut-wrenching seemed to be coming from him. And it was bad. He was about to lose something that had occupied the majority of his time and energy for all of his adult life. Yes, he had his new company, but it was like trying to replace a beloved pet with another one.

In other words, it couldn't be done.

"You need to get ready for the rodeo," his mom announced, getting to her feet. "And don't take it so hard if you don't win again."

He heard some under-the-breath comments about his mother's "if" instead of "when," but Lucian let it slide. They all put their signed papers on the desk and were all leaving. He didn't want to toss out some snark to delay their exit.

When they were out of the room, Lucian glanced out the window again. No Karlee, of course. She had already left with Corbin to do whatever she was planning on doing. Maybe getting started on finding that life she'd always wanted.

His heart sputtered some when there was a knock at his door, and for a moment he thought Karlee had indeed come back to the ranch without him knowing. But it was Abe who came in. Today, he was wearing a Rolling Stones T-shirt with a fraying collar seam, and near the belt buckle was a hole that looked like an off-center belly button.

Abe glanced at the papers, and while it was possible

he'd already heard what was happening, his attention didn't stay on them for long. "You put Jerry's balls in the right place."

"What balls he had left, I did," Lucian assured him.

He nodded in approval, crossed the room and dropped a paper bag on Lucian's desk. Because the bag seemed bulkier than usual, Lucian eyed it and then Abe.

Abe lifted his shoulder. "It might work on Karlee. Might not," he quickly added.

Despite everything, Lucian smiled. It wouldn't work, but it was good of Abe to give it a try. "Thanks."

"Hell, don't go all gushy on me," Abe growled, and he walked out, reminding Lucian that sometimes fatherly love and concern came in brown paper bags delivered by a bad cook in a Mick Jagger T-shirt.

Lucian gathered up all the signed documents and put them next to his copy. Which was still blank on the signature line. He picked up the pen, the point hovering over that line. And hovering.

And hovering.

What if he was wrong about this? Not just wrong about the business decision. Being wrong about that was actually something he could live with. He'd built Granger Enterprises up, and it seemed only fitting that he would be the one to dismantle it.

But what about Karlee?

What if he was wrong about her?

Well, shit.

KARLEE HAD ONLY been at the rodeo fairgrounds for a couple of minutes when she figured out that everyone knew about Lucian's and her breakup. There were too many whispers for it to be solely about her partial walk-of-shame clothes. The housekeeper had likely heard enough of her conversation with Jordan to get the scoop, and then promptly spread that scoop through Wrangler's Creek.

Not that Karlee needed more proof of what folks knew, but she got it with each step she took. Despite holding the hand of a cute little kid and doing a decent job of smiling, people looked at her with sad, sympathetic eyes, which meant they'd be using those same eyeballs to give Lucian some stank. He'd be the bad guy in this—again. Of course, now it wouldn't matter. He no longer had to play the role of the nice guy.

She spotted Jordan at a food truck called All Things Fried, and when Jordan turned around, she had what appeared to be a giant fried chunk of wood. A vanilla ice-cream cone was dripping in her other hand, and Jordan was taking frantic licks off it, but the ice cream was winning.

"There you are." Jordan went to them, immediately handing off the cone to Corbin, and she leaned in, putting her mouth close to Karlee's ear. "Everyone knows about Lucian and you."

Karlee nodded, tipped her head to the fried chunk. "What is that?"

"A one-pound brick of fried chocolate. Hey, don't judge. It's been a stressful past couple of months."

Yes, it had been. Karlee might order some bricks for herself.

"Lucian's in the arena," Jordan said a moment later, and that's when Karlee realized she was looking around for him. "If you talk to him, don't mention the business. He sold Granger Enterprises today."

Another nod. "You mean Jerry's shares."

"No. I mean all of it."

Her breath swooshed all the way down to her freshly painted toenails. That had been the fix? It sounded like a case of throwing out the baby with the bathwater.

"He sold Jerry's shares to the loan sharks." Jordan whispered the last two words, though Karlee was certain a half dozen people still heard her. There were suddenly a lot of folks milling around them. "And Lucian sold his shares to...her."

Karlee followed the direction of Jordan's gaze, and she saw Candy making a beeline toward them. Finally, here was someone with more inappropriate attire than Karlee. Candy was wearing super-skinny jeans and a red top with enough sparkles and sequins to trigger a seizure. Her five-inch heels had "sprained ankle" and "I don't belong here" written all over them.

"Go ahead." Candy outstretched her arms, causing all those sequins to flash off the sunlight. "Congratulate me on the sweet deal I made with Lucian." She didn't give them time to do that, though, because she just kept talking. "I'm now the primary shareholder of Granger Enterprises. Of course, I'm changing the name. Maybe to Hoo-Poo, Too. What do you think?"

Karlee thought no cattleman would ever do business with a company with that name, but that wasn't her problem, so she just gave a noncommittal smile and nod. Corbin, however, wasn't quite as diplomatic.

"Hoo-Poo, Too," he repeated while still licking his ice cream. "Dat's a funny."

Candy didn't smile about that, and before she could say anything to the boy, Karlee jumped into the conversation. "Aren't you worried about being business partners with loan sharks?"

"Heck, no. You'd be surprised at the sort of creeps you have to deal with in the feminine hygiene business."

"Hoo-Poo, Too," Corbin repeated with a giggle.

This time it was Jordan who jumped into the conversation. "Say, it's nearly time for Dylan's ride. Come on, Corbin. Let's go watch Daddy."

The bronc-riding competition wouldn't start for another thirty minutes, but Jordan whisked Corbin off as if it would take them that entire time to go the thirty yards or so to the arena.

"I should be going, too," Karlee said. Not a total lie. She did need to figure out a way to get Lucian the "gift" that Jerry had given her. Then after the bronc competition, she could go to her apartment, where she could eat that brick of chocolate and finish having her cry. "Congratulations," she added to Candy, causing the woman to smile.

Good. Karlee had made at least one person happy today. She doubted the gift would do the same to Lucian though. With all the surprises Jerry had sprung on them, there was no telling what was in the box. Since it was possibly another round of bad news, she would hand it off to someone who could in turn give it to Lucian after his ride. And she soon spotted a someone.

Lawson.

He wasn't riding today, so he was at the corral with his family. Eve, their daughter, Tessie, and toddler son, Aiden. They were all eating various fried stuff while watching the handlers parade the bulls out for everyone to see.

Eve and Tessie greeted her with a hug, but Lawson definitely wasn't in a hugging mood when she took the box from her purse and handed it to him. "Jerry wanted Lucian to have this."

Lawson looked at the note Jerry had written and read it aloud. "'Give this to Lucian, and tell him something for me. Tell him, Goodbye, Son.'"

Lawson promptly handed her the box right back. "No way in…Hades. You give it to him."

Eve nodded, apparently pleased that he hadn't said "hell" instead.

"What's in the box?" Eve asked.

"Maybe a vial of Ebola since it's from Jerry," Tessie mumbled.

While that was a bit of an exaggeration, Karlee thought Tessie was on the right track. "I need someone to give this to Lucian after his ride," Karlee explained.

All of them stared at her, including Aiden. "Because you're going home to cry." Tessie again.

"Yeah, we know about the breakup," Lawson added. "Lucian told us about it when he was gawking at you from his office window."

The gawking wasn't a surprise. She'd seen Lucian there, but Karlee had thought it was just a glance. Gawking meant that this was eating away at him. Of course, it was. He truly hadn't wanted to hurt her.

"Roman's around here somewhere," Lawson went on. "Why don't you have him give the box to Lucian?"

Lawson had probably suggested that because Roman wouldn't mind giving Lucian bad news. Yes, they were on better terms these days now that the land dispute had been settled, but it was hard to forget years of bad blood.

While Roman would have agreed to being the gift messenger, Karlee wanted Lucian to get it from someone who might actually show him some sympathy if it did indeed turn out to be bad.

She said goodbye to them and went into the arena in search of Regina. Lucian's mom would definitely be able to lend a sympathetic shoulder if he needed it. Regina wasn't anywhere in sight, though she did spot some Grangers.

Lucian's cousins.

Sophie McKinnon and her husband, Clay. Their twins were running around, dripping identical ice-cream cones to the one Corbin had had, and Sophie was making her way through a chocolate brick. Roman's wife, Mila, was with them, and so was Garrett's wife, Nicky, and their two children.

"We heard the news," Sophie said, immediately pulling Karlee into a hug.

Karlee wasn't sure which news exactly, so she just gave another noncommittal nod. If she kept this up, folks were going to think she had developed a nervous tic or something.

"Are you okay?" That from Nicky.

"I'm so sorry." That from Mila.

So this was likely about the breakup.

"I'm fine," Karlee answered.

Again, she got looks from the entire crew. She must have looked downtrodden because Sophie's daughter offered to share her cone with Karlee. Karlee declined but thanked her and wondered if this was the best candidate to give Lucian the gift. It was hard to be too blue when around a cute kid.

"Oh, there's Garrett," Nicky gushed when Garrett came out and waved at the crowd.

They all cheered, and he flashed a smile that reminded

Karlee why everyone called him the Golden Boy. Like Dylan, Garrett had gotten plenty of the Granger charm.

"There have been six other riders," Nicky explained, "but none has stayed on the eight seconds."

So it was still anyone's buckle to win.

"I hope the judges don't hold this against Lucian," Sophie added while Garrett headed to the gate area to the bronc he'd be riding.

Karlee figured her downtrodden-ness morphed to a confused look, and it took her a moment to realize where this was going. Staying on the bronc for eight seconds was only part of the competition. The judges also scored on more subjective things, like the rider's control of the horse, the way he used his spurs and kept the toes of his boots outward. If the judges didn't deem the ride "fluid" enough, then the rider could lose.

Crap.

Yes, that could indeed be held against Lucian. Of course, that was assuming he could stay on for eight seconds, but if he managed it and lost because of this breakup, then Karlee would never forgive herself. In hindsight, she should have waited until after the rodeo to end things. Now she had to do the next best thing—damage control.

"I was the one to end things with Lucian," Karlee told his cousins. "Spread the word, please."

Again, she got blank looks. Sophie's daughter offered her the cone again. Sophie offered her the chocolate brick. Karlee declined, said a friendly goodbye and set off to find Regina.

She'd only made it a few feet, though, when Garrett started his ride, so she stopped to watch. It was easy to see the time because there was a massive timer tick-

ing off the seconds in red lights, and it was also easy
to see Garrett since he stayed near the center. Karlee
hated to cheer against the nice-guy reigning champion,
but the only real chance Lucian had of winning in his
last rodeo competition was for Garrett to get bucked
off before the timing ran out.

Garrett stayed on.

Karlee wasn't an expert judge by any means, but
she did see a couple of areas where Garrett could lose
some points. Or maybe she should just admit that she
was biased and applaud like everyone else. So that's
what she did.

She finally saw Regina in the top row of the stands,
but before Karlee could start up to her, Dylan came out
of the gate for his ride. Once again, the timer started, so
Karlee watched. Eight seconds later, Dylan was still on
the bronc, and it was as if the blood-bay gelding cooperated to get him the smoothest dismount possible. Dylan
sort of glided right off to make it all look easy peasy.

Well, shoot. Now Lucian had two times the competition since it looked like a flawless ride to her.

With the crowd still on their feet cheering Dylan,
Karlee started toward Regina, but then stopped again.
This time when she saw Lucian go to the gate for his
ride. As if he knew exactly where she was in the sea
of people, he looked right at her. No smile. In fact, no
expression whatsoever.

She'd seen him do this event for years, but this was
the first time he hadn't been wearing his battle-ready
face. Maybe because he had had to put on that face too
many times over the past couple of months.

He was wearing all the right gear that always got her
attention. The vest, chaps and jeans. But even with the

vest she could see the bulk in the right side of his shirt. He'd stuffed something in there. Maybe something for good luck? Karlee had heard that Vita Banchini had paid him a visit, so maybe the old woman had given him some sort of charm or potion. If that's what it indeed was, it was a true testament to Lucian's need to win this because he always steered clear of any of Vita's offerings.

When Lucian got on the back of the palomino he'd drawn to ride, her heart jumped to her throat. Her stomach went in the opposite direction, and she thought it landed somewhere around her ankles. Karlee squeezed her eyes shut and waited.

And waited.

And waited.

Time must have stopped because those handful of seconds seemed to last an eternity. It didn't help that the crowd went as silent as the grave. The only sounds were that of the palomino whipping Lucian around.

Then the grumbles came, followed by a spattering of applause. Not very enthusiastic applause, either. Oh God. Lucian had lost.

She finally opened her eyes when she heard someone let out a loud whoop. Skeeter. He was right up by the fence. Regina started whooping, too. That's when Karlee spotted the timer.

Eight seconds.

And Lucian was still on the bronc. For a heartbeat longer, anyway, before he jumped from the saddle.

She hadn't known she was also going to whoop before the sound came out of her mouth, and it was significantly louder than Skeeter's or Regina's. Much, much louder, too, than the unenthusiastic applause. Lucian noticed all right. The moment he was out of the arena, he gave her another glance.

The announcer tapped the microphone. He was Buck Leonard, who had won a national bull-riding championship back in the seventies, and after a few more taps, his crackly voice poured through the arena. "Well…" Static. "…ride for…" More static. "…Granger."

Since she could see Buck's face, and he wasn't scowling or anything, he'd likely said something good about Lucian.

"In just a few minutes," Buck managed to get out before the mike did its snapping and crackling again. "…have final scores…" Totally unrecognizable gibberish. The crowd booed and yelled for him to speak up. Buck spoke up, making the gibberish even louder until finally something made its way through the static. "…who'll be taking home that prize rodeo buckle."

"At least it'll be a moral victory for Lucian," Jordan said. Until her friend had spoken, Karlee hadn't even known she'd walked up behind her.

A moral victory but not a real one since Jordan was in agreement with Sophie. That Lucian wouldn't win because he just wasn't likable enough. Too bad because in many ways he was the most likable person that Karlee had ever known. Loyal. No BS. You always knew where you stood with Lucian.

And that's why she was in love with him.

That really didn't help her stomach and her heart, and Karlee turned to leave. She'd give Lucian Jerry's gift some other time. For now, she needed to get out of there before she started crying.

She made it all the way to the doors when Buck

came back on the mike. "Cowboys and cowgirls, we got a winner."

Karlee glanced back over her shoulder to see the riders lined up on the opposite side of the arena by the fence. All but Lucian. He wasn't there, causing her to glance around for him. Maybe he already knew the outcome and didn't want to face anyone. Of course, her first instinct was to go to him, to try to comfort him, but she forced herself to stay put.

"And the winner is…" Buck paused. A very long time. Then repeated it. "Uh, it's Lucian Granger." The static cooperated for just that one sentence because it came through loud and clear.

If Karlee had thought it was quiet before, she'd been wrong. *This* was quiet. It seemed for just a couple of seconds everyone had sucked in their breath and held it. It didn't last. The gasps came, followed by whispers, grumbles of disbelief—all peppered with some outrage. Skeeter and Regina whooped, and Corbin joined them.

"Lucian, come on up to the podium…" The static returned. "…your buckle," Buck said.

Now everyone was looking around for Lucian. Riders scattered, no doubt hurrying to bring him in front of the crowd for his victory moment. It was Dylan who finally came back with him, and Lucian looked thunderstruck, as did a good 70 percent of the onlookers. However, he did go on the podium, again at Dylan's urging.

"Congrats, Lucian," Buck grumbled. Or rather, *hiss*, *pop*, *sizzle*, "Congrats, Lucian." And Buck handed him the buckle.

For a man who'd just accomplished the number one thing on his bucket list, Lucian didn't seem that interested. He didn't even spare the rodeo buckle a glance, but he did take the mike from Buck.

"Karlee?" Lucian looked at her. "Can we…?"

Dang it. The static ate the first part of the last word, but it was either "talk," "walk" or "stalk." She doubted he'd make a public announcement about stalking, or even walking, for that matter, so he wanted to talk.

Suddenly, all eyes were on her, and it was silent again. Everyone seemed to be waiting for her to respond. Everyone including Lucian.

So she nodded.

That set off a chain of whispers and other sounds that people made when they weren't sure what was happening. Karlee was right there with them. She didn't know what was happening, either. Lucian perhaps fell into that same boat, as well. But he clearly wasn't finished with the mike. That's because he added one more thing to his conversation request. And Lucian did it while looking her straight in the eyes.

"Karlee," he said, "I…" For crap's sake. It sounded like bubbly farts. "…you."

"What?" a whole lot of people yelled.

Lucian huffed, obviously as frustrated by the mike as everyone else. He rammed it into his pocket, shoved the buckle into the waist of his jeans and cupped his hands around his mouth, probably hoping his voice would carry.

It did. It carried just fine.

"Karlee," he shouted, "I need you."

CHAPTER TWENTY-THREE

UH-OH. IN HINDSIGHT, it just hadn't been a good idea for him to yell that *I need you* out to Karlee.

He heard and saw the reaction of the onlookers. Or rather, Lucian heard their silence. But there was only one reaction that he was tuned in to right now, and that was Karlee's. He saw her mouth move, but since she was all the way on the other side of the arena, he couldn't hear what she said.

Hell. His stomach was already one big knot, and he had to know if he'd just poured out his heart only to have it stomped on. Which was a strong possibility since Karlee had been the one to end things.

"*I need you*?" someone yelled. "That's the best you can do?"

No. It wasn't, but folks here wouldn't understand that those three words were the ones hardest for him to say to anyone.

"Y'all meet in the arena," someone else called out. The rumble of agreement rippled through the crowd.

Yeah, they'd like that. Karlee and him on display, and most of those rippled rumbles probably wanted him to get what they felt was coming to him. In other words, they wanted to witness Karlee reject him. If that was indeed what was going to happen, it'd soon get around anyway, so that's why Lucian stepped down into the arena. However, he did that with plans to go to Karlee and take her someplace private so they could talk.

"Meet him in the middle," several folks said. They'd moved on from rippling to chanting now, and they aimed those chants at Karlee.

Karlee glanced around, the kind of glance a cute bunny would make when surrounded by coyotes, but she must have figured out that folks wouldn't actually be able to hear what they were saying because she went through the gate and into the arena.

Lucian had never seen anyone take such hesitant steps toward him, which told him plenty. He'd waited too late to figure out his feelings for her. He'd let her slip away. And that did indeed make him a dickhead. A very sad one.

Since Karlee was wearing heels, it took her some snail-crawling moments to get to him. He considered just letting her talk, letting her give him a piece of her mind, but he was feeling desperate, so he pulled out the brown paper bag he'd stuffed inside his shirt. It hadn't fared well in the ride and was crushed, but he handed it to her anyway.

Most women would have probably been disappointed or at least confused by the offering, but her eyes had a little awe in them. "From Abe?" she asked.

Lucian nodded. "He thought it would help."

She opened it carefully, almost reverently, but that wasn't a reverent look when she saw what was inside. Karlee took it out, examining the sandwich, and then glanced at the one still in the bag.

"That one's mine," he explained.

With her nose wrinkled, her forehead bunched up and plenty of confusion dancing over her face, she lifted the bread as if she expected to find gold. Or a rattlesnake. She smiled when she saw what was there. "Peanut butter. Your favorite."

Abe and Karlee were the only two people who knew that. "Abe was worried about my protein intake," Lucian said, but there was no need to make a joke of it. No need to explain. When his life had been going to hell in the nearest handbasket, Abe had been the one to make sure he got something he loved.

And now Abe had done that for Karlee. Well, more or less. Since it wasn't actually Karlee's favorite, it was more symbolic.

"So, now you know all my deep dark secrets," he said. He'd just thrown the gauntlet to give her a chance for the air clearing he thought she needed. And while she was at it, if she wanted to spill some secrets, that was good, too.

"I've had a crush on you since fourth grade," she blurted out. She frowned and put the sandwich back in the bag with his. "All right, second grade. And no, I didn't know what a crush actually was, but I did know that when you walked into the room that I'd forget how to breathe." She paused a heartbeat. "Right now, I'm forgetting how to breathe, too."

Lucian wasn't sure if that was good or not, and he took hold of her arm just in case she fainted from lack of oxygen.

He hadn't known about the crush. It was probably like the lighting-up thing he'd missed for so long, but he thought maybe he saw a glimmer of that light now. Or maybe that was the glare of the arena lights.

"Speak up," someone yelled. He realized it was his mother. Later, he'd give her a scowl for that, but he didn't

want to sport that particular facial expression now because Karlee might think it was for her.

"I want you to repeat what you said," she whispered.
"Just to make sure I heard it right."

Oh. Well, this was easy. In fact, Lucian wouldn't mind
if she asked to hear it a couple of times. "I need you."

She smiled, just a little, and caught onto the front
of his shirt, pulling him down to her for a quick peck
on the lips.

"That's the best you can do?" Roman shouted. "Are
you sure you're a real Granger?"

Lucian would owe him a scowl, too, but for now he
apparently needed to prove that he could do a whole
lot better. He snapped Karlee to him and kissed her the
right way. Long, deep and hard.

That got mixed reactions from the crowd. He got
some whoops of approval, several *get a room* yells,
but somehow his mom's voice managed to waft above
the others.

"I need you?" Regina shouted like a challenge. "Roman's right. Can't you do better than that?"

Lucian huffed. No way did he want to have a yelling match to explain that there was nothing better than
that, but judging from Karlee's smile, she got it. And
she was the only one who mattered.

"Well, I need you, too," she said.

The relief came. Man, did it. Relief the size of Niagara
Falls. Then the giddy feeling following. He smiled, and
he kissed the living daylights out of her. Karlee didn't
get to stay on the receiving end of things though.

She kissed him right back.

A raging hard-on would have followed that if Lucian
hadn't remembered where they were, and he knew it

was time to do something about this public display of mutual affection.

"Get a room," someone shouted again.

"I think he's got the right idea," Lucian told her. "I can have you out of those jeans in no time flat, and I don't need any instructions from this crowd on how to do it."

It was only after he finished saying every single word that Lucian realized it was a lot louder than it should have been. And that's when he remembered the microphone that he'd stuck in his pocket. For the first time in at least a decade, the blasted thing had apparently decided to start working with perfect clarity.

Some of the women in the crowd were fanning themselves. Men were nudging some of those fanning women. Some had covered their children's ears. All signs that he needed to get the hell out of there.

Since he'd already made a spectacle of himself, Lucian decided to give Wrangler's Creek something else to talk about for years to come. Dropping the sandwich bag, he scooped up Karlee in his arms and started walking toward the exit. It not only gave him a chance to kiss her again, but it got them to the gate a whole heck of a lot faster than it would have with her in those heels.

Moving a whole lot faster soon became a necessity, though, because the silver rodeo buckle that he'd tucked in his jeans was now squished between Karlee and him, and it was gouging into his hip. Maybe he wouldn't need stitches. Best not to bleed all over Karlee when he had so many things to tell her.

And do to her.

Of course, like that kiss, she'd be doing some things to him, too.

There was a swarm of cowboys on the other side of

the gate. Some who'd finished their competition, others waiting for theirs. Karlee and he had to endure a few catcalls, winks and wolf whistles before Lucian ducked into the first place that had the potential to give them some privacy. The tack room. It was better than continuing the trek through the entire fairgrounds and to the parking lot.

Lucian threw open the door and found Roman's teenage son, Tate, making out with his girlfriend, Arwen. They weren't naked, but there was clearly some third-base stuff going on.

"Leave, and I'll give you a kidney if that ever becomes necessary," Lucian bargained with the teens. Because, yes, this time with Karlee was that important to him.

Arwen and Tate made a few adjustments to their clothes and scurried out. Lucian not only shut the door, he also put down Karlee long enough for them to drag some hay bales in front of the door to block it. With all the moving around, Karlee dropped not just her purse that she'd had hooked on her shoulder but the little white box she'd been carrying.

"Oh," she said when she saw he'd noticed it. "Jerry asked me to give it to you."

Talk about a big-assed step back in the good-mood department. Lucian didn't want to know what was inside, but he doubted it was going to make him feel as good as one of Abe's peanut-butter sandwiches. Still, he didn't have a choice about seeing the contents. The box opened during the fall, and he spotted the rodeo buckle. Not the one he'd just won. This was his grandfather J.L.'s, the one that Lucian had donated to the historical society.

"There's a note," Karlee said. "You want to read it?"

No. Wait—yes. The mood was gone, no trace of a hard-on now, so he might as well finish this so he could get back to Karlee.

Lucian scooped up both the buckle and the note, and he read aloud what Jerry had written: "'I bargained with Lois Fay and got this back for you. I gave them a bunch of your great-granddaddy's stuff instead. I know this doesn't make us even, not by a long shot, but it's just something I wanted to do. Have a good life, son.'"

Hell no, it didn't make them even, but Lucian was glad to have the buckle back. Glad, too, that he felt just this little sliver of peace when it came to his shithead of a father.

Karlee came back to him, pulling him into her arms. Like her kisses, it was hot and sweet as well because the gesture put his chest against her equally hot and sweet breasts. She kissed him, making things instantly better.

"You okay?" she asked.

Lucian hadn't planned on clothing removal with her—not here, anyway—but he had to get some things off his chest first. Off his hip, too. He moved the buckle to his back pocket.

Where he encountered the microphone that was still on. Shit.

He flicked off the button, only to hear a loud collective groan from the crowd in the arena. Apparently, they'd all still been listening. Lucian didn't have time to hang on to the annoyance about that, though, because Karlee chuckled and pulled him back to her for a kiss.

Man, oh, man. She had the cure for annoyance, doubt and even hip gouges. That hot, sweet mouth of hers could possibly even make him forget that there were probably folks listening at the door. That's why this couldn't turn into sex. Or maybe it could, if she kept kissing him like that, but he had to say some things to her first.

Lucian forced his mouth from hers since he needed that particular body part to talk. Karlee occupied herself with his other body parts, though, by bumping herself against him.

"I see the light in you now," he said, keeping his voice at a whisper. "I see a lot of things, and one of them was that I was really stupid to let you walk out of my bedroom this morning. I should have never let you go."

There. It was all out in the open. Well, all but that one more thing, and while it was important, it wasn't nearly as much of a big deal as his *I need you*. Still, he said it to Karlee.

"I love you."

She smiled again and just studied him as if savoring this moment. "That crush I mentioned earlier? Well, it turned to love a couple of years later. It's nice that you've caught up."

Yeah, it was, and that meant he had to make up for lost time. That's one of the reasons he slid his hand under her top. Mercy, she felt good, and he especially liked that little hitch sound of pleasure she made. But then she stopped and glanced around.

"This is a glorified barn, and you don't like barn sex, remember?" she pointed out.

"My views have changed a bit on that, too. A quickie here. Then I can take you back to the ranch for something not so quick."

Of course, when they walked out, everyone would know, but at the moment Lucian cared more about getting in Karlee's pants than he did that. Besides, even if they didn't have sex right now, folks would assume they had—and that he was bad at it because it had been so quick.

Kissing her, Lucian lowered her onto the hay bales they'd stacked. A sort of second "lock" to ensure no one walked in on them. And then he finally got his hand in her pants. Or rather, her panties, which he quickly shimmied off her.

"You forgot how to breathe when I walked into a room, huh?" he whispered. "Right now, I can't remember my own name."

"I know your name," she whispered back. "You're Lucian Granger, reigning bronc-riding champion and the person I love. You're also the man about to get down and dirty with me in this hay."

Karlee was so right. That's exactly what Lucian was—and it was exactly what he did.

* * * * *

Texas cattleman Callen Laramie hasn't been back to his hometown of Coldwater for years. But when his beloved foster father invites him to his Christmas wedding, Callen knows it's time to return. The hardest part will be resisting the man's daughter, the one woman he's never been able to forget...

Don't miss Lone Star Christmas,
a Coldwater, Texas novel
by USA TODAY *bestselling author Delores Fossen,*
on sale in October 2018!

COWBOY BLUES

CHAPTER ONE

NICK HASKINS HEARD the sounds in the bunkhouse the moment he stepped from the shower. Sounds of footsteps and somebody moving around on the creaky hardwood floor in the adjacent room.

Hell's bells.

He checked the time, a little past 10:00 p.m., and he scowled. No one else should be here now that the other hands had moved to the new bunkhouse on the west side of the Granger Ranch. And if a straggler had returned for any reason, Nick darn sure wasn't in the mood for company or an interruption of any sort.

Man, he hurt.

He had a bruise on his ribs where a temperamental gelding that he'd been training had thrown him, and it was throbbing. Almost as bad, his head was trying to compete for the award of the body part with the most pain. Nick figured both his head and side were in a dead heat for that award, because they caused him to wince and grunt every time he moved.

Doing more of that wincing/grunting, Nick wrapped the towel around himself and came out of the bathroom so he could make quick work of getting rid of whoever was clomping around in the other room. But he froze in the doorway when he looked in the bunkroom and

saw the butt. Not one of the hands or even one of his
bosses—they were all men.

This butt belonged to a woman.

She was facing away from him, leaning down over
one of the beds, which meant all he could see of her
was her back, butt and legs. She was wearing jeans that
framed the part of her body that had grabbed on to his
attention and was holding it hostage. Of course, anyone
would have gotten his attention at this point, because
no one should have been in there.

With annoyance sliding through him, Nick cleared
his throat to get her attention. And he got it all right.
She turned, not a whirling motion of someone who'd
just been startled, but slow and easy movements as if
she'd expected the throat clearing.

And expected *him*.

Nick got an instant jolt of recognition. He knew that
face, and for just a split second he thought it was Carol
Ann Gavin, his old high school girlfriend. However,
when she cocked her head to the side and smiled, he realized it wasn't Carol Ann but rather her identical twin,
Lindsay. Carol Ann definitely wouldn't have been smiling at him like that.

Or skimming her gaze over his body.

Nope. Not only was Carol Ann happily married, but
she also hadn't undressed him with her eyes in a very
long time. Not since high school.

Only then did Nick remember that at the moment
there wasn't much of him to undress. He was wearing
just a towel and a scowl. Neither the lack of clothing
nor expression seemed to bother Lindsay. In fact, her
smile widened as if there were something to actually
smile about.

There wasn't.

This wasn't exactly a welcome reunion. Yes, he'd dated her sister for two years way back when, and Lindsay and he had been friendly enough—in a hands-off, keep-his-distance sort of way. Since she worked at a large ranch just one county over and often came back to town to visit her sister, Nick had seen her from time to time.

And he'd run into her *that night*.

A night about six months ago at the Longhorn Bar that he'd tried hard to keep in his "stuff to forget" box. It hadn't worked. He still remembered that he'd noticed then what he was noticing now.

That she had curves in all the right places.

Something he really wished he hadn't spotted right off. Actually, he wished her face hadn't caught his attention, either. She was a looker, always had been. He'd especially seen it that night at the Longhorn, but he'd blamed that on too much beer and too little sleep.

"Nick," Lindsay said. She went to him, outstretching her arms as if she might hug him. She stopped, though, and glanced at the towel. A long glance. "I should probably save a friendly hug for later, or it might go beyond the friendly point." Then she chuckled.

Again, Nick saw nothing chuckle-worthy about this, especially since he'd noticed things about her that he shouldn't be noticing about his ex-girlfriend's sister. And he was also confused.

"Why are you here?" he asked.

Lindsay shrugged. "I moved back to Wrangler's Creek."

As if that explained everything, which it most certainly didn't, she turned and went back to the bunk where he'd first seen her. The bunk that was just below his. She opened a suitcase that she'd put on the bed and started unpacking.

Nick made sure he got a good grip on his towel, and barefoot, he padded across the room. "What do you think you're doing?"

She smiled, lifted her eyebrow. "Well, it's generally called unpacking." She tipped her head to his bare chest. "Is this a peep show I'm going to get every night, or is this a special occasion?"

Nick was certain there was a big-ass dumbfounded look on his face, and apparently it was effective because her forehead bunched up. "You don't know?" she added. "Dylan didn't tell you?"

Dylan was almost certainly Dylan Granger, his boss and one of the owners of the Granger Ranch, where Nick had worked for ten years, since he'd turned twenty-three. "Dylan got called out of town." To handle some snags on a cattle deal he'd put together. Nick wouldn't mention that, though, to an outsider.

Except maybe Lindsay didn't fall into that "outsider" category.

The uneasy feeling went through him, and Nick didn't think it was because of his lack of clothes or the way Lindsay kept glancing at him. The suitcase, the fact that she was here and mentioning Dylan all added up to one thing.

"You're the new horse trainer Dylan hired," Nick concluded.

"Bingo." That smile came again, and she gave her long, dark ponytail an adjustment before she started removing more clothes from the suitcase.

Nick took hold of her hand. Not the brightest idea he'd ever had since now not only was he touching her, but the looser grip caused his towel to shift, and the darn thing nearly slid off his hips before he caught it.

Her attention shifted from his re-grip on the towel to her hand that he'd touched and then to the suitcase that kept snagging his volleyed gaze. "You didn't know I'd be staying at the ranch until my own place is ready?"

Now it was his turn to say "bingo" because Lindsay had nailed it.

"Well, I'm having some repairs done on the house I just bought. It's the little cabin at the end of Creek Road that Mrs. Farley used to own. It has an acre of land and a small barn to hold a horse, but the place won't be ready for a week or so."

A week was way too long. Heck, five minutes was. But at least Nick had a fix for this. "This is the old bunkhouse. There's a new one, and that's where the other hands stay."

Her quick nod made him think his fix wasn't the solution she had in mind. "It's full. Well, with the exception of a cot that's in the corner of an unfinished room. That's why I'm here."

He hadn't known about the full part, but Dylan had said something about taking on extra hands for some seasonal work. Still, if there was a cot, even if it happened to be in an unfinished room, that's where she should be. Or her sister's place. Though come to think of it, Carol Ann's house was on the small side, and she did have a toddler.

She stared at him, not annoyed. More like amused. "You don't know how jealous I always was of Carol Ann," Lindsay said before he could speak.

Nick stared at her, confusion now mixed with his own annoyance. He was about to point out that he'd been her sister's boyfriend and that she shouldn't have been having thoughts like that about him, but that would be like the pot calling the kettle black.

Because he had indeed had thoughts like that about Lindsay.

Nick figured that was natural since they were identical twins, but it had always made him want to kick himself for noticing anything about her. That she was more outgoing, for instance. A risk-taker. Whereas Carol Ann had always made it clear she had deep roots in Wrangler's Creek and had wanted to have and raise a family here.

The family plans hadn't actually appealed much to Nick since he'd been a teenager, but Carol Ann was the "safe" twin. She had the good-girl label whereas Lindsay had been dubbed the wild child. There'd been no risk of getting in trouble or being arrested while he was with Carol Ann.

Staying out of jail had been a big priority for him in those days, since his dad had had repeated run-ins with the law. His father had been a screwup, and Nick had seen how it messed up his life. No way had he wanted to be Screwup Junior.

Nick still didn't want that label, and while he was no longer concerned about arrests and such, that didn't make this situation all right. Far from it. Because Lindsay could be a big problem.

He'd learned his lesson about taking his hand off the towel, but he used his head to motion to various parts of the room. Other than one chair, a small table and the bunk bed frames, there was no furniture. In fact, there were only two mattresses on the frames because the others had been taken to the new bunkhouse. Everything was scuffed, frayed or just plain old, and the smells of livestock and sweat had seeped permanently into the wood.

"Obviously, this isn't a good place for you to stay," he clarified.

She glanced around at the same things he'd just pointed out with his head tips. "It's better than sleeping under the roof with sixteen other hands. Plus, if it's good enough for you—"

"I want to be here," Nick growled. Of course, that was a bad argument, one that only caused Lindsay to lift her eyebrow again.

"So do I." She opened her mouth, probably to give him a better argument than the one he'd just given her, but then her expression changed when he shifted his position.

At first Nick thought that was because the towel had gaped in the wrong place and he'd flashed her, but she wasn't looking at his groin area. She'd noticed the fist-sized bruise on his side. The one that was contributing significantly to his pissed-off mood. Of course, Lindsay's being here sure wasn't helping.

"What the heck happened to you?" she asked.

"A piebald gelding named Gumball. Trust me, there's nothing sweet about him."

Since Lindsay was a trainer, too, he nearly launched right into some details of the plan he had for future training sessions, but this wasn't a conversation he wanted to continue. Somehow, he had to convince her to leave and go anywhere but here.

"The Grangers have a guesthouse you can probably use," he added.

If Lindsay heard him, she didn't respond. She went

straight to the open kitchen, threw open the freezer. It was practically empty except for a frozen pizza. That sent her looking in the fridge, and she grabbed a cold beer before she headed back to him.

"Hold this," she instructed when she thrust the bottle into his hand, then she dug through her suitcase to come up with a tube of something. "It's an herbal lip balm," she explained.

Sitting down on the edge of the bunk so that she was eye level with his side Lindsay began to dab the goo onto his ribs. Or at least that's what she was doing before he stepped back.

"It works," she assured him. She took hold of him, catching on to his hip, and pulled him closer.

Nick wanted to move, but the idiot part of him behind the towel started to react. Not just to the fact that she was touching him but also to her warm breath hitting his bare stomach. He just stood there, gritting his teeth and hoping for a quick end to the torture.

Apparently, though, Lindsay didn't think that was enough to drive him crazy, because she stood, then bent down to continue the goo-smearing. Her hip brushed against the front of the towel.

And against the front of *him*.

She obviously figured out that he was a man with full working parts, because she moved back a bit. "Sorry," she said, standing so that they were face-to-face. Breath-to-breath.

Their gazes held for a couple of seconds before she smiled. Again, there was nothing to warrant that grin.

"Well, I hadn't expected you to react to me like that," she added. "But it's a nice perk. Now, hold that cold beer on your side to bring down the swelling."

Since she'd run all those words together, it took Nick a moment to process the first part. He wanted to deny that he had any kind of thoughts about her that didn't involve her leaving now. But it was difficult to lie when he had the beginnings of a hard-on.

"You're sleeping here tonight," he concluded when she took a pair of pj's from the suitcase.

Lindsay nodded, smiled again and said something that Nick was certain would come back to haunt them.

"You'll never even notice I'm here." She added a wink. "And if you do notice, then all the better. Good night, Nick."

CHAPTER TWO

LINDSAY COULDN'T SAY she'd had the most restful night of sleep, but it had been *interesting*. Actually, everything about her return to Wrangler's Creek had fallen into that category.

She'd landed her dream job at the Granger Ranch, would be working with some of the best horses and best equipment that money could buy—thanks to the Grangers' deep pockets and love of the cowboy way of life. And she'd spent the night under the same roof as Nick.

He was the reason for both the interesting homecoming and why she'd had a less-than-perfect sleep cycle. Hard to relax when she'd seen so much of him in that little towel.

Good grief, the man got better looking with every passing day, and that was saying something since he'd been one of the hottest guys around in high school. He could still hold that hot label despite the scowls he'd continued to give her not just the night before but also this morning when he'd gotten up, grumbled something about needing a shower and headed into the bathroom.

Lindsay doubted he'd give her a second towel peep show, but her memories were clear enough that she didn't need another visual. Though she wouldn't have turned one down.

She winced at that thought. Somehow, she was going to have to rein in these feelings. Or not, she quickly amended when Nick came out of the bathroom and she got another eyeful of him. No towel this time, though. He was dressed in his work clothes—jeans, a blue shirt and boots—and he somehow managed to look almost as good dressed as he had naked.

Almost.

She finally decided that he was amazing no matter what the situation, and she was going to have to deal with the feelings that she'd had for him for years. It'd been a lot easier not to think about those feelings when he'd been out of sight, but even that hadn't been a fix. Especially since she had seemed to run into him every time she'd come back to visit her sister.

The last visit had been especially memorable.

"I made coffee and scrambled eggs," she told him.

It was a sort of peace offering, but Nick was still sporting that scowl. A scowl that would likely get worse when she told him what she'd learned from the phone call that she had made while he was dressing.

"Someone's using the Granger guesthouse so I can't go there," Lindsay explained. "Dylan said he'd get someone to fix up the room in the new bunkhouse but that he wouldn't be able to spare anyone to do it today. I told him that I understood, that you and I were both adults and that we could share the same space. Besides, this place suits me just fine."

Nick had already started pouring himself a cup of coffee, but he stopped mid-pour to stare at her. No longer scowling, but he clearly wasn't happy because he was filling in the blanks on that conversation. Maybe he was also wondering if Dylan had picked up on the fact that Nick hadn't wanted her there.

"I didn't mention the towel incident," she clarified, and since that made her want to smile—something she definitely shouldn't do—Lindsay quickly added, "How's your Gumball injury?"

"Better." You wouldn't have guessed that, though, from his grumpy tone. A tone that made it all the way to his expression and his sizzling blue eyes. He drank some coffee, then huffed. "You can't think us sharing a bunkhouse, *alone*, is a good idea."

It depended on the definition of *good*, so there were several ways she could interpret that. Maybe he was referring to his very male reaction when she'd put the lip balm on him. Or something else. Both, or either, would be weighing on his mind, so she decided to go ahead and get that thousand-pound gorilla out into the open.

"I'm sure you remember a group of us ended up at the Longhorn Bar after a charity rodeo," she threw out there. "You and I drank some beer, danced, and when we ended up going outside for some fresh air, you kissed me."

Nick stared at her for what felt like hours and then cursed. "I apologized for that. I was way out of line."

Lindsay frowned, but that was exactly the answer she'd expected. "Clearly, you and I have a different take on things. You kissed me, and I liked it. No apology was necessary."

"You can't argue with the *out of line* part," he grumbled. Nick did more of that cursing. "For Pete's sake, you're my ex-girlfriend's sister. That makes you off-limits."

Apparently, his feelings on that hadn't changed in the

past six months. Of course, her feelings hadn't changed, either. Somewhere in between the dancing and the kiss, Lindsay had fallen hard for Nick. Probably best not to blurt that out, though, or it would send him running.

It had nearly sent her running, too.

She hadn't been "in the market" for falling for a man. It hadn't even been on her radar. In fact, until that kiss from Nick, she'd decided that the life her sister had would never be hers. Not that she envied what Carol Ann had now. Nope. But Lindsay had just about decided that being in love wasn't something she would ever experience. She wasn't in love with Nick, not yet, anyway, but she could see it as being a possibility. No way would Nick see it that way.

Lindsay smiled when she looked at him. Not especially hard to manage that, since he was hot eye candy in addition to being a decent guy. Her exes hadn't quite qualified for decent status, and as Carol Ann liked to say, Lindsay was a turd magnet. Lindsay had totally agreed with her.

Until that kiss.

"When you kissed me that night, it felt as if something clicked," she confessed. She went closer to him. Probably too close. But she didn't want him to miss any part of this. Besides, it was just nice being next to him, especially when she took in the scent of his soap and the leather from his boots. "In that moment, I realized I couldn't settle for another turd."

In hindsight, she should have explained that better or at least given him a detail or two about the "turd" label. "Huh?" he asked. His forehead bunched up.

She would have explained herself, probably would have also moved closer to test his off-limits comment, but there was a knock on the bunkhouse door. Lindsay frowned, but it wasn't as deep as Nick's, and while checking his watch, he went to the door.

Lindsay checked the time: 7:00 a.m. Early by some people's standards, but their workday would start in about a half hour. Apparently, it was early enough for the boss, too, because their visitor was Dylan Granger.

He stepped in, his gaze sweeping around the bunkhouse before it landed first on Nick, then her and then on Nick again. The corner of Dylan's mouth lifted.

"Did you two sleep all right?" Dylan asked.

It wasn't just an ordinary question. Mainly because Dylan had seen the tail end of that kiss at the Longhorn, and judging by his expression, he hadn't forgotten it any more than Lindsay had.

"Fine," Nick snapped. "I just hadn't thought I would have to share the place with anyone."

Dylan lifted his shoulder. "I'm working to get Lindsay into the other bunkhouse. Just making sure that's what you want."

"It is." Nick was still snapping. Dylan was still half smiling. Lindsay made as noncommittal a sound as she could make.

"All right, then," Dylan said, his tone noncommittal, as well. "Well, I just wanted to make sure Lindsay was settling in." He looked at her. "Nick will show you the ropes."

No scowl or frown that time from Nick, but he did pull back his shoulders. "You usually have Bree work with the new trainers."

"Usually," Dylan repeated. "But I need her to go up to Abilene and take a look at some Appaloosas I want to buy. Showing Lindsay around won't be a problem, will it?"

And just like that, the scowl had returned. "Can we have a word?" Nick asked, but he didn't wait for Dylan to answer. Nick just headed out the back door.

Dylan didn't immediately follow him, though. He looked at Lindsay. "Is this about the kiss?" Dylan asked her.

She could have softened her response with a *maybe* or even a *possibly*, but it would have been a lie. Lindsay nodded. Dylan just sighed and went outside where Nick was waiting.

Since Nick clearly wanted the conversation to be private so he could gripe to Dylan about why this sleeping— and perhaps the working—arrangement wasn't going to cut it for him, Lindsay went out the front door. She could go around the massive main house and then make her way to the barn. At least that way she could get a start on the job she'd been hired to do. However, when Lindsay made it to the house, she spotted someone in the driveway.

Her sister.

Carol Ann was just getting out of her minivan and came her way the moment she saw Lindsay. "I know it's early, but I wanted to catch you before you started work. I won't stay long," Carol Ann immediately added. "I have to get back fast, because Craig needs to leave for work at the store."

Craig was her husband along with being the manager of the hardware and feed store. Since Carol Ann was a stay-at-home mom, that meant she'd need to get back to their son, Tanner.

"I just wanted to drop by and wish you good luck on your first day here at the ranch," Carol Ann added.

"Thanks." Lindsay hugged her. "I was on my way to the barn. You want to walk with me?"

"Sure. Just don't let me get in the way of anything you have to do." Carol Ann fell in step alongside her as they walked around the house. "So, how is it being here?"

As she'd done with Dylan, Lindsay went with the truth. "Nick and I are staying in the same bunkhouse. Alone. Just the two of us." And she left it at that.

"Oh." There was both surprise and concern in her sister's voice. "You think that's a good idea?"

Lindsay nearly smiled, because that was a version of the question that Nick had asked. "According to Nick, no. I think he's being cautious after the kiss at the Longhorn." A kiss that Lindsay had told her sister all about.

Carol Ann dragged in a long breath that could mean she was gearing up for a long response. Or maybe she was steeling herself. "I can definitely see Nick's side of this. It was weird for you two to kiss."

Lindsay frowned. When she'd first told Carol Ann about what'd happened, her sister hadn't considered it peculiar. Looking back, though, Tanner had been throwing a tantrum, and Carol Ann had been getting over a cold. Maybe it hadn't actually sunk in.

"I kissed your husband back in middle school before he was even on your radar—or you on his," Lindsay reminded her. And yes, Carol Ann knew all about that kiss, too.

Her sister gave Lindsay a flat look. "You were both twelve. That doesn't count."

"You were seventeen and eighteen when you were with Nick," Lindsay argued.

"Big difference. Nick and I were together, as a couple.

It wasn't just an innocent peck under the bleachers after a football game. Or a kiss after a night of drinking."

Lindsay frowned at that, too. Her sister's first description had been dead-on. The kiss with Craig had been a peck. Not the one with Nick, though, and she didn't like that Carol Ann had dismissed it with the "night of drinking."

"Nick was my actual boyfriend," Carol said as if she needed to bolster up her argument even more.

"But you never had actual sex," Lindsay pointed out. Well, there'd been no sex unless Carol Ann had failed to tell her. They hadn't been as close as most twins, because they'd always been complete opposites, but Lindsay believed they'd spilled the truth about the big stuff. And this would have been *big*.

"No, I didn't have sex with Nick," Carol Ann muttered several long moments later. "But we came very, very close a couple of times."

Lindsay wasn't sure whether to feel relieved about that or not. *Very, very close* could include things she definitely didn't want to think about, especially since she had been fantasizing about doing those same things, and more, with Nick since the kiss at the bar.

"I believe it would bother Nick to be with you," Carol Ann went on. "It should bother you, too. I mean, how would you know he wasn't thinking about me when he was kissing you?"

Good point. It would be impossible for Nick to push something like that out of his mind. It was a part of his past, and while it didn't lessen the heat Lindsay felt for him, it tightened her stomach until it was in a knot.

While Lindsay mulled that over, they made it to the barn, and she immediately saw the focus of her mulling. Nick. He was at the corral fence, sipping his coffee and looking at a gelding. Maybe Gumball, since he was a piebald. No Dylan, but one of the local large animal vets, Allie Devlin, was examining a bay mare on the other side of the corral.

"I should go," Carol Ann said the moment her attention landed on Nick. She made it a step but then caught on to Lindsay's shoulder as if balancing herself.

That got Lindsay's attention, and she took hold of her sister's arm. "Are you okay?" Lindsay asked.

Carol Ann sighed. "Just a little dizzy spell, that's all. I'm pretty sure I'm pregnant. Don't tell anyone yet, not even Craig," she quickly added. "We've been trying for a couple of months now, and I don't want to get his hopes up if it turns out I'm wrong." She smiled softly. "I'm not wrong, though. I just need to get the test to verify it, and then I can give him the good news on his birthday in two weeks."

Lindsay hugged her sister. "I'm so happy for you." And she was.

Carol Ann certainly didn't say the same thing to her, and when she brushed a kiss on Lindsay's cheek, she added, "Remember what I just told you about Nick."

Lindsay doubted she'd ever forget it, but the possibility of that happening went up a notch when Nick turned around, his gaze going to hers. And there it was. The build-up of heat became an avalanche.

Good grief.

Because he was a man she'd known for most of her life, it stunned her that she could feel something so strong that hadn't been there before the kiss. It was as if his mouth had unlocked something. And no, that wasn't purely sexual, though it was a huge part of it.

Why couldn't she just get him out of her thoughts, and why did her eyes think it was a wonderful idea to mentally undress him and get another look at what she'd seen the night before? Lindsay didn't have those answers, but she steeled herself and went closer.

"We need to talk," Nick said right off, and he motioned for her to follow him into the barn.

She did, dreading every step. His expression definitely wasn't one of a friendly "showing her the ropes." Thankfully, there wasn't anyone else in the barn, so there wouldn't be an audience in case this turned ugly.

"Did you talk Dylan into firing me?" she came out and asked.

His expression immediately changed—his eyes widening—and he looked at her as if she'd sprouted an extra ear or something. "No. Hell no," he added, and he scrubbed his hand over his face. "I just wanted to let him know that there could be a problem. Because of... well...because of the kissing."

Oh.

She'd never seen Nick flustered, but Lindsay was pretty sure he was now. It made her want to smile, just a little, because she was certainly flustered with her feelings for him. She doubted a smile would go over very well, though, and besides, he'd brought up a subject she felt needed some clarification.

"Did you think about Carol Ann when you kissed me that night at the Longhorn?" she asked.

He belted out another "hell" and then added another "no." Nick hadn't hesitated on that, either, which meant Carol Ann had been wrong. And that made Lindsay smile.

"What else did you tell Dylan about the kiss?" Lindsay pressed.

Nick looked at her for several dragging moments. "I didn't talk to Dylan about what had gone on at the Longhorn. I told him there was a strong possibility that there'd be other kisses. With you."

Lindsay could have sworn her heart dropped all the way to the heels of her boots, and it took all the air in her lungs with it. "What?" she managed to say.

But that was the only word that came out of her mouth before Nick pulled her to him and put his mouth on hers.

Wow. That was the first thought that went through her head. More wows followed as the memories of the other kiss collided with this one.

She'd thought the other one had been memorable, but this one was the king of kisses. All fire, need and a whole lot of touching as Nick yanked her against him. It was as if he was trying to work out his frustrations, cool his temper and give her an orgasm all in the same deep kiss. Lindsay didn't know if it worked for the first two, but she was pretty sure she felt the third one coming on.

Just as Nick ended it.

And with a single word of bad profanity leaving his mouth, he snapped away from her and stormed off.

CHAPTER THREE

NICK HAD TAKEN more cold showers in the past week than he had during his entire lifetime. And he could only blame himself for the extreme need for all that icy water. He'd been the one to launch right into that kiss with Lindsay, and now he was paying the price for it.

By wanting another kiss.

By needing to get her in his bed.

He couldn't do either of those. He'd figured that out a split second after he'd taken his mouth off hers. That's why he'd walked away, started working, and been working as hard and as long as possible—along with trying to cool down his body with the cold showers.

The work and showers had helped. More help had come when Dylan had assigned Lindsay to pair up with another trainer to deal with those new Appaloosas he'd brought in. That had put her on the other side of the ranch in the barn just off the back pasture. And the final help had come when she'd moved to the house she'd bought from the widow, Mrs. Farley, who'd relocated to Dallas to be closer to her kids. Being in her own place had gotten Lindsay out of sight in the evenings. So far, nothing had worked for getting her out of his mind for all the hours in the days and nights.

Nick put Gumball through the paces of training, careful of the gelding's hind legs. Like the other horses he had on his training schedule, Gumball had settled down plenty since that first day Nick had worked with him. Nick still didn't have him to the point, though, where just anyone could ride him, and he was too skittish around the cattle.

"You got any idea what they do with horses that don't live up to expectations?" he grumbled to Gumball. "It's not pretty. It starts with *g* and rhymes with *loo*."

Gumball looked over at him and made a sound that could have only been interpreted as "bullshit." Which is was. The gelding wouldn't be shipped off to the glue factory had there been such a thing, but if he didn't settle in, then he'd be sold to someone who didn't mind a persnickety horse who couldn't do the job of getting hands to and from all parts of the ranch.

The next look Gumball gave him let Nick know he had no concerns about that whatsoever. And maybe he didn't. Dylan had been the one to buy him, and he had a knack for seeing potential in a horse. That meant it was Nick's job to polish that potential, and he could do that by following the training plan.

By following the rules, he mentally added.

Rules worked. They kept things running as they should and lessened the chances of complications. And yes, a big reason for why he believed that was his godawful upbringing.

Nick heard the laughter coming from the other side of the corral and looked up to see Lindsay riding up on a paint gelding. *Rules work*, he repeated to himself.

But he frowned.

Sometimes, rules sucked, too, when they held you back from kissing a woman you wanted to kiss.

Lindsay was riding up with Skeeter Muldoon, the

oldest hand at the ranch. Nick wasn't sure how old Skeeter was exactly, but the man's wrinkles had wrinkles, and he'd been around during the days when Dylan's grandfather had run the place.

After they got off the horses, Skeeter and Lindsay chatted awhile and laughed a little longer before she finally looked at Nick. He'd spotted her a time or two over the past week, but she'd always waved, smiled and gone on her way. Probably because she knew he was trying to keep some distance between his mouth and hers. Today was different, though. She said something he didn't catch to Skeeter, and the old hand took the reins of both horses and headed into the barn with them.

And Lindsay came his way.

He was about to warn her of Gumball's moody tendencies, but the gelding went to Lindsay as if they were old friends and gave Lindsay's shoulder a gentle nudge.

"Such a sweet boy," Lindsay purred, and Gumball gave Nick a gloating glance before he sauntered—yes, sauntered—toward the water trough.

Lindsay was still smiling when she walked closer to him. "Skeeter said rain was coming in an hour or so. Said he could feel it because he had a 'mighty powerful ache' in the bone he broke in his arm when he was twelve." She sounded skeptical when she glanced up at the sky. Not completely cloudless but close. "How accurate is he on weather predictions?"

"A hundred percent," Nick verified without hesitation. "Take an umbrella if you're headed out anywhere."

She nodded and seemed both unconvinced and amused. "Skeeter also said I was to be careful or I'd end up in your bed. How accurate is he about predictions like that?"

Now he hesitated. It took some effort for Nick not to curse over the old ranch hand's doling out a bed warning. "No percent whatsoever."

Of course, it meant that Skeeter, who was partially blind and hard of hearing, had still seen the attraction between Lindsay and him. Not a good sign if it was that obvious.

"It's Skeeter's birthday," Lindsay went on. "He won't say how old he is exactly, but he claims if we buy him enough beer, he might spill. Anyway, a group of us are getting together at the Longhorn to celebrate. You're invited."

"The Longhorn?" he repeated.

Lindsay shrugged. "Not many places for an adult birthday party in Wrangler's Creek. Worried about returning to the scene of the crime?" she joked.

Yeah, he was.

Of course, now the barn fell into that category, too, because he'd also kissed her there. He'd thought enough about her during the showers and his sleepless nights that they weren't exactly Lindsay-free zones, either.

"I shouldn't have kissed you again," he said.

Another shrug. "I think we get a little mindless when we're around each other. Like now, for instance. I'm thinking things about you that would make you blush." She chuckled.

Then *she* blushed.

Nick didn't want to know about those thoughts, because he was having some bad ones himself. That's why he was about to decline the invitation, but Lindsay spoke before he could say anything.

"Come if you can," she added. "I'll understand if you can't make it."

That was it. A no-pressure pitch as she walked off,

giving him a nice view of the jeans-clad butt that had garnered his attention that night in the bunkhouse. It was still an attention-getter.

Lindsay gave Gumball a neck pat before she left the corral and headed in the direction where the hands parked their vehicles. No doubt so she could go home and get changed for a celebration. One for a man Nick had known his whole life. The party would include lots of beer. Probably dancing, too.

The two things that had led up to that first kiss.

Except this time he wouldn't be there. Plenty of the other hands would be, though, and he'd already heard a couple of the guys talking about hitting on Lindsay.

Crap.

Nick cursed himself. Then cursed those party-bound ranch hands and this blasted attraction that wouldn't cool down. He put up Gumball and went to his bunkhouse so he could shower and change. He opted for cold water again, and if he'd thought ice packs would help, Nick would have tried that, too.

He went ahead and ate to give everyone else time to get to the Longhorn. He definitely didn't want to be the first to get there, but the minute he arrived, Nick realized that wasn't a problem. It appeared that half of Wrangler's Creek had shown up to celebrate Skeeter's birthday. And despite the wall-to-wall crowd, he had no trouble spotting Lindsay.

She was standing next to Skeeter at the bar, and as expected the hands from the Granger Ranch were surrounding her. She didn't have on jeans tonight but rather a blue summer dress that hit several inches above her knee. Her legs managed to grab his interest as much as her butt had.

He'd seen her like this before, he realized. Laughing, drinking a beer and having fun. She probably didn't know that her face lit up when she was happy. Probably didn't know that it made her even more beautiful than she already was.

The ranch hands noticed, all right. Nick saw a couple of them give her long, slow glances, and while that didn't please him one bit, he couldn't blame them, because he was doing the same thing.

Nick stood there and watched her for a few seconds, feeling another wave of that heat wash over him. His belly tightened, and there was some tightening below that, too, behind his zipper.

She was mid-laugh over something Skeeter had said when she spotted Nick, and he saw the surprise in her eyes. And he felt the energy sizzle between them. He was sure if he had a mirror that he'd be seeing the same sizzle in his own eyes.

"I'm glad you came," someone said. Not Lindsay. She was still at the bar. This was Jolene Millhouse, who worked at the hardware and feed store, and she stepped directly in front of Nick.

Like he did just about everybody else in Wrangler's Creek, Nick had known her for years, and for most of those years, she'd looked at him the way he'd just been looking at Lindsay. Jolene and he had even hooked up a time or two. Nothing serious, though, which pretty much described all his relationships since high school. Which got him thinking.

Had it actually been serious between him and Carol Ann?

He wanted to say no, but that's because the idiot part behind his zipper was encouraging him to believe that if it wasn't serious, then maybe Carol Ann wasn't a real ex. But as a general rule, Nick didn't like lying to himself. Yeah, it'd been serious and exclusive between him and Carol Ann.

And that had happened fifteen years ago.

"Aren't you even going to take your eyes off Lindsay long enough to say hello?" Jolene asked.

Until she'd said that, Nick hadn't even realized he'd been staring at Lindsay, but now he shifted his gaze to Jolene. She studied him over the top of her drink and smiled. "You got it bad, Nick. Wanna know the cure for it?" She didn't wait for him to say no, that he didn't want to know. "Sex."

Jolene winked, letting him know that she could help him out with that "cure." He wouldn't take her up on that, even if he hadn't been lusting over Lindsay.

"Well, another time then," Jolene said, glancing back at Lindsay. "Another time for me, anyway. It looks as if you've made your plans for the evening."

He hadn't. In fact, Nick was still waffling back and forth on whether to make the mistake with Lindsay now or have another go at taking a shower to cool him down so he could try to resist her.

Lindsay already had a beer in her hand, but she snagged another one and headed his way. "I've been meaning to ask," she greeted, "is there an expiration on the man rule of not being with your ex-girlfriend's sister?"

"According to what Carol Ann told you, no." He took the beer, had a long pull, while he continued to look at her.

"Yes," she said, then paused. "Do you wish that I'd never come back to Wrangler's Creek?"

"No." He meant it, too. "This is your home."

He started to say more, but then he realized there were several people interested in this conversation. Jolene for one, but also the two ranch hands she was chatting with. Even Skeeter was aiming some glances their way. Apparently, folks were waiting to see where this was going so they could start the rumor mill.

Since there was nothing Nick could do about the gossip, he could at least minimize what the gossips could hear and see. They'd just have to make up the real details for themselves.

"Let's go this way," Nick told Lindsay, and he led her through the main bar and out back. Of course, that made him an idiot because there was a pitfall to privacy, and that was the privacy itself.

With Lindsay.

That didn't stop him from continuing. Nick took her to the back porch beneath the old tin roof where he could see and hear the rain. Yes, the very rain that Skeeter had predicted. Skeeter would be wrong, though, about Lindsay getting into his bed. For the time being, anyway.

The porch was empty but wouldn't stay that way. Soon, someone would come out for a smoke or in search of the fresh air that had led him and Lindsay to their first kiss. That's why Nick knew he had to hurry so they wouldn't be interrupted.

He turned to tell her that he was driving himself crazy with these thoughts of her, but it wasn't a good idea to turn. Or look. Because Nick felt the same punch that he'd felt the other times he'd seen her like this. He didn't bother to curse himself or fight it. He just slid his arm around the back of her neck and kissed her.

Their beer bottles clinked and clanged between them, but without breaking the lip-lock, Nick took them and put them on the window ledge next to them. That not only freed up their hands, but with nothing between them, he could pull Lindsay right against him.

He could have sworn his body said, "Thank you!"

But Nick didn't think his brain would be in on that gratitude. That's because the kiss was even better than the others, and he knew he'd never forget that taste. Like a good party and a feast all rolled into one. He'd never forget the feel of her in his arms, either. Hard to forget how her breasts pressed against his chest. And even if he developed some kind of memory block, that sound she made would stay with him.

A soft, silky moan that had another "thank you" ring to it.

Great. It couldn't be good that both of them were going to be stupid about this at the same time, but apparently that was the case. Because not only did they deepen the kiss, the touching and the body-to-body contact went up a notch.

Before she hooked her arm around his waist and gave his butt a hard push, Nick hadn't thought they could get any closer while standing outside, but he'd been wrong. Of course, it helped that it was the right kind of contact. His zipper against the front of her dress. It gave him a huge reminder that he wanted her out of that dress. Out of her bra and panties, too.

But not here.

Not on the back porch of the Longhorn Bar.

That warning thankfully blared through his head. "We're leaving now," Nick insisted. He took hold of her hand and hurried her down the steps and into the rain.

CHAPTER FOUR

THE RAIN DIDN'T cool down Lindsay one bit, and while she hadn't seen this coming—not so soon, anyway—she welcomed it.

Thankfully, they hadn't hurt themselves with the breakneck race from the back of the Longhorn to the side parking lot. She could add another thanks that no one had seen or stopped them along the way. Lindsay wouldn't have cared if someone had spied them, but she doubted Nick wanted the word out until he'd worked through his man rule and his feelings for her.

Of course, it was possible the only thing he was feeling for her was lust. But she thought something more was there, just beneath the surface. And no, she wasn't talking about his jeans and boxers.

Lindsay got another round of things she welcomed and was thankful for when they got into Nick's truck and he immediately pulled her into his arms. She got another kiss, and his mouth was pure magic.

All the feelings and the heat he could bring out in her, and better yet, the reaction was mutual.

The kiss was hard and hungry, as if he were starved for her. All that skirting around each other they'd done for the last week had been an insane kind of foreplay.

"Go to my place," she insisted when he broke the kiss to start the truck. "It's closer." Even though closer sud-

denly didn't feel near enough. Still, it was better than
going seven miles or so back to the Granger Ranch.

Nick nodded and started driving, but they hadn't gone
far when he glanced at her. Uh-oh. Common sense—or
rather what he thought of as common sense—was returning now that he didn't have an immediate source
of the scalding attraction.

Lindsay did something about that.

She dropped a quick kiss on his mouth and then
lowered her head to go after his neck. That way, Nick
could still see out the windshield while she stoked the
fire. It turned out, though, that stoking wasn't that hard.
One kiss, then a lick and nip on his neck, had him cursing her.

Nick pulled off the side of the road, both the truck
and his motions jerky and hurried, and the second they
were at a stop, he took her again. This time, his hand
went into her hair. This time it was even harder than the
other kiss and had a Texas-sized amount of urgency to
it. Lindsay hadn't lost any of her own urgency, but that
revved her up to the next level.

"We should get to my house now," she insisted. Best
not to have sex while pulled off on Creek Road. It wasn't
exactly a hotbed of traffic, but there were four houses
on the road, and one of the other owners could drive
up at any time.

That brought on more cursing from Nick, and he
let go of her to throw the truck into gear. They made
it about a block before he pulled over again and kissed
her. This time, his hand went up her dress.

And then inside her panties.

Lindsay saw stars. Maybe the moon. Heck, an entire
galaxy, and the revving up skyrocketed her straight to

a need that made her not care one bit that they were on the side of a road, in a truck.

Nick seemed to care, though. He pulled back his hand, let go of her and, with yet another round of cursing, he started driving toward her house. Even though it was only about three more blocks away, they stopped two more times. And the last time, Lindsay put *her* hand in *his* pants. Turnabout was fair play, but like the touching he'd done to her, it only made them crazier than they already were.

Nick pulled into her driveway and nearly plowed the truck into the porch of the small house. Lindsay didn't mind, because it put them closer to being inside. Only then did she realize something.

"My key is in my purse at the Longhorn," she said, her breath gusting. "I left it on the bar."

If he was upset about that, he darn sure didn't show it. He just gave her another of those scorcher kisses, this one so hot that it possibly melted every thread of her underwear, and he hauled her out of his truck. He didn't stop the kissing, which made her thankful for yet something else—that she didn't have neighbors right on top of her.

They were already soaked from the run from the Longhorn, but a second soaking came when they got out of the truck. It probably would have gone a lot faster and Lindsay wouldn't have bashed her elbow on the steering wheel if they'd stopped kissing and groping, but that hardly seemed like an option.

Nothing did.

Except for her having Nick.

Nick was on the same page there, too. They kissed their way up the steps onto her postage stamp of a porch and finally made it to the door. With his arms wrapped around her and his mouth on hers, Nick rammed his shoulder into the door and sent it flying open, along with shattering some of the wood frame that had held it in place.

"I'll fix that later," he mumbled around the kiss.

At the moment repairs of any kind were way down on her list of concerns. Ditto for bruises and torn clothes. Even air for her lungs. The ache and burn had gone to a full-scale blaze, and Lindsay wanted a fix—now.

Nick had enough sense to shut the door and drag a chair over in front of it to hold it in place. And he did all of that while still kissing her blind. Obviously, he had no trouble multitasking with his smooth, fluid movements.

Lindsay's movements, however, weren't quite as slick. She hoped Nick shared her views about torn clothes not being a problem, because when she went after his shirt, she heard a button pop and then ping to the floor.

"I'll fix that for you later," she assured him.

His shirt fought her every step of the way, but Lindsay got it off him. Finally! And she got to touch and kiss all those wonderful muscles on his chest. He was ripped. Perfect, too. But then she'd already known that because of the towel peep show in the bunkhouse.

She kissed her way down to his stomach while she got him unzipped, and she would have just continued that if Nick hadn't hauled her back up. So he could go after her dress, she realized. He pulled it off over her head, hitting himself in the face along the way, but that didn't deter him. He rid her of her bra and had a touching, kissing fest on her body as she'd done to his.

"Perfect," he drawled.

There was nothing perfect about her body, but Lindsay was glad he thought that. Glad, too, that with the next set of kisses, he hooked his arm around her waist and got her moving to her bedroom. Or what he likely thought was her bedroom. It wasn't, so Lindsay shifted directions and kissed him all the way there.

Before today, they'd kissed twice, and now she'd already lost count of how many times they'd shared that particular pleasure. She was fairly sure that the number was going to skyrocket before this night was over.

There were still unpacked boxes on the floor, which they tripped over, but it was a small room with a big bed so they landed on the mattress. With him on top of her. All in all, not a bad place, because she could feel more of him this way and felt yet even more when she slipped her hands into his jeans.

He didn't curse this time, but his eyes met hers. So intense. So on fire. He groaned out something she didn't understand, and he ravaged her mouth again. Her breasts, too. If she hadn't already been so close to the brink, she might have let him linger there awhile. But Lindsay wanted a different source of pleasure-giving right now.

She got him unzipped and accidentally punched him in the stomach. He grunted, pushed her hand away and finished the job himself. Boots, jeans and boxers—all gone. And she finally got a great look at what had been behind the towel.

"Perfect," she concluded.

The corner of his mouth hitched in the shortest history of short smiles. It ended when he got on the condom he took from his wallet and then pushed into her. A lot of things ended for Lindsay in that moment, too.

Sanity, for instance. Ditto for any other thoughts. Everything vanished except for Nick and the pleasure. Not bad things to hold on to.

It turned out that Nick didn't just look perfect. He also hit the mark on that with lovemaking. Definitely not too gentle. Not too fast, either. But he certainly was thorough. He moved harder, deeper, and swept her right into the rhythm that Lindsay knew would take her to only one place.

A giant climax.

Thankfully, it was really the only place she wanted to go, anyway, and since Nick had been the one to deliver on being "perfect," she took him right along with her.

CHAPTER FIVE

IT WAS HARD for Nick to feel too bad over a broken man rule when the rest of him felt so darn good. Even harder to feel bad when he was next to Lindsay in her bed—a place she'd spent not only the night before but most of Saturday morning.

Since it was already 10:00 a.m., they'd eventually have to get up, but Nick wasn't pushing it. They'd worn themselves out with the sex, and he was considering seeing just how much more wearing out they could do since neither of them would have to be back at work until Monday morning.

He silently groaned at the thought of the weekend being over. Not just because he and Lindsay wouldn't be able to stay in bed but also because he'd have to answer a question or two. After all, they had left the Longhorn Bar without so much as a goodbye. She'd even left her purse there. Someone would have realized that, and while it was almost certainly safe, plenty of people could have noticed when he'd kissed Lindsay on the back porch. Or the way they'd made a run through the rain to his truck and then driven off.

Yeah, there'd be questions all right.

From the other hands. And eventually from Carol Ann when word reached her. Before that, though, Nick needed to figure out some things for himself just so he stood a chance of answering those questions.

Since that reminder was now fixed in his head, it meant he wouldn't be going back to sleep. Nick eased from the bed, gathering up his clothes—at least the ones he could find—and he headed to the shower. Not the one in the master bedroom where Lindsay was still sacked out. He didn't want to wake her, so he used the guest bathroom across the hall. After he was done, he pulled on his jeans and went in search of coffee. And he found it.

Found Lindsay, too.

She was in the kitchen, her back to him as it had been that night when he'd seen her in the bunkhouse. Except there were no jeans this time. She was wearing a bulky T-shirt and nothing else. He got a nice view of that "nothing else" when she reached into the cabinet for cups, and he saw her bare butt.

Nick found himself going to her. She turned, already smiling, and as if it were something they'd been doing for years, she pulled him into her arms. Any kiss from her was a good one, but a smiling kiss had some extra kick to it.

"How'd your bruised ribs hold up to our marathon of sex?" she asked.

"Just fine. Didn't even notice the pain." But he sure as heck noticed her. He pulled her back to him and brushed his mouth on the top of her head. "Just how much of a monkey wrench will this put in your life?"

She eased back, met his gaze. "Big enough, depending on how my sister handles it." Lindsay paused, and the smile returned. "Monkey wrenches can be fun, though." She chuckled and set the cups aside so she could give him a real kiss. Definitely not a top-of-the-head peck.

Fun.

So that's what this was. Nick wasn't sure whether to feel relieved or troubled that she hadn't thought it was something more. Or that it could at least lead to more. Soon, though, he was neither relieved nor troubled. That's because the kiss continued, hot and pressing as their other kisses had been, and he knew this one was going to take them straight back to bed.

Or to the floor, since it was closer.

He got more proof of that as he slid his hands down to her bare butt. Lindsay, of course, did her own version of sliding. She took her mouth to his neck and her hands to his jeans.

"Let's see how fast I can get you out of these," she purred when her mouth came back to his.

Nick soon learned the answer to that.

Fast.

NICK GAVE GUMBALL a warning glance before he walked up to the gelding. It was early, an hour or more before the hands would start their shift, but he'd wanted to jump into work and hoped that it would clear his head.

Over the last decade, he'd worked with plenty of smart horses who could let him know right off what they were thinking, but this gelding was the best at that. With the flick of his white tail and the indifferent look he gave him, it made Nick think they'd finally reached some kind of truce.

Good.

Because he sure as heck needed one part of his life

to be trouble-free, and he couldn't say that about anything else.

As expected, there'd been talk all right, and it'd started as soon as he'd gotten back to the bunkhouse on Sunday night. It had continued through this Monday morning and likely would until all the other hands had exhausted their gossip and crude comments. Of course, he had gotten some "way to go" looks and knowing winks. He'd scowled at all of it and hopefully sent a clear message for them to keep their noses out of his business.

Nick put Gumball through the training routine, and the gelding aced it, giving him hope that this would be the last session they'd need. Next up was a chestnut mare he would have gotten started on if he hadn't seen Lindsay. She was in the parking area, next to her truck, and she wasn't alone.

Carol Ann was with her, and he could tell from both women's body language that they were having a heated discussion. When the morning breeze shifted and the sound of their voices carried his way, he could hear it, too.

"I can't believe you did this," Carol Ann said.

Well, hell.

Since this had to be about Lindsay and him, Nick left the mare in the corral and hurried to the women. Lindsay saw him coming, but Carol Ann didn't. She just kept on talking.

"You knew my feelings about this," Carol Ann went on, "and you did it, anyway."

Nick cleared his throat to get Carol Ann's attention, and she whirled around to face him. No tears, thank goodness, but she was pissed off. And maybe hurt.

"I was the one who started things between Lindsay and me," Nick volunteered. "I kissed her. Many, many times," he added. "And yes, I had sex with her. The many, many applies to that, too."

Both Lindsay and Carol Ann opened their mouths to say something, but Nick lifted his hand to silence them. When he finished he'd give them a turn. A turn that Carol Ann might not want once she heard what he was about to tell her.

"I know you see that as some kind of broken rule," he went on, staring at Carol Ann, "but that was a lifetime ago. We were kids. Lindsay and I aren't, and what I feel for her is going on now, and it's not kids' stuff."

From the corral behind him, Nick heard Gumball whinnying out what seemed to be a thumbs-up.

Again, Lindsay started to say something, but this time it was Carol Ann who cut her off. Carol Ann folded her arms over her chest. "And what exactly do you feel for my sister?"

He darn sure hadn't wanted this to be done as a threesome, but that air needed clearing. "I care a lot for her. In fact, I'm falling in love with her. Now, I'm sorry if that hurts you, and maybe you feel you can never accept it. But don't take this out on Lindsay. Don't let it ruin your relationship with her. Especially since this is just fun for her."

Crud. He hadn't meant to blurt out that last part. Gumball's next sound, a fluttering snort, let Nick know that the gelding hadn't thought it such a good idea, either. It had a "you idiot" ring to it. And maybe he was an idiot for putting this all out there, but it was something that had been bugging him since Lindsay had been so casual about what was between them. Yeah, they'd had plenty of fun, but it had meant a whole lot more to him than that.

Carol Ann still had her arms folded over her chest when she turned to her sister. "And how exactly do you feel about Nick?"

Lindsay had a "deer caught in the headlights" moment, followed by a look of discomfort. A look that Nick figured was on his own face.

"I've already done the falling," Lindsay finally said. "I'm head over heels in love with him."

That got the look of discomfort off his face, and he smiled. Until he remembered Carol Ann was still right there. He steeled himself for the verbal blast and fallout that Lindsay's twin was no doubt about to give them. Then maybe he could find a quiet spot and talk things out with the woman who'd just admitted she was in love with him. And not just in love, either. Head over heels.

He grinned.

Then Nick quit grinning when Carol Ann turned to him. He opened his mouth to tell her, firmly, that he wouldn't be held to an old man rule, but Carol Ann stopped him with a lifted hand as he'd done to her earlier.

"All right then," Carol Ann said, and she smiled. Actually smiled, and it didn't look as if it was one of the *I'm planning revenge* ones. "I figured it would take you a while to get it all out in the open, and I think this helped."

Then Carol Ann did something that would have stunned him to silence had he not already been quiet. She brushed a kiss on his cheek. "I just want you and my sister to be happy," she added.

Again, there was no revenge plot or maniacal hint to it. It was genuine.

Nick had to shake his head. "When I walked up, you were chewing Lindsay out," he said.

Carol Ann made a quick sound of agreement and also added quickly narrowed eyes at her twin. Eyes that didn't stay narrowed for long, though. "That's because Lindsay spilled to Craig that I was pregnant."

"No," Lindsay argued. "I was worried about you. When you called me last night and said you'd had another dizzy spell, I was concerned. I just mentioned to Craig that he should keep an eye on you."

Carol Ann huffed. "That's a big red flag because the only time I get dizzy is when I'm pregnant." She huffed again, but there didn't seem to be any anger in it. In fact, she kissed Lindsay's cheek. "Why don't you and Nick come to dinner this weekend? We can celebrate the new baby, Craig's birthday and this." She motioned to Nick and Lindsay, and then took hold of her sister, moved her to Nick's side and maneuvered Nick's arm around her. *"This,"* Carol Ann amended.

With her smile even wider, Carol Ann waved and headed toward her car. "You can kiss her now, Nick," Carol Ann added with a chuckle.

Nick wanted to do just that. Man, did he. But he looked at Lindsay to see if she was as confused about this as he was.

Lindsay just shrugged. "Once she realized this wasn't just a fling, she was okay with it." She paused. "It's not just a fling, is it?"

"No. It's the real thing." And he took that kiss.

Nick claimed her mouth, and he let that hit of heat slide right through him.

"Sorry," he added when he eased back from her. "This isn't the place for a kiss like that. There are rules about this sort of thing."

"Good thing for you that I've always been a rule breaker." She grabbed on to a handful of his shirt and pulled him to her.

Yes, and later when they were alone, he'd see just how many rules they could break. For now, he simply kissed her again.

Behind them, Gumball neighed, and Nick could almost hear the horse say, "It's about damn time."

* * * * *

Can't get enough romantic suspense?
Then USA TODAY *bestselling author*
Delores Fossen's Cowboy Above the Law *has got*
you covered. Sexy Deputy Court McCall won't rest
until the person responsible for shooting his father
is brought to justice. Even if it means going after a
woman from his past, a woman he's never been able
to forget...

Read on for a sneak peek at this gripping
Harlequin Intrigue book!

Chapter One

Deputy Court McCall glanced down at the blood on his shirt. *His father's blood.* Just the sight of it sliced away at him and made him feel as if someone had put a bullet in him, too.

Court hadn't changed into clean clothes because he wanted Rayna Travers to see what she had done. He wanted to be right in her face when he told her that she'd failed.

Barely though.

His father, Warren, was still alive, hanging on by a thread, but Court refused to accept that he wouldn't make it. No, his father would not only recover, but Warren would also help Court put Rayna behind bars. This time, she wasn't going to get away with murder.

Court pulled to a stop in front of her house, a place not exactly on the beaten path. Of course, that applied to a lot of the homes in or near McCall Canyon. His ancestors had founded the town over a hundred years ago, and it had become exactly what they'd intended it to be—a ranching community.

What they almost certainly hadn't counted on was having a would-be killer in their midst.

Court looked down at his hands. Steady. That was

good. Because there was nothing steady inside him. The anger was bubbling up, and he had to make sure he reined in his temper enough to arrest Rayna. He wouldn't resort to strong-arm tactics, but there was a high chance he would say something he shouldn't.

Since Rayna's car was in her driveway, it probably meant she was home. Good. He hadn't wanted to go hunting for her. Still, it was somewhat of a surprise that she hadn't gone on the run. Of course, she was probably going to say she was innocent, that she hadn't had anything to do with the shot that'd slammed into his father's chest. But simply put, she had a strong motive to kill a McCall.

And then there was the witness.

If Rayna tried to convince him she'd had no part in the shooting, then Court could let her know that someone had spotted her in the vicinity of the sheriff's office just minutes before Warren had been gunned down. Then, Court would follow through on her arrest.

He got out of his truck and started toward the porch of the small stone-front house, but Court only made it a few steps because his phone rang, and his brother's name popped up on the screen.

Egan.

Egan wasn't just his big brother though. He was also Court's boss since Egan was the sheriff of McCall Canyon. By now, Egan had probably figured out where Court was heading and wanted to make sure his deputy followed the book on this one.

He would.

Not cutting corners because he wanted Rayna behind bars.

Court ignored the call, and the ding of the voice mail

that followed, and went up the steps to the front door. This wasn't his first time here. Once, he'd made many trips to Rayna's door—before she'd chosen another man over him. Once, he'd had feelings for her. He had feelings now, too, but they had nothing to do with the old attraction he'd once felt.

He steeled himself and put his hand over his firearm in case Rayna wasn't finished with her shooting spree today.

"Open up," Court said, knocking on the door. Of course, he knocked a lot louder than necessary, but he wanted to make sure she heard him.

If she did hear him, she darn sure didn't answer. He knocked again, his anger rising even more, and Court finally tested the knob. Unlocked. So, he threw open the door.

And he found a gun pointed right in his face.

Rayna's finger was on the trigger.

Court cursed and automatically drew his own weapon. Obviously, it was too late because she could have fired before he'd even had a chance to do that. She didn't though. Maybe because Rayna felt she'd already fulfilled her quota of shooting McCalls today.

"Put down your gun," he snarled.

"No." Rayna shook her head, and that's when he noticed there was blood in her blond hair. Blood on the side of her face, too. Added to that, he could see bruises and cuts on her knuckles and wrists. "I'm not going to let you try to kill me again."

"Again?" Court was certain he looked very confused. Because he was. "What the devil are you talking about? I came here to arrest you for shooting my father."

If that news surprised her in the least, she didn't

show it. She didn't lower her gun, either. Rayna stood there, glaring at him.

What the hell had happened here?

Court looked behind her to see if the person who'd given her those injuries was still around. There was no sign of anyone else, but the furniture in the living room had been tossed around. There was a broken lamp on the floor. More blood, too. All indications of a struggle.

"Start talking," Court demanded, making sure he sounded like the lawman that he was.

"I will. When Egan gets here."

Court cursed again. Egan definitely wasn't going to approve of Court storming out here to see her, but his brother also couldn't ignore the evidence that Rayna had shot their father. There was definitely something else going on though.

"My father's alive," Court told her. "You didn't manage to kill him after all."

She looked down at his shirt. At the blood. And Rayna glanced away as if the sight of it sickened her. Court took advantage of her glance and knocked the gun from her hand.

At least that's what he tried to do, but Rayna held on. She pushed him, and in the same motion, she turned to run. That's when Court tackled her. Her gun went flying, skittering all the way into the living room, and both Court and she landed hard on the floor.

Rayna groaned in pain. It wasn't a soft groan, and while holding her side, she scrambled away from him. Court was about to dive at her again, but he saw yet more blood. This time on the side that she was holding.

That stopped him.

"What's wrong with you? What happened?" Court snapped.

She looked around as if considering another run for it, but then her shoulders sagged as if she was surrendering.

Rayna sat up, putting her weight, and the back of her head, against the wall. She opened her mouth as if to start with that explanation, but she had to pause when her breath shuddered. She waved that off as if embarrassed by it and then hiked up her chin. It seemed to him as if she was trying to look strong.

She failed.

"When I came in from the barn about an hour ago, there was someone in my house," Rayna said, her voice still a little unsteady. "I didn't see who it was because he immediately clubbed me on the head and grabbed me from behind." She winced again when she rubbed her left side. "I think he cracked my ribs when he hit me with something."

Well, hell. Court certainly hadn't expected any of this. And reminded himself that maybe it was all a lie, to cover up for the fact that she'd committed a crime. But those wounds weren't lies. They were the real deal. That didn't mean that they weren't self-inflicted.

"I got away from him," she continued a moment later. "After he hit me a few more times. And I pulled my gun, which I had in a slide holster in the back of my jeans. That's when he left. I'm not sure where he went."

That didn't make sense. "If someone really broke in an hour ago, why didn't you call the sheriff's office right away?"

Rayna lifted her head a little and raised her eyebrow.

For a simple gesture, it said loads. She didn't trust the cops. Didn't trust *him*.

Well, the feeling was mutual.

"I passed out for a while," she added. She shook her head as if even she was confused by that, and she lifted the side of her shirt that had the blood. There was a bruise there, too, and what appeared to be a puncture wound. One that had likely caused the bleeding. "Or maybe the guy drugged me."

"Great," he muttered. This was getting more far-fetched with each passing moment. "FYI, I'm not buying this. And as for not calling the cops when you were attacked, you called Egan when you saw me," Court pointed out.

"Because I didn't want things to escalate to this." She motioned to their positions on the floor. "Obviously, it didn't work."

He huffed. "And neither is this story you're telling." Court got to his feet and took out his phone. "Only a couple of minutes before my father was gunned down, a waitress in the diner across the street from the sheriff's office spotted you in the parking lot. There's no way you could have been here in your house during this so-called attack because you were in town."

She quit wincing so she could glare at him. "I was here." Her tone said *I don't care if you believe me or not.*

He didn't believe her. "You must have known my father had been shot because you didn't react when I told you."

"I did know. Whitney called me when I was walking back from the barn. I'd just gotten off the phone with her when that goon clubbed me."

Whitney Goble, her best friend. And it was entirely

possible that Whitney had either seen his father get shot or heard about it shortly thereafter because she worked part-time as a dispatcher for the sheriff's office. It would be easy enough to check to see if Whitney had indeed called her, and using her cell phone records, they could possibly figure out Rayna's location when she'd talked to her friend. Court was betting it hadn't been on Rayna's walk back from the barn. It had been while she was escaping from the scene of the shooting.

"This waitress claims she saw me shoot your father?" Rayna asked.

He hated that he couldn't answer yes to that, but Court couldn't. "She was in the kitchen when the actual shot was fired. But the bullet came from the park directly behind the sheriff's office parking lot. The very parking lot where you were right before the attack."

Judging from her repeated flat look, Rayna was about to deny that, so Court took out his phone and opened the photo. "The waitress took that picture of you."

Court didn't go closer to her with the phone, but Rayna stood. Not easily. She continued to clutch her side and blew out some short, rough breaths. However, she shook her head the moment her attention landed on the grainy shot of the woman in a red dress. A woman with hair the same color blond as Rayna's.

"That's not me," she insisted. "I don't have a dress that color. And besides, I wasn't there."

This was a very frustrating conversation, but thankfully he had more. He tapped the car that was just up the street from the woman in the photo. "That's your car, your license plate."

With her forehead bunched up, Rayna snatched the

phone from him and had a closer look. "That's not my car. I've been home all morning." Her gaze flew to his, and now there was some venom in her eyes. "You're trying to set me up." She groaned and practically threw his phone at him. "Haven't you McCalls already done enough to me without adding this?"

Court caught his phone, but he had to answer her through clenched teeth. "We haven't done anything."

She laughed, but there wasn't a trace of humor in it. "Right. Remember Bobby Joe," she spat out. "Or did you forget about him?"

Bobby Joe Hawley. No, Court hadn't forgotten. Obviously, neither had Rayna.

"Three years ago, your father tried to pin Bobby Joe's murder on me," Rayna continued. "It didn't work. A jury acquitted me."

He couldn't deny the acquittal. "Being found not guilty isn't the same as being innocent."

Something that ate away at him. Because the evidence had been there. Bobby Joe's blood in Rayna's house. Blood that she'd tried to clean up. There'd also been the knife found in her barn. It'd had Bobby Joe's blood on it, too. What was missing were Rayna's prints. Ditto for the body. They'd never found it, but Rayna could have hidden it along with wiping her prints from the murder weapon.

The jury hadn't seen it that way though.

Possibly because they hadn't been able to look past one other piece of evidence. Bobby Joe had assaulted Rayna on several occasions, both while they'd been together and after their breakup when she'd gotten a restraining order against him. In her mind, she probably thought that was justification to kill him. And equal justification to now go after Court's father, who'd been sheriff at the time. Warren had been the one to press for Rayna's arrest and trial. After that, his father had retired. But Rayna could have been holding a serious grudge against him all this time.

She'd certainly held one against Court.

He heard the sound of the vehicle pulling up in front of Rayna's house and knew it was Egan before he glanced out the still-open door. He also knew Egan wouldn't be pleased. And he was right. His brother was sporting a scowl when he got out of the cruiser and started for the door.

Egan was only two years older than Court, but he definitely had that big brother "I'm in charge" air about him. Egan had somehow managed to have that even when he'd still been a deputy. Folks liked to joke that he could kick your butt even before you'd known it was kicked.

"If you think Egan is going to let you walk, think again," Court warned her.

"I won't let him railroad me," she insisted, aiming another scowl at Court. "I won't let you do it, either. It doesn't matter that we have a history together. That history gives you no right to pull some stunt like this."

They had a history all right. Filled with both good and bad memories. They'd been high school sweethearts, but that "young love" was significantly overshadowed by the bad blood that was between them now.

Egan stepped into the house, putting his hands on his hips, and made a sweeping glance around the room before his attention landed on Court. "Please tell me you're not responsible for any of this."

"I'm not." At least Court hoped he wasn't, but it was

possible he'd added some to the damage when he tackled her. "Rayna said someone broke in."

Court figured his brother was also going to have a
hard time believing that. It did seem too much of a coincidence that his father would be shot and Rayna would
have a break-in around the same time.

"You shouldn't have come," Egan said to him in a
rough whisper.

Court was certain he'd hear more of that later, but he
had a darn good reason for being here. "I didn't want
her to escape."

"And I thought he'd come here to kill me," Rayna
countered. "I pulled a gun on him." She swallowed hard.
"Things didn't go well after that."

Egan huffed and grumbled something that Court
didn't catch before he took out his phone and texted
someone

"Court didn't do any of the damage in this room,"
Rayna added. "It happened when an intruder attacked
me."

That only tightened Egan's mouth even more before
he shifted his gaze to Rayna. "An ambulance is on the
way. How bad are you hurt?" he asked and put his phone
back in his pocket.

She waved it off, wincing again while she did that.
Yeah, she was hurt. But Court thought Egan was missing what was really important here.

"She shot Dad," Court reminded Egan. "We have
the picture, remember?" Though he knew there was no
way his brother could have forgotten that. "It's proof
she was there. Proof that she shot him."

"No, it's not." Egan groaned, scrubbed his hand over
his face. "I think someone tried to set Rayna up."

Court opened his mouth to say that wasn't true. But then, Egan took out his own phone and showed him a picture.

"A few minutes after you stormed out of the hospital," Egan continued, "Eldon Cooper, the clerk at the hardware store, found this."

"This" was a blond-haired woman wearing a red dress. An identical dress to the one in the photo the waitress had taken. But this one had one big difference from the first picture.

In this one, the woman was dead.

Chapter Two

Rayna slowly walked toward Egan so she could see the photograph that had caused Court to go stiff. It had caused him to mumble some profanity, too, and Rayna soon knew why.

The woman in the photograph had been shot in the head.

There was blood. Her body was limp, and her lifeless eyes were fixed in a permanent blank stare at the sky.

Rayna dropped back a step, an icy chill going through her. Because Court had been right. The woman did look like her. The one in the first picture did anyway. The second photo was much clearer, and while it wasn't a perfect match, the dead woman looked enough like her to be a relative. But Rayna knew she didn't have any living relatives.

"Someone killed her because of me?" she whispered.

Neither Court nor Egan denied it.

She felt the tears threaten. The panic, too. But Rayna forced herself not to give in to either of them. Not in front of Court anyway. Later, she could have a cry, tend to her wounds and try to figure out what the heck was going on.

"Who is she?" Rayna asked.

"We don't have an ID on her yet, but we will soon. After the medical examiner's had a look at her, then we'll search for any ID. If there isn't any on her body or in the car, we'll run her prints."

It was so hard for Rayna to think with her head hurting, but she forced herself to try to figure this out. "Why would someone go to all the trouble of having a look-alike and then leave a car behind with bogus plates?"

Egan shrugged again. "It goes back to someone setting you up." He sounded a little skeptical about that though. "Unless you hired the woman in that photo to pose as you. You could have gotten spooked when something went wrong and left the car."

Even though she'd braced herself to have more accusations tossed at her, that still stung. It always did. Because this accusation went beyond just hiring an impostor. He was almost certainly implying that she had something to do with the woman's death, too.

"No. I didn't hire her," Rayna managed to say though her throat had clamped shut. "And I didn't shoot your father. I haven't been in town in weeks, and that wasn't my car parked near the sheriff's office."

Egan nodded, glanced at Court. "She's right about the car. The plates are fake. I had one of the deputies go out and take a look at it. It's still parked up the street from the office. Someone painted over the numbers so that it matched the plates on Rayna's vehicle."

Again, Egan was making it sound as if she had something to do with that. Good grief. Why was she always having to defend herself when it came to the McCalls?

Of course, she knew the answer.

She'd made her own bed when it'd come to Bobby Joe. She had stayed with him even after he'd hit her and called her every name in the book. She had let him rob her of her confidence. Her dignity.

And nearly her life.

But Egan and Court—and their father—hadn't seen things that way. Bobby Joe had kept the abuse hidden. A wolf in sheep's clothing, and very few people in town had been on her side when Warren McCall had arrested her for Bobby Joe's murder.

"You're barking up the wrong tree—again," Rayna added. "I didn't have anything to do with this. And why would I? If I were going to shoot anyone, why would I send in a look-alike? Why would I pick a spot like Main Street, which is practically on the doorstep of a building filled with cowboy cops?"

Egan shrugged. "Maybe to make us believe you're innocent and knew nothing about it."

"I am innocent," she practically yelled. Rayna stopped though, and peered at the mess in the living room. "But maybe my intruder is behind what happened in town and what happened to that woman, as well. He could have arranged to have your father shot, killed her and then could have come out here to attack me. His prints could be on the lamp. It's what he used to bash me over the head."

Court looked at her, and for a split second, she thought she saw some sympathy in his intense gray eyes. It was gone as quickly as it'd come, and he stood there, waiting. Maybe for an explanation that would cause all of this to make sense. But she couldn't give him that.

Rayna huffed. "If I was going to do something to fake an assault, I wouldn't have hit myself that hard on my head or cracked my ribs. And I wouldn't have broken my grandmother's lamp."

It sickened her to see it shattered like that. In the grand scheme of things, it wasn't a huge deal, but it felt like one to her. It was one of the few things she had left of her gran. And now it was gone—much like what little peace of mind she'd managed to regain over the past year.

"Who do you think would have done something like this?" Court asked, tipping his head toward the living room.

"Bobby Joe," she answered without thinking. She knew it would get huffs and eye rolls from them, and it did. "You think he's dead, that I killed him. But I know I didn't. So, that means he could still be out there."

Court didn't repeat his huff, but she could tell he wanted to. "So, you think Bobby Joe set you up for my father's shooting and then came out here and attacked you? If he's really alive, why would he wait three years to do that?"

Rayna gave it some thought and didn't have an answer. However, she wouldn't put it past Bobby Joe. At the end of their relationship, he'd threatened to kill her. Maybe this was his way of doing that. Bobby Joe could be toying with her while also getting back at Warren McCall, who hadn't managed to get her convicted of murder.

But there was something else. A piece that didn't seem to fit.

"Tell me about the waitress," Rayna insisted. "Who was she, and why did she take the picture of the woman in the parking lot?"

"Her name is Janet Bolin," Court answered. "She

said she took the photo because she thought you…or rather the woman…was acting strange."

Egan groaned. Probably because he was agreeing with her theory of an ill-fitting puzzle piece. "I'll get a CSI team out here to process the place." He pressed a button on his phone and went onto the porch to make the call.

"You know this waitress?" Rayna asked Court.

He shook his head. "She's new, has only been working there a week or so, but I've seen her around. We'll bring her in for questioning."

Good. Because it meant Rayna was finally making some headway in convincing Court that she hadn't fired that shot or had anything to do with that woman's death.

She hesitated before asking her next question. "How's your father?" Warren was a touchy subject for both of them.

A muscle flickered in Court's jaw. "He's out of surgery but still unconscious. We don't know just how bad the damage is yet."

He might have added more, might, but the sound outside stopped him. Sirens. They were from the ambulance that was coming up the road. Since her house was the only one out here, they were here for her.

"I don't want an ambulance," she insisted. "I'll go to the hospital on my own." And it wouldn't be to the one in McCall Canyon. She would drive into nearby San Antonio.

"That's not a very smart thing to do." No pause for Court that time. "We're not sure what's going on here. Plus, your ribs could be broken. You don't need to be driving if they are."

She couldn't help it. Rayna gave him a snarky smile before she could stop herself. "Worried about me?"

That earned her another glare, but this one didn't last. And for a moment she saw something else. Not the sympathy this time, either. But the old attraction. Even now, it tugged at her. Apparently, it tugged at Court because he cursed again and looked away.

"I just wanted to make sure I didn't hurt you when we fell on the floor," Court said.

"You didn't." That was probably a lie, but Rayna was hurting in so many places that it was hard to tell who was responsible for the bruises and cuts.

Court's gaze came back to her. "Was there anything… sexual about the assault after you got hit on the head?"

"No." Thank God. That was something at least. "In fact, I'm not even sure he intended to kill me. I mean, he could have shot me the moment I walked into my house—"

"Maybe he didn't have a gun. He could have been robbing the place and got spooked when you came in."

True. But that didn't feel right. Neither did the spot on her ribs, and Rayna had another look. Too bad that meant pulling up her top again, and this time Court examined it, too. He leaned in, so close that she could feel his breath hitting her skin.

"It looks like a needle mark," he said. "And you mentioned something about passing out?"

She nodded. "But the man was gone by the time that happened." Of course, he could have come back. Heck, he could still come back.

That made her stomach tighten, and she gave an uneasy glance around the front and side yards. There were plenty of places on her land for someone to hide.

"You're sure it was a man?" Court asked. He was using his lawman's tone again. Good. That was easier to deal with than the old attraction. "You said you didn't get a look at the person, so how do you know it was a man?"

"I've had a man's hands on me before so yes, I'm sure he was male." She immediately hated that she'd blurted that out, even if it was true. But Rayna didn't like reminding anyone, especially Court, of just how wrong she'd been about Bobby Joe. After all, she'd let Court go to be with him.

"After he clubbed me with the lamp," Rayna added, "he hooked his arm around my throat. My back landed against his chest so I know it was a man."

Court took a moment, obviously processing that, and he looked at the lock on the front door. "There's no sign of forced entry. Was it locked, and did you have on your security system?"

Everything inside her went still. With all the chaos that had gone on, it hadn't occurred to Rayna to ask herself those questions. "Yes, it would have been locked, and the security system was on. I never leave the house without doing that."

"Even if you were just going to the barn?" Court immediately asked.

"Even then." She gathered her breath, which had suddenly gone thin again. It always did when she thought of the woman she'd become. "I honestly believe Bobby Joe is alive and that he could come after me."

Court looked ready to grumble out some profanity, but Rayna wasn't sure if that's because he felt sorry for her or because he thought she was crazy for being so wary about a man he believed was dead.

"The front door was unlocked when I got here," Court continued several moments later. "Is it possible your intruder had a key?"

"No. And I don't keep a spare one lying around, either." She kept her attention on the ambulance that stopped behind the cruiser. "Plus, he would have had to disarm the security system. It's tamperproof, so he couldn't have simply cut a wire or something. He would have had to know the code."

With each word, that knot in her stomach got tighter and tighter. She had taken all the necessary precautions, and it hadn't been enough. That hurt. Because she might never feel safe here again in this house that she loved. Her gran's house. That didn't mean she would leave. No. She wouldn't give Bobby Joe the satisfaction of seeing her run, but Rayna figured there'd be a lot more sleepless nights in her future.

Egan was still on the phone when the medics got out of the ambulance and started for the porch. Rayna went out to tell them they could leave, but she spotted another vehicle. A familiar one.

Whitney's red Mustang.

"You called her?" Court asked.

Rayna shook her head, but it didn't surprise her that Whitney had heard about what happened and then had driven out to see her. They'd been friends since third grade, and even though that friendship had cooled a little after Rayna had gotten involved with Bobby Joe, Whitney had usually been there for her. Whitney was also one of the few people who'd stood by her when Rayna had been on trial.

Her friend bolted from the car and ran past the medics to get to Rayna. Whitney immediately pulled her

into her arms for a hug. An uncomfortable one because
Rayna felt the pain from her ribs, and she backed away.

"I came as fast as I could get someone to cover for
me at work." Whitney's words rushed together. "My
God, you're hurt." She reached out as if to touch the
wound on Rayna's hand, but she stopped. "It must be
bad if the ambulance came."

"No. They were just leaving." Rayna made sure she
said that loud enough for the medics to hear.

"They're not leaving," Court snapped, and he motioned for them to wait. No doubt so he could try to talk
Rayna into going with them.

Whitney volleyed puzzled looks between Court and
her. "Is, uh, anything going on between you two? I
mean, you're not back together, are you?"

"No," Court and Rayna answered in unison, but it
did make Rayna wonder what Whitney had picked up
on to make her think that.

Whitney released her breath as if relieved. Maybe
because she knew Rayna wasn't ready for a relationship. Especially one with Court McCall.

"What happened here?" Whitney asked, glancing
inside.

"Someone broke in," Rayna settled for saying. She
planned to give Whitney more information later, but
her friend filled in the blanks.

"And you think it was Bobby Joe," Whitney concluded. But she immediately shook her head after saying
that. "It seems to be more than that going on. I mean,
what with Warren being shot."

Court made a sound of agreement. "Do you have a
key to Rayna's house? And no, I'm not accusing her of

anything," Court quickly added to Rayna. "I'm just trying to figure out how the intruder got in."

"No key," Whitney answered. "Bobby Joe wouldn't have one, either. Rayna changed all the locks after she was acquitted. She had the windows and doors wired for security, too. Did she tell you that she has guns stashed all around the house?"

Rayna gave Whitney a sharp look to get her to hush. But it was too late. After hearing that, Court was probably even more convinced that she was about to go off the deep end.

"So, are you coming with us?" one of the medics called out. He sounded, and looked, impatient.

Rayna knew him. His name was Dustin Mendoza. A friend of Bobby Joe's. Of course, pretty much every man in McCall Canyon in their midthirties fell into that particular category.

"No," Rayna repeated.

She figured Court was about to do some repeating as well and insist that she go. He didn't. "I'll drive Rayna to the hospital. I need to ask her some more questions about the break-in."

Dustin didn't wait around to see if that was okay with her. He motioned for his partner to leave, and they started back for the ambulance.

"I also think you should consider protective custody," Court said to her. "The intruder obviously knows how to get in your house, and he could come back."

That had already occurred to Rayna, but it chilled her to the bone to hear someone say it.

"You can stay with me," Whitney suggested. "In fact, I can take you to the hospital."

It was generous of Whitney, and Rayna was about to

consider accepting, but Court spoke before she could say anything. "That could be dangerous. For Whitney. If this intruder is still after you, he could go to her place while looking for you."

That drained some of the color from Whitney's face. Obviously, it wasn't something she'd considered when she'd made the offer.

"It's okay," Rayna assured her. "I can make other plans."

She didn't know what exactly those plans would be, but she might have to hire a bodyguard. And put some distance between her and the McCalls. Whatever was going on seemed to be connected to them. Rayna didn't think it was a coincidence about the timing of Warren's attack, the break-in and the dead woman.

Egan finally finished his call, and the moment he turned to walk toward them, Rayna knew something was wrong.

"Is it Dad?" Court immediately asked.

Egan shook his head. "It's the waitress. Janet Bolin. She's dead. Someone murdered her."

Don't miss Cowboy Above the Law
by Delores Fossen
Available in August from Harlequin Intrigue!

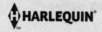

INTRIGUE
EDGE-OF-YOUR-SEAT INTRIGUE, FEARLESS ROMANCE.

Save **$1.00**

on the purchase of ANY Harlequin® Intrigue book.

Available wherever books are sold, including most bookstores, supermarkets, drugstores and discount stores.

Save **$1.00**

on the purchase of any Harlequin® Intrigue book.

Coupon valid until September 30, 2018.
Redeemable at participating outlets in the U.S. and Canada only.
Not redeemable at Barnes & Noble stores. Limit one coupon per customer.

52615782

5 65373 00076 2   (8100)0 12368

® and ™ are trademarks owned and used by the trademark owner and/or its licensee.

© 2018 Harlequin Enterprises Limited

HIEJCOUPBPA0718